MAY McGOLDRICK

The FIREBRAND

ONYX

Don't miss the other books in the Highland Treasure Trilogy....

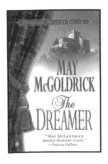

Praise for *The Dreamer*
"An enchanting tale not to be missed."
—*Philadelphia Enquirer*

from

ONYX

HIGHLAND TREASURE:
The Firebrand

May McGoldrick

AN ONYX BOOK

ONYX
Published by New American Library, a division of
Penguin Putnam Inc., 375 Hudson Street,
New York, New York 10014, U.S.A.
Penguin Books Ltd, 27 Wrights Lane,
London W8 5TZ, England
Penguin Books Australia Ltd, Ringwood,
Victoria, Australia
Penguin Books Canada Ltd, 10 Alcorn Avenue,
Toronto, Ontario, Canada M4V 3B2
Penguin Books (N.Z.) Ltd, 182–190 Wairau Road,
Auckland 10, New Zealand

Penguin Books Ltd, Registered Offices:
Harmondsworth, Middlesex, England

First published by Onyx, an imprint of New American Library,
a division of Penguin Putnam Inc.

First Printing, November 2000
10 9 8 7 6 5 4 3 2 1

To the talented members of Bucks County and
New Jersey Romance Writers—may the
gods and goddesses of publishing smile upon all.

And to Hilary Ross—for your encouragement
in bringing out the best in us.
This book would not be what it is without you.

Prologue

"Your father is dead."

Frowning through the mud that covered his lined and weary face, the knight looked steadily at the three young women. They stood together by the hearth, their stunned faces golden in the glow of the small fire. Only a few candles lit the small abbey chamber.

"You should know that he died true to his beliefs. Like Thomas More and Bishop Fisher, he couldn't be forced to sign the King Henry's Oath of Supremacy. No matter what they did—no matter what the torture—Edmund Percy would not be crushed."

He fixed his eyes on the youngest daughter as tears, glimmering like watery diamonds, suddenly splashed from her cheeks onto the stone floor.

"They murdered him in his cell. They feared to bring him to Westminster for a trial, so they came at him in the night like vile and bloodthirsty cowards. A guard I know told me the blackguards cut Edmund's throat. He fought them manfully, but a dog's dagger put an end to his worthy life."

Benedict, the tall monk standing by the door, rasped out his concern. "Where is his body? Will it be returned to Yorkshire for proper burial?"

"Nay, the body was carried to . . ."

A small sob escaped the youngest daughter's lips as she suddenly bolted for the door. No one attempted to stop her as she brushed past the monk and disappeared into the blackness of the corridor.

"Continue," Benedict ordered, motioning to the other two sisters to remain. "There is more that we must learn."

*   *   *

Grief clawed at her insides, tearing the very breath from her lungs.

Leaving the chapter house, Adrianne stumbled down the three steps, ignoring the hands that reached out to help. As she ran across the abbey courtyard toward the stables, she saw only the blur of her own tears.

He was dead. Her father was gone. Forever.

She flew into the stables, her hand finding the mucking shovel by the door. Adrianne's shoulder banged hard against the rough wood of the stalls, but her body was numb to the pain. She staggered through the dark, finding her way to the empty stall. Grief turned to fury, and she lashed out with the wooden shovel, flailing away at the stone and wood walls.

An entire year of hoping, praying, that Edmund Percy would be released from his unjust imprisonment had all been for naught. Her father was dead.

Adrianne kicked at an empty feed bucket and slung the shovel into a corner. She punched at the stable wall until blood ran from her knuckles. But she was senseless to the pain.

Images of years past flashed through her brain. Her father, tall and handsome—the gentle warrior whose heart always shone through his clear blue eyes. Her mother Nichola—the serene beauty who ruled Edmund's heart with the same affection with which she shaped the lives of the three daughters. The family she'd had. The love they'd shared. Gone. Gone.

"Gone!" She spit out the words in anger as her bloody fist again slammed the wall. The sharp pain in her hand this time broke through the wall of insensibility, and she sank to the ground, the tears once again flowing freely.

The images were burning in her brain—of Edmund Percy's arrest, of their mother frantically trying to hide their daughters, of the massacre of innocent servants, of blood that had been left staining the walls and floors of their manor home. It was all too clear.

Sobs shook Adrianne's slender frame. Helplessness like nothing she had ever known drained her very soul. She leaned her head back against the stone wall and wept.

When Catherine entered the stables, the sight of her younger sister collapsed in the stall added yet one more wound to a grieving heart. Adrianne's black hair had come loose from its braid. The gray dress, torn at the sleeve, was covered with dirt and straw. As the youngest Percy daughter looked up, the streaks of blood and dirt, mingled with tears, drew Catherine immediately to Adrianne's side. She lay the wick lamp she carried carefully in the straw.

"What have you done?" She touched a bruise on her sister's forehead, another scratch on her cheek.

"Don't!" Adrianne brought a hand up to ward off her sister's gentle touch. But Catherine's gaze immediately fell on the bruised and bloody knuckles.

"By the Virgin! Adrianne, what have you done?"

"Please don't!" A sob escaped the younger woman's lips. "Please don't lecture me on what I should or should not do. Not now. And please don't pretend that this news of our father is another lie."

There was a long silence. Two matching pairs of blue eyes met, each sister seeking consolation in the other.

"This time, I believe it," Catherine said at last. "This news of Father's death was first taken to the Borders to the far north. Mother sent this knight back to us. He had a sealed letter from her. He delivered it to Laura and me after you left the abbot's chamber."

Adrianne dashed away at the tears on her face and straightened where she sat. "What does the letter say? What news is there of Mother? Is she safe where she is?"

"She assures us that she is safe, but as always she does not concern herself as much with her own well-being as with ours." Catherine took a kerchief out of her sleeve and started wrapping it around Adrianne's knuckles.

"Did she say anything about the Treasure of Tiberius?"

"Aye, but 'tis all a jumble of riddles . . . as always! Words about 'the map' and our responsibility to keep it safe as our father did before us. References about how we should protect the sections of the map that she will send to us. The only thing that is truly clear is how real the dangers will be from those who will pursue us for it."

"So this game we have been playing." Adrianne met her sister's gaze. "Laura's elaborate plans we three have been carrying out. All the wee caskets we've been burying in every corner of Yorkshire. All those sketches and riddles to lead those who seek the treasure on to the next false destination— do you believe 'twill still serve any purpose?"

"Aye, that it shall." Catherine nodded. "Especially now, for Mother believes that 'twill be only a matter of days before a warrant is issued for the arrest of the three of us, as well. In fact, she mentions the king's Lieutenant, Arthur Courtenay by name. He has been just waiting for this opportunity to come after us."

Rage rushed into Adrianne's face. "He wouldn't dare do so while Father was alive. Well, let him come. This time we will fight him to the last drop of our blood. There will be no imprisonment . . . no waiting . . ."

"Adrianne—" Catherine's hand firmly clasped her sister's chin—"our mother does not wish to lose any more of her loved ones. She wants us safe. She wishes for us to leave England."

"Leave England? Does she want us in the Borders with her?"

Catherine shook her head. "She doesn't consider the Borders safe for her daughters. Nay, she has planned for the three of us to be sent to remote corners of Scotland."

Adrianne shook her head in confusion. "Separating us? Hasn't it been enough to live with losing our father . . . with losing her? The three of us staying together has been the only sane thing in this entire year of madness. We each need the other two to survive!"

"Adrianne, we are sisters. Nothing can change that. No distance between us can crumble the foundation of strength and love that has been built." Catherine's hand swept the dark strands of hair out of Adrianne's face. "But I believe we should do as she bids us. The ploy of hiding the Treasure of Tiberius will buy us some time. Surely, Sir Arthur Courtenay's interest will lie in unearthing the treasure first. We have been given a task of carrying out our father's wishes. This is his legacy to us. We must follow Mother's plans."

Tears once again rushed into Adrianne's eyes. "And lose the last of what we have by being separated? By going blindly to the ends of the world? By going where one and all will surely hate us for our English blood?"

"We are all half Scottish. Nichola Erskine is our mother, so there will certainly be some tolerance in the way we are received." She turned toward the door. "Come out of here, Adrianne, Laura is still looking for you."

The two sisters both pushed themselves to their feet. Catherine picked up the wick lamp and continued. "The way I see things, Mother has planned for me to be sent to Balvenie Castle where, through the generosity of the earl of Athol, I will be able to open the school I have so long dreamed of. Once I am settled, I see no reason why you and Laura cannot join me there. We are all well educated and know how to tutor others. We must think of this as only a brief separation."

"And Laura? Where is she being sent?"

"Farther to the north. To a place on the eastern sea called the Chapel of St. Duthac."

"And I?"

"To the western isles. You are being sent to an island called Barra."

"An *island*?" Adrianne exclaimed. "But one needs a boat or a ship to get to an island."

"Aye! I believe 'tis too far to swim, little sister."

Her bandaged hand unconsciously pressed to her stomach. "But why did our mother have to send me to an island?"

Catherine started ushering her sister out of the stall. "You'll survive the journey. And once you are there, you will be cared for perfectly . . . until such time as you can join me at Balvenie Castle."

"An island," Adrianne murmured with dismay. "So few people. So little to do."

"Just think of all the hardships we have faced, Adrianne. Compared to all we have been through this past year, I am certain that life on Barra will be heaven!"

Chapter 1

The cry of anguish from the wooden cage hanging high above the rocks brought nods of approval from the throng huddled together at the base of the castle wall.

"And I'm telling you, Wyntoun, she is too obstinate a vixen to die of a wee bit of weather!"

The gust of the bitter Hebrides wind carried the nun's declaration up the stone walls of the castle to the inhabitant of the swinging cage. The boxlike prison of wood and rope hung suspended from what looked like a ship's bowsprit projecting out from a corner of the main tower of the castle.

From the confines of the cage, Adrianne Percy peered down at the cold stare of the Abbess of the Chapel of St. Mary. Fighting the bile in her throat and the numbness of her bare fingers clutching the wooden slats, she strained to hear every word.

"Surely, considering the ice and the rain and all, the woman must have endured enough punishment already . . ."

"The lass has been up there just a few short hours!" the nun snapped accusingly. "Three days! She will remain up there three days—"

Adrianne shook the cage, drawing up all eyes. "Make it three hundred days, if you like, for this punishment is preferable, by far, to everything else you have meted out to me since arriving on this accursed island."

The abbess howled upward into the wind. "Any less than three days and I will not even consider giving her leave to beg for forgiveness."

The young woman shook the cage again. "Beg for forgiveness? Never!"

"Five days," the abbess shouted.

"I have done no wrong, and if there is any forgiveness needed, 'twill be granted by me only." Adrianne's voice rose over a gust of wind. "Do you hear? By me!"

Adrianne felt the satisfaction and despair blend and curl in her chest at the sight of the ancient nun mumbling and making her way carefully over the rocks toward the main entrance of the keep. The abbess only stopped long enough to call out her answer before continuing.

"Seven days, vixen!"

"Hell's gate! Just *try* to keep me here for seven days! For even one day. Virgil, be my guide," she intoned. "I'd raise hell's demons, except that they're probably already wearing an abbess's wimple!"

Adrianne sniffed at the horrified gasps from the men below the cage. Glancing down, she looked at the newly arrived man—the one the abbess had called by the name of Wyntoun. He was standing apart from the rest with his arms crossed over his chest, and frowning up at her.

A surge of anger made her want to spit down on him—and on the rest of them. But her present battle lay with the abbess. Fighting her unsettled stomach, queasy from the wind-blown motion of the cage, Adrianne shifted from one side to the other to watch the nun's departure.

"You will not be escaping me! This pitiful pile of rock you call a castle is too small. You cannot escape hearing me . . . hearing my curses, you—"

"By the saints, wench!" the burly steward standing near the newcomer called up to her. "If ye do not hold yer rattling tongue, ye'll be hanging up there until ye rot."

"Nobody called for you to speak, you muddle-headed scullion." She had the satisfaction of seeing a wave wash seawater up between the rocks and soak the man. "In fact, if it weren't for your wagging tongue delivering lies about what I had done, I wouldn't be here." A gust of wind had the cage again shake and swing precariously from the beam. Adrianne sank down on her knees as her stomach heaved from the jerky motion.

An icy rain had begun to fall in earnest. The wind, picking up as the tide came in, added a bitter chill to the wintry dusk settling over them.

She could handle the cold, even the soaking of her blanket and clothes with the icy rain. But she couldn't deal with the illness caused by the rough movements of the cage. She despised this weakness. Taking a chestful of cold salty air, she grabbed the large shell and the food that was left in it and pushed herself back to her feet.

"And I'll not be so easily poisoned, either, you fish-faced pox mongers." She cast the dish and its contents fiercely downward. The food carried outward in the wind, falling on some of the onlookers as the shell itself shattered on the rocks not far from the newcomer's feet.

"Come. All of you!" The abbess stood in the entryway to the castle. "Leave her."

At the nun's sharp order the heads of the half-dozen men snapped around, and all but the newcomer climbed over the rocks, filing into the keep behind the diminutive woman.

Still clutching the slats fiercely in her numb fingers, Adrianne wondered the reason for the man's arrival. She had seen the ship sail into the bay just as they'd been hanging the cage from the tower that morning. She had also seen the boat that had been rowed ashore with this man in it. She was certain that this was the same man, for he was easily a head taller than the others who had been standing on the rocks below. And then, there was his short black hair—the same color as his black attire. Very different than the others who lived on Barra. But as far as the rest of his looks, it was too long a drop to the wet rocks to notice anything else but his fierce glower.

Watching him silently, Adrianne wondered why he had stayed behind.

"Do you realize that your perch is higher than the uppermost rigging of most ships? You must not be afraid of the heights," he called out. "Though I know many a man who would swallow his tongue at the threat of being hung in a cage from Kisimul Castle."

"Well, that says a great deal for the men of Barra!"

A wave splashed up onto his boots. Lithe as a cat, the tall

newcomer moved easily from rock to rock, passing under the cage and stopping on the far side.

Adrianne shifted her hands on the slats and moved to the other side of the cage, so she could peer down at him.

"So, what terrible crime did you commit to deserve this grim punishment?"

She'd committed *no* crime, but she chose silence as an answer. Since her arrival on Barra, no one had yet believed anything she said, anyhow.

"You can talk to me. I've already tried to speak on your behalf. I *could* be a friend."

She snorted loud enough to make sure he heard.

"I may not yet be convinced of your wickedness. I only just arrived on the island and—"

"I saw you sail in," she exploded. "You're a Highlander, and therefore vexatious baggage . . . like the rest of them."

"You have too much mouth for a helpless English damsel."

So he knew something of her background. "I am anything but helpless, you buffle-headed clackdish."

"Buffle-headed? You must be confusing me with someone else. But you do appear helpless from where I'm standing. And from all I've heard since stepping foot on Barra, you seem to have committed some unforgivable sin. And an unmentionable one, I might add, since no one appears to want to speak of what exactly you did to rile the most gentle and mild-tempered abbess in the entire Western Isles."

She looked frantically about the cage to find something else to throw at him. But there was nothing that she would dare give up.

"To start, my recommendation would be for you to change your manner of speaking with her."

Temper had already formed hot replies in her throat, but she had to forego her answer as a blast of wind lashed the swaying cage with more icy rain. Her white fingers clutched the slats of wood, as she fought down another lurch in her belly.

"I've been acquainted with that gentle nun for a good portion of my life, and I'd say there is no man or woman or child living who would lend a hand to anyone bold enough to defy the wishes of that . . . well, that saint of a woman."

"I don't need or wish for help from any of you. I didn't ask for it, and I never will. You are all nothing but spineless, cowering toads, and you deserve what you get at her hands." Frustration forced her to shake the cage. Her voice rising to match the wind. "And despite what you fools want to believe, that woman *is* a tyrant."

"Nay! She is a respected and loving leader who is highly regarded by the people of Barra . . . and by their master, as well."

"Humph! I have heard about that one, too. And how convenient! Rather than minding her own corner of Barra by running her paltry abbey, the 'good' woman controls the entire island while the *master*—that, perpetually absent minnow of a nephew—stays away. I think the milksop is afraid to deal with this tyrant's wrath."

"Minnow? Milksop? Is that the best you can do?"

"Nay, I can do better!" she retorted sharply. "The 'great' MacNeil is a roistering, shard-borne scut! From all I can tell, he's merely a venomous, bunch-backed puttock, a—"

"Actually, mistress, he's a MacLean. His mother was a MacNeil."

Adrianne glanced to the side to see the steward standing against the castle wall, watching the exchange.

"M'lord!" The portly servant cleared his throat, sounding serious. "The abbess . . . she wishes to speak with you."

After giving a departing look at the cage, the Highlander headed across the rocks to the entryway into the castle. Holding the slats of the cage in each fist, she watched him disappear. The chill wind buffeted the cage within inches of the ancient tower wall, and the endless rain finally managed to bring about a wave of desperation. She frowned and gazed down at the arrogant steward who was lingering below— gloating up at her from the safety of the rocks by the castle wall.

"Who is he?" She had to ask. "That Highlander! That fainthearted puppy who ran as soon as the abbess whistled for him."

"That 'puppy,' ye sharp-tongued vixen, is Sir Wyntoun MacLean, the abbess's nephew and the master of Kisimul Castle." She could see the man's grin even in the dusk. "He's the fiercest warrior ever to command either ship or raiding party. And after what ye said about him, I'd say 'twill be a fortnight before he'll be letting us feed ye, never mind let ye out of that cage of yers. Aye . . . a full fortnight, I'd be wagering, ye quarrelsome chit."

She glared at him until he disappeared into the castle again. The words should have frightened her, but Adrianne felt no remorse over what she had said and done. Five months. For five months she had been practically a prisoner on this island. For five months she had been corrected, condemned, made a fool of, and punished repeatedly for no reason. And it all had come to this moment.

She looked down at the sharp drop. The sea was boiling up a little farther with each swell of the tide. The salty spray stung her face as the waves now washed over the rocks and battered the wall of the castle.

Uncoiling one hand from the slats of the cage, Adrianne reached inside the waistband of her skirt beneath the cloak and drew out the small dagger she had hidden there. Reaching above her head, her fingers slid through the wide slats of the cage and took hold of the single thick rope that connected the cage to the beam.

Aye, it had all come down to this, she thought, cutting away at the rope.

Chapter 2

The black shadow of the diminutive nun loomed huge on the eastern wall of the Great Hall.

"The young women in my care are sent to this blessed island to focus on Almighty God. Their desire is to be free of the disturbing distractions of life. I tell you their wish is to embrace the stillness, to achieve the inner peace and tranquillity that they cannot find in the world abroad."

The abbess stopped her pacing before the master's table and waited until the Highlander lifted his gaze from the ledger book open before him. She nodded curtly. "For the past five months, Wyn, these poor creatures have not gotten any semblance of the prayerful solitude promised them . . . or promised their families. And our failure . . . every single disruption . . . can be laid at the feet of one person. That bullheaded, barbed-tongued banshee . . . Adrianne Percy."

"For certain, Aunt, in your vast years of experience, you must have had other spirited young women who have shown similar restlessness in their disposition."

"Ha! Restlessness? Ha! 'Restless' does not even come close to describing this wild-eyed Fury." The pacing started again. "I've had others. 'Tis true enough. But none . . . I can assure you . . . none of the others in my charge have ever dreamed of spreading open revolt beyond the walls of our little abbey. Why, the Chapel of St. Mary may never be as 'twas. Aye, Wyn, 'Fury' is the right name for Adrianne Percy. For certain, she's the lassie that cuts the Thread of Life—mine! And I do not know what I did to deserve her."

The Highlander closed the ledger book and nodded to the steward standing patiently at the end of the table to come and take away the record of the island's business. Gesturing to a lean man who'd just entered the Great Hall, Wyntoun half-listened as the abbess churned on.

"First, she started in at the abbey. Breaking every rule— ignoring our routines—preaching anarchy among the youngest women. But that was only the start."

Wyntoun watched his trusted shipmaster cross the torch-lit floor of the Hall. Although his graying thatch of hair belied his young age, Alan MacNeil was—in Wyntoun's mind—the most knowledgeable and the most level-headed man sailing the seas. From the man's shoulder, an oiled leather satchel hung.

"Alan!" The abbess erupted, turning as he passed in front of the blazing hearth and moved to the seat next to his master. " 'Tis about time you left that precious ship of yours and granted us the pleasure of your exalted presence."

"Good day, Aunt." Alan bowed quickly to the abbess and sat down, drawing a roll of vellum from his satchel. A serving lad quickly ran in with a bowl of steaming liquid for the unsmiling newcomer, who sipped it as Wyntoun unrolled the map before them.

"Where was I? Oh . . . that wee vixen!" The abbess began to pace again. "No convent walls could hold that wild thing. Why the creature was not here a week before she took to walking the entire length and breadth of the island! Alone! 'Taking its measure,' she tells me. Stopping in at every hut, I come to find out. Breaking bread with the good and the ungodly! And her foul mouth . . . where do you think *that* came from? I'll tell you . . . 'twas from mixing with the fishermen and some of the roughs and rascals that idle their time away on Barra."

The nun waved a finger at the two men. "I know what you're thinking. Our own kin, she's talking about. Aye, I know. And I'm ashamed of all of them. But I'll tell you something. There has not been a single person on this blessed island that Adrianne Percy has not sought out. Why, that lass has deliberately tried to make everyone's business her own. And if you think anyone can suffer a fever or a hangnail on Barra without the meddling mistress poking her nose into it, you're greatly mistaken!" The abbess snorted derisively. "And do you think she has even once told me where she's going or when she'll be back? Or—when she does get back—how she could possibly have gotten so muddy? Nay. In she comes with her skirt torn and her hands looking like a stable worker's . . . and acting as if nothing in the world was amiss!"

"Aye, Aunt," Wyntoun said vaguely, still looking at the charts.

"And don't think that was the end of her transgressions!" Planting her small fists on her hips, the abbess came to a stop before the two men. "The Rule of Ailbe! You know it, Wyntoun. What is the Rule of Ailbe?"

The knight lifted his head and met the old woman's piercing green eyes.

"St. Ailbe calls for meditative quiet in the lives of the religious."

"I'm glad you recall, nephew. 'Let his work be silently done when possible. Let him not be talkative, but rather be a man of few words. Be silent . . . seek peacefulness, that your devotion might be fruitful.' "

"Aye." Wyntoun's gaze dropped to the map.

The nun was not finished. "And now, 'tis for you to ask me what the Rule of Ailbe has to do with Adrianne Percy."

The knight frowned and looked up from the table. "Well, Aunt, and what does all of this have to do with Adrianne Percy?"

"Everything!" she exploded. "And before you lose interest and go back to your maps and other worldly pursuits, let me answer the question you asked me about what she's done to deserve being hung in that cage!"

Wyntoun remained still, making a show of attentiveness to the abbess.

"I've already told you that young woman's sole purpose since arriving here has been to break every rule that pertains not only to her, but to everyone else on this island."

Wyntoun slapped his palm on the table impatiently. "Aye, Aunt. You have!"

"But I haven't said a word about her latest misdeed." She raised an accusing finger and pointed at the corner of the castle where the Englishwoman's cage was hanging outside. "Two days ago, Adrianne Percy burst into the cloister of the monastery, her hair unbound and her skirts flying about her ankles, screaming 'Fire!' and nearly giving old Brother Brendan apoplexy!" The abbess leaned over the table and lowered her voice to a whisper. " 'The Rule of Ailbe be damned!' the vixen kept shouting. 'There's a fire!' "

"From what we heard from the lads bringing stores aboard from the village, the incident at the monastery was—"

"You mind your maps, Alan."

The shipmaster reddened to the roots of his prematurely gray hair, but pressed his lips together in a thin line and looked back down at the map.

The nun turned her fiery gaze back on Wyntoun. "There was *no* fire . . . to speak of. Her purpose is to ruin us. To ruin the peace of the people living on this blessed island. To ruin God's work here."

The Highlander sat back, pushing the maps away from him. "Very well, Aunt. I hear your complaint. What do you wish me to do?"

There was a pause—and a quick flash of surprise in the old woman's wrinkled features.

"I . . . well, there is the question of her mother's wishes. Nichola Erskine Percy. Her wishes were for the daughter to stay here until such time as she would be sent for." A note of pique quickly crept back into the woman's tone. "But the Lady Nichola did not mention a word of Adrianne's unruly disposition. Nay, there were no warnings, at all, in any of her correspondence. Truly, if there were *any* hint of this, I would never have—"

"What do you wish me to do, Aunt?"

The repeated question silenced the old woman for a moment. She walked to the hearth and stared into the leaping flames. She then turned back to her nephew.

"I want you to take her away. Return her to her mother. Take her back to England or wherever 'tis Nichola is residing now."

"Done!" Wyntoun abruptly pulled the maps close again. Alan began pointing out the likeliest route along the coast.

"You are not mocking me, now, Wyntoun? This is not a jest?" she persisted. "You *are* taking her away!"

The knight's green eyes flashed like emeralds in the light of Great Hall's torches. "You know me, Aunt. I never jest."

The abbess nodded, but she did not retreat as the two men turned back to the map. The serving lad ran in again and replaced the pitcher of ale on the table. Another appeared carrying huge chunks of peat, which he proceeded to stack high in the blazing hearth. No fire, though, would be hot enough to disperse the chill from the Hall.

"And my decree of punishment for her?" she asked after a pause.

"'Twill stand . . . if you insist on it." Wyntoun put one map away as Alan unrolled another, spreading it on the surface of the wooden table. "But I warn you . . . when the ship's stores are restocked and the weather clears, we will be setting sail. And if the time I choose to leave precedes your release of the English lass"—a deep frown challenged the abbess's—"then you may have to keep her until spring. I do not know when I will be sending another ship that can convey her back to her mother."

The abbess pursed her thin lips with displeasure.

"I will not trust another crew and ship," she said finally, eyeing both men. "And I say this as much for Adrianne's sake as for my own."

Alan glanced quickly at his leader, but Wyntoun fixed his eyes on the map.

"She is hell's fire on earth, Wyn. She's a firebrand in a grain barn." The abbess turned and stared at the hearth. "'Tis a miracle the ship bringing her here didn't sink at sea. I don't understand how that crew was able to keep her under control for the journey from England."

"And you want *us* taking her back?" Alan pushed his cup of ale away. "What are you trying to do, Aunt? Get rid of us all?"

The abbess dismissed the sailor's comment with a wave of her hand. "You can handle it, Alan," she replied, coming back to the table. "You're my own kin. And if anyone trusts my opinions, 'tis my own family. But you must be warned.

She has the ability to charm both man and woman into believing what she says . . . into following her disruptive impulses . . ."

"I've seen her 'charm' in action, Aunt." Wyntoun looked up, his face serious.

"Nay, Wyn," she persisted. "She has something special in her. She can speak sweetly enough when she cares to. People follow her, I tell you . . . and men are the first to fall before her bonny looks." Neither man moved nor showed the slightest curiosity. After a long moment, the abbess nodded with satisfaction. "There we are, then. Adrianne stays in her confinement until you are ready to set sail."

"As I was coming ashore, the rain was changing to snow." Alan addressed Wyntoun instead of the abbess. "Would it not be better for you to put her in the prisoner's hole . . . or even hang her cage here in the Great Hall?"

"I'll not have it." The abbess shook her head adamantly at the two men. "We've done that. Two days ago, when we first brought her down from the abbey, I had her cage hung right there from that rafter. Why, in a few moments, the brazen creature was amusing herself entertaining everyone below with her wicked tongue. And I do not mind telling you that I myself was the butt of most of her impudent mockery. Nay! That will not do, at all. Why, inside of an hour, she'd managed to win a number of those listening to take her side against me!"

Again Alan directed his words to the master. "Half-Scot she might be, but the lass was raised an English lady. She may not survive the night out there."

"I had blankets put in the cage for her. She'll survive." The nun wrapped both of her hands around the ornate silver cross hanging around her neck, and a small smile broke across her thin lips. "I am pleased, though, that my prayers have finally been answered. Once and for all, we will be ridding Barra of that wee scourge."

Sudden shouts coming from the courtyard drew everyone's eyes to the doorway as the burly steward ran into the Hall.

"The cage, m'lord!"

Wyntoun shoved the map in Alan's direction. "What about the cage?"

"The cage fell. The thing is crashed on the rocks. The rope must have given way."

"What of her?" Wyntoun walked around the table and quickly crossed the floor with Alan and the abbess on his heels. "What of the Englishwoman?"

"She went down, too, m'lord . . . on the rocks. The men heard her scream. And that was that. By the time we got out there, the tide had washed away most of her . . . Lord bless her soul."

The steward made the sign of the cross, and Wyntoun glared back at the ancient nun.

"It appears your prayers have been answered sooner than you expected, Aunt."

Chapter 3

The night wind, black and bitter, tore at the flaring torches, threatening to extinguish them and . . . at the same time . . . snuff out Wyntoun's hopes. Still, though, the old woman continued to rail at the knight.

"Get back to your ship, I tell you. You need to be ready to set sail with the tide."

Wyntoun swung the smoking torch abruptly around and glared with annoyance at the face of the nun looking on.

"We set sail when *I* am ready, Aunt." The mix of rain and snow driven by the wind stung his face, but as he looked at her, the aged nun seemed oblivious to the storm. He frowned, gentling his tone. "I advised you to stay indoors and leave the search to the men."

"I am telling you, Wyn, you have to go."

The Highlander turned and faced the roiling surface of the bay. His ship—not an arrowshot from the castle—was riding the waves easily. From the rise and fall of the torches, though, he could tell that the small boats working just beyond the castle's rocks were clearly struggling to stay afloat and still continue the search. Men on the shore, waist deep in the frigid waters, clung to half-submerged boulders and looked for the young woman's body. "We are not leaving. At least, not until we find some trace of her."

A shout came from one of the boats. Wyntoun moved into the water himself, edging closer to where the torches flared in the wind.

"A blanket, m'lord!" One of the men shouted to Wyntoun.

"More pieces of the cage." The call was from Alan on the right.

The Highlander turned in that direction.

"Listen to me, Wyn," the abbess called from the shore. "You're wasting your time here."

The knight disregarded the abbess's comment and raised his torch higher in the air.

"By the saints! 'Tis her hair!" The steward's shout was almost a moan. "Och, the blessed lass. Here's a lock of her hair caught between these slats."

Wyntoun waded back to the shallows and climbed up to where the steward stood with a handful of long wet curls. The abbess reached the spot ahead of him and snatched the hair out of the man's hand.

"I do not care to repeat myself, Wyntoun, but in this case I am making an exception. Take your men this instant and get back to your ship."

A flash of temper crossed the Highlander's expression.

"Look at it."

Wyntoun's anger quickly subsided as he glared at the hair the nun held up for him to see. He took it and, studying it in the light of the torch, frowned at the straight cut of the tresses' ends. Hardly the look of hair that had been torn out.

"In the abbey I have some documents and correspondence regarding Adrianne that I need to get for you . . . before you sail."

"I'll meet you there."

"Nay!" The woman shook her head vehemently. "If you do not get back to your ship immediately, she'll be arranging for your men to sail that vessel to sea without you . . . and with herself at the helm!"

As the narrow door of the shipmaster's cabin opened, the tiny windows at the stern of the ship swung wide. Wyntoun crossed the cabin, pulled them shut, and latched them before turning to his man.

"She's aboard, Wyn . . . just as you said."

The Highlander turned and gave a satisfied nod to Alan.

"And you left her in hiding?"

"We did. Not an alarm raised. We did not even touch the wet clothes she must have tucked into a coil of rope on deck when she first climbed aboard. She's a game one . . . I'll give her that."

"You're having her hiding place watched."

"Aye, she's in one of the empty water barrels . . . Coll heard her moving about inside. And we're keeping an eye on her." Alan closed the door behind him. Muffled shouts from above deck told Wyntoun that the crew was readying the ship to set sail.

"How did she get out here? Swim?"

"Aye. She must have."

Wyntoun hung his sword belt on a peg across the cabin. "Any word from the abbess?"

"They tell me she still insists on coming aboard, rather than giving Ian whatever 'tis she has of the Englishwoman."

The knight's green eyes couldn't hide his satisfaction as he reached into a traveling bag he'd dropped on the cabin bunk. Removing a folded parchment, he carried the letter to where Alan had seated himself at a small worktable by the narrow cabin door.

"I had my doubts, Wyn. But it all worked out well." Alan picked up the letter and glanced at the contents. "You were right in not mentioning to the abbess the real reason behind taking the Englishwoman from Barra."

"The less anyone knows, the better."

"When do you intend to tell the lass?" Alan folded the letter again and put it back on the desk. "Or rather, how long are you planning to let her hide in that barrel?"

"For as long as she wishes. 'Tis much easier to keep her there in her barrel than anyplace else on this ship."

"Surely she's wet to the bone."

"Once we set sail, we'll lure her out."

"So far, everything she's done has played right into your hand."

"And we have to make sure that all her future moves, as well, work to our advantage . . . until we reach Duart Castle."

"Are you going to send word to her sisters?"

"Not just yet." Wyntoun crouched beside the worktable and slid open a secret panel on the side of the desk. With a satisfied glance at his cousin, he placed the letter in the chamber and slid the panel closed again. "Of course, everything I plan is subject to change, depending on the contents of these precious documents our aunt is entrusting me with on behalf of the Percy lass."

"I believe she's here."

Alan had no sooner come to his feet when there was a knock. At Wyntoun's command Ian, one of the MacNeil warriors, pushed open the door and stepped back, letting the abbess squeeze by him before following her in.

"Well!" The nun's critical eye took in the neatly arranged furnishings of the cabin. "I have to give you credit, Wyntoun. Your sense of order even shows in this wee closet you call home for a few days of the year. Put that chest here, Ian."

As the warrior placed a small wooden chest on the table, Alan headed for the door. "I'll leave you two. I want to be ready to sail at first light."

"Ian, wait outside for the abbess," the knight ordered. "Our business here shall be quick. My guess is the abbess has no desire to sail with us."

The woman snorted and sat with a sigh on the chair as the door closed behind the departing men. "Have you found her?"

"We have, Aunt. She is resting comfortably in one of the empty water barrels we'll be refilling when we reach Mull."

"I knew it." She reached inside the neck of her woolen dress and produced a heavy key hanging on a chain. "You might not think five months is enough time to get to know someone well, but I tell you, having witnessed this young woman's antics, having observed how determined she can be, I knew in my bones that she had already found her way to this ship."

"But why the ship?" Wyntoun asked, watching the nun's long fingers as they put the key into the lock of the wooden chest. "What made you so certain that she would come here, rather than hiding in the keep . . . or in some crofter's hut on the island?"

The lock clicked dully and the abbess pushed open the top of the chest. "I knew she'd come here. From the first week that she arrived on Barra, she has been trying to leave. To escape this island."

"But where did she want to go? From what you've told me, she has no one else near."

"To her two older sisters," the abbess announced, taking a thick leather packet out of the wooden chest. "She has been determined to leave Barra and find her sisters. They, too—from what she told me, were sent to the Highlands by their mother after Edmund Percy was murdered in the Tower of London."

"Do you know where the others are?"

"Nay. If I had any information on their whereabouts, I would have sent word to come and remove the vixen months ago." The abbess laid the packet on the table and placed a protective hand over it. "With your connections, Wyn, I am certain you can find Nichola Percy in no time. I can only tell you that in her original correspondence, she wrote that she was taking shelter in the Borders . . . with some of the families that had close ties to her father, Thomas Erskine."

"Finding the mother should not be too difficult," Wyntoun assured her.

"Now, in returning the daughter to her, you must also return this package—sealed as 'tis—to Lady Nichola."

The abbess picked up the packet and held it out. Wyntoun took the packet from her hand. "What does it contain, Aunt?"

"In truth, I do not know. But Lady Nichola's instructions were clear when she sent it to me." Her sharp green eyes met and held the Highlander's. "I was to hide this wooden casket and its contents. I was to protect it as if the key to the very Gates of Heaven lay within it."

"And?"

"And I was to continue the watch over it until such time as Adrianne was secure in her place of safety."

"You could have given this to her on Barra." Wyntoun turned the packet over in his hand. The wax seal showed the Percy and Erskine coats of arms linked. "She was safe there."

The nun snorted with disgust. "But she was never secure. The greatest danger that young woman faces comes not from those pursuing her as it does from herself." She shook her head. "Nay! She was certainly not ready to receive this packet at any time that she has been on Barra. So as it came to me, I want you to return it to Lady Nichola . . . along with her daughter. Let the woman make other arrangements."

Wyntoun casually tossed the packet back into the wooden chest and nodded reassuringly to the old woman. "I shall take care of everything, Aunt."

"Very well!" The abbess rose to her feet and stepped toward the door. "And you *will* look after her?"

"I will."

"You *will* be patient with her. She is, after all, quite young."

"I can assure you, Aunt, no discipline I come up with for the English firebrand will be any harsher than hanging her in a cage from the top of Kisimul Castle on a midwinter's eve."

"Humph! That was nothing!" She waited for Wyntoun to open the door for her and then glanced back at him. "And you'll find out soon enough that Adrianne has no fear of heights or anything else. Putting her out there was only a test of her skill. When I had her suspended in the Great Hall, it took her only a few hours before she'd worked herself free and was climbing down the rope on the far side of the Hall. I believe the cold must have slowed her down a wee bit tonight."

Wyntoun frowned at the old woman's serious expression, unsure whether her words had been spoken in jest . . . or out of admiration.

"Have no worries, Aunt. I shall see to it that she is safely united with her kin."

"Very well! I'm done with it." The nun waved a hand at her nephew and stepped into the narrow gangway, pushing Ian ahead of her toward the ladder leading to the deck. "Lead on, you hulking oaf. I want to get my feet on solid ground again."

Wyntoun walked back inside the cabin and, as he closed the door behind him, his eyes never left the open casket on his desk.

"Far easier than I would have ever thought."

Wyntoun sat himself at the desk, picked up the packet, and broke the seal without a moment's hesitation. Unwrap-

ping the leather, he gazed for a moment at the contents. A
letter addressed to Adrianne Percy on fine parchment . . . and
a smaller folded packet of vellum.

He pushed aside the letter and reached for the folded vellum. Carefully opening it, he stared at the marks and symbols on the sheet.

The map. Well, part of it, anyway, he decided.

"Tiberius!" he whispered.

There was no warning. Suddenly, he felt the cutting edge
of the dagger pressed tightly against his throat, the woman's
small hand having taken a firm grip on his hair.

Wyntoun dropped the map on the table.

"Very good, clackdish! But you *know* you shouldn't be
touching things that don't belong to you!"

Chapter 4

Adrianne's hand kept a steady pressure with the small dagger as her eyes glanced over the map on the table before the Highlander. He turned his head slightly and the weapon cut into his skin. Blood beaded up on the taut skin of his neck.

"The next time you move will be the last time."

In spite of the trickle of blood now running down into the neck of his black shirt, Adrianne knew that her threat had not struck fear into the knight's heart. In fact, as green eyes turned and looked up at her, she wondered whether he was taking her seriously at all. His intense gaze swept downward from her face, taking in what he could see of the rest of her, and Adrianne suddenly felt her skin grow warm under his bold scrutiny.

Anger quickly replaced surprise, and she jerked his head backward, holding tight to his short black hair.

"Do not push your . . ." She paused as men could be heard passing the cabin door.

"Do not push what, wee one?"

He turned in the chair, and Adrianne quickly sidestepped to keep her advantage.

"Stop your moving, or I'll cut your throat. I swear I will!" Wyntoun MacLean in the flesh was clearly a great deal more dangerous than she had anticipated while hanging in her cage off Kisimul Castle's wall. And though the shade of green was darker, he had the predatory gaze of a cat on the hunt.

"And then what?"

"I . . . I have no time for these games. Be quick now. Wrap everything you took out in the leather again."

The Highlander not only ignored her command, he sat back in the chair, stretching his booted legs before him. The muscles in his tanned face relaxed, one corner of his mouth quirking upward insolently. The rogue even had the nerve to look bored.

She jerked his hair even harder, wiping the smirk off his face.

"I gave you a specific order. Now, if you wish to live long enough to see the first rays of dawn—"

The small dagger flew out of her hand and clattered loudly across the wooden floor of the cabin as the chair he was sitting on toppled on its side. Adrianne hadn't even time to let out a gasp before the Highlander's rock-hard forearm was around her, pinning her against him.

Kicking, twisting, punching at him wildly, Adrianne felt the hand she'd held the dagger in going numb from his sudden blow. Her strength seemed to drain from her completely as she realized her attempts were having no effect whatsoever on the blackguard. The brute simply twisted one of her arms behind her back, applying pressure and pulling her tighter to him.

She winced from the pain, but refused to cry out as he pinned the second behind her, as well.

"Now, you listen to me, hellcat," he said, snarling into her face.

She butted him with her head and this time had the satisfaction of seeing surprise and annoyance register in his arrogant features.

"What the hell . . . ?" he growled. Holding both her hands behind her in one viselike fist, he grabbed her wild tangle of hair with the other and held her solidly anchored in place.

"They were not jesting on Barra," he said, frowning at her. "You *are* truly dangerous."

Her head pounded with the impact of the blow she'd given him, but she ignored it, glaring at him fiercely.

"You should have listened with greater care, knight, as I will be cutting your throat as soon as I free myself of your loathsome grasp." Her gaze fell on his rigidly set jaw. She glanced up past the stern line of full lips—so close to her face—to his eyes. Wyntoun MacLean's eyes were assuredly the greenest she'd ever seen in her entire life. Far greener than the abbess's . . . and far more dangerous.

She swallowed the rest of her words and looked in the direction of the door. Escape suddenly seemed out of the question.

The warrior tugged again on a fistful of her hair and Adrianne's head snapped back. She watched as his eyes moved over her face, her mouth. He forced her body backward, his bold gaze taking in even more.

"You are much more . . . much older than I thought you would be."

The meaning of his words was unmistakable, as was the object of his attention. Adrianne felt a strange tingling in her breasts beneath the wet wool of her blouse. She struggled, but he again pinned her tightly against him.

"Let go of me," she squirmed, finding her face too close to his own. Strange feelings were racing through her. Part panic, part . . . something else. So close to him, she could smell his masculine scent—that unexpected smell of sea and storm. The saltiness of the west wind. His scent was too paralyzing, too . . . exciting. She tried to push away from him again.

"You will stop your squirming if you know what is best for you."

She paid no attention to his words and again tried to wriggle free of his hold. "If you don't release me this instant, by the Virg . . ."

The words once again withered on her lips as his strong arm pulled her tightly against his groin. This time she couldn't stop the gasp that escaped her as she felt the ridge of hardness against her hip. She knew what it was. It was that peculiar condition she knew men suffered when they were enticed in a certain way. Adrianne froze, looking up in shock at his face.

"I warned you to stop your squirming."

"I'm no scullery maid, villain. And I did *not* summon you."

One dark brow arched questioningly. "What are you talking about?"

"You have no reason for . . . for getting like this."

There was a small twitch at the corner of his mouth, and she gave him her fiercest and most contemptuous scowl.

"You think I need to be summoned, hellcat?" He pulled her tighter. "You think a man waits to be summoned?"

"Of course!" she challenged.

"A better man than I, perhaps." His eyes narrowed as he stared into her own. "But how do you know so much about this business of . . . summoning?"

Adrianne felt his manhood throb against her and tried again to get free of his hold, but he wouldn't release her.

"Did someone on Barra . . . touch you . . . or teach you of such things?" His face took on a murderous cast.

"I have had an endless experience with such matters. But what I know, I learned years before I ever stepped foot on your pitiful island."

An eyebrow shot up. "*Years* before?"

"Let go of me, clackdish." She twisted again, trying to break loose of his hold. Suddenly, the heat in the cabin had become unbearable.

"Years?"

She stopped, momentarily taken aback by the caressing softness in his tone, at the smoky look that had crept into his green eyes. Adrianne suddenly found it increasingly difficult to breathe. She forced herself to stare at the neckline of his black shirt, at the darker spots where she had drawn blood with her dagger.

"Aye, years," she retorted as sharply as she could. "I was fourteen when I first learned of this. That is considered years, I'd say."

"And who, might I ask, was the rogue that took it on himself to teach you such delicate and private matters? Some wandering friar, no doubt."

"You shall not slander the good name of God's lowly servants!" She hesitated, looking up at him. "As a matter of fact, there was not *one* rogue. There were many."

His look of desire quickly sharpened to a glare. "Many?"

"Of course, there were many." She nodded firmly. "Many men and one woman."

"A wom—?" His glare turned to a look of shock. "And where did these lecherous acts take place?"

"In the stables of our estate in Yorkshire. The last stall on the left was the favorite meeting place."

"Were . . . were your parents aware of such . . . such indiscreet behavior?"

"Of course not. But my sisters knew everything."

"And they didn't stop you?"

"Why should they?"

He was glaring at her. She glared back.

"It only began by accident . . . and quite innocently, too!" Her wrists ached from his powerful grip. "They knew I liked to go and learn by watching the men. And I never tried to rescue Catherine from herself when she would get lost in her books and daydream most of a day away. And Laura! She was worse with her lists and schedules and ordering everyone around."

"I hardly think your sisters' pastimes were quite the same thing as your . . . well, the fact that you would find pleasure in escaping to the stables."

"You condemn me without knowing anything about it." She tried to twist her arms free, but he continued to hold her. "And you're yelling at me."

"Someone needs to."

"And why is that?" she stormed. "You don't know about my family. If you knew anything about us, you'd understand that my nature and my talents are as valuable to our cause as my sisters' contributions."

"Your *cause*? And how is that?" His voice dripped with mockery. "Don't tell me. I suppose you plan to sell your services . . . and expertise . . . for money to take care of all three of you."

She frowned and met his piercing gaze. "Actually, the thought has crossed my mind many times. And I will tell you something, I would go through with it if there were ever a need for us to look after ourselves."

His face was the very picture of angry discontent.

"I *am* as good as any hired man."

"Hired *man*? This from Edmund Percy's daughter?"

He abruptly released Adrianne's hands, keeping his grip on her hair as he quickly righted the chair. Whirling her around, he sat her firmly in the chair and let go of her tangled locks.

"What business is it of yours if I—"

"I believe . . ." he growled, towering over her. "I believe I've learned more than I care to know about your flawed character."

"Flawed? How dare you!" She tried to stand up, but he pushed her back into the chair. "Just because I am more capable than most hired warriors . . . certainly more than an apelike mercenary like you . . . there is no reason for you to attack my character. I could easily disguise myself as a man, and I can fight as well as any of you. I can cut down a rider with a sword. I can jump a ditch or scale a castle wall. I can ride a horse better than most men, and I—"

"Perhaps you can, but we are discussing something quite different."

"I disagree!"

She reached for the map on the table, but he slapped her hand away. Taking hold of her chin, he raised it until their eyes met again.

The jolt Adrianne felt in her belly when he touched her was followed by a fluttering sensation that whirred upward through her with surprising speed. As she stared, she realized that, for the first time in her life, she was flustered by a man's good looks. Strong jaw. Full, firm lips. A weathered face with skin angling sharply over perfectly proportioned cheekbones. Wyntoun MacLean's piercing green eyes seemed to bore right into her, setting off sparks that seemed to burn holes right through the pulsing wings that continued to flutter inside of her.

"When you spoke of watching the men and learning, what were you talking about?"

"Watching them train for battle, of course."

The hard lines of his jaw visibly softened, and Adrianne was even more shocked to see the glint of humor in the warrior's eyes. He let go of her chin and straightened.

"Before we go any further, Mistress Percy, I am not a paid

mercenary—apelike or otherwise. I came to Barra at the request of your sisters."

She'd already heard as much while she hid amid the weapons stored in the shuttered cabinet beneath the cabin's bed. But there were other things that she'd heard, too. Things that made her realize she should not trust him.

"Tell me again, though. What was it exactly that you did when you went to the stables in Yorkshire?"

Though she had a few questions of her own to ask, she could see the determination in his eyes as he again focused his gaze on her.

"I watched my father's men training from a place in the loft."

"And you started doing this when you were fourteen?"

She snorted, shaking her head. "Nay! I started that when I was a child, old enough to reach the first rung of the ladder. I used to go up into the haylofts and lie there for whole afternoons, watching the men train with swords and spears, axes and halberds. The courtyard was alive with fighting in those days."

"And what exactly happened in the last stall to the left when you were fourteen?"

Adrianne felt her face flushing with heat. "I watched the scullery maid."

"Who?"

"The new scullery maid who had come to us from the village. After that, she would often meet there with men from the household and the farms."

"She met men?"

"Aye, she summoned them . . . you know . . ."

"Nay, I don't."

Adrianne glanced up, realizing that he was toying with her, and her temper flared. Spinning off the chair, she shoved it at him as she snatched the map off the table.

"I'll take that." His voice was low, threatening, and his eyes dark again with anger.

With her back to the table, she knew she had no clear path of escape. But at the same time, she wasn't ready to surrender, either. She held the map behind her.

" 'Tis mine and you know it. You were not to touch it—not to break the seal."

"I was entrusted with protecting the contents of that casket . . . and I do not take on a responsibility unless I know what 'tis that I'm protecting."

"You lie. You said nothing of this to the abbess."

"I am the master here . . . not the abbess." Drawing himself to his full height, the Highlander's head nearly brushed the cross-beams in the cabin ceiling. "Give me the map."

Adrianne edged back farther until her hip bumped the table.

"I heard you and the other man talking before. Who is really your master? I do not believe my sisters sent you here."

The two gazed at each other for a long moment of unbroken silence. His anger seemed to disappear. At the dull sound of heavy chain clanking and men shouting on deck, he nodded at her.

"You may believe what you want, but 'twas at the request of Catherine and Laura that I came after you."

"Why?"

"Is it so strange that those who are kin to you—?"

"Do not treat me like a fool. Why did my sisters need to send someone after me? Why now in the middle of winter? Why not wait for spring?"

With a look that bordered on amusement, he raised a hand over his head and leaned lazily against the cross-beam. "You are far too untrusting . . . you ask far too many questions."

She tried not to stare at the muscles of his arms bulging through the black sleeves of his shirt. "And you are giving far too few answers."

As he'd done before, his gaze drifted down the front of her body in a way that made a strange heat suddenly pool in her belly. She knew she was still wet. She could feel the weight of the wet wool of her clothes, even without the tartan shawl she'd stripped off her shoulders when she'd climbed aboard the vessel. Without the wrap, she was still dressed in a woolen blouse and a skirt made of MacNeil plaid. Still, there should not have been anything about her attire that should warrant so much of his attention.

"I know you are trying to distract me with your insolent

gaze. But it will not work." Holding the map in one hand, she moved it close to the flame of the wick lamp burning on the table. Though he made no visible movement, she saw his eyes narrow with concern as they followed the movement of her hand. This was better than a sword to his throat, Adrianne decided silently.

"Perhaps now you will be persuaded to answer my questions." The green eyes shifted back to her face. "Who, if anyone, really sent you here?"

"You already know everything that concerns you."

"Answer the question." Clenching the map tightly in her fist, she held it closer to the flame.

"You will not burn it."

Adrianne raised her chin in challenge. "Are you so certain?"

"'Tis part of your heritage. The honor of your family's name depends on that which you hold in your hand. You will not destroy the map to Tiberius."

"You know what this is. You mentioned it before." A heavy weight settled in her chest. Her hand moved still closer to the flame. She could feel the heat on her fingers. "But you are wrong. I *will* destroy this to stop the likes of you from ever getting hold of it. I will not let you meddle with what is sacred."

Adrianne steadily held his gaze, but suddenly the ship heeled to one side, forcing her to take a step for balance. This was all the advantage the Highlander needed, and he was on her in an instant. Once again, she found herself overmatched by sheer strength.

Holding tight to the hand that held the map, the warrior pushed her behind him, prying open her fingers as she punched him with her free hand. Finally, biting his arm just above the elbow, she found herself being spun around and pressed flat against the wall of the cabin. She continued to fight him, but he had her fist open and the map out of it in a moment. Shoving the document into the thick belt at his waist, he turned to her.

"You have forged on to the very end of my patience," he

growled close to her face. "I'll have you shackled and caged until we reach our destination."

"I'll escape." She glowered at him. "And before you know it, I'll be back in this cabin with my knife to your throat. And this time I won't give you a warning. You'll be dead before you have a—"

One strong hand encircled her throat, and she choked back the rest of the words. The ship leaned, and his body pressed more intimately against hers. She fought back the tumult of sensations at the feel of his aroused manhood. She lifted her eyes to his. Behind the deep green, she saw anger and fire.

"Now that I think of it, I have a better place to keep you."

The breath caught in her throat as his hand released her throat and moved slowly downward. She felt the brush of callused fingers against bare skin just above her right breast. Glancing quickly down, she stared at a long tear on her blouse—where his fingers were tracing a seductive path on the exposed curve of her breast.

"I . . . Stop!" She struggled against him, and he moved, allowing her to bring a hand between their bodies and pull the torn material together. "I . . . I must have torn that climbing aboard."

He was no longer touching her, but Adrianne could still feel the scorching heat of his hand on her skin, the strange tightness in her belly that his closeness seemed to be making worse with each passing moment.

"I warn you . . . my passion runs far cooler than my aunt's. But if you continue to provoke me . . ." At his pause, she looked up and met his eyes again. "If you push me too far, I can devise far more creative . . . treatment . . . than anything you've encountered so far."

The fight drained out of her in an instant as his hands moved up and cradled her face, holding her head motionless against the wall. She watched his eyes linger on her lips.

His mouth descended until his words were just a breath upon her skin.

"This is only a sample of the consequences that await you, if you should choose to provoke my passions."

Chapter 5

He might as well have hidden in a grave.

The incessant chattering of Gillie's teeth echoed dully inside the damp wooden staves of the barrel. For hours, it seemed, his legs had been alternating between feelings of pins-and-needles and total numbness. Pressing his thin chest tighter against his kilted legs, the boy blew on his hands, trying to breathe some warmth into the chilled bones.

The bay's water had been much colder than he'd thought it would be. The swim to the ship, much farther in the whipped-up water than he'd ever tried swimming in winter. Halfway to the ship, he had felt his mind starting to wander, but he'd forced himself onward. Onward in pursuit of his protector—his friend—the one person in the entire world who had cared enough to treat him with any kindness. Onward in pursuit of Mistress Adrianne.

The salty brine was still in his nose, and Gillie snatched the wet tam off his head to smother the sneeze that he felt coming on. The burning itch in the skin of his face was driving him mad. It was a hundred times worse from the sea-water, and he scratched at it carefully with the tam. It didn't help, but Gillie knew how agonizing it would be if he really scratched it as he wanted to. The crusty patches would just open up again, fiercely painful and oozing pus.

The boy forced himself to think of other things. Of Mistress Adrianne.

Hiding amid the rocks on Barra's shore, he'd kept watch over Mistress Adrianne from the time they'd hoisted the cage up the wall of Kisimul Castle. When the shipmaster had dropped anchor in the bay, and the steward had sent one of

the other lads calling for Gillie to help with the stores going
to the ship, he'd kept his silence and watched that cage
swinging in the winter gloom.

But it wasn't for her protection that he'd kept his vigil.
Gillie knew better than anyone that his mistress was braver
and more capable of taking care of herself than most men.
He'd been waiting for her to escape. And he'd known where
she was going.

For the past five months, for as long as he'd known Mistress Adrianne, she'd been waiting for a ship. Waiting for a
way to escape the Isle of Barra and get back to her family.
Seeing the tall masts and dark sails swing around the eastern point, Gillie had known that—cage or no—Mistress Adrianne was going to find a way to get on that vessel before it
sailed from Barra.

If she ever left the island, the boy had decided months
ago, he was going, as well. Gillie had decided that the first
moment she had taken the time to notice him.

Aye, he'd known he had to go with her. Except for the
fat steward when there was work to be done, no one would
miss him if he were to disappear forever. No one here cared
about Gillie the Fairy-Borne. Gillie the Scar-Face. Gillie the
Bringer of Bad Luck. Nay, no one here would miss him.

No one but Adrianne Percy.

He covered his nose and mouth again to smother another
sneeze.

True, Mistress Adrianne cared for everyone. She had always been there to help a wife haul kelp up for a garden,
or to lend a hand when a fishing net fouled on the rocks.
True, she always watched over a sick child while a woman
tended her wee ones. But Gillie knew that she cared for him,
as well. Perhaps even more than she cared for the others.

Through the darkness, he'd heard her scream, heard the
crash of the cage onto the wave-swept rocks. When he'd
seen the men out searching the waters around the castle,
though, he'd known that she'd escaped them . . . again.

And standing on the shore, watching the flaring torches
and the small boats bobbing about in the bay, Gillie had even
known where Mistress Adrianne had gone. He'd looked at

the ship and, without a moment's hesitation, he had stepped into the icy waters.

The ship was pitching and rolling with the movement of the sea, and Gillie was certain they had gotten underway. He could hear the commands and shouts of the sailors on deck. Each time the ship would roll, the bumping and squeaking of the barrels straining at their lashings would fill his ears. There was a shudder of the ship's timbers that Gillie felt in his bowels. Shifting his body, he pushed up slightly at the heavy cover of the barrel. Immediately, the foul smell of ship's bilge filled his lungs, and Gillie smothered another sneeze in the wool cloth of his cap.

The ship pitched forward with another lurching motion. It was even colder outside the barrel, and the boy tried to quiet his chattering teeth. His ragged clothes did little to keep out the winter cold. Wet as they were, they did even less.

In searching for a hiding place when he'd climbed hastily aboard, Gillie had seen a pile of old sailcloth that had been cast aside in the dark hold where he'd found refuge. Deciding that the old sails might offer more warmth than the damp barrel, he raised the cover completely and stood up, pausing to listen.

Aside from the shifting cargo and the water sloshing far below him, the noises were muffled, coming from above decks. The hold was dark as a cave. He pulled the wet tam onto his head and started to climb out of the barrel.

He had one leg out when a pair of sneezes exploded from his head, filling the darkness of the hold. In his rush to cover his mouth, he slipped and fell—boy and barrel cover—on the rough wooden planks.

The barrel cover rolled noisily across the deck, and Gillie scrambled after it. When it crashed into a bulkhead, the boy was nearly upon it. Grabbing it as it fell on its side, he held it and peered upward at the closed hatch doors.

Gillie's sigh of relief turned quickly to a gasp, though. From the darkness behind him, the talonlike hands of a sailor grasped him by the arms and held him up in the air while another sailor peered closely into his face.

*   *   *

It was only a brush of the lips. But it was also a step toward a chasm that Wyntoun knew held great danger. He was standing at the edge. As he looked into her eyes, he knew that she felt it too. The desire sizzled in the narrow space between them . . . and he saw her struggling against it.

With his lips still hovering just over hers, he watched her violet blue eyes grow round with awareness. The wild beat of her pulse beneath the tips of his fingers spoke of her agitation, and as he looked down at her parted lips, the thrill of conquest—and desire—surged in his loins. How he longed to feast on those lips!

He released her abruptly and took a step back.

"Remember this," he growled. He saw her clutch tightly at the torn section of her blouse. "Next time, there will be no stopping. And I assure you, if you are foolish enough to arouse my passions another time, our dealings will not end with a kiss . . . summons or no."

She remained still, her back to the wall of the cabin. Her face was flushed, but she continued to remain silent. As he'd expected, all the fight had washed out of her. Wyntoun eyed her with amusement, pushing back thoughts of his own physical reaction to this untamed beauty.

He pulled the map from his belt and placed it with the letter inside the leather pouch. Adrianne continued to watch his hands, but still she didn't move.

"Do you want to hear why I was sent after you?"

He glanced at her and saw her eyes flicker back from a spot across the cabin floor. Following her gaze, he located the small dagger that he'd knocked from her hand earlier. She was no quitter, he thought with grudging admiration.

He walked over and picked the weapon up off the floor and turned on his heels. Returning to her, Wyntoun held the dagger toward her with the hilt pointing out.

"Take it."

She stared at the weapon in his hand for a moment in surprise. "Why?"

"You are here on a ship with a crew of men who love three things—a bloody fight, a goodly drink, and a lusty wench. You'll need to protect yourself, I'd say."

Her hand reached up and encircled the hilt.

"And I am giving you this, not because I want to lose any of my fine crew, but because I trust you to use it only when you must. Oh, and not on me."

Her eyes—alert and blue enough to stir any man's blood—narrowed, belying her calm exterior. He watched her tuck the weapon in the waistband of her skirt. She was more confident with that weapon than many a man he knew. He looked up at the cut section of her dark tresses, falling so seductively across her brow.

The drama! She'd cut her hair to be certain that those who found the remnants of the cage would suffer with regret. Her only means of escape had been to climb up the single rope and over the beam to the castle wall.

She *was* a dangerous opponent. He would need to use all the finesse he could muster to keep her off balance.

"Your mother has been captured by the English king's men."

Her body snapped to attention at his sudden news.

"I was visiting my friend William Ross at Blackfearn Castle when the letter arrived. It came soon after his wedding to your sister Laura."

She opened her mouth, but no words came out.

"I have a great deal of information for you. So if you'll promise not to murder me with that wee dagger of yours, I'll tell you what I know." Granted, he thought, it was a poor enough effort at lightening the mood. He watched her move away from the wall and sink down onto the chair by the table. The stunned look on her face didn't change.

"My mother," Adrianne croaked, her voice barely a whisper.

"She is alive and will stay alive if Henry's demands are met."

He saw her fingers tremble as they reached up again and clutched at the torn blouse. "And Laura . . . she's married."

"Both of your sisters are married. Catherine has married John Stewart, earl of Athol. As I was leaving Blackfearn, a messenger brought word that she is bearing their first bairn."

"A bairn," she whispered. She turned her face away from

him, but not before he spotted the glint of tears in her eyes. "Tell me . . . tell me more about my mother."

"All I know is from the ransom letter that was sent to William Ross and from there to Athol."

"What did it say?"

"The letter came with an offer of exchange."

"Exchange for what?"

As Adrianne continued to clutch at her shirt, he considered acting as an honorable knight, the concerned host, and offering her dry clothing of his own to wear. But the look of entreaty in her eyes told him that she would have nothing to do with any of that until she knew the rest of his news.

"Treasure . . . in exchange for the life of your mother. Before they light the fires of Midsummer's Eve, you and your sisters must produce a certain treasure."

Her voice was barely a whisper. "Tiberius."

"Aye. That was why I broke the seal and searched out the map. Each of your sisters already has her own section of it."

"And all three pieces are needed."

"Laura has already sent word that you three agree to the exchange."

The temper flashed in her face as she turned to him. "There is nothing in this world I hold more dear than our mother, but that would not have been her wish. We are to protect the Treasure of Tiberius and keep it away from the likes of that foul English king, no matter what the hardship . . . no matter what the sacrifice."

Wyntoun paused, watching the emotions play across Adrianne's face.

"I believe your sister was only trying to buy time until an alternate plan could be devised."

Adrianne gave a small nod, a flush of embarrassment darkening her cheeks. Her voice was gentler when she spoke again. "Our instructions were to protect the map. But what if Nichola knows the whereabouts of Tiberius? This will give our enemies the chance to force the information from her. The treasure needs to be moved."

"Together, the three of you have the ability to find Tiberius. The journey to locate it should not be a difficult one."

The young woman came to her feet. "But what about our mother? We must raise an army! We must go south and free her before 'tis too late!"

The Highlander frowned at her. "You don't know where she is being held."

"It doesn't matter." She paced across the cabin. "Someone must know. We go to the Borders and take one castle at a time, if we have to. We—"

"I understand now why your mother saw fit to have word sent to your sister Laura."

Adrianne whirled to face him, blue eyes flashing, the revealing tear in her blouse already forgotten. The young woman was the very image of a storm about to break.

"No army Athol or William Ross could raise will match the English king's if she is being held south of the Tweed River. We tried that once, at Flodden Field, and lost many of Scotland's finest."

"I will not sit back and let her be murdered as my father was."

"Aye, no one could blame you for feeling that way. But sometimes, you must use forethought in dealing with such a delicate matter. You must plan your course as if you were sailing your ship through the reefs off Mull."

"You sound very much like Laura," she scoffed.

"I take that as a compliment."

"'Twas not intended as a compliment."

The ship suddenly dove downward into a trough, and Wyntoun knew they had moved into the open sea.

Adrianne pressed a hand to her stomach, reaching out to steady herself with the other. "What . . . what is Laura's plan?"

"I am to take you to Balvenie Castle, Athol's stronghold in the Highlands near Elgin. Laura and William Ross are to go there as well. When you are all together, you three and your sisters' husbands will agree upon a final plan."

"But that's not where you are going, are you?" The look of distrust was alive again in her eyes.

"Nay, not directly."

"And why is that?"

He studied her for a long moment, considering whether to answer or not. Moments before, when she'd been wild and reckless—when she'd held the dagger to his throat—the decision would have been easy. He would tell her nothing. Now, however, he was beginning to understand her.

"The weather in the Highlands can be a dangerous thing at this time of the year. Once we make the mainland, it could take as long as a month of hard travel to reach Balvenie Castle." He went to a small sea chest by the bed and returned with a map. Spreading it open on the table, he waited until she was leaning over it, too.

"My plan is to go to Duart Castle first. Depending on the wind, we should be there tomorrow . . . or the next day."

"Where is Duart Castle?"

He pointed at the map. "'Tis here, on the Isle of Mull. 'Tis the MacLean stronghold. From there, I could send men to the south into the Borders—and beyond if need be—to find out about your mother's possible whereabouts. And while we wait, I'll put together an escort to take you to your sisters."

Wyntoun studied her profile as she gazed intently at the map. Some time during the past few months, she'd obviously adopted the dress of the island women. The undyed wool blouse. The red and black and green MacNeil plaid skirt. When she'd climbed aboard the ship, she had discarded the wet tartan shawl that would complete the picture. Aye, he thought, with her wild mane of loose dark hair and her sun-kissed skin, she had the look of an islander. A stunningly beautiful islander.

He shook his head and looked down at the map. But he had not come to Barra looking for a woman to bed. Not even when that woman managed to heat his blood with a mere show of skin. She was a bonny thing, though, to be sure.

Nay, he told himself decisively, he'd come here to take

possession of the youngest of the Percy sisters for a reason . . . a reason far nobler than simple lust.

She pointed a slender finger at the map. "Where is Balvenie Castle?"

"Here," he replied, pointing to an empty space beneath the cross marked "Elgin."

She shook her dark locks. " 'Twould be a waste of time for me to go north to them. I will travel there only to turn around and go south again. If it takes as long as you say, the Treasure of Tiberius will be surely lost . . . and my mother, too."

"Your sisters' wishes were clear regarding what you were to do."

There was a knock at the door. She ignored it and turned to him. "But that was because . . . well, I love them both dearly, but they are incapable of acting swiftly."

"I gave them my word that you would be delivered safely." The knock was louder this time. Wyntoun turned irritably to the door. "Aye, what is it?"

Alan pushed open the door.

"I have bad news, Wyn. We've cleared the point and made the turn toward Ardnamurchan. But Coll just brought up the stowaway from the hold, and 'tis not the lass—" The shipmaster stopped dead as he noticed Adrianne standing behind the knight. "On the other hand . . ."

"Mistress Percy is accustomed to traveling in better quarters than an empty barrel." Wyntoun cast a quick glance in Adrianne's direction and found her frowning at him. "Stay to your course, Alan. Our guest managed to find this cabin with no help from any of us."

The sound of shouts and laughter from the deck above them raised Wyntoun's brow.

"And what is all that about?"

"We did find a stowaway in the barrel." The shipmaster seemed to have some difficulty tearing his eyes away from Adrianne.

"And who might that be?"

"The foundling you came across years ago. The scar-faced lad they call Gillie the Fairy-Borne."

There were more shouts and laughter from above.

"What's all the noise about?" Wyntoun asked again, stepping around Alan and cocking an ear toward the ladder as a loud cheer from the sailors reverberated throughout the cabin.

"I believe the men just threw the lad overboard."

Chapter 6

"Overboard!" Adrianne cried out. "They cannot throw Gillie into the sea!"

She made it only to the door of the cabin before the knight caught her and tossed her roughly in the direction of the shipmaster.

"Let me go! I have to get him out of that icy water. The lad will die!"

"Alan, keep an eye on this hellcat until I get back."

Adrianne struggled for a moment against the man's grip, but the rolling of the ship suddenly sent a wave of sickly heat through her, causing her knees to weaken beneath her. She paused and drew a breath in alarm. The cabin was suddenly close and warm. She pushed away from him again in an attempt to move toward the door. The shipmaster held her firmly by the arm.

"Mistress Percy, you've no reason to fight me. The master will bring the lad back. The men may have him tethered to a line yet."

His voice was gentle, soothing, but she looked at the man called Alan in alarm.

"Tethered to a line?"

"Aye," he answered. "To see how long he can stay afloat. Everyone knows the servants of the de'il cannot bear the water."

"Servants of the devil? Gillie's just a young boy!"

"These men are just sailors, mistress. They have their superstitions and their old beliefs . . . just like everyone else."

"But—"

"Wyntoun can handle them," he said, easing his grip. "All will be well. Just wait, mistress."

He dropped his hand from her arm, and she moved to the small, shuttered windows at the far end of the cabin. She turned her back on him and tried to pull together the torn edges of her blouse.

"You might want to be using this."

Adrianne glanced over her shoulder at the Highlander as he picked up a blanket off the single bed and held it out to her.

"You're soaking wet, and Wyntoun wouldn't be too happy if you were to catch a chill before we reach Duart Castle." He glanced at her clutching the blouse. "And I'll have some-one—nay, I'll bring down a needle and thread from my things for you to mend that."

Adrianne studied more closely the confident and serious set of the man's features. She was sure he was younger than he looked, in spite of the gray thatch of hair and the skin weathered by sun and salt air. His green eyes were so much like Wyntoun MacLean's that she wondered for a moment if they were brothers. She took the blanket from him and wrapped it around her shoulders.

"Why would the sailors think Gillie was a servant of the devil?"

"His face, mistress. One look at him and they decided he's one of . . . of *that* kind. The kind that brings bad luck."

"But he's only a lad with a birth scar of sorts."

"He's sure to bring bad luck, all the same, as far as sailors are concerned."

She tightened her hold on the blanket as the sound of shouts and activity came from above. As the ship rolled again, she sat down on the single chair.

"This is the same nonsense I heard on Barra. Villagers not allowing him in their huts. Fishermen beating him if he got too close to their boat. Even the nuns from the chapel going wide around him if they were to meet him on the path."

The shipmaster shrugged and leaned against the bulkhead by the door. "I told you before, everyone knows the lad brings bad luck."

The ship heeled over sharply, and Adrianne knew the vessel was turning.

"But what proof has anyone of this foolishness? Has the lad been the cause of great fires, or storms, or plague? Has there been a great flood?" She continued to frown up at him. "Has there been one sickness or death in human or animal that the lad has been responsible for?"

Alan cocked an ear toward the open door for a moment as a loud commotion could be heard overhead. As he stepped out the threshold, Adrianne sprang to her feet, thinking to follow the Highlander on deck. An instant later, though, he was back in his place, shaking his head.

"Well, I've an hour's work getting this ship back on course. The lad's not bringing *me* any luck."

"That's no answer," she persisted. "What is it that Gillie has done?"

"'Tis not what *he* has or has not done, mistress," Alan responded calmly. "I feel badly for the lad, as well. 'Tis just that bad luck follows him about. Things . . . bad things happen to people when they let the lad tarry near them. A cow stops giving milk. A net full of fish breaks. 'Tis nothing that he does. 'Tis just that things happen."

"Well, he's been following me about for almost six months and nothing bad has happened to me."

The man shrugged again as the first hint of a smile threatened to appear on his weathered face. "Well, mistress, I would not call hanging in a cage from the ramparts of Kisimul a *good* thing."

"That was my own doing . . . and the doing of the abbess."

"Maybe so. Anyway, some folk are not affected by bad luck. Wyntoun is like that. He was the one who found Gillie the Fairy-Borne in the first place and brought him to Barra. And just like you, nothing bad ever happens to him."

There were more shouts coming from the deck above, and Adrianne bit at her lip as a wave of nausea struck her. She forced down the feeling.

"They might need help. Are you sure Sir Wyntoun will get him back aboard?"

"Aye, mistress. The water's a wee bit cold, but the lad can swim."

The matter-of-factness of his answer only eased her fears a little. She let another moment pass before rising and pacing the length of the cabin, occasionally stopping and gazing in the direction of the door.

"What will he do with the lad?"

Alan thought a moment. "We pass by a wee island called Muldoanich. The master may just cast him ashore there. The fishermen will be stopping there come spring, so the lad should survive. Someone will take him back to Barra."

She shook her head in disagreement, eyeing the door of the cabin uneasily. "I know how the fishermen treat him. And that is even if he could survive out there alone through the winter."

The Highlander stared at Adrianne, then spoke more softly. "You don't have to worry, Mistress Percy. Wyn has even more of an interest in Gillie than you do yourself. He'll do right by the lad."

"And why is that?"

"I said before that he found him in a bank of gillieflowers . . . all bundled up in a rag and left in the hills for the fairies . . . or the beasts to take. Now, the way that wee thing looked—with that devil's . . . with that mark covering half of his tiny face—and weak enough that he didn't have any voice left even to whimper." He shook his head at the memory. "Most men would have walked away and let the poor creature take his last breath and thought no more on it. But not Wyntoun MacLean."

Adrianne frowned deeply. She knew the realities of life in the Highlands . . . and in these wild windswept islands. Life was hard here for those trying to eke out an existence. And superstitions here were no stronger than in Yorkshire, where she grew up. Having a bairn here—just as having a child in her native country—was good only as long as you could count on him or her to help with the work. Woe to the child born "different," though. Ignorance had a dark and frightening power.

"They call him 'fairy-borne,' " she murmured softly, recalling her first view of the lad's face. Half of his face handsome, dark, and brooding. The other half misshapen—the flesh beneath his eye sagging, the skin red and raw, covered with scaly, encrusted patches. Whatever was wrong, the innocent boy had been plagued with the condition since infancy.

"Aye! Gillie the Fairy-Borne." Alan leaned against the wall, eyeing her with his arms crossed over his chest. "Borne by the fairies into Wyntoun's own hands."

The ship heeled over again and shuddered as the wind caught in the sails. The wooden chest slid across the table. Adrianne reached for it and caught it before it fell to the floor. Placing it back where it was, she leaned gingerly against the cabin wall. The movement of the box had set the room spinning around her.

"I have . . . I was just hoping that your master would give me leave to see the lad before putting him off on the island."

The Highlander cast a knowing look in her direction but said nothing.

"I've grown fond of Gillie these past months." There was another dipping motion, and Adrianne's stomach lurched uneasily. "I'm certain he stowed away on this ship to be close to me. He's grown somewhat attached to me, I believe."

"I can see how that could happen."

Adrianne, surprised by his statement, glanced quickly at the man. His face had lost its guarded look for an instant, and tenderness was evident in the green eyes. She opened her mouth to speak, but a feeling of nausea—caused by the ship's movement—swept over her, silencing her.

"Mistress Percy, are you weak-legged when it comes to the sea?"

She stared at the man blankly. "Of course not! I've sailed a number of—"

The ship rose and then dropped with a sideways rolling motion that was too much for her. Suddenly, she was running for the small windows and holding her hand to her mouth.

As she emptied the contents of her belly into open air, the gray-green ocean rose up in swells high enough to spray her with stinging brine.

In a moment, a pair of hands drew her back in and she found herself on her knees and retching into a bucket.

On and on it went. A nightmare of sensations! A most horrible weakness! She willed herself to stop and tried to force open her eyes. But one glimpse of her own bile in the bottom of the bucket and she was heaving again. Her stomach was empty, and yet—as the ship rolled or lurched or dove into the bottomless well between two waves—she continued to retch.

Time passed. She wasn't sure how much. Vaguely, she was aware of voices in the cabin. People around her. With her arms wrapped around the bucket and her head buried in it, however, she couldn't find the strength to look up. With every movement of the ship, her body convulsed. The only conscious thought she had now was the desire to die.

". . . Wrap the lad . . . dry blanket . . . Nay, I'm fine . . . set your course as you . . ."

The knight's voice. And Alan's. Another, too. A moaning sound that she realized was coming from her own body. With a will, she raised herself above her misery enough to sense the presence of young Gillie, as well, but immediately sank again without being able to open her eyes fully. She would live out her life with her two arms wrapped tightly around the bucket.

". . . not much of a sailor . . . I do not know a woman who . . ."

Something in the tone of the new voice penetrated her stupor. Scorn.

This was everything that she hated. Helplessness—the inability to protect herself. Seasickness was the one weakness that she could not conquer, and her mother knew it very well. Adrianne knew it was the reason Lady Nichola had arranged to have her sent to an island. Her mother wanted her in a place where leaving . . . where escaping . . . would be next to impossible. Even for her.

Fighting the sickness, she realized that her body was shivering violently. The cramping of her belly was like a red hot poker jabbed into her entrails. She was obviously in her final death throes.

"Coll, go find a dry blanket . . . and fetch a clean bucket, as well."

Adrianne felt someone sweep back her hair. Strong hands took hold of her shoulders, supporting her.

"I can take the lad back to the galley and keep an eye on him there, master."

"Nay! I'll not go!" Gillie's voice.

"Leave him here for now."

The sound of the cabin door penetrated. One of the hands moved to her back. She could feel the warmth of it through her blouse. She lifted her head enough to rest her forehead on the back of her hand. She would not die with her head in the bucket.

"You'd best go on deck, Alan."

"Are you sure you can deal with this yourself?" There was a note of teasing in the shipmaster's voice. Somehow, she just didn't see any humor in the fact that she was dying.

"I'll call up for you if I need help."

Footsteps. The door of the cabin closing. Adrianne desperately wished the knight would just go away, too, and let her suffer her last moments of agony alone. Suddenly, to her great disappointment, her wish was granted as the warm hands dropped away. She heard his boots scrape the rough floor as he stood and took a step back.

The ship shuddered before dropping about a mile straight down, and Adrianne heaved again, twisting in pain as the cramping seized her middle again. This was so much worse than her journey to Barra, and far, far worse than the trip to France that she'd taken with her father when she'd been a young child of only seven. Well, she'd never see twenty-seven, of that she was certain.

She couldn't help it as tears sprang to her eyes. The ship lurched again and her stomach retched again in response. She thought she heard the sound of his boots moving away.

"Don't . . . don't go." Her voice was little more than a moan. The violent shuddering again wracked her body. She was cold. Cold and wet to the bone.

"I'm not going anywhere, lass."

Adrianne felt the weight of a blanket being wrapped around

her. Then she was surrounded again with heat, with warm and steady hands, rubbing her shoulders, infusing heat into her shivering body.

"Take a sip of this. Wash your mouth out with it."

The thought of taking anything revolted her, and she desperately shook her head.

"You can do it." The bucket was wrenched away from her shaky hands and Adrianne found herself being pulled back until she was nestled against his body. "Just a sip."

She pried open her eyes enough to see a cup as it was being pressed against her lips. She stared into the green eyes above the cup. Short hair the color of night. The lean, muscular face unmarked by scars. Adrianne knew she must be terribly weak, feverish, perhaps even delirious in her last moments, for Wyntoun MacLean looked like some warrior angel, waiting to guide her home. His magnificence took her very breath away . . . though it could have been the room that was spinning behind him.

"Come, Adrianne. A sip. A wee one. Enough to wet your mouth."

Totally helpless to disagree, she allowed him to pour a mouthful of the liquid past her lips. Miraculously, the drink slipped down her raw throat. And she held it down. She closed her eyes and felt herself drawn tightly against his chest, and in a few moments the ship seemed to be rising and falling with less violence than it had been doing before.

Opening her eyes, she stared vaguely across the floor. The cabin had taken on a dreamlike quality. None of the edges of things were sharp, and she could not bring them into focus. Then she saw the anxious eyes of Gillie peering at her from a corner of the room.

As she watched him, the boy sneezed. Adrianne dove forward for the bucket as another retching sensation convulsed her body. The strong arms of the knight held her, and drew a clean bucket closer. There was nothing left in her belly, but that didn't seem to matter much.

"She won't die, will she, master?" She could hear the worry in the lad's voice.

"Nay, Gillie. Not as long as we keep any food away from her for the rest of this journey."

Callused fingers gently lifted the hair away from her face and drew her head back against his chest. The cup again appeared at her lips, and she had no fight left in her as the Highlander poured a small taste of it into her mouth.

A strange taste, this drink he was giving her. She had more of it this time. It was warm on her tongue, numbing the places that it touched.

"Are you poisoning me?"

"Nay. Taking care of you."

His fingers were soothing as they caressed her hair, her brow. She felt knuckles brush against her cheek. A drug of some kind, she sighed. A potion.

Her eyes drooped, and Gillie's image across the room wavered and then faded into the warm colors of a summer afternoon. She reached for the strong arm at her side, resting her cheek against his solid chest. Vaguely, she could hear the sound of a strong heart beating.

And then she slept.

The thin light of a gray dawn filtered through the single narrow window, an arrow slit high up on the wall of the stone tower room. The floor that had allowed access to that window had long ago been pulled away. Lying awake on the narrow cot, Lady Nichola Percy stared blankly upward at the window and the beams above and tried to make some sense out of the distant noises coming through the solid, iron-banded door of her prison chamber.

But there was nothing she could hear that triggered any memory. No distinct accents, no familiar smells, not even the normal sounds of castle life could be heard rising to the tiny window. Nothing that would give her a clue as to where she was . . . or as to the identity of her abductors.

She and a company of trusted friends and warriors had just left the ancient tower on St. Mary's Loch, west of Jedburgh. The attack had come out of nowhere, and as the skies rained warriors, Nichola had been snatched from her horse and carried off. Blindfolded and bound, she had heard the sounds of battle being fought in her wake. But they had her now. Whoever they were.

She didn't know how long they'd traveled. Passed from hand to hand, she guessed it was days, but she couldn't be certain. Faint from exhaustion and hunger, the time just blurred into a gray-black haze. She had no idea where they had taken her. North, south, east . . . she couldn't tell.

Even once she had been deposited in the dark hole of some castle, she had not been told anything. In the entire month she had spent as their prisoner, she'd been moved three times. Always the same way. Each time with great secrecy. Each time blindfolded by nameless and faceless men and whisked away in the middle of the night to another windowless hole in some ancient keep.

No one would talk to her, and not knowing why these men were treating her this way was about to drive her mad.

Death held no terror for Nichola Percy. After her husband's murder in the Tower of London, Nichola had been more than prepared for her own fate. Her daughters were safely scattered across the Highlands. Catherine already wed, and Laura and Adrianne hopefully wed soon.

Marriage. She wondered what her daughters' marriages would be like. As good as her own had been? Indeed, there were nights when the ache inside of her for her loving Edmund struck her so sharply that she would have welcomed death.

If the English king wanted her, she would stay where he could find her. She would not venture too far north into her native land. All she had to do was remain alive and free until the good news from Laura and Adrianne reached her, as well. Until she knew that her plans of their future had borne fruit. Then she would follow willingly after her dearest love.

But there was nothing about these people that told her she had fallen into the hands of Henry Tudor. There had been no attempt on her life. After the initial journey, there had been no real hardship imposed upon her . . . with the exception of the silence. Her imprisonment seemed so different from Edmund's swift and brutal end.

But if these men were not in the English king's service, then who were they?

No interrogation, no questions of any kind. In the back of her brain, the thought kept nagging at her that perhaps her capture and imprisonment had nothing to do either with Henry's hatred of the Percys or with the whereabouts of the maps.

But if she was being held against her will for some other reason, then none of this made any sense.

A heavy door squeaked on old hinges somewhere beneath where she lay. Last night, Nichola had come through that door herself before climbing the twenty-seven steps to a landing and her chamber. After the iron-banded door had shut behind her, she'd simply been left alone to remove the blindfold herself.

Quietly, she sat up and placed her feet on the oak floor. She could feel air pushing up through the old timbers. Nichola stared at the door, desperately hoping for someone to come through it. Anyone, she thought.

After a few endless moments, a bar lifted on the far side, and Nichola stood as it opened just enough for an old woman to enter. The heavy door swung shut behind her.

A dark cloth served as a covering to the woman's head. What might be visible of her face, Nichola could not see because of the pronounced bend on the woman's back. She disregarded the tray that was placed on the single table by the wall. Instead, she focused on the frail old creature as she made her way around the room, checking the chamber pot, stacking some peat in the small brazier that burned smokily in the corner, though it did little to take the edge off the winter chill. The ancient woman never looked up at her once.

"Good morning to you, mistress," Nichola offered.

There was no response. But then again, there had been no response to anything she'd said or demanded in the last two places that she'd been kept.

She crossed over to the table and poured some of the water from a pitcher into a bowl. She glanced again at the woman's back. The difference this time over the last two keepers was that *a woman* had been sent in to see to these basic needs. Nichola considered that a positive sign.

"Is it still raining outside?" The ride had been wet the previous day. Her own horse had slipped a number of times as her captors had led her to this keep.

Again, the old woman gave no sign of answering. No movement of the head. No straightening of the back. Not even a glance of curiosity.

Nichola dipped her hands into the icy water and raised them to her face. The cold against her skin felt good, and she glanced again at the woman as she turned to the door.

"Can you stay? Just for a few moments to keep me company while I eat?"

No acknowledgment. Only a heavy shuffling toward the door.

Nichola watched as the spotted, blue-veined hand rose and rapped on the heavy oak. A frown pulled at the prisoner's mouth as the iron-banded door opened again only enough for the visitor to slide through and disappear. In a few moments, Nichola heard the heavy door at the bottom of the stairwell open and close.

"Who are you people?" She found her temper rising and made no attempt to check it. "What do you want from me?"

Chapter 7

Wyntoun stared at the gray line of Ardnamurchan's coast rising above the mists. On a clear day, the worn crags of Bienn na Seilg would be visible from here, but the day had been anything but clear and darkness was closing in fast. He turned his attention up to the sailors scurrying through the rigging. In a couple of hours' time they'd be running into the smoother waters of the Sound of Mull. And assuming Argyll's men at Mingary Castle didn't take a fancy to sending a few cannon balls their way as the carrack passed, he'd be dropping anchor in Duart Bay before dawn, if the breezes held.

In front of him, Alan shouted orders upward at the men in the rigging before walking aft to where Wyn stood at the stern rail. The shipmaster took note of the wind to the south, eyed the coastline, and nodded—his unsmiling face giving no indication of satisfaction. Wyntoun knew from experience, though, that Alan would take his ship home without mishap.

As the two men stood in comfortable silence, Coll, one of Wyntoun's oldest and ablest sailors, came up from below and mounted the short ladder to the aft deck.

"Any change?"

Coll shook his head, his blue eyes as clear as the day he'd gone to sea as a lad. "The drink ye gave must have been a strong one, master. The lassie ne'er stirred a finger the whole watch."

"And the lad?"

"Nary a blink from that one." The sailor pulled off his tam and scratched the bald spot on top of his head. "He's still huddled at the foot of the bed, guarding the lassie. He's got spunk, the lad does."

"But he doesn't seem to have brought us much bad luck in the crossing, would you say?"

Coll's face turned a shade of red as he shook his head at his master. "Nay . . . but ye know I do not put much faith in such rubbish, master. I did hear the men saying that we had no trouble because ye locked the lad up in yer cabin . . . there was no way he could spread his bad luck from down there."

"I say we spread the word that the ducking Gillie got in that cold water yesterday must have washed off all of the lad's bad luck." Wyntoun's comment brought a chuckle from Coll and a nod from Alan. "The lad will be staying at Duart Castle for a while—at least until we have another ship going back to Barra. And the last thing I want is for our men to be bringing any rubbish ashore about the lad."

"Aye, master, I can spread the word. I've found, though, from place to place folks think much the same about lads like him . . . without much encouraging."

"Then we'll just have to look after him."

Wyntoun turned his back on the sailor and frowned at the solid gray mass of sea and sky to the west. What Coll said was true. From the time that Wyntoun had found the infant years back, such ignorance must have been dogging the lad. He'd only seen him a handful of times while stopping at Barra, but never—during any of those visits—had he realized the depth of the hostility those islanders held against Gillie. These sailors were rough men, hardened by a life of battling both the sea and other men. It had been little more than a diversion dropping the lad overboard into the icy waters, but Wyntoun still seethed, thinking that the boy could have drowned because of such foolishness.

"Should we try to wake the mistress, master . . . before arriving at Duart Castle?"

"Let her be for now." The ship shuddered as a strong gust swept in from the west. In a moment a blast of stinging rain struck the men. "The closer we get to the castle, the less problem we'll have dealing with her."

A wry glint showed in Alan's eye. "Wyn, I never knew you to cower before a challenge, no matter how unpleasant the possible outcome."

"The woman is *not* a challenge," the Highlander growled. "Just a nuisance."

As he moved away from the two, it occurred to him that he'd do well to remind himself of that point time and again. Adrianne Percy was nothing more than a nuisance.

He'd forced himself to keep his distance since yesterday, when she'd finally fallen asleep in his arms in the cabin. He'd had to. Seeing her so wretchedly seasick and then holding her as she so willingly melted against him as the drink had taken effect had been torture. He'd felt it then. He felt it now. Something had happened as he'd sat there with her beautiful face pressed against his pounding heart, with those magical blue eyes looking up at him so trustingly before slowly closing.

The vision was still too alive in his memory. Far too alive.

His manhood hardened as he thought of her body, so perfect as he had stripped off her wet clothes and worked her limp arms into a wool shirt of his own. Wyntoun was almost glad that Gillie the Protector had been sitting in the corner of the cabin, eyes riveted to the floor, as he'd tucked her into his bed. Almost glad.

Wyntoun filled his lungs with the cold salty air and let the rain beat at his face. He stared at the surging gray-green waves and tried not to think of the smooth ivory skin of her shoulders; the firm, orb-shaped breasts; the rosy nipples, puckered into hard, tight points in the cold air of the cabin. He exhaled sharply, puffing his cheeks. He needed to try harder not to think of such things, he told himself.

Adrianne Percy was far more of a handful than he'd thought she would be. Somehow, in spite of what he'd heard, he'd thought she would be more like her sister Laura. In reality, though, they couldn't be more different. As he'd mapped out his scheme, Wyntoun realized now, he'd clearly miscalculated when it came to the youngest Percy.

He frowned into the biting wind. But it wasn't Adrianne's willfulness that was going to cause him trouble. It was his own irrational attraction to her.

"Distance, by the devil," he swore under his breath. "Bloody distance."

*   *   *

The ship seemed to have stopped its insane rolling and
pitching . . . and so had her stomach. Adrianne slowly pried
open her eyes.

There was no spinning of the chamber, no undulating walls,
only the sound of sea birds and the lapping of water somewhere. Gillie's worried face came into view above her, and
Adrianne smiled.

"Mistress," the lad gasped with relief, touching her hand.
"You're finally awake. The master did say that you'd be sleeping for a wee while longer, but I've never seen anyone who
could sleep so long."

"How long, Gillie?"

"A night, a day, and a whole night again, mistress." The
boy's face brightened. "And you look very well this morning. Not green the way you were when I was fetched out of
the water and brought in here by the master."

"You look very well, too, Gillie. All dried out?"

The boy suddenly flushed. Scurrying away, the lad popped
back a moment later with his wool tam, as usual, covering
much of the scarred half of his face.

"You don't have to wear that around me, Gillie."

"I do, mistress. I always have to."

Adrianne shook her head in disagreement. "I think you are
the most handsome of lads—just as you are."

Gillie's visible cheek turned a darker shade of red as he
scrambled to his feet. Crossing the ship's cabin, he poured
her a cup of a water from a pitcher.

Her mouth was dry as dust . . . and tasted about as badly.
She smiled at him appreciatively as she raised herself on her
elbows. It was then that she noticed the change in her ap-
parel.

Gone was her wet dress of two days ago. Her torn blouse.
She was now wearing only a man's shirt. A rather large man's
shirt. She peered quickly under the blankets and stared with
dismay at her bare legs.

"You would have caught your death, for sure, if he'd not
got you out of those wet clothes."

Adrianne did her best to keep the note of panic out of her voice.

"He?" she managed to croak.

"Aye. The master . . . Sir Wyntoun." The boy crouched beside the bed, his spindly legs hidden beneath his ragged kilt of red, black, and green plaid. "I was right here, though, mistress. The master did nothing . . . well, you know . . . he was right quick about it."

She pushed a shock of hair out of her face and spotted her clothes spread on the single chair by the worktable. A strange heat prickled in her belly, working its way outward, and she gnawed at her lip. Well, she couldn't change what was past.

"You must be thirsty, mistress." Gillie held the cup out to her.

Adrianne forced herself to focus on the boy, and reached for the cup. "This will not make me sleep more, will it?"

"Nay!" he replied, watching her drink. "Auld Coll said you've had enough sleeping to last you a fortnight."

"And who is Auld Coll?"

"He is one of the sailors, mistress. The one who found me hiding in a barrel."

"And one of the men who threw you overboard?" She sat up in the small bunk and gathered the blankets tightly around her bare legs.

"Nay, not him." Gillie shook his head. "He says he has been sailing the seas too long to be believing in fairy nonsense. He says luck is one thing, and curses is another. He had nothing to do with them when they tied me to a line and threw me to the fish. In fact, Auld Coll was a help to the master when he pulled me out."

"I'm sorry that happened, Gillie." She touched him gently on the side of his face. "Were you frightened?"

"Nay, mistress . . . well, a wee bit." An impish smile tugged at his lips.

"I believe I like Auld Master Coll." Adrianne swung her feet to the floor, bringing the blankets with her. A flash of lightheadedness swept through her, and she waited a moment. "The ship's not moving."

"We're anchored in the Bay of Mull, mistress. If you look out that wee window there, you'll see we're but a stone's throw from Duart Castle."

"A speedy journey," Adrianne whispered, watching with amusement as Gillie moved across the cabin and returned with a trencher on which someone had placed a bannock cake and some salted fish. Putting it on the bed next to her, he then shook out a tartan shawl that lay folded at the foot of the bunk and put it around her shoulders.

"Auld Coll came in a while back and said I should be letting him know as soon as you're up and about. The sailors are running boats back and forth from the stone quay down the hill from the castle. I think he had in mind that you'd be needing to—"

"Gillie!" The boy stopped dead, waiting obediently for her to speak. "Why don't you go and let them know."

"Auld Coll said that unless the master himself comes down to relieve me, I should not be leaving you alone, mistress."

"Gillie!" she said more forcefully this time. "I'd like a moment to myself to get into my own clothes. So just run along."

"Aye, mistress."

"But do not go too far," she called gently after him. "I don't believe I have my strength back, so I'll be needing your protection."

The boy's quick grin was precious. He nodded once and quietly slipped out of the cabin.

Pushing the covers aside, Adrianne pushed herself to her feet only to stretch a hand out quickly for the closest solid object. She was weak and extremely wobbly on her feet. Still though, she managed to make her way eventually across the cabin to the table, where she found a bowl of water. After washing herself, she removed the shirt and hurriedly donned her own blouse and dress.

The effort took a great deal of energy, but the two small windows at the stern of the cabin beckoned to her. Adrianne crossed the chamber and opened them. She closed her eyes and filled her lungs with the fresh sea air. Her stomach, achingly empty, did not complain at all as the gentle swells of the small bay rocked the ship.

From above the windows, she could hear the sounds of men talking and laughing somewhere on deck. A boat pushed away from the side with the wooden clap of oars against their pegs. She opened her eyes as the boat came into view beneath the stern—four men rowing, five barrels stacked and tied fast in the stern.

She turned her gaze on the shore and the castle, standing so proud above the bay.

With its great tower and stout stone walls, Duart Castle was a magnificent structure of strength and beauty. Smiling wistfully, Adrianne recalled the memory of days not so far in the past, when her sisters Catherine and Laura had teased her for seeing beauty in the powerful set of a curtain wall, or in the crenellated tops of a tower, or in the magnificent workmanship of an iron gate.

As Catherine would dream for hours of books and teaching, and as Laura would find enjoyment in finding a solution to everyone else's problems, Adrianne had always been fascinated with structures—to the art of building something so significant that would outlast the destructive power of storms and time . . . and men. She loved the lines of the fortress, the moat, the keep, the tower. It said to your enemies, *I can protect myself and my own.*

Self-preservation and independence. They were the reasons behind her lifelong drive to school herself in the art of handling knife and sword.

Not that it had done her much good when it came to dealing with Sir Wyntoun MacLean, Adrianne thought with a frown.

Pushing the short locks away and gathering the rest of her hair to one side, she combed her fingers through the thick locks before beginning to braid it. But the situation had only gone from bad to worse, she thought. And in light of the shirt she'd found herself wearing upon awakening, perhaps it was best not to think about him at all. Maybe what she needed was a tower and a moat of her own.

A knock on the door brought a smile to her lips. Her affectionate and devoted gentleman protector . . . aged ten.

"Come in, Gillie," she called loudly over the sound of men's voices from the quay.

The door opened at her summons, but her heart jumped a beat when she saw Wyntoun MacLean duck across the threshold into the cabin.

"I hope you do not mind, but your wee warrior was needed on deck."

For some reason, she couldn't quite find her voice.

"Coll will watch out for him, so you needn't fret. And Alan's about, as well. The lad needs to know he's earning his keep."

Adrianne, feeling strangely short of breath, deftly finished braiding her hair and pushed it back over one shoulder. His gaze rested momentarily on the tear in her blouse.

"I see you have already found your clothes."

"I . . . I have." She stopped, trying to calm the wild beating of her heart. What was done, was done, she told herself. His gaze still lingered on the tear in her blouse. She gathered it quickly.

"I must mend this as soon as I have a chance . . ."

One of his eyebrows arched. "Not on my account, I hope."

Adrianne felt the heat rising in her face, and she turned her gaze away. "That . . . that drink you gave me when I was ill. I slept like the dead. What was in it?"

"Folk of the west are not known to part easily with their secrets." He went to the bunk and picked up the tartan shawl Gillie had offered her before.

When he placed the tartan around her shoulders, she felt the strength in her legs suddenly drain out. She could smell his good masculine scent of sea and leather, and the effect of his nearness was dizzying.

"We're at Duart Castle," he said, stepping back. Adrianne quickly crossed the ends of the tartan over her chest, covering the tear in her blouse. "Anytime you're ready, a boat will take you ashore."

"What about Gillie?"

"The lad will be staying at the castle for a while."

She nodded, considering the best way to ask him his intentions for the boy. Though he couldn't know how difficult life was for Gillie on the island, she knew this was probably not the best time to press him on the matter.

"Your stay at Duart Castle will be brief." He closed and latched the small windows in the stern. "As I told you before, you'll be remaining here only until I can equip a number of trusted men to take you north."

"The map?" Adrianne asked, crossing to the table. There was no sight of the packet or the wooden casket.

"Fear not. It has already been brought safely ashore. I will hold it until such time as you're ready to depart. We both know it will do no one any good without the portions that your sisters possess. 'Twill be safely kept, mistress."

What he said was true. It made no difference. Nichola's letter to them had said as much—all three portions of the map were needed to find the Treasure of Tiberius.

"We'll say nothing to the laird of it, however."

"The laird?" she replied, surprised at his words. She had assumed that Wyntoun was laird.

"Aye. My father, Alexander, is the MacLean and laird of Duart Castle. He has already been told of your arrival, but I've said nothing to him of the map . . . or the treasure."

She watched him as he crossed to a sea chest. Inside, oiled leather packets lay stacked in tidy rows beside a black leather-bound book of some sort and a stack of carefully folded garments. The very vision of order, she thought.

"I have also sent word up to the castle of your . . . of your lack of clothing necessary for traveling into the Highlands, so Mara is having someone see to your needs."

"Mara?"

"My father's wife. She will make certain that your stay at Duart Castle will be comfortable and uneventful."

She nodded again as she hastily tucked the ends of the tartan shawl into her skirt, trying to create some semblance of order out of her ragged and ill-used island clothing. Adrianne started at the sound of a knock. Wyntoun tore his attention away from the contents of the sea chest.

"If you're ready, a boat has been prepared for you." He

stood and turned to her, his face serious. "Have a pleasant stay, mistress."

She let her gaze travel upward, fixing on those eyes of green. This man seemed so different from the one whose throat she held a dagger to less than two days ago. That man had been reckless and dangerous. He'd been a man of daring . . . one with no fear of death. One who, in fact, had considered her threats to be no challenge whatsoever.

This one standing before her seemed so . . . so trustworthy. True, this Wyntoun MacLean was somewhat distant, and yet he was so compliant to her wishes.

Suddenly, she wondered which of the two was the real Wyntoun MacLean. Suspicion narrowed her gaze. "You are not coming ashore?"

"I will, mistress. But later." He moved around her to open the door. "We will certainly meet again before you depart for Balvenie Castle."

"Was there no letter from my mother in the packet with the map?"

"Aye. Of course, I'll have it brought up to you once you are settled in. I also have letters from your sisters that you're surely anxious to read."

Adrianne nodded and paused at the door. "And is there anything else you'd like to tell me about . . . your family?"

An odd smile broke across his lips, a flicker of amusement glinting in his green eyes.

"Trust me, mistress, you'll learn nearly everything that there is to know about the MacLeans *and* the MacNeils before this day is out. In fact, I'd wager you'll learn more than you wish to know."

Duart Castle crouched atop the rocky headland overlooking the bay, a great gray cat poised to spring on any who dared to come within range of her lethal claws.

Adrianne tore her gaze away from the impressive structure and looked into the ruddy faces of the three sailors rowing her toward the shore.

"Can you tell me, Ian, how old is this castle?"

The redheaded sailor sitting closest to her arched an eyebrow, obviously pleased that Adrianne had remembered his name. "They tell me 'tis over two hundred years Duart Castle's been here, mistress."

"And was it built by the MacLeans or was it taken over from another clan?"

The man shook his head. "Nay, mistress. A MacLean clan chief built the place and has defended it ever since."

"But you are a MacNeil, Ian, are you not?" she probed gently. "I gathered from what I heard on deck that you and the ship's master and many of the sailors are of the clan Mac-Neil."

"Aye, mistress. Many of us are MacNeils. But that's because 'tis a well-known fact that a MacNeil can outsail a MacLean any day!" He looked over his shoulder at the two sailors behind him. "Is that not true, lads?"

The graying sailor in the center of the boat said nothing, but the younger man in the bow laughed, calling out his concurrence.

"And there is no trouble between the clans, then?"

Ian shook his head. "Nay, mistress, there hasn't been much feuding at all between the clans since Sir Wyntoun's mother— bless her soul—married Alexander MacLean some thirty years ago. No trouble at all, to speak of."

The sailor in the bow added his voice in agreement.

Adrianne smiled at the silent sailor in the middle, the oldest of the three who were rowing her ashore. "And you are . . . Master John, I believe?"

The two other men gave a hearty laugh and the man in the bow of the boat spoke up. "You must have a bit of the fairy in you, mistress, to be so good at guessing names!"

"Do you think so?" She squinched up her face. "Then you must be . . . Master Kevin?"

"By the devil," Ian chimed in. "The lass is good."

Adrianne held back her own smile at the compliment. It hadn't been too difficult to learn the names of the sailors as she'd waited on deck.

"So, Master John? You must be a MacLean, then."

Kevin spoke up for him. "He is, mistress, and has been

living with the same sweet lass in the same tumbledown cottage since long before my da was even borne."

Ian turned and looked past John at the young man. "I shouldn't be giving John too hard a time, if I were you, lad. When your darling Agnes is ready to deliver your first bairn in the next month or so, you'll be on your knees for sure at the door of that 'tumbledown cottage,' begging for Auld Jean to come running."

Adrianne turned again to John. "Your wife Jean is a midwife?"

Kevin answered for him again. "And a healer. To be honest, mistress, Auld Jean has helped with the birthing of every bairn on this end of Mull for at least forty years." The young man grinned and jerked his head toward Ian. "Unfortunately, she's even helped to bring scurvy rogues like the one sitting before you into the world."

Ian glared back at him.

"Tell me, Master John," she pushed on. "Do you have many children and grandchildren of your own?"

The old sailor, silent still, simply shook his head and gave her a gentle smile before looking out to sea.

Adrianne felt a knot form in her throat as she looked at him. The thought of growing old and not having children or grandchildren to gather at your hearth was something she had never thought about before. She wondered how lonely that would be.

She tore her eyes away from the man's rough profile and stared up at the castle, rising higher above them with each stroke of the oars.

Starting anew, Adrianne silently reminded herself. Barra was behind her, and she was determined to do better here at Duart Castle.

Aye, that's it! To start anew!

Though advancing in years, Alexander MacLean was all that Adrianne had imagined a clan chief could be. Handsome. Powerful. Charming. Entertaining.

And, apparently, a pirate.

Bathed and dressed in clean clothing that had been sent

in for her, Adrianne sat momentarily stunned at the dais, a forgotten leg of roasted duck halfway to her mouth. As she stared at the gray-haired warrior sitting in the laird's chair, the Highlander beamed with unabashed delight at her response.

"You look like you've swallowed a bone, lass!" the laird shouted, his laughter booming out across the Great Hall. "Mistress, don't look at me as if I'm the first pirate you've encountered in your life."

Adrianne lowered the food to her plate and looked about her at the faces of those sitting at the table. The rest who had gathered in the Hall for the meal sat looking on in amused silence, waiting for her answer. She glanced at the empty place to her right—the seat saved for Wyntoun should he come ashore in time to join them. She wished he'd given her some type of warning.

Pirates! Nursery tales of mist-dwelling thieves who waylaid innocent travelers ran through her mind. Half-remembered stories of Moorish cutthroats who roamed the Barbary Coast, pillaging and looting, came to mind. Even the names used to strike fear into the hearts of children along the western sea—names like Bloody Hugh Campbell and Mad Alex Macpherson—came back to her, raising gooseflesh on her arms and neck even now. And there were more recent tales that she'd heard on Barra. But this was no time to think of them. She shook her head.

"Nay, m'lord, you are the first pirate I've had the pleasure of meeting."

This time the laird's loud laughter was echoed by the rest of the occupants of the Hall. Adrianne forced a smile and glanced in the direction of Mara, Lord Alexander's tiny, middle-aged wife. Though the woman's pale face was barely visible above the thick mantle of fur that she wore, what Adrianne could see told her that Lady Mara did not share her husband's amusement.

"Well, lass, you're wrong in that, as well," the laird boomed.

Adrianne focused her attention on the man as he wiped away the tears of laughter that were now streaming down his face.

"I don't know why you should say that, sir," she announced, perhaps more strongly than she should have, considering her position as a guest. "I assure you I have *never* met another pirate until today."

Again the Hall erupted with laughter.

"And how did you get here, lassie?"

"M'lord, you are assuredly teasing me, now. You're well aware how I came to Duart Castle." Adrianne pushed the trencher of food away from her and faced the laird. "I was brought here on one of your ships. A man named Alan Mac-Neil is the shipmaster."

"Aye, a good man, to be sure. And who else?"

"There were a number of sailors who rowed me ashore—"

"Whose ship was it, lass?" The laird cut in over the chuckling mirth of the crowd. "Who was entrusted with bringing you back from Barra?"

The merriment of the group ebbed for a moment as Adrianne found the heat rising in her face at her inability to understand the laird.

"Why, your son. Sir Wyntoun brought me here, m'lord."

The laird turned to the Hall, banging his huge fist on the table as he roared out with laughter. "And the lass thinks the Blade of Barra is no pirate!"

Chapter 8

The silent monk fixed his steely gaze on the dais where John Stewart, the earl of Athol, sat holding his wife's hand.

Although she still did not show it, everyone knew that Catherine was carrying the earl's child. Here within the stout walls of Balvenie Castle, surrounded with her new family and people, the woman was the very picture of security and happiness. So unlike the days that she and her sisters had been scurrying to flee their home—and in so doing, making a farce of hiding the Treasure of Tiberius.

And what had she or *any* of her family done to deserve the great trust that had been bestowed upon them so long ago? He turned his head to conceal his disgust.

Beside him, the fat fool Brother Bartholomew continued to chatter on incessantly. The other three monks sitting with them were listening with varying degrees of interest, stuffing themselves with food at the earl's table. As the pitcher of ale passed down the table, he looked back at the dais where the Percy bitch was gazing dreamily into her new protector's eyes.

By God, he hated her . . . and the other two sisters, as well!

Bartholomew's grating voice broke into his reverie. "So, Benedict, I understand you had a most pleasant interview with the countess this day."

"With the *earl* and the countess." The monk snapped, correcting the portly cleric. Benedict's piercing gaze riveted on the woman as she rose to her feet and made excuses at the head table. The bairn that she was carrying was not due until spring. If she lived so long, he thought, watching Athol escort her from the Hall.

"Aye, with the earl and the countess!" Bartholomew
replied. "Balvenie's master has not been the same since he
laid eyes on our lovely Catherine. Why, when I first arrived
here, the earl personally spoke with all of us . . . even though
Mistress Catherine knew us from childhood. Why, even
though I myself had taught her geography, the laird asked
me the most penetrating questions."

"Is there a point to this?" the monk snapped.

"Of course, Benedict," the jovial cleric rolled on. " 'Twas
just that you have been so close to Sir Edmund Percy and to
the family, I'd imagined the earl would trust you to meet with
his wife—"

" 'Tis late." The monk placed a misshapen hand on the
shoulder of the portly brother and rose to his feet. He was
tall, though bent a bit from torture he had so recently endured at the hands of an "ally." "There is work that I need
to see to tonight. Come, Jacob."

As a small, wiry monk leaped up from the table, Benedict limped toward the door of the Hall. In spite of his dis-
ability, the tall cleric was almost to the door before his
diminutive underling caught up to him.

"The message you received earlier"—Jacob asked under
his breath—"was it of any value?"

Benedict silenced him with a sharp look and continued
past the carved oaken doorway. In a moment they were outside. Wet, feathery snow was still falling on swirling gusts
of wind, brightening the darkness of the courtyard, and muf-
fling all sounds. The monk turned toward the smaller man,
grasping him by the cowl and yanking him close.

"What happens at the gatherings of the Knights of the Veil
is always of value. Do you think I would risk using my connections to get the information, otherwise?"

"Nay . . . nay, I did not mean to . . ." Jacob stuttered. As
Benedict eased his grip, the wiry monk tried to recover himself. "What I meant to ask was whether the message had any
information of the Blade of Barra? Has the pirate secured
the youngest Percy?"

The monk pulled his dark hood over his head, hiding his
battered features from the wind and the snow.

"You ask too many questions, Jacob. I will tell you what you need to know." He started across the courtyard. "But the night is still young, and our game but beginning."

The wiry man shook his head, following. "But time is running short for me. Everyone here is waiting for Laura Percy and her husband to arrive. They are expected any day now. I just cannot remain hidden in the shadows, hoping they will not recognize me."

The tall monk stopped, turning on the older man. "You said Laura barely glanced at you when you tried to take her from the convent on Loch Fleet."

"Aye . . ." Jacob's hands fiddled with the cord at his waist, his eyes avoiding those of his superior. "'Tis true. I thought that . . . at first. But we cannot chance it. These Highlanders are savages . . . ruthless in protecting their own. If the new husband . . . this William Ross . . . if he gets any idea that I am the same monk that went after them . . . !" The man's eyes were fearful as they scanned the snowy courtyard. There was a note of growing panic in his voice. "He was there himself . . . pretending to be some dying peasant. He was there . . . and I fear what might happen if he recognizes me."

The tall monk paused for a moment before turning away and starting again down the yard. Jacob hurried after, keeping pace.

"We must do something, Benedict. Send me away. Find some excuse for me to go. I can come back again when they've gone from Balvenie."

"'Tis too soon after our arrival," the monk growled. "'Twill raise their suspicions. You will remain."

"But I cannot!" Jacob whined. "If I am recognized . . . if they decide to torture me to get answers . . . I do not know how strong I can be. Such a course puts all in jeopardy. It could be fatal for you, as well."

"You have lost interest in our sacred cause." Benedict stopped again; his voice was low, like the sound of a dog before it attacks.

Jacob faltered, squinting into the darkness of the monk's eyes.

"Nay . . . I have not," he replied quickly, his words tumbling out. "I only ask that you send me away for a short time . . . for the good of our cause. I only say that I will be more useful alive than dead at the hands of one of these filthy Highlanders."

In the deep shadow of his hood, Benedict's face was a mask. The two stood in silence for half an eternity, the snow and darkness around them like a shroud. A broken, gnarled hand extended from the tall monk's sleeve, taking hold of Jacob's shoulder. Clearly, it was all the old monk could do to stop himself from recoiling from his master's touch.

"Of course, you are correct in your reasoning, Jacob. And it has just occurred to me how we can put an end to your dilemma and still push forward our plans. Come," he rasped thickly. "Come with me now, and we shall . . . we shall correct this problem."

The roar of laughter in the Hall was deafening, and it took Adrianne a few long moments before the meaning of the laird's words sank in. She glanced at Wyntoun's empty seat and then stared at the weave of the tartan beneath the trencher of food before her.

The Blade of Barra! It was a name she knew very well.

During her five months of living among the people of Barra, there seemed to have been so many stories told, over and over, about the islanders' beloved pirate. Everyone, it seemed, had a tale to tell about him. Everyone had been eager to share, telling their story with gratitude shining in their faces as they told of how this pirate called Blade had bettered their lives.

Some of the tales, Adrianne was quite sure, had been pure invention, the product of those long winter nights during the stretch of seemingly endless winter. Tales of the pirate singlehandedly conquering vast fleets of Englishmen and Danes, of killing sea serpents with only the broken blade of a dirk, of sailing to China just to bring a mysterious medicine home for a fisherman's ailing bairn. Adrianne had simply attributed the tales to the separation of this rugged folk from the mainland. These stories simply sprang from the needs of these islanders to create imaginary heroes and to honor them.

Her disbelief was also based on the fact that, in all the time she had been on the island, there had never been any sign of the Blade of Barra himself. Even when she'd asked out of curiosity who the pirate was, she had gotten no answer. She had always assumed he was a member of the MacNeil clan, if he existed, at all. There certainly had been no hint at any time that the renowned pirate hero was the islanders' young master. But of course, she realized belatedly, Wyntoun MacLean's mother had been a MacNeil.

As Adrianne reached for her cup, those in the Hall continued to revel at her discomfort.

"That is *quite* enough!"

Lady Mara's words, spoken quietly, had an immediate effect in the Hall. Silence reigned for a long moment, until Lord Alexander cleared his throat and everyone at the long tables went about their business of eating their meal.

Adrianne glanced gratefully in the direction of Mara and found the older woman in a hushed conversation with the laird. Although she couldn't hear the words, the scolding that the laird was getting from his diminutive wife was obvious. Mara continued to whisper and Alexander continued to shake his head in agreement. Then, to Adrianne's great amusement, the white-haired giant simply stopped his wife's lecture with a sound kiss on the mouth.

Mara, her red hair touched with wisps of gray, had a complexion the color of lilies. Now, however, her nearly translucent skin took on a lively, fiery hue. Her pale blue eyes spit flames, as well, and she rose sharply.

"Oh . . . Alexander!" Mara said as her husband chuckled heartily.

"Yes, my love? You were saying?"

"Oh . . . you are the devil!"

As the laird laughed, Mara pulled the fur mantle tighter around her throat and turned to Adrianne.

"Come with me! Sometimes the company here"—she arched a thin eyebrow in her husband's direction—"is not fit for civilized people!"

Though Adrianne had always been one to resist authority, at this moment she had no problem with obeying. She rose to her feet and, receiving a wink from the smiling Highland chief, quietly followed Mara and her waiting women from the Great Hall.

When Adrianne had arrived that morning, all she had seen of the castle was the Great Hall and the circular stairwell that had led to her room on the second floor of the west wing. There, she had been surprised to find a tub being prepared for a bath. Once she had bathed, Adrianne had changed into a clean dress of midnight blue, styled after the latest French designs. The handmaid named Makyn, who had remained to wait on her, told Adrianne that the dress had been brought to her at Lady Mara's direction. And as she finished dressing, Adrianne had been delighted to have the letters from her mother and her sisters delivered to her chamber door.

The letter from Catherine, with the news of her marriage and the bairn that she was expecting in the spring, and of the school that she was opening shortly thereafter. And then Laura, the ever careful planner. Even from her letter, Adrianne could tell Laura had fallen desperately in love with a man so different from herself. The irony was delightful.

Adrianne had then pored over Nichola's letter, obviously written months earlier, before any of the daughters had left Yorkshire. The same cryptic advice about protecting the map and the Treasure of Tiberius.

Now, following Lady Mara, Adrianne pulled herself out of her thoughts of family and secret treasure. The diminutive woman led her to a door that opened into a large antechamber to the laird's apartment. From the looks of things, Adrianne surmised that this was where the older woman spent a great deal of her time.

What shocked her, however, was the chamber itself. It had the feel of an oven to it.

As the door closed to her back, Adrianne stared at the fire blazing in a hearth that had been added to one end of the chamber. Shifting her gaze around the room, the thought occurred to her that there were entire castles in England with fewer furnishings than this single chamber contained. A half dozen carved chairs with pillows. A large settle by the fireplace and two tables covered with elaborate candleholders.

French, Spanish, and Italian tapestries of exquisite workmanship covered nearly every inch of gray stone wall . . . from floor to timbered ceiling. The heat was intense, and the tightly closed shutters seemed to bring the walls in even closer.

Adrianne stood hesitantly by the door and watched the laird's wife drop her fur mantle into the arms of one of her maidservants and seat herself in a comfortable chair by the hearth. An elderly servant moved close and laid a heavy blanket of quilted silk over Mara's lap.

" 'Tis chilly in here. Not much better than that cave of a Hall, I'd say. Add more peat to that fire, will you, Bege?"

A trickle of sweat ran down Adrianne's back as she watched the serving woman add more fuel to the flames.

"Did you find your chamber comfortable, Adrianne?"

"Aye, m'lady." Adrianne judged that her bedchamber was probably directly above this one. She glanced at the closed shutters again and found herself yearning for a breath of fresh sea air. The two women entering with them, apparently unaware of the heat, seated themselves near the hearth and pulled pieces of sewing into their laps. "I am grateful to you for giving me a room with such a beautiful view of the bay, m'lady."

Mara shook her head disapprovingly, her pale blue eyes scolding. "Enough of this 'm'lady' business. You will call me Mara. And you should not open those shutters at this time of year. The wind from the west is bitter cold, and the walls of this pile of rock have more holes in them than the fishermen's nets. I'll send Auld Bege here up to seal those windows tight. She'll be sure that the others keep a good-sized fire going for you." She looked at Adrianne sharply. "They *did* bring up a brazier for you, did they not?"

"Aye, m'lady . . . Mara," Adrianne added quickly. "But that won't be necessary. I already closed the shutters and . . . and there was a good fire going there when I came down."

Moving to the farthest point in the room from the source of fire, Adrianne patted away the beads of sweat that were forming on her forehead. Casually removing the tartan shawl on her shoulders, she folded it over her arm and sat down on a three-legged stool.

With any luck, she thought, smiling into Mara's piercing eyes, she would not suffocate.

"The dress. The one I sent you. That is the one you are wearing, is it not?"

She was relieved to have the subject of heat dropped for now. "Aye, m'lady . . . Mara. And thank you—"

"'Tis too big."

"'Tis fine." Adrianne responded quickly, grateful to be wearing something dry and clean and lacking in revealing tears. Most of all, she was happy to be wearing something *not* belonging to Wyntoun MacLean.

"Any foolish creature can see that 'tis far too big in the waist and in the chest," For the first time, an odd half-smile broke over the woman's thin lips. "Why, we could put two of you in the bodice of that dress."

Adrianne looked down at her own chest and smiled, as well. "Well, I'd say three—perhaps four. But I like it. It makes me look much more substantial, don't you agree?"

There was a chuckle from the women by the hearth, and Adrianne looked up, only to be shocked by the transformation in Mara's face. The older woman was actually pretty when she smiled, and she was really smiling now. In fact, there was a glint of mischief in those pale blue eyes.

"You are not at all what I expected."

Adrianne nodded, frowning at the comment. "I see that my reputation has preceded me."

Mara's eyes shone with intelligence. "You know the way men talk. They gossip more than women . . . in spite of the foolishness that some people believe. But I have learned not to believe much of the mindless chatter that I hear from them."

"Well, Mara, in this case I advise you to believe everything . . . and then some."

Mara turned to the old servant by the fire. "Bege, bring in some dried fruits and a pitcher of wine for us," she said, turning to the other woman, as well. "Leave us."

Mara fiddled with the rings on her fingers and did not speak again until the chamber was left to Adrianne and herself.

"Young woman, you shall not belittle yourself before me or anybody else again."

Adrianne's jaw dropped open at Mara's scolding words, but she quickly recovered herself. "I was not belittling myself, but I am not about to hide who I am or anything I did at Barra."

"Then tell me, child. Who are you?"

She was taken aback again, but the gentleness that had replaced the sharp tone in Mara's voice was the cause for her surprise this time. Interest now lit the woman's face.

"I believe you know who I am. But if you would like to hear about my family . . . about my two sisters and my mother . . ."

"I only want to hear about you. Who are *you*, Adrianne?"

"I don't understand."

"I believe you do." Mara pushed the blanket from her lap and settled back, clasping two small hands around a large handworked gold cross that she wore on a chain around her neck. "We all know you are the youngest daughter to Nichola Erskine and Edmund Percy. We also know that your father was murdered for defying the English king while your worthy mother was chased from that country she chose to live in, running for the Borders to escape her own imprisonment . . . or worse. We know that you and your sisters have been left without home or future, largely deserted to fend for yoursel—"

"We were not deserted. We were sent north to . . ."

Adrianne hesitated as Mara held up a hand, requesting her silence.

"I only care to hear about you, child. Tell me about this firebrand of a lassie who has successfully burned down every building on the island of Barra . . . if any of these stories are to be believed. Tell me of this hellcat who wreaked havoc not only on the lives of those islanders, but managed to shake the composure of that nun . . . that ice mistress . . . that abbess of the Chapel of St. Mary."

"I see you are fond of her, as well."

"My disagreements with that old Nero in a nun's habit are older than you are, but I have no desire to get into any of that with you now. But for the moment, we are discussing you." Mara's eyes showed her admiration. "I hear she hung you in a cage from Kisimul's tower wall."

"She did."

"And you escaped?"

Adrianne shrugged. "I have never been fearful of heights. 'Twas not much of a challenge."

A mischievous smile brightened the woman's face. "What was she accusing you of?"

"Those who were quick to tell you of my sins must surely have told you—"

"Not sins, Adrianne. No one said that. I heard only tales of bravery, compassion . . . and stubbornness." The older woman smiled conspiratorially. "But I do not consider any of that a sin. Tell me."

Adrianne shrugged again and met the pale blue eyes. "To be honest, 'twas simply one thing after another. The abbess wished to exert control over me—to have me behave like some docile milk cow, staying put when she ordered. She wanted me to be as manageable as her other nuns. But I could not be that way. I need my freedom. I need to come and go and be useful . . . not only useful within the confines of an abbey. Even on a island as small as Barra, there is much to do."

"You knew no one there. Perhaps she was concerned about your welfare . . . your safety."

"How far could I have gone?" Adrianne shook her head. "Nay, Mara. I don't believe 'twas that. The abbess simply expected me always to remain where she wanted me. She wanted a grateful young woman attending her . . . but instead she ended up with . . . well, with me." She paused and looked at her. "You called me a 'firebrand.' The reason she had me hung from Kisimul tower was because she claimed that I had set a fire in the little monastery there."

"And had you?"

"Of course not. There was a fire, but I did not start it. But I also was not about to wait until the mass in the chapel was finished before warning the monks. The flames were leaping out of the windows of the chapter house."

"And did you tell her that?"

"Aye." Adrianne felt her temper rising inside of her at the memory. "But she did not believe me—did not *want* to believe me!"

In the long moment of silence that followed, Adrianne stared at her hands, listening to the fire's occasional hiss and crackle. The sounds of people still at their meal in the Great Hall could be heard through the closed door. As the moments drifted by, Adrianne felt her anger subside.

"I will not ask you if anyone stepped forward on your behalf . . . as the answer is already clear to me. Obviously, no one did." Mara turned the cross in her hand and gazed vacantly at it. "But my question to you is this. Was it worth it? Considering the trouble and the punishment she brought down on your head, was it worthwhile being so . . . so unmanageable?"

"Unmanageable?" Adrianne frowned. "This is who I am. I am no one's fool. And I would do it all again. I might have been a nuisance to a few on Barra, but I was a help to many others . . . and to the wee lad who followed me onto Sir Wyntoun's ship. That I know."

"You must mean this lad . . . Gillie . . . is that his name?"

She nodded. "Aye . . . but do you know where he has been sent? I haven't seen him since coming up to the castle."

"You have no need to worry about him. Wyn has made the arrangements. He seems to have taken a liking to the lad. And once the Blade has bestowed his favor on someone, no one would dare do the child any harm."

She still wanted to see Gillie—to make sure that the boy was truly better off here than he had been at Barra—but she fought the impulse to excuse herself.

"So what road stretches out now for Adrianne Percy?"

Adrianne rubbed her palms on the wool of her skirt. "I cannot say. I suppose I will go to my sisters. They are north, beyond the mountains, near Elgin."

Mara shook her head and pulled the wrap back on her lap. "A very long and dangerous journey, considering the time of the year. But again, knowing Wyntoun, he'll find you the best of escorts and the sturdiest of horses."

Blade! Wyntoun! Two names, one man. Adrianne let the names dance in her head. And she had seen them both. Blade, the reckless pirate who considered a knife at his throat no threat. Wyntoun, the compassionate knight who'd offered the comfort of his arms when she'd been sick. That handsome face, the intense green eyes, one man answering to both names.

"Why is it that you have asked no questions about him?"

For the first time since entering the room, Adrianne was thankful for the extreme heat. Her blush would hopefully go unnoticed. Strange . . . Mara had broken into her reverie as if she could read her very thoughts. "Whom do you mean?"

"Come, now. Wyntoun, of course."

"I . . . I didn't know what to say . . . or ask."

"You were clearly surprised when my husband told you of Wyntoun's . . . vocation."

"I was."

Mara nodded. "Alexander loves a good jest, but truly he wanted you to know. At Duart Castle, we do not believe in keeping much a secret."

"That's quite unusual . . . considering."

"'Twill not seem so unusual, once you get to know my husband better." The older woman's eyes softened. "But I believe in this case, he has good reason for being so open. And he is very proud of his son."

Obviously seeing Adrianne's confusion, Mara continued.

"Since Wyntoun lost two caravels on the Irish Sea last year, Alexander has urged him to spend more time on Mull, preparing to take his place . . . when the time is right. But being a pigheaded MacLean—just the same as his father— Wyn has been ignoring Alexander's suggestions, excusing himself for the most pitiful of reasons or simply disappearing on a midnight tide for months on end. His father just laughs, telling me he'll just have to live another twenty-five years or so, but . . ." She paused, changing directions. "And Wyntoun says he'll not rest until he has replaced his lost two ships with a new galleon . . . which makes me think he's planning a trip south where he can take one from the Spanish king."

"Do pirate chiefs always plan so?"

"I can hardly tell. But Wyn certainly does."

Adrianne fought back a knowing smile. She had been correct in comparing Wyntoun MacLean to her sister Laura. "But couldn't . . . couldn't this openness about Wyntoun being the Blade of Barra be harmful if it were to be widely known?"

"Aye, I should say so! But Alexander would only reveal such things to certain . . . well, a select few."

"But the Hall was full of people!"

"Aye, but they were all of the clan. You were the only guest."

"Still! How does he know to trust me?"

"Did I not already speak of Alexander's motives?"

Adrianne looked blankly at the older woman. The twinkle of mischief was back in the blue eyes. "Do these . . . motives have something to do with . . . with me?"

"Wyntoun is not the only planner and plotter in this family, my dear."

"Mara, for the second time this day, I feel that I am being led around with a sack over my head." She rose to her feet and took a step toward the shutters—desperately hoping for some air—but there was none. She turned around. "Please speak frankly."

"Can you not see it, lass? Alexander is planning on you becoming Wyntoun's wife. Sit down, Adrianne. 'Twould not do for the Blade of Barra's bride to faint dead away, now would it?"

Chapter 9

Leaving Lady Mara's chambers, Adrianne put her question to Bege, the aging maidservant, waiting in the dark corridor leading to the staircase.

"Aye, mistress. He's come ashore and is in with the MacLean himself in the Great Hall."

"Would you have someone ask him if I might have a few moments to speak with him . . . when he is free?"

"Aye, mistress. I'll tell him myself. Where can I tell him ye'll be?"

Adrianne frowned. By no means did she wish to give him a wrong idea by meeting him in her bedchamber. Not after all the confusion over her mention of "summoning."

"Perhaps 'twould be best if Makyn here showed you to the antechamber of his own apartments, mistress." Bege nodded to the same serving lass who had helped her to dress earlier. "He uses it as a work room of sorts."

Adrianne nodded. "That would be very helpful."

Bege lowered her voice to a confidential whisper. "Sir Wyntoun even has books that he keeps there."

"I won't tell anyone."

At Adrianne's request not to pass through the Great Hall, the serving woman led her silently down the spiral staircase through a maze of corridors, past locked storerooms and stalls filled with great casks. Finally, they climbed another spiral staircase into a newer building.

Adrianne knew they must be in the wing that extended past the Great Hall. This east wing, obviously newer than the Great Hall, appeared to be a mirror image of the section of the keep where the laird's apartments were located—and where she had been given a room herself.

As she peered down the torchlit corridors, Adrianne could see great attention had been paid to maintain a sense of symmetry and complement the original design of the keep.

"Makyn, what is located on the floor above?"

"Two bedchambers, mistress. Same as the west wing."

Adrianne hesitated by the stairwell.

"Sir Wyntoun's apartments are this way, mistress."

Adrianne nodded and followed the other woman. As Makyn opened the door into the anteroom, though, the two women were both surprised to find the laird's son standing by the small fireplace. Makyn curtsied and departed, closing the door behind her.

"You are . . . already here."

"Aye." His eyes flashed in the light of fire and candle. His handsome face, chiseled as an ancient statue, showed no emotion. No one man had a right to be this handsome, she thought, fighting her own jittery response to Wyntoun MacLean. She tore her gaze away from his face, staring instead at the ornate brooch that held the tartan at his shoulder. She glanced from the brooch to the painted shield hanging above the hearth and then back again at the colored gemstones on the intricately jeweled brooch.

Both depicted a red fist clutching a blue cross.

A blue cloth fringed with gold hung behind the shield above the hearth. Something clicked in her memory. Something from her childhood.

"'Tis the same design . . . my brooch and the shield." He spoke quietly, drawing her gaze. "You sent word that you wished to see me."

Adrianne rubbed her damp palms on the wool of her skirt and nodded curtly before looking away. She thought back on Lady Mara's words.

This wasn't as easy as she'd thought it would be. Walk in, say what she had to say, and be done with it. That had been her plan . . . such as it was. Granted, she had always been known more for her impulsiveness than her planning, but she needed to clear this situation up as quickly as possible. Or, at least, before he secured her an escort to the Highlands.

Now, feeling his piercing gaze on her face, she was struggling even to find her voice, never mind remember exactly how she'd wanted to word this.

This was his fault, damn him! It had been so much easier dealing with Wyntoun MacLean when she'd thought he was just another thieving villain.

"I assume you've found your quarters comfortable."

She gave a small nod, realizing that he was trying to help her. Small talk. That's it. Start slow. She turned away and sat in a nearby chair and placed her hands demurely in her lap. She let her gaze wander about the anteroom. She looked at the furnishings, the tapestries on the wall. Even the books. Every detail, large and small, received her attention.

She looked at everything but him.

"This chamber is quite beautiful. The entire wing is a very pleasing addition to the rest of Duart Castle. Lady Mara mentioned that you oversaw the building of this section yourself."

"What do you want, Adrianne?"

The devil take him. He was *not* helping her. She snapped her gaze back to him and found him leaning one broad shoulder against the hearth. Muscular arms crossed over his chest.

"This cannot be a friendly visit?"

He shook his head. "I do not believe so."

"How can you be so certain? You know so little about me."

The hint of a smile actually broke out on his lips, and suddenly she thought "handsome" was no longer a sufficient word to describe the man.

"I know much more about you than you are aware of."

She let out a groan and rose to her feet. "I forgot. My sister Laura. You spent some time with her."

"The letters that I had sent up to you earlier said as much, did they not?"

This time she was the one who smiled. It had been so wonderful to read them.

She looked up to find Wyntoun gazing at her with a somewhat different expression. The intensity in those green eyes fired up that strange heat in her body, and she quickly looked away.

"They did. Thank you for sending the letters up to me."

He moved away from the hearth and walked to a desk where a candle gleamed on an inkhorn, a goose quill, an assortment of other tools of a scribe, and a number of sheets of vellum.

"You do understand that your sister Catherine's letter did not reach you earlier because no ships generally brave the winter seas to go to Barra. After being asked to come after you by Laura and William Ross, I came across one of the earl of Athol's messengers. The poor fellow might have had to wait until spring to find a boat going to Barra."

"I understand." She watched him move behind his desk, putting as much distance as possible in between them.

"I have already arranged for a group to depart by the end of the week for Balvenie Castle."

Damn, he was efficient. Say it, she urged herself. Say it! But different words spewed out. "Considering we only arrived this morning, that is quite . . . expeditious."

One eyebrow arched momentarily, but he quickly seated himself behind the desk and glanced down at the sheet of vellum. "I could have arranged for you to leave sooner, but I assumed that you would need some time to recover from the journey from Barra . . ."

She squared her shoulders, stepping forward until she stood directly across the desk from him. He was clearly losing interest in this discussion. Her time was running out.

"Now, if that is all you wanted to see me about—"

Adrianne leaned forward and planted her palms on his desk. Wyntoun's gaze snapped up from his correspondence, fixing on her face.

"What is it?" he asked, his expression showing his surprise.

"I need you to marry me."

*   *   *

The wooden pitcher hit the floor with a loud thud and bounced several times before rolling to its side and coming to rest.

"You cannot hear!" Nichola's blue eyes flashed with understanding. To confirm her insight, she picked up the pitcher and again threw it with all her force against the floor. But again there was no sign of awareness in the old woman who continued to tend the small peat fire in the corner of the chamber.

"Deaf!" Nichola whispered to herself. Crossing the room, she clapped her hands loudly behind the woman's head. Not so much as a twitch. "Stone deaf."

Her mind racing as to how she could use this newfound knowledge, Nichola stood silently as the old woman finished her work with the fire and got slowly to her feet.

Nichola put a hand on the servant's arm. Startled, the woman hesitated, but the bowed back never straightened. Inquisitive eyes never peered out from the shadows of the hood of her cloak.

"You cannot hear me, can you?"

Again, she received no response from the servant except a gentle pull to free herself from Nichola's grip. She gently reached over and pushed back the servant's hood.

Nichola forced herself not to recoil at the sight of the woman's face. Age and disease had both left their mark, though disease clearly had left the deeper scars.

The servant's gaze never lifted from the floor as Nichola gently drew the hood back in place.

"I'm sorry," she whispered softly.

Before the woman could move, however, Nichola gestured for her to wait. Taking an intricately carved wooden cross from around her neck, she looped it quickly over the old servant's head.

Nichola crouched down to pick up the pitcher, and the old woman shuffled to the door. But as the door opened a little to let the servant out, she could have sworn that the ancient creature was clasping the cross to her heart.

Chapter 10

S he was as predictable as the rising sun.

It was difficult to refrain from smiling as she looked down at him, her violet blue eyes so full of hope. The only surprise was how damned near impossible it was not to drag her across that desk and onto his lap. The act of kissing that mouth of hers properly would not be conducive to letting her argue him into consenting.

And that's what he knew he had to do. Let her think she was convincing him.

"Would you care to say that again?"

"I need you to marry me." She said it this time with a little more hesitation, with a note of questioning in her tone.

"And what is the reason for this . . . this somewhat surprising request?"

Adrianne started to straighten up, but he leaned forward and grasped one of her wrists. She froze in place.

"I . . . I had a talk with Mara earlier." She casually tried to pull her hand free, but he continued to hold her. "She . . . mentioned that your father is hoping . . . that . . . 'twould be convenient . . . that I should become wife to the next MacLean."

"You must have made a better first impression on them than you did on me."

"Well, I didn't hold a dagger to anyone's throat, if that's what you mean. Let go of me."

Wyntoun covered his amusement with a frown. "My father has been trying to get me to marry since the day I turned sixteen. In the years since then, it has become a favorite pastime of his." He could feel the blood pulsing beneath the soft skin of her wrist. "But when I am ready to choose a wife, my father will have no voice in the selection."

Temper raised a pretty blush in her face and Adrianne tried to pull away, but he continued to hold her captive.

"I appreciate your candor. Now release me."

"What is wrong, Adrianne? Did you leave your fire on Barra?"

She raised her other hand, her fingers clenched in a fist, but he caught that one, too, as it shot toward his face. Her eyes were flashing as she glared at him across the desk.

"And where is that lively tongue of yours? Don't disappoint me and tell me you left that behind, as well?"

"You are a bully and a boor to bait me like this while I am a guest at Duart Castle." She spoke through clenched teeth. "Your father and Lady Mara are decent people. You, clackdish, must have been a foundling . . . no doubt left behind by the devil, himself, for that tyrant aunt of yours to raise!"

"Mild! Far too mild. You are clearly not yet recovered enough to travel." He came to his feet and leaned toward her. He saw her swallow hard. "But getting back to your proposal of marriage, what in the world makes you believe that you're good enough to be wife to a MacLean clan chief?"

"The offer is withdrawn," she snapped. "I'd forgotten that *you* don't qualify to be a husband to a Percy!"

Still holding her wrists tightly, he moved around the desk—careful not to come too close to her. Never mind the fact that the woman was quick and cunning—he still had a cut on his throat as proof of that—Wyntoun was too aware of his own aroused condition whenever she was near him.

"Sit!" He pushed her down on the chair and let go of her hands.

"Start again . . . from the beginning."

"I am finished speaking."

He abruptly placed both hands on the carved arms of her chair and leaned forward until his mouth was a breath away from hers. Her blue eyes widened in surprise. "From the beginning, Adrianne."

Time hung suspended between them for a long torturous

moment. Wyntoun could almost feel the texture of her lips beneath his own. The taste. He wondered if the inside of her mouth was as soft as the outside. Then, as abruptly as he had approached, he pulled himself away, seating himself on the corner of his desk.

Her chest was rising and falling, and when she spoke, her voice was husky. "But I . . . I already have your answer . . . so there is no reason—"

"Talk, Adrianne. You have suggested marriage without giving me your reasons for asking." He let his eyes travel down her body. "And right now my thoughts are running wild with why you might possibly desire—"

" 'Tis a combination of things! Many things," she blurted quickly. "The idea of asking you to marry me, that is. What I learned of your background from your father. Then my talk with Mara. And before that . . . reading those letters from my sisters. I know I am not much of a planner, but everything somehow comes together to recommend it. I truly believe it could work. At least, 'tis worth trying."

"Worth trying? Marriage? You would do better to go slowly in explaining yourself, Adrianne."

She stared down at her hands, two restless creatures that seemed to have a life of their own.

"My sisters," she started again. "Both are married. From what I've read in their letters, they have kept nothing from their husbands. This John Stewart . . . and William Ross . . . they apparently know everything of the Percys' secrets. They seem to know everything about the maps and the Treasure of Tiberius. Even you know more than you should!"

He crossed his arms as she rose to her feet. He watched her pace across the room and knew that this restlessness was so characteristic of her. Aye, restless and impulsive.

"So I thought . . . for me to go north to Balvenie could take weeks, if not months, considering the winter and the mountains and all. 'Tis too long and a wasted trip. Taking the time to go there would jeopardize our chances of rescuing my mother." She pushed back a stray lock of hair that had escaped the thick braid. "And I have another reason for not wanting to go to my sisters right now."

"And that is . . . ?"

"Once I reach Balvenie Castle, and we have the three maps together, the chance of my sisters and their husbands allowing me to go along with them to get Tiberius and then attempt a rescue of our mother is slight." She stopped her pacing and met his eyes. "I have to be there. I must be part of it. And that is why when I learned you were . . . well, the Blade of Barra, it just made sense."

"What does that mean, exactly?"

"You are a knight. You are a pir—a seagoing warrior who is both admired and feared. And you have been trusted by my sisters to come after me. Do you not see it? You have all the necessary qualifications."

"To do what, Adrianne?"

"To go after Tiberius *and* save my mother!" She rubbed her palms on her skirt and gentled her voice. "My sisters trusted you to come after me . . . but—" Adrianne stopped, frowned at him, and then crossed the room, pausing before the hearth and staring into the flames. "But why am I saying this, since none of it matters? You have already rejected my offer."

"I have yet to hear an offer. You only made a demand before . . . a demand that still requires some explanation."

A flash of hope brightened her face. She immediately came toward him, halting a step away. "You will consider?"

"I haven't said so."

"Nay, but you haven't thrown me out of your apartments yet, either."

She smiled, and Wyntoun realized that Adrianne had no idea of how formidable a weapon her beauty could be. Which made her all the more dangerous, he thought, willing himself to ignore the tightening in his loins.

"If we were to marry this week . . ." She reached out and put a hand on his arm, clearly with no thought other than to silence any objections he might have.

He said nothing. How could he speak? Her fingers were burning him through the material of his sleeve. He could feel the heat shooting up his arm . . . into his brain. He liked the feel of that touch.

"If we were to marry right away," she continued, "then you could still send a messenger north to Balvenie Castle. Rather than being encumbered with me and with an entourage, he could travel the distance in far less time. He could bring the news of our marriage to my sisters. And this messenger can carry word of our plan . . . of you and me going after Tiberius and our mother."

She dropped her hand and gave him another bright smile. "'Tis so clear. They will send back their portions of the map, and we will be on our way."

He studied her critically. "Just a moment. Though I haven't met your older sister Catherine, Laura did not strike me as one who would just part with something as precious as her portion of this map, and leave everything to a reckless younger sister." His comment obviously stung her, and Wyntoun felt a pang of guilt. But he shook it off. "I don't believe this plan of yours has a chance in hell of succeeding."

"I disagree." Adrianne leaned against the desk and crossed her arms over her chest, mimicking his pose. "Answer these questions for me, Sir Wyntoun. Are my sister and this new brother, William Ross, aware that you are the Blade of Barra?"

"William knows. I would guess that John Stewart, the earl of Athol, knows as well. And I also assume that they have, by now, divulged that to your sisters."

"And knowing your reputation, they trusted you to come after me?"

"They did."

"Do they consider you a man of courage?"

"I assume so."

"And well connected with other Scottish lairds?"

He frowned at her impatiently. "Cut to the bone here, Adrianne."

She nodded with obvious satisfaction. "'Tis *you*, sir. They'll send those maps to us because they trust *you*. They already realize that time is of the utmost importance."

"I believe I have the trust of William and Athol, but that does not ensure that your sisters feel the same way. In fact, they may have serious misgivings already."

"On the contrary . . . because of the bonds of marriage,

my sisters will trust you in the same fashion that they trust their own husbands." She nodded confidently. "You become . . . family . . . and as such, you become one who is entrusted with the Treasure of Tiberius. I tell you, it *will* work!"

He remained silent and thoughtful for a long moment, just gazing at her and watching as she returned his gaze. Confidence was written all over her . . . from the smile on her face to the easy balance of her carriage. He knew she was offering him a way to achieve his goals in a way that would prove far quicker than his own previously laid plans. But there was also a shadow of doubt in the depths of those violet blue eyes. Behind the façade of confidence, and logic, and conspiring together, she didn't really trust him.

"What is in this for me? What are you offering in trade for my services?"

Hiding a pang of regret, he watched the shadow lift in her eyes. He'd passed her test. Now she *knew* he was the pirate that she wanted him to be.

"I assume goodwill and my family's gratitude is not sufficient."

"Hardly." He frowned at her. "You require my services not only as Sir Wyntoun MacLean but as the Blade of Barra, as well. What do you have that you are willing to bargain?"

The rush of color to her cheeks spoke of her discomfort. "My hand in marriage . . . I . . . I could bear you an heir, if you require it . . . as your family wishes. Of course, that part of the bargain must take place after we have accomplished our goal of moving Tiberius to a safe place . . . and rescuing my mother."

"We might never be able to save your mother. You would only back out on your part of the bargain."

"Nay, I will not. I will bear your children, if . . . if you require it of me."

Wyntoun thought himself worse than the lowest born knave for saying it, but he knew it must be said. He summoned up the most scornful look he could muster. "Any woman can deliver a bairn. And I assure you, m'lady, finding a suitable match would not be difficult for a man in my position."

Inwardly, he marveled at the way she handled the callousness of his remark. Turning to pace the room again, she nodded with understanding and pressed her trembling hands into the folds of the full skirt.

"Then I assume wealth must motivate you."

He didn't answer. She would have to make her own assumptions.

"The Treasure of Tiberius . . ." She paused, a slight tremble in her voice. "Though I have spoken of our duty regarding the treasure, if it comes down to the life of my mother or the safekeeping of Tiberius . . . then I would prefer to free Nichola and have someone . . . like you . . . rather than Henry of England . . . take the— "

"Is that your decision to make?"

"I'm willing to face my sisters with such a—"

"And face them alone, I suppose." His voice sounded like steel scraping on bone. "I am *not* interested in any bauble or fortune where the price of obtaining it would include dishonor in the eyes of those who consider me a friend. Those like William Ross and your sister, who sent me to convey you in safety to them."

She visibly brightened at his answer, but he shook his head and stood up, putting on the pretense of disgust with their discussion.

"'Tis late," he said gruffly. "And though you have had the luxury of sleeping for the past two days, I am anxious to—"

"Wait! There *is* something that I can offer you." She raised a hand to her mouth to cover a smile. "Did Laura tell you about my late father's ships?"

"Nay, only that all your family's wealth was confiscated by the English crown."

"Not all," she blurted excitedly. "A galleon that belonged to my father did not fall into their greedy hands. You can have it!"

"I have no plans of scouring the coast of England for a ship that may well be sitting at a London quay. You do not know if this galleon of your father's escaped being seized."

She shook her head. "I know this ship escaped their clutches. This galleon, recently built for my father, was being kept at the Isle of Man. 'Tis still there for you, once you help me."

He eyed her with suspicion. "How do I know your sisters and your mother will agree to give up the ship to me?"

"They will all gladly relinquish their claim on it. Consider what you are willing to do for us. To risk your life . . . your own ships!" She nodded with certainty. "But if you have any doubts, I will write a letter to my sisters so your messenger can take that to Balvenie Castle, as well. My sisters will give their blessing on the arrangement, mark my word on it."

He studied her, rubbing his chin and feigning an attitude of veiled avarice. "A new-built galleon, you say."

She seemed to be holding her breath.

"I guess I could use a galleon."

She threw herself forward to take his hands, but stumbled, falling into his arms and nearly toppling them both to the floor.

His arms wrapped around her, drawing her up hard against his chest. He dipped his head and inhaled the sweet scent of her hair, feeling her arms slip effortlessly around his neck. The soft skin of her throat beckoned to his lips as his manhood hardened at the thought that—despite all the clothing—her body fit so perfectly against his. How exquisite it would be to test that fit when they had both shed these encumbering garments.

Damn, he chided himself. His body was getting ahead of the game. He could not afford to let his guard down, could not afford to lose his focus . . . no matter how desirable the temptation.

He reached up abruptly and drew her arms from around his neck. As if stung, her face flushed with color as he pushed her an arm's length away. Whether from embarrassment or disappointment, he could not tell.

"I will go along with this, Adrianne, but there are conditions." Strangely, it hurt him somewhere close to his heart to see the bafflement in her violet blue eyes. "This marriage of ours, 'twill be in name only."

Her gaze dropped. She nodded. "Of course, as you wish

it. After our task is accomplished . . . and you have your reward . . . I will go away."

" 'Twould be best that way." He said the words as much to convince himself as Adrianne. There was so much about him that she didn't know. But this necessary deception was certain to surface one day. Then, once she learned the truth about what he'd done, her hatred and her anger would cut deep.

The problem was, if they were to give in to their desires, the pain would cut both ways. It was safest for her to go away untouched and with no attachments.

"Annulment," she said matter-of-factly. "We can request an annulment when we are finished with what we have to do. When we are finished with this . . . marriage."

He nodded in agreement but then turned away and went around his desk, putting distance between them. "I know a bishop who will get us the annulment from Rome, but I prefer to keep our agreement regarding this marriage private. There is no reason for anyone else to know that we have no intention of keeping our vows."

"Of course. I don't believe my sisters would be so willing to go along with this . . . this plan of ours if they knew the truth of the matter."

He wished she would look at him. Nay, he was glad she would not.

He forced his face to remain impassive as he sat down on the chair. "I will give the news to my father and to Mara this night. The wedding could take place tomorrow or the next day."

She nodded, all the while averting her gaze and gnawing at her lip. She looked as if she were having difficulty breathing, but he did not dare to ask.

"I will arrange for a messenger to leave immediately after the wedding, so if you wish to prepare the letters for your sisters—"

"I will. They will be ready."

He placed his elbows on the table, his hands in a steeple. He studied her for a moment. Her emotions were lashed down

as securely as a hatch cover, but he knew they were just beneath the surface. "Then I suppose we're finished here."

"We are!" she whispered softly, rubbing her palms on her
skirt and turning to the door. She paused, though, before
pulling it open, and glanced at him over her shoulder. "What
will you tell them . . . Alexander and Mara? What will you
use as the reason for choosing me as your wife?"

Your loveliness. Your courage. Your wit. The passion that
I know you can barely contain within you.

"Your colorful manner of speaking. I will tell them that I
have discovered my weakness lies in being cursed at by a
wee fiery vixen."

Chapter 11

Adrianne rolled onto her back for the thousandth time and stared up through the darkness at the stout wooden beams of the ceiling. It was no use. With morning only an hour or two off, there would be no sleep for her. Ever since the castle noises had subsided so long ago, her mind had been a bubbling hodgepodge of images and words and empty promises.

Her mother's letter. Courage leapt off the page, warming her soul, giving her strength for what she was about to do . . . for what she *had* to do. Adrianne had read the words over and over, a dozen times before going to bed. And then there were the letters from her sisters. The images of Catherine and Laura's happiness that had come through the words so clearly! What must it be like to be so much in love? To have a husband desire you as much as you desire him? How unlike the disturbing attraction she felt toward Wyntoun MacLean . . . and the total disinterest he had in her.

Not that she deserved any better, considering the lie she'd given him. A galleon in exchange for his offer of marriage? True, her father had a galleon sitting by the Isle of Man. But what she had failed to tell the Blade of Barra was that the promised prize was no more than a burned hulk of a ship. A worthless skeleton of charred timbers that had caught fire and burned before ever leaving the dock.

Adrianne pushed the covers aside and sat up in the bed. She'd been desperate to get him to agree. Somehow, before this entire ordeal was finished, though, she would have to reimburse him for his troubles. Somehow, some way, she had to make it worth the pirate's while.

The castle was still quiet when Adrianne washed up and

pulled on her dress. Taking a wool tartan from the chest, she left the bedchamber and tiptoed down the stairs toward the Great Hall. At a turn in the stairwell, though, she nearly tripped over a small bundle of blankets. Crouching low, she found Gillie fast asleep.

Adrianne smiled at the familiar sight and pulled the blankets higher on the lad's shoulders. There had been many a day on Barra when she had readied herself to leave the convent, only to find the boy sound asleep by the door, or in the kirkyard. Always near, always waiting for her to come out, so they could spend the day roaming the island.

Well, she wasn't about to wake Gillie now. The day had not yet begun for the rest of the world. Besides, she needed to find her own way about the island before she would feel safe allowing him along.

With the exception of a dog or two raising a head and wagging a tail, no one else stirred as she walked through the Great Hall and out into the courtyard.

The air was sharp and cold, and yet it felt good on her face. Taking a few deep breaths, Adrianne looked about her and smiled to see the heavy portcullis of the castle gate already open. A half dozen sleepy-faced men and women, their shoulders hunched against the predawn cold, were just entering through the gate and heading toward the kitchens. A man and a woman looked at her, their eyes popping open with surprise at seeing her.

Adrianne wrapped the wool tartan tightly around her shoulders and nodded to them. The night sky was only starting to lighten slightly in the east as she walked through the gate and headed down the hill toward the cluster of cottages that hugged the curving shoreline.

She had no destination in mind, no purpose other than seeing the village that lay beyond the castle walls. Smoke was beginning to rise from the smoke holes of a dozen or so of the huts, and she stopped on a knoll to survey the tidy scene. Many of the huts had low walls around them, and a cow or a pig could be seen in the enclosure. All had small garden plots, many finished for the winter. Brown, communal fields of oat and barley were just starting to become visible inland of the village, the stubble of harvested stalks looking like an old man's whiskers.

The smell of salt air mingled with the peat smoke, and Adrianne felt a fleeting sense of well-being course through her.

Just above the first of the cottages, she spotted a single stone cottage that was tucked away from the others. There were no animals visible around the place, no dog trotting out to growl or sniff at her suspiciously. As Adrianne approached she took in the remnants of a large garden surrounding the cottage. She decided it must have thrived in the spring and summer, for the soil looked surprisingly dark and rich. A few steps from the cottage door, blocks of peat and clumps of seaweed were piled neatly by a smoky fire. Great slabs of fish, covered with herbs, had been suspended over the fire.

She approached the fire and held her bare hands over the low flame, enjoying the heat and the smell of the fish. Something in the aroma of the herbs set her mind whirling again, and she thought back on her childhood studies and the little she'd learned about herbs. She pursed her lips at the memory of the two monks, Benedict and Bartholomew, arguing over the teachings of a physician named Paracelsus and the value of herbs in healing. What had they argued about?

Adrianne promptly withdrew her hands from the fire as a familiar face emerged from the cottage.

"Good morning, John," she said cheerfully, nodding to the aging sailor.

The man's gentle eyes lit upon her, and the quiet man nodded and gave her a friendly smile before pulling a cap over his head and turning his steps toward the village.

Adrianne watched the man go. She too had things to do this morning. The castle would surely be abuzz by the time she got back, for Wyntoun was going to give Alexander and Mara the news of the upcoming marriage last night after she'd retired to her chamber. She had no idea what would be waiting for her but she knew that she would surely be expected there.

"And you must be the wee English lassie everyone has been chattering about on the island."

Adrianne turned and smiled at the gray-haired woman who was leaning heavily on a stout stick in the doorway of the cottage.

"And you must be Jean the midwife. I was hoping that I would have a chance to meet you."

"Come inside. Come inside, mistress. Surely, this winter air is far too chilly for a gentle soul such as yourself."

"I don't mind the cold," Adrianne confessed, approaching the old woman. "But thank you, I'd like to visit."

The older woman turned in the doorway and struggled a little with the stick that she was using. Adrianne came near enough to be able to offer assistance only if she were asked.

"I wish I could say the same thing about this wretched weather," Jean complained, hobbling in and motioning for the younger woman to follow. "I've had a lifetime of this cold and damp, but lately it seems to cut the legs out from under me."

Adrianne let the stiff leather flap that served as a door close behind her. The cottage glowed in the golden light of a small hearth fire. Dried flowers and herbs hung down everywhere from the low, thatched roof. Woven cloths, colorful shells, carved wooden spoons and animals, and baskets of every size and shape and color adorned walls and windowsills. She gazed about her in wonder.

"This is what happens after you've helped kin and friend and foe for nigh onto forty years. You end up with a cottage filled with gratitude." The woman chuckled to herself and hunched over a bubbling kettle suspended from an iron hook. "They keep bringing you gifts of thanks until you find yourself forced out of your home by the things."

"They are so beautiful." Adrianne shook her head in disbelief as she approached the fire. As Jean lowered herself into a settle, the visitor sat on a short stool across from her.

"Aye, that they are! And every one holds a special meaning." She waved a hand in the air. "But I keep threatening these folks, telling them 'no more.' Why, my John is already warning me that he will be burning some of these instead of peat if I don't put a stop to this hoarding of things."

Adrianne met the woman's sparkling gray eyes. "So he *does* talk!"

A hearty laugh escaped the healer's lips. "Aye, that he does, mistress. He talks plenty when he has something to say."

Jean reached into a basket of wool beside her and took out a piece and a sharp-toothed comb, untangling the fibers as they talked.

"Coming ashore from Sir Wyntoun's boat, I heard the men talking of you and all the bairns you've delivered for so many folks on the island." She picked up a sprig of rosemary from the floor and twisted it around her fingers. The scent wafted up around her. "Did you help to bring Sir Wyntoun into this world, as well?"

"I wish I had," Jean said soberly, shaking her gray head. "But, being a MacNeil, his mother Margaret had her mind set on delivering her bairn at Kisimul Castle on Barra. And she was a strong-minded woman . . . though it all went against her in the end, poor thing."

"Did she have a hard time with the birthing?"

"She didn't survive it." Jean frowned. "'Twas a shame. So bonny and young she was. From what I hear, young Margaret struggled for days with the labor. And when 'twas over, she kissed the bairn's dark hair and sent a blessing to heaven, before closing her eyes one last time."

Emotion burned in the back of Adrianne's throat, and she looked away at the fire.

"I did have a hand in raising that darling rascal, though, after Alexander brought him back to Duart Castle. True, he had a wet nurse, and some ten years or so later his father married Mara, giving the rogue a new mother. But Wyn spent many hours as a lad playing on the floor of this hut. And as he grew, I soothed many a bump on his head, or sewed up a cut on his arms or his feet. That stern-faced laddie, Alan, came in here with him many a time, too, but young Wyn always seemed to be the one doing the more dangerous things, I believe." She grinned. "He was the one who always managed to get the most battered, anyway."

Adrianne tried to imagine him as a child. A head of wild,

dark hair. Green eyes that must have lit up his mud-spattered face. She couldn't help but let her mind wander with him as he roamed the wild moors of heather and bracken. She could see him clearly—there, amid the twisted oak and the pine. And there, climbing the rocks along the shore in search of bird's eggs and falcons. With every season growing stronger and more handsome . . .

How many hearts he must have broken with those good looks before becoming the man he was now! The Blade of Barra!

"You've fallen to his charms, I see!"

Adrianne snapped herself out of her reverie and met Jean's smiling eyes. "I haven't."

"Say what you will, lass." The older woman teased as she dropped the wool back into the basket. "But you've nothing to fear. Your secret is safe with me. In fact, I don't believe I'd mind it if you were to follow your fancy and settle here on the island."

Adrianne looked down into her lap. She knew there was no point in denying anything, for the news would be out soon enough. But still the young woman found herself unable to tell her new friend of the upcoming wedding. Perhaps it was because the vows she and Wyntoun would soon exchange were nothing more than a lie.

Seeing Auld Jean struggling to reach for the pot bubbling over the fire, Adrianne jumped up, lifting it off the hook and placing it on the stone hearth. The brew smelled sweet and clean, like a warm spring day. When Adrianne offered, Jean gave her a wooden bowl to use to fill a larger pottery ewer that sat by her feet. There were other herbs that Jean wanted, as well, and Adrianne was delighted to let the conversation shift. She was also happy to be of some help.

"Bring me two good sprigs of that feverfew, will you, lass?"

Adrianne reached up where Jean pointed and brought the herb down. "What is the feverfew for?"

"'Tis a strengthener of women's wombs. We'll pour this decoction over the dried blossoms and then strain the wee

things out. 'Tis a powerful medicine. I am making it up for
young Agnes in the village."

"Oh! That's Kevin's wife. They're expecting a bairn soon,
I heard."

"Very good, lass. You listen."

As Jean worked over the medicine, Adrianne's gaze was
again drawn to all the herbs drying beneath the roof.

"'Tis fascinating to me that so much good can come from
plants that grow wild."

"'Tis the same with some people," Auld Jean murmured
without looking up.

Adrianne stared at the woman's capable hands. "'Tis even
more wondrous that there can be so much healing in a person's touch."

"Come now, lass. What we're doing is no different than
what a cook does in preparing a meal, or a seamstress does
in sewing a dress."

"I doubt there are too many cooks and seamstresses anywhere with as many treasures as you have received, Jean."

The old woman gave Adrianne a warm smile. "John was
quite right in praising you, lass. Your heart is as pleasing to
look upon as your bonny face."

Adrianne shook her head, feeling herself redden.

"I hope you will be staying on the island for a time."

"I hope so, too," she found herself murmuring. "And while
I am here, may I come back and visit you from time to time?"

"You are welcome any day and anytime, lass."

"Perhaps I might even be of some help?" Adrianne brightened. "I can do whatever you find is wearying for you. Help
around the cottage. Carry your baskets."

Jean placed a hand on top of Adrianne's. It was warm and
strong. "Child, you are a lady."

"I don't know that I was cut from the cloth needed to be
a lady, Jean. I cannot sit idle while there is work to be done.
Please give me a chance to be of some use. I learn quickly,
and I'm a good worker."

"As I said before, lass, you are welcome here anytime."
The woman's smile was filled with tenderness. "Och, but what
kind of friend am I to be! Why, here you are coming down

from the castle long before the kitchens were serving anything to eat, and I don't even offer you anything to keep body and soul together. I still have some warm bread and—"

"Nay, thank you, Jean. But, in truth, I should get back to the keep. I didn't tell anyone where I was going when I left, and they may be wondering . . ." She frowned at the thought of how much trouble she got into at Barra. "But is there anything I can do before I go? Perhaps I could deliver your medicine to Agnes's cottage? Is she in the village below?"

"Aye, she is! And that would be a blessing, lass."

Holding the medicine carefully, so as not to spill a drop, Adrianne left the cottage. The winter morning sky would hold no sun for quite some time, but the air was fresh and clear. As she moved along a path, the low sea grass tugging at her skirts, Adrianne felt a sense of peace wash through her. It was the first time that she had felt this way for a long time. It was the first time since the awful day when her family was torn apart. She stopped and looked back at the cottage. Jean was hobbling out to the fire to tend her smoked fish.

This island. That cottage. The kindly old woman who not only healed the body, but somehow also considered the soul. That visit had changed things for Adrianne. She looked down at the ewer of medicine in her hands.

It was all different now.

Escape. Escape. Escape.

Stepping out into the brisk air of early morning, Wyntoun filled his lungs, happy to be beyond the confining walls of the keep. No wonder he had fought the notion of marriage for so long.

The Great Hall and the kitchens were already in an uproar, with Mara tearing about like a warrior chief readying her charges for battle.

Wyntoun's plan, however, was to stay as far away as possible from the commotion surrounding his upcoming wedding. He had no desire to be drawn into the preparations any more than he had to. More important, he had no intention of spending any more time with his future bride than he absolutely must.

Perhaps he was being a bloody villain, but that was exactly what he needed to be. He was not marrying the Percy woman for life. Because of his lie, their future did not hold the prospect of bairns and respect and contentment—things that he felt should go along with marriage. He was marrying Adrianne Percy only temporarily . . . and for the sole purpose of fulfilling his task. And his task, he reminded himself, was to locate and secure the Treasure of Tiberius.

As Wyntoun strode across the courtyard toward the stables, though, the face of the enchantress lingered in his mind.

Adrianne Percy. The youngest daughter of Edmund Percy, a late brother in the Knights of the Veil. When Wyntoun had agreed to accomplish this task so many months ago, though, he'd never foreseen marriage to the youngest Percy as the means of achieving his goal.

The knight shrugged off his misgivings. He had a job to do. He had to secure all three sections of the map. This was the first step toward finding Tiberius before someone else did. And Wyntoun's initial plan—having Lady Nichola captured and kept imprisoned until an exchange could be made—had become unworkable. After meeting Laura, the middle sister, at Blackfearn Castle, and then Adrianne, he'd soon realized that the solution lay in becoming one of them. In joining their circle. And here he was, marrying the only available sister. Simple enough.

Ha!

He heard her laughter ring out clear and true across the courtyard, and he turned his head.

A feeling struck him then that every sailor has felt at least once out in a stormy sea. First the stinging rain and winds that have been lashing your face—driving cold spikes into your bones—suddenly ease, making your body feel somehow lighter. The frothy waves that had been threatening to sweep you off the deck for days suddenly diminish to rolling swells. And then, in the distance, that first single ray of sunlight bursts through the heavy clouds, glittering, fiery, ablaze on the surface of the lowering sea.

Seeing Adrianne's face as she emerged from the dark gate beneath the curtain wall stopped Wyntoun in his tracks. Like sunlight ablaze on the sea after a storm, the light in her face captured him, and he stood still, unable to move, staring like a man enthralled.

And then he saw her smile brilliantly at a man who was passing through the gate with her.

Wyntoun was halfway across the courtyard to them before he even knew his legs were moving. The sharp stabs of jealousy were knife thrusts in his gut. His hands fisted as he charged toward them, his gaze now locked on the blackguard who was striding along beside her.

Somewhere from the back of his head, an awareness formed that he knew the man. Aye, it was Kevin, one of his own sailors, a young man of promise. A young man who would not live to fulfill that promise. Wyntoun's strides carried him quickly toward the rogue. Before he could reach them, though, the knight saw the young sailor casually hand Adrianne a basket and turn his steps toward the kitchens.

Wyntoun hesitated as a flash of common sense suddenly asserted itself. What the hell was he doing? What was possessing him to go after this young man? By the devil, what was going through his head?

The knight halted abruptly. Before he could gather what remained of his wits, though, he saw Adrianne spot him and smile. He was still wrestling with his temper when she reached him.

" 'Tis early," he managed to snarl. "Half the household—the half Mara could not rouse—is still asleep. Where have you been?"

"And good morning to you, too, Wyntoun." She ignored his question and instead smiled into his face. "Or are you the Blade today?"

Her face was flushed and healthy looking from the cold and exercise, her eyes so blue they mocked the sky. She was so calm and composed that he had to fight the urge to throttle her. She was so beautiful.

" 'Tis difficult to know how I should act. Do you go by different names on different days? Being as orderly as you are, you surely have some system that I can learn so that I can address you properly when we meet each day?"

His fingers ached to dig into that silky mass of ebony hair. His lips hungered for the taste of her full mouth. He'd touched those lips before, felt their softness. Now he wanted more.

"I certainly like this attitude in the morning," she continued. "This brooding stillness. This silence. It means I can say what I will and do as I wish, I assume."

"You assume incorrectly," he responded gruffly. "I spoke to Alexander and Mara last night. Two days. Though I do not believe your nature will ever change, two days are all that remain of your wild and reckless youth."

She moved the basket from one arm to the other and studied him with an obvious interest. "Is this a threat, Sir Wyntoun? Are you trying to scare me? Perhaps I should dive into the sea and swim to the mainland."

"Are you a coward?"

"Nay, that I am not."

"You must be a cheat, then, to wish to break our bargain so quickly."

Her back stiffened. "I want nothing of the kind. 'Twas *my* proposal that you consented to, and I will fulfill my part in it."

"Then let us begin again. Where have you been this morning, Adrianne?"

Her eyes flashed with challenge. "Knowing where and when I go and what I do was not part of our pact."

"In two days you will become my wife."

"Very true. But as you said yourself, I still have two days of wild and reckless freedom left." She paused a moment, obviously measuring his patience. "And even if we were already wed, I distinctly remember our agreement is that we are to wed in name only. I see no reason, therefore, that I should report every step I take. I certainly do not believe you need to know every secret I possess."

"Are you trying to drive me mad, Adrianne, or are you trying to make me back out of our arrangement?"

She hesitated, her eyes narrowing. "Are you a coward?" she said finally.

"That I am not."

She tossed him another one of her enchanting smiles and went around him.

"Then do not try to cheat me, either."

Wyntoun turned to watch her go.

Chapter 12

Like a thief, like a fraud, Adrianne stood back and watched the commotion created by the wedding.

Two days! That's what Wyntoun had threatened her with. Two days for Mara and Alexander to set up the wedding and the accompanying feast. In spite of the Advent season, the pale old abbot from the small monastery overlooking the Firth of Lorn had been easily persuaded to come to the castle for the wedding. Indeed, in spite of the short notice, there seemed to be no shortage of help. Duart Castle immediately swelled with people who, under Mara's dictatorial direction, practically turned the place upside down in preparation for the nuptial celebrations.

"Dinna move, mistress."

Adrianne felt a needle brush past the skin on her back. The nearly toothless and wrinkled face of the seamstress peeked at her around her arm.

"I didna stab ye now, did I mistress?"

Adrianne shook her head and glanced longingly toward the door. She wished she had remained in Auld Jean's cottage that morning and not returned to the castle. She wished she could walk out that door and simply disappear until this entire complicated mess was done with. But there was no chance of that. Mara had already given her a list so organized that it would have made her sister Laura envious. Places to go. Sauces to taste. People to meet.

She couldn't breathe.

"Raise yer arm, mistress. Aye, like so." Adrianne obediently did as she was told and watched as the old seamstress pulled the silky sleeve over one bare arm and adeptly pinned it in place.

"Canny, ye brazen fool, stop yer sulking. Come and lend a hand with this."

Beyond the kerchief-covered head of the seamstress, Adrianne watched the blond-haired, shapely young woman come abruptly to her feet, dumping all the fabric on her lap onto the floor.

"Och, Canny, look what ye have done now!"

"But she's too tall for me to be fixing that sleeve."

"Tall? She's but a wee thing! Och . . . very well, then! Ye can stitch her back as I finish the sleeve, can ye not?"

Adrianne gave the serving lass a friendly smile as the young woman brushed past her. But there was no warmth in Canny's blue eyes as she glared back.

She should have foreseen what was coming. The first thrust of Canny's needle pierced Adrianne's flesh. She didn't make a sound, but the seamstress must have seen her wince, for in a moment the buxom young woman was sent scurrying out to fetch another helper.

"She doesn't appear to like me," Adrianne said as Canny closed the door on her way out.

"Dinna mind her, mistress. She'll come around when ye become Sir Wyntoun's wife . . . or I'll see that she gets a whipping a day for her foolishness!"

"Nay, I wouldn't care for that to happen." Adrianne continued to stare at the door. "Her dislike . . . is it because I am half English?"

The woman's gray eyes held Adrianne's for a moment. She finally shrugged.

"I know 'tis not my place to tell, but with ye having no woman kin of yer own here, I suppose someone must tell ye." Adrianne used her left hand to hold the sleeve on the right shoulder as the seamstress continued to sew. "Master Wyntoun has always been a favorite with the MacLean women. Of course, the menfolk would follow him anywhere. 'Tis just that the young lasses—like that fool Canny—are a wee bit fonder of him than they should be. 'Tis not ye, mistress. They'd not be happy with *any* woman he'd be choosing for a wife."

Well, they don't have to worry much, Adrianne wanted to say, as this marriage would only be a temporary match.

"Now, the lassies about here were that way about the MacLean himself when he lost his first wife and came back with the wee bairn of a son. Himself was a widower for ten years before he took Lady Mara as a wife. Of course, his brother Lachlan was laird then . . . but that's a long story. The womenfolk soon came around for her, though, let me tell ye." The woman's eyes twinkled with mischief. "Now that's one woman who knew how to train and keep a husband, never mind putting all the other lassies in their place when it came to their dealings with her husband."

"Her size is no measure of her will." Adrianne smiled. "I like her."

"I'm glad to be hearing that, mistress, as everyone already knows that she's taken a shine to ye. Let me tell ye, Lady Mara would never have gone through all this fuss about the wedding on such a short notice, otherwise." The seamstress gave Adrianne a knowing wink. "Now, as far as handling Master Wyn and putting all these other women in their place, I'm telling ye that ye should have a talk with Lady Mara. Liking ye the way she does, she's sure to share some of her tricks with ye."

She wouldn't be needing any advice, Adrianne moped silently. He'd already told her that he didn't want her as a real wife. This morning's meeting in the courtyard had been proof enough of that. It galled her a little even thinking about it. Her . . . friendly and happy to see him. Him . . . cool and distant. Ugh!

Don't think about it, she told herself. Their arrangement was for the best. It would be far better to have few ties and fewer regrets after the treasure was relocated and her mother was saved. It would be far better to go away. Far away.

And if Wyntoun, while he was . . . well, married to her, wanted to bring other women to his bed, who was she to complain? Adrianne found her jaw tensing as an ache formed in a strangely hollow place in her chest. Gnawing at her lip, she realized that she didn't like the way she was feeling at the thought of him sharing his bed with another.

Nay, she didn't like this one bit. Maybe she would have a talk with Mara, after all. If for nothing else, perhaps she should learn a few things about keeping the competition at arm's length while she feigned this sham of a marriage. She needed to prepare herself.

Aye, prepared. Armed and ready to be the Blade of Barra's wife.

One day left to the wedding. Mara was fretting. Alexander was grumbling. The seamstress complaining. Throughout the keep, chaos still reigned amid the mountain of work that needed to be done. And yet, everything had halted. The household waited. An eerie, whispering silence had descended on the Great Hall.

It was already midday, and the bride was again missing.

Wyntoun had brought the problem to Duart Castle, so there was no escaping his responsibility.

Setting out on foot for the village, the Highlander left the gates of Duart Castle and started down the hill in search of his runaway bride. The steady freezing rain that had started sometime before dawn had coated the ground with a crust of ice. The rising wind tugged at his cloak, and the chill rain stung his face.

She had taken no horse out of the stables. Because of the deteriorating weather, no boats of any kind had left the harbor. He could see the fishermen down on the rocky strand, huddled against the rain and working on their boats and nets. The bloody woman had to be nearby. Of course she wouldn't go far. The aggravating wench would naturally want to stay close enough to enjoy watching his temper boil over. Why else would she be out causing mischief and testing his patience with just a day left to the damn wedding?

He had heard enough about Adrianne's headstrong nature from his aunt on Barra. He frowned fiercely as he pushed toward the village. Perhaps he should have taken her words more to heart. Perhaps he should have thought of a different solution for finding Tiberius. People do not change, everyone knew that. The way you were born was the way you died. By the devil, he was a fool to think that she could change her temperament and rein in her unruly impulses. He was an even greater fool to think she would pretend to be an obedient wife for the short time that they had to stay together.

He had forgotten everything.

Arriving at edge of the village, he stood and peered past low walls and cottages toward the market cross by the stony strand, but he could see no sign of her.

As he was considering going from cottage to cottage, Ian and Bull, two of his sailors, trudged up from the fishing boats and approached when they saw their master.

"John saw her, m'lord," Ian said, responding to Wyntoun's question. "For the second morning in the row, he saw the mistress coming out of the mist toward his cottage when he left. She must be visiting with Auld Jean."

"But I saw Kevin this morn," Bull added, scratching his head. "And he told me that the lass . . . I mean, Mistress Adrianne has been settin' with his Agnes both yesterday and today. Wee Agnes has been feeling poorly, master, ever since we dropped anchor and—"

"Now that you mention it," Ian added, "I saw someone taking a basket of something into the widow Meggan's cottage not an hour ago. That must've been the mistress."

Wyntoun turned to see Coll and Ector, two more sailors who had joined the group.

"Aye, that was her," Coll put in. "I saw her chasing Meggan's youngest one and drag him out of the dungheap and back into the cottage."

Ector wiped the rain out of his face. "But I swear I heard someone say that they saw the lass heading to Effie's cottage about noon."

"That's halfway around the blasted bay!" Wyntoun exploded.

Ector shrugged sheepishly. "It could have been just talk, master. I mean, Coll's eyes are dimmer than an auld cow's. Ye'd think she was everywhere else this morning. I mean, she wouldn't be tracking across the island, when she had a nice dry keep to sit in, would she?"

"I'm telling ye, I saw—"

"Hush, Coll." Bull nodded his big head toward a nearby hut. "Here she is now, master, coming out of Lame Gerta's cottage."

Wyntoun turned as Adrianne closed the driftwood gate of the tiny garden enclosure around the cottage. Her dress was dark with mud practically to her knees. She had thrown a MacLean tartan over her head and shoulders. But even from here, he could tell that the wool was soaked through.

"Be off with you," Wyntoun growled as he pushed through his men and started toward the object of his search.

She did not see him, practically colliding with him before looking up. "Wyntoun!" she exclaimed breathlessly. "Or is it Blade, this morning!"

Damn, he thought, why couldn't she look more like some pop-eyed sow? Her cheeks carried a blush of wild rose from the cold. Her eyes, large and clear and violet blue, gave no hint of trouble or chaos or even mystery. By the saints, she looked like a goddess.

"Adrianne!" he said, finally finding his voice. "Where have you been?"

"Wyntoun, there are far more interesting ways to start a conversation than saying 'Where have you been?' all the time."

"I'm sure there are far, far more things I might have said, but I was attempting to be civilized."

"And is that a struggle?" she asked sweetly as the pirate felt his temper rise another degree. She patted him on the arm and looked over his shoulder toward the castle atop the hill. "If we are heading in the same direction, I would be more than willing to give you a quick lesson on the topic of conversing properly."

He knew he was scowling with a ferocity that made men cower before him, but she didn't seem to pay any attention to it, skipping around him and starting up the hill toward the keep.

Wyntoun paused for a long moment in disbelief and watched her go. She appeared completely unconcerned with the magnitude of his anger or with the fact that she had caused it.

"Adrianne," he growled, striding after her.

"Very well! So you've decided to walk with me," she said brightly when he caught up to her. "Now, the proper way to—"

"I don't give banning hag's ballocks about the proper way to start a conversation."

"Oh, I've never heard that one before!" She glanced at him with surprise. "Is this a sailor's curse? Could I use this with your men?"

He took hold of her arm roughly and yanked her to an abrupt stop. She had to be daft to not feel threatened in the face of his fury.

"Nay, you may *not* use it in talking with my men. In fact, since we are talking about proper conversation, you will not curse at all while you are my wife. And another thing, you will not leave the castle without telling someone where you go. Adrianne, you will not behave irresponsibly during the *short time* that our marriage lasts . . . even though you have behaved this way for your entire life."

Adrianne looked hard at his hand gripping her arm, and then met his gaze. He could see the blazing fire in them, and almost laughed. She might put on an attitude of calm, but the fire was always smoldering just beneath her skin, ready to burst forth at the smallest provocation.

"And what, may I ask, is the reason for your harsh words and rough treatment of me this morning?"

He let go of her arm, oddly disappointed that she chose not to lash him with her barbed tongue. He frowned, prodding her further. "And why am I not surprised? 'Tis only natural that you should be oblivious to others around you."

His words clearly stung her, but she came back at him after only the shortest pause.

"I do not care to repeat myself, Sir Wyntoun, but in this case I will make an exception." A small finger poked him in the chest. "'Twas your wish that our marriage be in name only. Therefore, I will show you due respect when we are in the presence of your people. But beyond that, do not expect me to stop breathing. I will not be worn like an ornament, wife or no. I will never be some docile creature who puts her own intelligence and will on a shelf to pacify the whims of a 'masterful' husband."

"Then 'tis best that we made the arrangement that we did."

"Aye, 'tis best." Her hand dropped to her side. As she turned her head, he caught a glimpse of a tear welling in her eye. "I have no time left for riddles or rhymes. Blast me if it suits you, but do it as we walk up to the castle. I'm certain a legion of workers are awaiting my return. I wish to cause no further hardship for anyone else. Do not detain me any longer."

"Very well!"

"Very well!"

She turned and glided away from him, climbing the hill effortlessly. Standing and watching her slender back, Wyntoun couldn't help but feel as if he had been the one scolded. As if *he* were the one at fault! How did *that* happen? he thought, frowning.

This was not good. The blasted woman was playing with his mind.

The huge pawlike hand of Alexander MacLean drew his wife's smaller one from the depths of her fur cloak and gathered it in his own. He frowned at the troubled lines marking her fine, pale brow.

"Mara, my love, there is nothing more to fret about. You've done excellent work preparing for this wedding. Wyn finally has found a suitable match, and they are about to take their vows."

She nodded absently and glanced over her shoulder at the large throng of clan folk who had gathered in the little kirk. The crowd spilled out the door and into the kirkyard, and Mara could hear the celebratory sounds of pipers and singing already starting outside. Inside, the brightly appareled company was restless with anticipation.

"I know what troubles you. You're upset that we did not wait the three weeks for the reading of the banns."

She shook her head and gave him a dismissive slap on the arm.

A devilish gleam crept into the laird's eyes. "Ah, I have it! You regret not having the time to send for Wyntoun's aunt from the MacNeil side. You wished the abbess could have come in from Barra for the ceremony . . . I think that is a very lovely thought, Mara. You certainly are a—"

"I wished for no such thing, and you know it!"

"Then what is the problem, my love?" He caressed her hand, his voice gentling to a whisper. "You're acting as if all the troubles of the great world are lying on your wee shoulders."

"Hush and look at the two of them, Alex," she said softly as the chapel quieted and the old priest turned to the altar and the ancient cross hanging above it.

"Aye," he whispered. "They're an impressive pair, those two."

"Nay," she shot back, frowning. "Look at them closely."

Alexander peered at the two standing before the altar. "They look well enough to me, lass."

She gave him an impatient jab in the side. "Look at the way the golden sunlight plays in her dark locks. Look at the blush that livens her skin. Look at the way the dress molds her body. Well enough? She looks like a heavenly spirit come to earth. Is she not the loveliest woman you've ever seen?"

"I am a happily married man, and the loveliest woman is standing beside me."

"You are a sweet old fool, Alex. But seriously, look at her. She's an angel."

"Nay, I'll neither look nor admit to such a thing."

She shook her head at him. "Then look at Wyntoun."

"Aye, the lad is magnificent." Alexander cocked his head and looked more critically at his son. "I did tell him that he should have worn his black clothes. After all, he is the Blade of Barra and has an image to uphold. Do you not think there is something infinitely more mysterious about him in black?"

The priest's voice rose and fell in the measured cadences of the mixed Latin and Gaelic. The congregation shifted restlessly behind them.

"I don't mean what he is wearing, you oaf," she scolded. "Look at the way he keeps his distance from her. He has not once touched her hand, nor even brushed a shoulder against her."

"Considering all the lad will be touching before this night is over, I do not believe—"

"This is not the time to be obscene, Alexander. I am serious."

"Aye, so am I." He shrugged, looking at his son again. "It could be the nerves. Wyn is a fighter and a planner, Mara. He fears no man, but he's avoided this marriage business for quite some time now. Knowing him, he is probably trying to think ahead to every complication this marriage might produce. Why, the lad is probably trying to devise a solution to some possible problem, at this very moment."

The priest raised up his hands in offering, and then turned and preceded his acolytes down from the altar. Wyntoun turned and faced Adrianne, and she hesitantly placed her hand in his.

"That's not it," Mara murmured quietly under her breath, staring at the safe distance that still separated the two. "But whatever is going on, I believe I will get to the bottom of it—and soon."

The intricate design of his brooch turned out to be her salvation. Adrianne only allowed her gaze to travel as high as the piece of jewelry during the entire length of the ceremony.

Repeating the vows that she intended to break, standing before a throng of people who were soon to think her a traitor for not living up to her part of the union, was distressing, to say the least. She was not good at playing the part of a fraud. She wondered for a moment if one would burn in hell for committing such a sin as this. Probably, she decided. And yet, she would go through with this farce, since it was her best chance of saving her mother.

The loud cheer of the congregation greeted them as the priest gave the final blessing on their union. Still avoiding his gaze, she followed Wyntoun's lead as he clasped her hand,

and they both turned to the clan folk crowding in around them.

"Kiss!" A woman's voice, which she could have sworn was Mara's, sounded from somewhere in the front. There were more shouts to the same effect, but as Adrianne frowned at the thought of how such a display might affect their appeal for an annulment, she found herself being spun around and clasped in the brawny arms of the MacLean laird, himself.

The hearty hug Alexander gave her was enough to break bones, but she could not help but smile at the affection that was so openly displayed. It was a moment she would cherish always.

"I want to be a grandsire, lass. Bairns. Do not forget . . . lots of bairns! Could you arrange that for a broken down old pirate?"

She raised her eyebrows and then smiled weakly at the laird. From behind her, Wyntoun pulled her elbow, and she turned and looked up into his stern face. He nodded toward the warriors, sailors, and well-wishers from both the MacLean and MacNeil clans who had formed a line extending right out the door of the kirk.

"They're waiting."

"I'd wager any of these men would gladly volunteer to give a lesson or two to you on how to kiss a beautiful new wife, Wyntoun."

Adrianne, surprised, glanced past her new husband to see Mara standing just beyond him, poking a finger into Wyntoun's side. The small woman's head did not even reach his shoulder, and yet the words drew response.

"Ma-ra!" he growled threateningly.

"You know I love you as my own son." She raised herself on her tiptoes and placed a kiss on Wyntoun's cheek. "And, by the Virgin, you've done well, choosing this bonny lass as your wife. Now let us see if you can continue to do well . . . by keeping her."

As quietly as she'd approached them, she drifted away and disappeared among the gathering.

Sensing his eyes on her face, Adrianne looked up and for

the first time this day met his gaze. Harsh words had passed between them the day before. At this moment though, none of that mattered, for as she realized his intention, her treacherous heart began to drum in her chest.

"For the sake of those who expect such things." His voice was a thick murmur as she watched his head descend—his gaze dropping to her lips.

It was a chaste kiss, a brush of lips. And yet, she began to tremble strangely at the feel of the softness of the touch, her heart racing at the memory of a similar kiss in his cabin. She couldn't pull her eyes away from him. A look of intensity was etched in his face. His green eyes were relentless in their study of *her* face, as well.

Her gaze fell on his mouth. The kiss had been so quick that she yearned to feel the texture of those lips again. She brought a hand up tentatively and touched his lips with the tip of her fingers. There was softness and yet strength.

"Present her," a voice called from the crowd. She recognized it as Alan's.

"Not yet," Wyntoun growled.

She could feel his strong fingers behind her neck, raising her lips to his. No longer gentle, the kiss this time was a plundering of her mouth, and all Adrianne could do was to clutch his tartan to stop herself from melting at his feet. He pushed down at her chin, and before she knew it, he was filling her mouth with his tongue, with his taste. His desire was so powerful that she found herself not helpless to it, but relishing it, rising to it, with feeling she'd never have imagined possible.

"You'll have plenty of time for all of this." The clap of Alan's hand on Wyntoun's shoulder caused him to break off the kiss. "Present her, you blackguard!"

Adrianne was certain her cheeks must look as if they were scorched. She glanced up to find him still gazing longingly at her mouth.

The time that they remained in the chapel was just a blur as Adrianne found herself aware only of *him*. And later, when the celebrations in the Great Hall were in full swing, she was again aware of the way his gaze drifted to her repeatedly.

"Is this part of what is expected, as well?" she found herself asking at one point when he entwined her fingers in his own and brought them to his lips.

His devilish smile caused a fluttery jump in her belly. "I will do whatever I must to keep Mara from thinking she needs to have someone beneath our bed to keep an eye on us. I believe she is going to want proof of the consummation of this marriage."

So it was for the sake of pretense, she thought, freeing her hand and hiding her face by bringing a cup of wine to her lips. She threw a quick glance in Mara's direction and found the older woman watching them intently.

Adrianne turned her attention back to her new husband and fell in with the ruse, hanging on his every word.

Rising from the table with him a short time later, Adrianne allowed herself to be escorted about the Great Hall, visiting with the colorful assembly of guests. More than once did she see a look of surprise pass over Wyntoun's face when she addressed clan folk and villagers by name.

His surprise turned to shock when she sat herself at the long table across from Auld Jean and John, and drew him down beside her. As always, John spoke only with his eyes and a nod or shake of the head, but his aging wife happily chatted away. Adrianne could see that the old midwife was clearly pleased with the marriage.

Later, during a short lull in the dancing, Adrianne saw Mara rise and motion for her to follow her. The bride turned her eyes questioningly on Wyntoun.

"You will be taken away from the Great Hall to be prepared for . . . for the marriage bed by these women. Mara will oversee everything, you can be certain." He nodded at the women who were gathering excitedly in the center of the Great Hall . . . and responding noisily to the calls and laughter of the wedding guests.

"Do you think this is necessary?" she whispered under her breath, watching a pair of pipers join the ebullient swarm. "Considering the . . . considering our arrangement."

"How can it be avoided?" He took her hand in his own and stared into her eyes. "Whatever you do, do not let Mara even guess the truth of our intentions. Remember, my chambers are in the east wing of the keep. We will have all the privacy we are after. There is no way she can learn the truth, Adrianne, unless we ourselves let her in on our secret."

She had no time even to give her assent before he leaned forward, brushing his lips across hers in a fleeting kiss. Stunned momentarily, she only moved when a group of laughing women approached, taking her by the arms and leading her to the merry throng.

"Nice gesture," Mara murmured quietly as Adrianne drew near. "But you two will need to work a wee bit more on your public displays."

Shocked by the words, Adrianne struggled unsuccessfully to come up with a response. It really didn't matter, though, for Mara quickly turned and gestured for the pipers to lead the procession out of the Great Hall, toward the east wing of Duart Castle.

Adrianne had already seen Wyntoun's antechamber the night she'd first brought up her proposal of marriage. Impressed as she'd been by the masculine furnishings and the obvious sense of order, she was now equally impressed by the subtle changes that had been made to make the chamber pleasing for a woman, as well.

Damask-covered pillows now softened the lines of the straight chairs. Delicate lace covered a small table by the hearth. Warm, colorful blankets adorned the back of a carved oak chair. A newly made mat of woven rushes covered the floor. A much larger fire burned in the hearth. She looked at Wyntoun's desk and noted the array of foods heaped up on golden trays. Feast would be a meager word to describe the amount and the variety of dishes that covered the table.

"The change in this room . . . 'tis absolutely beautiful!" She smiled at Mara before touching the edge of a silver platter piled high with cheeses and dried fruit. "But all of this . . . ! Mara, there is enough food here to feed a crowd as large as those already gathered in the Great Hall."

The women laughed, and Mara nodded as she put a gentle hand on Adrianne's elbow and guided her toward the door that the young woman knew must be Wyntoun's bedchamber.

"For what you two are *expected* to go through tonight and during the *next* four days—you will be needing a great deal of nourishment."

"Four days?" Adrianne asked with alarm, eliciting yet another laugh from her attendants. Mara drew her into the bedchamber, the others crowding in behind them.

"Tonight is the only night that you should worry about," Mara confided. "Survive this night . . . and perhaps tomorrow . . . and my guess is that you will *want* to have him to yourself . . . for a month, at least."

"Survive?" Adrianne asked, nervously turning to glance at Mara, but then the scene before her brought a smile of utter delight to her lips. "Oh, my!"

The room was adorned in a style befitting a royal couple. Everywhere Adrianne looked there were lit candles reflecting off of vases of gold and silver. Huge, richly embroidered pillows of velvet and damask had been beautifully arranged throughout the chamber. Nothing, though, could diminish the looming presence of the large, curtained bed that sat so prominently at one end of the chamber.

Mara gestured toward a chair that had been placed near a large fire crackling cozily on the stone hearth. "This is to keep your outsides warm until your husband arrives." She next waved her hand at a pitcher of wine sitting amid two sparkling crystal goblets on a small table beside the chair. "And the purpose of this is to warm your insides . . . again, until he joins you here."

The women filling the doorway giggled.

Adrianne nodded slowly, avoiding Mara's keen eyes and instead looking at Bege as she opened the curtains of the bed and held up a nightshift of the most transparent material Adrianne had ever seen.

"And this, my dear"—the older woman chuckled, motioning for Bege to bring the nightdress closer—"is for the purpose of making your new husband go mad."

She blanched at the thought of wearing such a garment anytime . . . never mind for Wyntoun MacLean!

"Go mad?" Adrianne questioned, watching the play of the fire through the sheer fabric.

"Aye! Mad with desire. Crazed with desire for you!" Mara grinned mischievously. "What else?"

Adrianne wiped the beads of perspiration that were gathering on her forehead. " 'Tis getting quite warm in here, don't you think?"

Mara and all of the attendants were delighted with her breathless response, and swarmed around her with a burst of good-natured teasing. As the back of the wedding dress was unlaced and the garment pulled from her body, each person present in the chamber seemed to have a bit of advice for Adrianne, some of it so bawdy that she blushed fiercely as the others laughed. The shift beneath her dress was disposed of in the same manner, but Adrianne had little time to worry about modesty as a tartan, for the time being, was wrapped around her.

Mara appeared in front of her. "Adrianne, in all seriousness, I haven't had this talk with you before, since I didn't know how . . . how knowledgeable you are about the matters of this first night . . . about the marriage bed."

"I . . . I . . ."

"I thought so. Completely inexperienced." Mara pushed her down on the chair. "Bess the seamstress warned me, and now I know."

Adrianne felt the clan women undoing the braids in her hair.

"Wyntoun is a man . . . and years ahead of you in . . . in this area. So you have some things you must learn."

"I—" A brush pulled at her hair, and Adrianne was silenced again as Mara shook her head.

"You need to remember that experience in a man is not necessarily a bad thing. In fact, once you learn to overcome your hesitancy regarding your husband and marriage bed—"

"I have no hesitancy."

"Well, you'll have plenty of opportunity to prove that, my dear." Mara took the brush in her own hand and started on Adrianne's hair. "As I was saying, once you are open to the responsibilities of married life, you'll realize that his experience with other women will bring you plenty of satisfaction."

"Mara, this is not a topic I want to—"

"Nonsense. This is knowledge every bride should acquire before her wedding night."

Adrianne stared straight ahead, feeling suddenly a little queasy. She was quite certain that she did not want to hear about his experience with all other women, but Mara was obviously determined to pursue the subject.

"Your husband is a very attractive man and, as all in this chamber will attest, he has for quite some time had his choice of the young wenches of the clan."

"And more than a few of the older ones, as well," one of the women chirped in, making the rest of them laugh.

"In fact, he's spent the greater part of his adult life fighting off the advances of lasses."

Adrianne was all ears now, suddenly wondering if he had bedded any of the women she'd visited in the village.

"So if we choose to be a *real* wife to our husband, the challenge for any woman lies in how we keep him interested enough in *our* company and *our* bed. Aye, that's the secret to having a successful conjugal life, rather than having a marriage in which we find ourselves relegated to being a wife in name only."

Adrianne winced. The bed part would be difficult, since Wyntoun had been clear enough about *not* wanting her there. Somehow his feelings on that score were rankling even more now than when he had first accepted her proposal.

"Of course, there are some women who are satisfied with sharing their husbands."

"I am not." Adrianne didn't know she had spoken the words aloud until she saw Mara's approving nod.

"I never really thought so," Mara said, patting her cheek. The older woman motioned for Bege to bring the nightgown.

Reluctantly, the young woman let go of the blanket and rose to her feet as the exquisite material was pulled over her head and onto her body. She didn't dare to look down as she could only guess at how absolutely indecent it must look.

"You have to charm him, lass, and yet retain your integrity. You have to appear willing and yet remain proud."

Simple words could not change who Adrianne was. Not that she herself could understand herself sometimes. But there was no reason for Mara to know her confusion. The ability to keep her own counsel was one quality that she suddenly had great use of at Duart Castle.

"Your knowledge on all of this is . . . is quite impressive."

Mara smiled. "Not really. 'Tis just that I've been married to Alexander for close to twenty years, and Wyntoun—with all his differences and independence—is still his father's son. He may have MacNeil blood in his veins, but he has a MacLean heart."

"I shall remember that."

Adrianne tried to pay close attention to everything else that Mara and her women said about the ways of luring and keeping a husband interested.

To all they said, though, she knew she would have to add her own emendations. Keeping him from straying was one thing. It was quite another to keep a man like Wyntoun MacLean from straying *and* make his family believe that she was keeping him interested.

Sometime during this lecture, it occurred to Adrianne that wielding a sword and facing an army of intruders was assuredly more pleasant than hearing all these wild tales about the marriage bed. After all, she would probably never have a chance to practice any of what she was being taught this night.

"Well, I suppose you are ready," Mara said finally, motioning for the attending women to back up.

Adrianne, glancing down at the sheer fabric that so clearly revealed her bare skin beneath, groaned inwardly at the image. She didn't dare voice a complaint, though, but smiled weakly as they all prepared to leave her. Casually, though, she pulled the long mane of black hair over her shoulders, covering the rosy circles of her nipples showing so blatantly through the delicate weave.

"Once we return to the Great Hall, it shouldn't be too long before the men carry him to your door. But you just stay put, just as you are, lass, and Wyntoun shall be undone the moment he lays eyes on you."

Adrianne smiled at Mara as reassuringly as she could and watched the crowd push toward the door.

"And do not forget everything that we've told you."

"I shall never forget," she called after the women, nodding at Mara as the diminutive woman backed out, closing the door behind her. Alone, Adrianne gnawed at her lip and tried desperately to figure how much time she had before her husband would arrive.

With any luck it would take as long as a journey to Balvenie Castle and back!

Chapter 13

Wyntoun had known that spending this first night alone with her would be the most challenging part of this entire charade. To last the night in the same room with her and not do what was expected of him—not do what he desired to do—was surely reason enough for sainthood. And he was no saint.

From the time he had kissed her at the altar, he knew that he would need all of his willpower, all of his wits, to withstand the power of his desire for Adrianne Percy. The woman had crept under his skin. In the days before, he would suddenly have to rouse himself as some waking dream or another seemed to take control of his mind and his body. Working in his chambers, he would find himself gazing at the buff-colored leather of some book and realize that his thoughts had been dwelling on the curve of her ear, on the color of her skin. Riding out across the rainy windswept moors of Mull late yesterday, he'd watched the hunters spreading out beneath him from hill to forested glade, and found his mind focusing on a pursuit of another kind. Even as he admitted such things to himself, a great red doe had leaped from the woods into the open meadow, fields now scored with the muted browns of the season, and Wyntoun had found in himself absolutely no desire to run down such magnificent beauty. He'd simply watched, fascinated with the grace and power of the animal.

And then he'd thought of Adrianne Percy—of her grace, her strength, her temperament, her beauty.

Raising his goblet of wine, he now tried to hide his growing frustration. It had been a long time since he'd wanted a woman the way he wanted her. Inwardly, he cursed himself, chiding himself for his weakness, for the desire he felt for her, the desire of a man for a woman.

And yet, he could not spread a pall over the clan's merrymaking. Looking around the Great Hall, seeing his father dancing happily within a jostling circle of farmers and fisher folk as the pipes sang out, he pushed back the tumult of feelings racing through him. He had raised far too many goblets of wine with this lively gathering of kinfolk to be showing any ambivalence now. Hell, he would face whatever the future would bring. His course was charted.

He just needed to get through tonight.

Moments later, the women returned and a final cup was raised to the happy couple. Alan formed an escort, the MacLean himself gave a drunken blessing, and a shoving, shouting, laughing throng of Highlanders carried Wyntoun along to his apartment and his new wife. At the massive oak door, the knight turned and faced them, scowling.

"Very well, you blackguards," he shouted. "This is as far as you all go."

"Nay, Wyn!" Alan turned to the others. "I say we do not let go of him until he is safe in bed with his bonny wife." The men gave a loud cheer at the shipmaster's words, but in an instant Wyntoun had his friend by the shirt.

"Back everyone up, my dear cousin, or blood'll be shed tonight—your blood!"

Alan's dark brows arched mockingly above green eyes. "Do as you will. I am too drunk to care. But you, my dear cousin, are as nervous as the night we were fourteen and the smith's young sister came to meet you at the cairn by the loch."

"Alan"—Wyntoun growled menacingly—"shut that maw of yours or I'll ding you so hard—"

"No fear, Wyn. I'll say no more." Alan's hand rested heavily on the knight's shoulder. "But you are a lucky devil, Wyn. We both know this one could have had the face of a sow, and you still would have taken her as wife."

"No more, Alan, you bloody fool."

"But she's no sow, is she? In fact, this lassie's more beautiful than any you or I ever—"

"That's enough," the Highlander growled, motioning for Coll to come and give him a hand.

"Be good to her," Alan said quietly. "She deserves better than she's getting. You might even give her a wee taste of the truth."

Wyntoun frowned as the shipmaster turned away.

"Very well, lads," Alan shouted to the others. "I believe there is a wee bit more drinking to be done this night! On, pipers, lead us back to the Great Hall!"

The knight watched for a moment as the boisterous crowd jostled and shoved their way down the corridor, laughing and singing as they went. Once they had disappeared, he turned and stared at the door.

Alan had known the truth from the beginning. Everything. All of his plans. All he would do to preserve the Treasure of Tiberius. The two had grown up together, trained together, sailed together, fought together. There had never been a moment's disagreement over what path they would take—not one instance of conflict over any decision regarding what they wanted to accomplish.

Be good to her, he'd said.

Wyntoun pushed open the door to his chambers and stepped inside the well-lit anteroom. He glanced wearily at the extravagant amount of food and drink adorning the table, and barred the door behind him.

Perhaps it was the wine they'd both drunk this night, but for the first time in all their years together, Wyntoun could sense a division between himself and Alan.

He shook his head. He'd be damned if he would let that happen because of a woman.

A beautiful woman, granted. But one who was only at his side for the present. Aye, he reminded himself. Just for the time being, and no more.

Pulling his tartan about him, Gillie listened to the pipes and the men moving back toward the Great Hall. Crouched in the shadows of the corridor, he kept up his vigil, his eyes riveted to the doorway where the master had just disappeared.

Tonight was no different from any other night. He'd kept watch over Mistress Adrianne since the night of their arrival at Duart Castle, just as he had kept watch over her on Barra. She was his friend. Even in becoming the wife of his master, she had not forgotten him. This morning before the wedding, Mistress Adrianne had stopped by the stables, looking for him.

If the other stable lads had been curious about the way Sir Wyntoun had shown interest in him, directing the master of the horses as to how Gillie was to be treated, this morning they had all stared—utterly stunned by the lady's attentions.

"I just wanted to make sure that you were settled," she had said with that sweet voice of hers, touching his face in the way that she always did. "I wanted to make certain that there were no troubles."

"No troubles," were the only words he'd been able to say, since she had looked so beautiful that he'd been ready to swallow his tongue.

Gillie glanced down the corridor to where the sound of merrymaking could be heard coming from the Great Hall. He was happy that Mistress Adrianne had decided to marry Sir Wyntoun. She would be good for him. Gillie had never thought his master to be very happy before—not the way that Ian, the old blind netmaker on Barra was happy—and he knew that his mistress would fix that.

And the master would be good for her, too, Gillie thought. Aye, Mistress Adrianne had a way of getting into mischief. But maybe now—being the master's wife—nobody would dare put her in a cage and hang her from some tower as punishment.

Deciding that they must be settled for the night, Gillie stretched his legs out before him and tucked his arms into his tartan. This was a new place for him, a good place. From now on he would be guarding the master's chambers. With Mistress Adrianne there—he curled himself into a tight ball— now he had the two of them to watch over.

He couldn't be happier.

*   *   *

Adrianne heard the outer door to the anteroom open and close and she hurriedly finished the last of her preparations. Standing back and giving her handiwork a final inspection, she hid her smile of satisfaction and waited expectantly for Wyntoun to enter the bedchamber.

The door to the chamber opened, and the tall figure of her husband filled the doorway. There was a deadly pause.

"By the devil! Whatever has happened here?"

She came around the bed and tried to look past him into the work room. "Are you alone?"

"By the . . . of course, I'm alone!"

As he entered, Adrianne quickly moved past him, glancing into the antechamber for herself before shutting the door. She came in and stood beside him. He was staring about the chamber in disbelief, and suddenly she was uncertain about some of the things that she'd done.

"Do you believe I have gone too far?"

He gave her a side glance that showed his agitation. "You mean you are responsible for this?"

She hesitantly nodded and watched him as he made his way to the hearth. He picked up the empty pitcher of wine.

"Did you drink all of it?" he asked, holding it upside down. A drop of wine fell to the mat of woven rushes on the floor.

Her temper flared in an instant. "Now, do I look like a person who could drink all of that wine and still be able to act as rationally as I have been?"

"Rationally?" he exploded, pointing at the mess around him. "You call breaking fine crystal fit for a king's table 'rational'? Do you call the act of tearing up good clothing, throwing food about, and upending furniture 'acting rationally'?"

"There is no reason for you to get upset," she scolded. "Everything I did here had a purpose and, after you give me a chance to explain it all, you'll see yourself that the . . . uh, damage . . . is completely justified . . . and well planned, if I do say so myself."

A loud snort escaped him, and he picked up a broken shard of wine crystal at his feet.

She stared at the broken pieces of the crystal. True, she *did* regret destroying certain items. Things as valuable as crystal, for instance. And having lived in the western isles for so many months, she was well aware of the scarcity of such luxuries.

"I had reason for breaking that," she said quickly, trying to fight back a sudden pang of guilt. "Will you listen to what I have to say?"

She saw him pick up a torn—and very sheer—nightgown. He held it up to the light and glanced back at her. "Very well, and perhaps you might explain this, as well."

Adrianne stepped toward him and snatched the transparent garment away. Bess had sewn this especially for Adrianne, and she was regretful of going so far as tearing it. Still, there was no point in letting *him* know of her regrets. "I will only explain if you agree to hear me out . . . from the beginning."

He glanced at her left hand, staring at the piece of linen she had wrapped around it. "And what did you do to your hand?"

"Only from the beginning," she repeated, placing the torn nightgown on a nearby chair and walking past him toward the hearth. She turned apprehensively and faced him.

"Begin, then."

"Will you please sit?"

"I prefer to stand."

She met his glare unflinchingly.

"I'll not have you towering over me." She motioned toward the chair again. "Will you be kind enough to sit?"

Adrianne breathed a silent sigh of relief when he finally did as she asked. She wiped one damp palm on the fabric of her blue dress and hid the linen-wrapped one behind her.

"Mara and her women had a talk with me tonight."

"Do not tell me you are planning to blame her for this madness!"

"Nay, I am not," she stated calmly. "All I am saying is that my handiwork here came as a response to what everyone goes through on their wedding night."

"*Everyone?*"

She wished he didn't suddenly look so amused.

"Well, it all begins with the wine," she started quickly, knowing her only salvation lay in getting through this explanation. "Since I am a . . . well, so inexperienced . . . you had me . . . had us . . . drink some wine."

He reached for the pitcher and turned it upside down again.

"A great deal of wine," she corrected, moving quickly to take the pitcher from him and putting it back where it was. "By the way, I poured the wine out the window. So please stop looking at me as if I were some drunken madwoman."

"A *drunken* madwoman could only accomplish half the damage you have done . . . but do continue."

"Very well."

As his eyes continued to take her in, Adrianne felt that strange heat pooling once again in her belly. The sudden tightening in her chest surprised her, though, and she drew a deep breath, forcing the air into her lungs. But he continued to look at her, his gaze wandering from her feet to the large wart she must have just grown on her forehead. She pushed her loose hair over one shoulder and wished she'd had time to braid it again.

"Well, becoming a wee light-headed after drinking all that wine, we crushed a wine goblet beneath our feet."

"Fine crystal?! Crushed on purpose?"

"Aye! 'Twas my idea. I thought 'twould be romantic. As the Jews do in Antwerp. My mother told me about it," she added belatedly. "But I am now truly sorry for breaking it, considering the value . . ."

She glanced nervously as he tossed the broken crystal into the fire without ever taking his eyes from her. A frown creased his face, but his green eyes showed no great anger about the loss. In fact, he didn't seem terribly angry, after all.

"Being somewhat . . . well, drunk . . . you . . . you chased me around the room."

"I *what*?!"

"You chased me. And that is the reason for the toppled furniture and the dumping of some of the food on the floor. If you think that's too much, though, I can pick up the food."

He said nothing, simply continuing to stare at her in disbelief.

She hurried on. "Then you caught me." She picked up the torn night dress and walked to a small table upended by the hearth. She held up the gauzy garment. "You . . . tore this off of me . . . right here."

Adrianne could feel the heat in her face. The thought of Wyntoun doing such a thing ignited a scorching hot flame inside of her. She didn't dare raise her eyes to him, but stood for a moment, frowning. Then she froze, hearing him chuckle under his breath. She dropped the shift back onto the floor and—still not looking at him—walked to the bed.

"'Tis natural, the women told me, for a man to be restless and throw the coverings off . . . as you see."

"And the feathers?"

A shiver coursed through her as she realized he was on his feet, approaching the bed.

"Playfulness?" she croaked, feeling his arm touch her shoulder as he came and stood next to her by the bed. "I . . . just thought . . . we . . . things became a wee bit rough . . . and the stitching on the pillows came loose."

"A wee bit rough? And you think that is customary?"

"I don't know anything about it! But I recall seeing—" She stopped, shooting him a look as she realized he was teasing her.

Taking a deep breath Adrianne pointed to the center of the bed.

"And that . . . is the proof that we . . . we consummated our marriage."

She tried to turn away from the bed, but his grip on her elbow held her in place. She did not look up, but knew he was staring at the stain of blood on the sheet.

"Mara wouldn't be convinced without it," she said nervously, too much aware of the heat in his grip. "She specifically told me that there would be blood, and I thought—"

"Let me see your hand."

"'Tis nothing. I—"

He quickly pulled the linen from her hand and stood studying the cut on her palm. She could see the concern in his

face, though when he raised his head, only a frown was evident.

"I cannot believe you cut yourself."

"I told you, 'tis nothing. I have been injured many times . . .
and far more seriously than a simple cut."

He didn't seem convinced. But as he wrapped the linen
around her palm again, she pulled away as if his touch were
more painful than the cut itself.

"And that is all," she said, turning sharply away from the
bed. "I believe we are prepared now."

"Only by half." He threw some of the coverings back on
the bed.

"What did I forget?" she asked, turning back to him with
alarm.

"In the morning, they will expect to find us . . . you and
me . . . in that bed . . . together . . . naked and exhausted after
a night of wedded bliss."

She swallowed hard and then glanced nervously at the bed
and then back up at his face. "You are jesting."

"I never jest."

"But—" She rubbed her hands again on the wool of her
skirts and tried to think of something to say.

"Knowing Mara"—Wyntoun crossed his arms over his
chest and leaned casually against one of the tall bedposts—
"she will be sending one of her women in here at the crack
of dawn to check on something trivial like the food . . . or
the fire."

Adrianne bit her lip trying to imagine a solution to this
problem. Getting into that bed with Wyntoun MacLean right
now seemed totally inappropriate. Nay! Such a thing was out
of the question!

"Of course, a woman who has seen as much as you have
would surely have no silly qualms involving modesty, now!"

Adrianne continued to gnaw at her lip, staring past his
wide shoulders at the bed. The memory of his kiss at the
chapel was suddenly the only thing that she could think of.
She could still feel the heat of his lips on hers. And there
was an unmistakable note of suggestiveness in his tone just
now.

"And 'tis not as if I haven't seen you naked already."

She closed her eyes, feeling herself wither with humiliation. She took a deep breath. "I was told that you . . . you only undressed me . . . but did not look."

"Nay, of course not. What man would look at a bonny lass who lies in all her unadorned splendor in his caring arms?" He straightened up, and she noted a huskiness that had crept into his last words, overshadowing the note of irony in his voice. He continued to stare at her, a fire lighting his green eyes, and her heart stopped as she felt him seeing her now, stripped of her clothing. "What's wrong, Adrianne? You do not trust yourself in the same bed with me?"

Nay, I do not, she wanted to say. Instead, though, she clutched a fistful of the fabric of her skirt with trembling hands.

"'Tis just that there are so many hours left 'til the morning. Lying there . . . waiting . . ." She shook her head. She wanted to be utterly exhausted, unconscious when she lay down on that bed.

His voice was matter-of-fact when he continued. "We could do something wildly unexpected, Adrianne—like sleep."

His commonsense attitude sent a shock of embarrassment through her. Perhaps, she thought suddenly, all of this was only her imagination. He was not affected at all. She felt herself sinking again. She was such a mess.

"Are you tired?" she managed to get out.

His eyes again swept suggestively over her body. This was definitely not her imagination, though the thought did little to buoy her spirits.

"Not very."

"Then lying abed with you will not do." She started pacing the room, trying to come up with some solution. Any solution. She stopped abruptly a moment later. "If we are not here, then there will be nothing more for them to see. I mean, there certainly is enough proof here—"

"Where do you suggest that we go?"

She looked hopefully toward the closed shutters. "For a ride. I haven't been on a horse in months."

"'Tis after midnight!" He looked at her incredulously. "Not

to mention that 'tis the middle of winter. A wee English thing like you would freeze to death in a trice."

"The moon is full, and the night clear." She moved about the room looking for her boots. "And I am only half English. I will not freeze. Please, I love the feel of a bracing wind in my face. I promise that you'll not hear a word of complaint."

"But there is nothing to see, nowhere to go. 'Tis dark . . . in spite of the moon."

"Humor me," she said softly from the other side of the room. "I believe we both need some fresh air."

He paused, considering.

Adrianne crossed the room and took hold of his arm. "Come, Wyntoun. We can always come back and get into the bed if the weather outside becomes unbearable."

Wyntoun reluctantly let her draw him toward the door. "If you think I plan to forfeit all sleep for the next month or so, while we push forward with your plan, then you are absolutely wrong."

"Have no fear." She patted him on the arm and tried to sound more convinced than she felt. "After this night, I will gladly let you sleep with me. I know I can count on your honor. I just cannot wait here tonight knowing someone is ready to barge in and find us in . . . in a compromising position."

As she dragged him into the antechamber, Adrianne did not dare look into his face, into those green eyes that were surely fixed on her. *Gladly let you sleep with me? Compromising positions?*

By the Virgin, she chided herself silently. Why couldn't she think before speaking?

Chapter 14

The dead monk's face was twisted with a look of fear. The rope burn around his scrawny neck was raw looking, but had begun to turn dark.

"Aye," she whispered. "He is the same monk who came after us last fall at the convent on Loch Fleet!"

Laura Percy Ross, clutching tightly to her husband's arm, tore her misty blue eyes away from the dead cleric.

"'Tis the same man." William Ross agreed. He turned Laura in his arms until she was facing away from the dead body. The thin scar that ran along the left outline of his lower jaw showed white in the torchlight. "Did the knave hang himself here in the crypt?"

"Aye, from there," John Stewart, the earl of Athol replied, pointing. "One of the scrving lasses came looking for him."

"What was his name?" Laura asked.

"Jacob. Or at least, that's what we were told." Athol nodded to those who would see to the body, and the three started out of the crypt. "He arrived here with the monk Benedict a fortnight ago. Benedict apparently guessed at this one's treachery, though, and even at a connection that Jacob might have had with the attempt to abduct Laura from Loch Fleet."

"I know Benedict," Laura said as they walked out of the chapel. The sharp Highland wind pulled at her long black hair. "He was a friend to my father and a tutor to us for all the years we were in Yorkshire. We were only separated from him when Catherine, Adrianne, and I left Jervaulx Abbey before being sent into the Highlands."

"Benedict told us that he met the other monk while he was on the way to Ironcross Castle. That's a holding to the south of here. It belongs to our friends and allies, Gavin Kerr and his wife, Joanna MacInnes." Athol walked beside the two as they made their way across the cobbled courtyard. "Benedict suspects that Jacob tried to get close to him, knowing of his connection with the Percy family. Later, he used the association he'd made with your old tutor to secure himself a position here at Balvenie Castle."

"Filthy bastard."

Athol nodded at William. "From what the monk Benedict says, Jacob became quite agitated upon hearing that the two of you were due to arrive from Blackfearn Castle. It looks like suicide, though for the life of me I do not know why he did not simply run for his life."

"'Tis a wee bit difficult to believe that our wives' enemies will simply kill themselves . . . saving us the trouble."

"True," Athol agreed, adding, "especially considering the trouble Catherine had with two other priests who arrived here earlier. Whoever these monks are—if they are monks—they seem intent on bringing this danger to our very doors."

"Has Benedict said anything else about why he didn't voice his suspicions sooner?" Laura asked, shivering. She continued to keep her death grip on William's arm. "What about Jacob? Did he mention any other names? Anything that might shed light on who is behind this terrible game? Jacob was not alone when he came after us at that convent."

Athol shook his head. "We only found the body this morning. Your arrival curtailed any serious questioning of Benedict. That monk is quite willing to talk, and I have a servant watching him. Once you've both had a wee rest and something to warm your insides, I'll see to it that we all have some time with the man."

The three climbed the steps to the massive doorway leading into Balvenie Castle's keep and entered the Great Hall. Laura opened her arms as a brown haired, blue-eyed, seven-year-old left Catherine's side and dashed across the Hall to them.

"Was he the ugliest thing you've ever seen?" the little girl asked, wrapping herself around Laura's waist. "Was he hideous and crawling with worms?"

"Miriam!" William gently scolded the child, hoisting her up and slinging her onto his back. "Come, lass. Your faithful steed awaits."

Miriam's blue eyes were the perfect match of William's as she looked over his shoulder. "So was he?"

"Aye, lass . . . worse even!"

"William Ross!" Laura chided. "You'll be giving her nightmares."

"Come on, lassie," he whispered loudly. "We'll leave Laura and your Aunt Catherine to their own devices, and I'll tell you all the gory details."

As he carried the child across the Hall toward the huge open hearth, Athol fell in step with them.

"You'd best lay the whip on that beast of yours, Miriam," the earl joked with a wink at the two women. "He looks a wee bit wild to me!"

Laura, misty-eyed, smiled and watched as father and daughter romped across the Hall, John Stewart in pursuit.

"She is the most beautiful child, Laura."

Laura turned and wrapped her arms around her sister. Tears, instead of words, were all that spilled out. The two women stood wrapped in each other's embrace for a few moments, until Laura thought about her sister actually carrying a child within her at this very moment!

"How do you feel?" she asked, wiping away a tear from the corner of her eye.

"I'm very well. I can feel him . . . or her . . . moving within me sometimes."

"Well, whatever 'tis, the babe will surely be a strong wee thing."

"To be sure! He's been using my ribs to practice scaling castle walls for the past month!"

" 'Tis a miracle, Catherine."

The two women fell silent for a moment, and then a tear splashed onto Laura's cheek.

"Come now," Catherine said encouragingly. " 'Tis not all as bad as it appears."

"I don't know what's wrong with me," Laura replied. "I . . . I mean, you are right. We've had it far worse than this. But for the past few days . . . anytime I think of Mother . . ." More tears welled up and spilled down Laura's cheeks.

Catherine ran a gentle hand over her sister's silky hair. "We'll find her and free her. I know deep in my heart that we will, Laura. Everything will be well."

Laura straightened up and, accepting a laced handkerchief from the older sister, wiped away the tears. "Of course, you're right. We need to be brave. By the Virgin, I wish Adrianne were here!"

Catherine nodded in agreement, and Laura's teary gaze lit on her sister's barely swollen belly.

"You look so wonderful . . . so beautiful," she said. As Catherine reached out and took her hand, Laura shook her head, hiccuping now. "I don't know what's wrong with me. I weep so easily these days. I've never been so . . . so weak-spirited."

"Don't be silly. We're all entitled to a good cry now and then."

Laura let herself be led to the nearest bench. "This morning, just seeing Miriam sitting with William on his horse Dread made me break down. Last night, just feeling my husband wrap his arm around me made me cry. Today . . . seeing you and your new family . . ." She wiped away more tears. "I cannot understand this. I am totally muddled with these emotions."

Laura buried her face in her hands and tried to take a few long breaths—to control her feelings. She couldn't let William or Miriam see any more of this silliness. She was certain they must already fear some madness had seized hold of her.

A few moments later she finally lifted her face only to find Catherine looking at her with scarcely concealed amusement.

"And what else are you feeling?"

"I don't know what you mean," Laura responded, casting a quick glance in the direction of her husband and Miriam. Athol was speaking seriously with William as Miriam peered up at them both attentively.

"Anything unusual?" Catherine persisted. "Feelings that

are new to you. Anything that you feel now that you didn't feel . . . say six months ago?"

"I am extremely happy!"

Catherine's burst of laughter drew the attention of others in the Hall. She immediately lowered her voice. "You didn't have to tell me that. I'd already guessed. Now think, Laura, what else?"

As she thought hard, Laura's hands drifted to her breasts. "They hurt?"

Dropping her hands immediately to her lap, Laura blushed furiously, and then nodded shyly. "Aye, they've been quite tender. Also, I believe they are growing. How could that be possible?"

Catherine's smile was anything but concealed as she patted Laura's lap. "What else?"

"I have half the stamina as I had before. Perhaps 'tis due to our traveling, but I could easily sleep the next fortnight away."

A frown furrowed Catherine's brow. "This sounds quite serious!"

"Do you think so?" Laura asked a bit nervously. " 'Tis not like me ever to become ill, though I sometimes cannot hold food down at all. I mean, when my belly started to pain me again a fortnight ago, I thought my old nervous stomach was back, but with these other symptoms—"

"Aye, quite serious!" Catherine repeated, bending over and placing a gentle kiss on her sister's brow.

"Please tell me," Laura pleaded, tears again springing to her eyes. "If I have some ghastly ailment that is going to take me away from my new family . . . I need to plan for it. I need to make some provision—"

Upon seeing Catherine starting to rise to her feet, Laura put a hand on her sister's arm. "Please tell me. I need to know!"

Catherine shook her head and then glanced mischievously in William Ross's direction. "Perhaps we should discuss this mystifying ailment with the one who caused it in the first place."

Laura stared blankly for a moment, and then felt her heart

leap as the realization of what Catherine was trying to tell her suddenly dawned on her. Her mouth dropped open, and she rose to her feet as Catherine nodded.

"Better yet"—Catherine whispered conspiratorially—"perhaps you had better wait here. I believe the laird of Blackfearn Castle might just need a place to sit when you tell him of the forthcoming addition to his family."

The thick forest of ancient oaks that ran nearly to the rocky shores of Loch Dan had lost most of its leafy foliage, and the darkness of the trail was lit by the great white moon that still hung so high in the western sky. But Wyntoun could have ridden this track blindfolded, for he knew these woods as well as he knew Duart Castle itself. He could hear the hoofbeats of Adrianne's mount close behind his own, and in a few moments they broke out of the woods into the open moorland.

As he turned to see her ride into open ground, the moonlight was so bright that the smile on her face fairly glowed. Putting the spurs to his steed, he raced ahead toward the rolling hills that led to bluffs above Loch Spelvie, his bride keeping pace and pressing him at every opportunity.

She was a skilled rider and a clever competitor. But it wasn't her competence in handling the sleek steed that he found so breathtaking, as the way her approach to riding reflected the way that she seemed to approach everything in life—with brashness and spontaneity, with a reckless kind of courage, and with passion. Always with that same fiery passion.

At the top of a bluff, Wyntoun reined his mount to a halt, gesturing for Adrianne to do the same. Her face was flushed with the exhilaration of the heady ride, and the flecks of sweat on her horse glistened in the moonlight as she patted his neck and murmured so soothingly.

Beneath them, the waters of the loch sparkled, and the dark peaks of Maol Ban and Druim Fada rose in the distance beyond. Wyntoun stared at Adrianne's profile as she straightened in her saddle and gazed in open awe at the sight spread out before them. The hood of her cloak had fallen back long ago, and silky tendrils of loose hair were dancing in the wind, teasing her brow, her delicate ear. As the puffs of mist continued to escape her parted lips, Wyntoun found himself suddenly hungry for the taste of her. The cold, the exercise . . . none of this had done anything to diminish the tantalizing image she'd conjured before they'd left their chambers at Duart Castle. To have her. To sleep with her. More. Looking out at the shimmering waters, he tried to tell himself this must all be the effect of too many cups of wine. What had happened to all of his good intentions, his sound reasoning? All that seemed to matter so little, now.

Wyntoun drew a deep breath and looked up at the moon, at the starry formations. He knew he would never again discourage Adrianne from talking him into something as ludicrous as riding out in the middle of the night in the dead of winter. The bracing salt air, the savage beauty of the land, the unadulterated thrill of night riding, all combined to satisfy some deep need in him. In five hundred years, he told himself, no one would remember that Wyntoun MacLean and Adrianne Percy had ever existed. There would be no record of this night. Who would know or even care that the two of them had breathed this air? That the two of them had felt this ground beneath them? That the two of them had looked up at that shining white disk coursing across the black night sky?

No one. Now was their time to live.

And he wanted her.

"Ready to start back?"

"We've only just arrived!"

"You *must* be tired by now."

She gave him a half glance and smiled. "Not very!" Her attention turned back to the scene before them. "This is absolutely beautiful. The reflection of the moon on the sea— the brightness of the night—'tis as if the fairies have lighted a road to heaven. I am certain that I can see the gates sparkling way up there . . . between those two blue stars."

He couldn't tear his eyes away from her face. In the soft light of the moon, she was far more beautiful than stars.

"Is it always like this? So serene? So lovely?"

"Serene? Hardly! But lovely . . . charming . . . ravish-ing . . . all those words work at times. But there are moments when no words sufficiently describe the beauty one sees."

She took a deep breath of cold air and seemed to hold it in for a long time. She then turned in his direction and found him watching her.

"I suppose, for someone of your experience, there is no magic in stars like these. To spend as much time as you spend at sea, there is probably nothing new and exciting to see."

"I wouldn't say that." He pushed his horse forward until his boot bumped her knee. He pulled off a glove and held out a hand in her direction. She gave him a shy glance and stared at his outstretched hand for a moment before uncoil-ing her own from the horse's rein, pulling off her glove, and placing her hand in his.

Her skin was as soft as the finest silk. He felt her shiver as his thumb traced a path on the back of her hand.

"You are cold." He reached over and took her other hand in his, as well. Carefully, he pulled her other glove off of her fingers. The horses shuffled their hooves, bringing them closer.

Clasping her smooth hands between his own, he brought them to his lips and blew his warm breath on them. She shiv-ered again.

"This will not do, Wyntoun." Before she could further voice a complaint, he reached over and took her horse's reins, tying them loosely to his own. Her eyes were huge when she realized his intention.

"I . . . I am . . . I am fine where—"

As easily as lifting a pile of feathers, he pulled her onto his lap. "I cannot let you end up getting a chill on our wed-ding night."

"I was not cold." She argued softly as he settled her against himself. He tucked her cloak around her, making sure she was well protected from the cold. She opened her mouth to speak, but then closed it as he cupped her face with one large hand.

"Tell me again that you are not cold." The silky skin of her face had the feel of ice. Her blue eyes—the color of a midnight sky in the moonlight—gazed into his own. He touched her brow lightly, her cheeks, the outline of one perfect ear. He ran his fingers down the barely exposed line of her throat. Grazing softly across the skin, his fingers traced the edge of her bottom lip, where rose met ivory, and heard her breath catch in her throat. He watched her eyelids close slightly.

He didn't pause, he didn't think it through, he did the only thing that his body commanded him to do. He crushed her lips beneath his.

She was sweeter than he remembered. Surely, this was the taste of the forbidden fruit.

Her hands were fisted for a moment, but then they fluttered open against his chest. As he pulled her tighter into his lap, he felt her softening, melting, her lips parting, yielding to his. He swallowed her soft moan of surrender as her body molded against his.

Wyntoun's hands were rough as they traced her back, pressing her to him so hard so there was not a breath of distance left between their bodies. He heard himself groan in frustration though as her tongue started shyly tangling with his, her arms moving up and encircling his neck. He let his lips travel along her cheek, her temple. He saw the way she looked at him, the way her desire and curiosity were carrying her along. When his mouth finally returned to hers, she was waiting, eager, ready to kiss him the way she had been kissed.

The wrong versus right. The unleashing of desire against reason. The battle brewing inside his head was short-lived as logic quickly bowed to passion.

She was already his wife. What else mattered?

Her tongue traced the line of his lips, urging him to continue where he'd left off. What she lacked in experience, she made up for in passion. And this was all the encouragement Wyntoun needed. With raw animal passion, he took possession of her mouth, devouring her lips, seemingly unable to get enough of her.

A sudden gust of wind swirled around them on the high cliffs, wrapping them in a spiral of desire.

"Still cold?" he asked unsteadily as her lips moved over his face, his skin, as his lips had done earlier.

"What cold?" she whispered, kissing him on the chin. "I feel . . . feverish . . . as if I am being scorched by the sun on a midsummer's day."

Wyntoun's mouth again took momentary possession of hers. His hands moved beneath the wool cloak and caressed her slender shoulders and her back, moving downward and feeling the curve of her buttock. He pulled her hip tighter against his hardening manhood.

"I never knew kissing could be this . . . this breathtaking." She nipped at his lips, teasing him, daring him to kiss her deeply again. "If there is this much pleasure . . . one gets from just kissing . . . why does anyone choose to go any . . . any further?"

Wyntoun groaned as much with pleasure as frustration as his hands traced the curve of her full breast through the thick wool barrier of the dress. He wanted to take her here—now. The desire that was driving out all other thought was that he wanted to be buried inside her. To feel her warmth all around himself. But she deserved better than this for her first time, and he physically forced back his own carnal desires.

"There is far more pleasure to be given . . . and received . . . than what we feel now."

She pulled back slightly and stared, in her gaze a hint of suspicion and yet wonder, as well. "More than I feel now?"

Her wondering question made him smile as he kissed her again, thoroughly, deepening the kiss with every thrust of his tongue. His fingers slid over her hardened nipples, teasing them through the dress. Then, he moved his hand slowly downward, feeling her body arch to his touch. Through the wool he pressed, urging her to part her legs and, as she did, he cupped her mound.

Gasping with surprise, she tore her mouth away from his. "I . . . these feelings . . . the tightness in my belly . . . this is more . . . more pleasure."

He suppressed his smile, placing gentle kisses on her face, all the while keeping the pressure on the juncture of her thighs, stoking, caressing, waiting for her body to take over its response to his probing fingers.

"This is far more." She leaned her brow against his lips. "This is so confusing . . . like some race . . . and I do not know how to reach . . . the end."

He kissed her brow again, her face, her mouth. No woman had ever put into words these things to him before. No woman he'd ever known had been anything like Adrianne.

"Tell me," he whispered in her ear, his mouth feasting on any skin that he could lay hold of. His hand continued its mission. "Tell me more of how you feel."

"Faster!" she moaned softly. "I have to go faster . . . the heat . . . the colors . . . but there is too much . . . too much clothing . . . my skin is . . . I need to feel—"

He too was aroused, his own breathing not much better than hers. When her beseeching and clouded eyes lifted to his, he savagely claimed her mouth. His one hand held her steady around the waist as the other pulled at her skirts. The layers of clothing were a nuisance, but he found his way. His fingers, creeping up along the silky skin of her thigh, were soon engulfed with the wetness and the warmth of her mound. He didn't know which of their gasps of relief was the louder.

She wrapped her hands more tightly around his neck. "I am . . . I cannot . . ."

He slipped a finger into her tight sheath. "Let it go, Adrianne." He kissed her with a need beyond control. "Let it go."

The moment before her release was almost frantic, her body writhing against his hand, and then she exploded with a cry of ecstasy beneath the starry sky.

For a long, long moment he could not think clearly. All he wanted was to take her, to bury himself in her, but instead he simply held her tight, soothing her with words of affection, kissing her with all the tenderness that she'd awakened in him.

Then, abruptly, Wyntoun found himself wheeling his horse about and spurring the steed toward Duart Castle with Adrianne wrapped tightly in his arms and her horse trailing behind them. Moments passed before she recovered enough to utter a word.

He wanted her more than anything else he'd ever wanted in his life. He desired her with an ardor and a desperation he'd never experienced before. But he would not take her here in the heather and the bracken or in a forest of oaks . . . devil take him! This was still her wedding night, and he would do it right.

Her head was tucked into the crook of his neck. Her warm breath and soft lips a welcome torture on his skin. She had one hand tucked inside his tartan and shirt, caressing the bare skin of his chest. For her sake he so hoped she wouldn't slide those fingers lower, or his intentions of waiting until they reached their warm bed would be all for naught.

"Where are we going in such haste?" she asked as the forest loomed ahead.

"Back to Duart Castle . . . to our own chambers."

He felt her head lift from his shoulders. Looking at her, he noted a pretty smile threatening to break across her lips.

"But there is still so much time left until morn. You do not seem ready to retire for the night . . . to sleep, I mean. What . . . what will we do until the sun rises?"

He pulled her tight and nipped at her lips. "There might be a thing or two I could suggest once we get there. A thing or two we could try out . . . you *did* mention 'compromising positions' earlier. I've just thought of some."

Her blue eyes rounded with surprise. "But what of the things *you* said earlier. Of your condition of—"

"To hell with everything I said," he growled. "Making love to my wife is the only condition I am interested in any longer this night."

This time Wyntoun was the one to miss the look. Anticipation mingled with blissful well-being on Adrianne's face as she tucked her head onto her husband's shoulder.

Chapter 15

Although everything was in place, Nichola Percy knew that timing the incident incorrectly would surely cost her own life.

Already, she had nearly broken her neck dragging the cot up on end against the crumbling mortar and stone and climbing up on it to stuff her blanket into the narrow window slit high on the chamber wall.

The cot was now leaning against the wall, a few steps from the door, another blanket draped over the knotted cords and wood frame. She would be hiding there when they entered the chamber. With any luck the smoke would be so thick that they wouldn't see her slip out, she told herself, sweeping a few more of the floor rushes into the loose pile she'd constructed.

Nichola stood back and frowned at her handiwork. The straw-filled mattress that she'd propped up would burn readily enough; she just hoped there would be enough smoke created to fill the chamber. She glanced up at the timbers. The smoke from the brazier was already hanging amid the blackened oak. The blocked window was having an effect.

"'Twill have to do," she muttered aloud.

She could not take a day more of this imprisonment and this silence. If she were to live out her life this way, then death offered no punishment, and only a passage to something better awaiting her in the next world.

Nichola paced to the door of the small room, listening intently for the distant sounds that would warn of her old caregiver's approach. Now was the moment.

"The tide must be taken at the flood, they say—"

The utter recklessness of her act struck her fully as she covered her hand with her cloak and pushed the brazier over, spilling the chunky embers into the rushes. She simply could not endure this endless entrapment any longer, but the extent of the possible consequences of this fire could be far-reaching. True, she had lost all patience—but what of the people who depended on this castle for their livelihood? True, whoever owned this keep had mistreated her by keeping her against her will and without any human contact—but what if innocent people were injured or killed fighting this fire? What if this fire got out of control? Was the fact that she was ready to scream out and batter down the walls of her prison a good enough reason to destroy someone's home or take someone's life?

The rushes flared up and the mattress quickly caught. In an instant, black smoke was billowing into the air, and Nichola gave a mirthless laugh at her own rash behavior. To think that now, after years of preaching patience and thoughtful deliberation to her daughters—especially to Adrianne—she herself was reverting to wild and reckless ways!

The situation was suddenly as amusing as it was grim!

The smoke now filled the upper regions of the chamber, and Nichola covered her mouth and nose with her cloak. As she ran to the door, the two candles sitting on the small table suddenly went out, and Nichola found her breaths coming harder. She could hear air whistling in from beneath the door, and as she crouched beside the entry, she saw flames beginning to spread along the floor. The ancient oak boards themselves were beginning to catch fire.

She turned her head at the sound of a heavy door squeaking on old door hinges somewhere on the floors beneath her prison.

"FIRE!" Nichola screamed at the top of her voice. "HELP ME! FIRE!"

The thought suddenly occurred to her—immediately evolving into a certainty—that her captors might not believe her cry for help. The old servant would not hear her, that was certain. What if no one else were within earshot? She could now feel the heat of the flames spreading across the floor. Her eyes burned from the stinging smoke.

"FIRE!" she screamed again. "FIRE!!"

Moving from the iron-banded door to the hiding place behind the cot, she waited, suddenly doubtful that someone would come through that entryway. Holding the cloak over her mouth, Nichola stared, not so much with fear as with an eerie acceptance that perhaps this *was* how she was intended to die. She hoped she would be the only victim.

Then, in the smoke, she saw the face of Edmund, her husband. Then her daughters were standing beside him. The three lasses, smiling. But so young. Dressed in pristine white linen dresses, they were just bonny young things. The image shifted. They were running wildly across the moors toward her, but she kept drawing away from them. She could see their shining dark locks flying in the wind. The blue eyes pleading, their wee hands waving at her, motioning for her to wait for them.

Nichola turned her face and saw Edmund, down on one knee beside her. She cried out with pleasure at seeing him alive— seeing him whole. The tears of happiness were quick to rush to her eyes as she thought of how empty she'd felt without him. She reached out to touch his face, but a cloud of smoke was all that swirled around her.

"Edmund!" she sobbed quietly. She saw him starting to fade away. "Please take me. Take me with you, Edmund."

The image of her children again presented itself—grown now and standing before faceless men. Catherine, her belly swollen with child, held a smiling Laura by the arm. Adrianne, a knight's hand resting on her shoulder, was holding out a blue cloth, fringed with gold. It was the cloth that hung in her husband's study.

"They look happy, Edmund," Nichola heard herself whisper. "Content. Take me . . ."

There was no one beside her. No blue eyes. No gentle face. No strong shoulder on which she might cry out her anguish and find solace. He was gone. In his place, Nichola saw only fire and smoke and three men frantically batting down at the flames with blankets. She looked at the door. It stood wide open.

She didn't hesitate. Stepping out onto the landing, she saw her aged caregiver tugging open a long narrow shutter on the stairwell in an attempt to let in some of the night air.

Nichola moved quickly past the woman and ran down the stairs in a frenzied rush. At the landing below, another door stood open, with a gallery leading off in one direction and more steps leading downward.

The shouts of men racing up the stairs panicked her for a moment, but she quickly recovered, darting along the gallery past closed doors. At the end of the gallery, a torch on the wall showed another set of stairs. On her left, unglazed windows looked out on a courtyard below, and she could see men and women scurrying about, torches in hand.

Running along the corridor, she started at the sound of people ahead of her and slipped through a doorway into a dimly lit chamber. A half-dozen men and women raced past the doorway hauling sloshing buckets of water, and she could hear more coming behind them. She turned and stared at the chamber she was in. A warm fire burned in a fireplace, throwing light on a nearby settle and on the walls. On a desk in the center of the room, a number of parchment scrolls had been spread, carved stone weights holding them open. There was no other door that she could see.

And then she stopped, her mouth dropping open. There, on the wall above a small hearth, hung a shield with a coat-of-arms that she knew as well as her own.

Even more startling, though, behind the painted targe a fine cloth of blue had been carefully arranged. As if drawn to it by some supernatural power, Nichola stepped toward the blue cloth, staring in disbelief at the fringe of gold sparkling in the flickering light of the fire.

"So, what *specifically* do you intend to do to me once we arrive back at Duart Castle?" Adrianne's head lay comfortably against Wyntoun's chest. She breathed in the musky masculine smell of sea and leather and the winter forest at night.

A thrill raced up her spine, and she tightened her hold on him.

"Adrianne . . ." His threatening growl caused her to smile mischievously. She placed a kiss on the exposed skin of his neck.

"But there is so much that I do not know. Perhaps if you were to begin giving me some instruction along the way . . ."

She could feel his manhood, hard and pressing against her hip. He shifted slightly, and pulled her even tighter against his chest.

"You continue this sort of talk, and there will be no arriving at Duart Castle this night."

She lifted her head off his shoulder and smiled into his face. "You know of a closer place where we could take shelter for the night?"

"Aye! So long as you do not mind the frozen ground as your bed, the night sky as your roof, and the weight of your husband as your blanket!"

"I shouldn't mind that, at all."

The sound of his laughter ringing through the night made Adrianne's heart ache with an affection for him that she'd not known could be so strong. She placed a hand on his cheek and saw his gaze lower to hers and linger there.

The oak trees formed a thick spidery canopy overhead. In the summer months, when the leaves covered the tree branches, it must be very dark here, she thought.

The knight slowed his horse to a walk, and moments passed before either of them spoke again.

"This game we are playing, Adrianne . . . you know there is a price to be paid."

"Is there?"

"Aye . . . consequences. We are about to get into something far more involved than we bargained for." He was staring straight ahead. Farther along the trail, she could hear the sound of the wide stream they had splashed across on their ride out to the bluff overlooking the loch. In her mind she could see the water tumbling over ice-encrusted rocks.

"Do you find the price too high, Wyntoun MacLean?"

"Nay, I do not," he said tightly. "So long as there are no regrets after all is done."

"In that case, I *will* tell you where I go in the mornings. Does this please you?"

"Aye, that it does," he chuckled softly, growing immediately serious again. "Though not everything between us will be righted so easily."

She remained tucked in his arms, listening to the wind rise and whistle through the branches overhead.

Adrianne's brow creased, and she gnawed at her lip as she considered his words. *After all is done . . . Everything being righted.* Did he still intend for her to go away once they had accomplished their task? Surely something had changed in their plans. Adrianne opened her mouth to ask the questions that had already begun to eat away at the moment, but she stopped as Wyntoun abruptly jerked the horses to a halt.

"What is it?"

"There . . . in the stream." He pointed off the path, turning the horses toward the water. "There is something moving."

She took the reins of the horses as he quickly leaped to the ground. She peered ahead through the openings of the trees. She could just make out the looming presence of Duart Castle in the moonlit distance.

"Someone is there. And it looks to be a wee one."

Adrianne scrambled off the horse herself and followed him to the edge of the water. Looking past his shoulder, she could see the shadow of a small figure huddled in the water.

"Wait here!" He walked out into the icy water, drawing his dirk from his wide belt.

Quickly tying the horse's reins to a nearby bush, she followed him without a second thought into the stream.

"I told you to stay back there," he growled, looking down. Her skirts were billowing out on the water at her knees.

She glanced down as well, but ignored his reprimand, moving past him toward the huddled figure. For an instant her thoughts ran to the possibility of it being some fairy creature, some river dweller. As she neared it, though, with Wyntoun beside her, she saw the thatch of dark hair, the slim shoulders hunched and shivering from the freezing water.

Gillie!

"By the devil, is that you, Gillie?" The knight sheathed his dagger and bent over the lad.

"Gillie, what are you doing here?" Adrianne asked, touching the boy's hair. There was ice in it. She drew his chin up so she could make sure he was still breathing. His teeth were chattering and his eyes unfocused. She quickly undid her cloak to put it around him.

"Not yet," Wyntoun ordered. "Let's get him out of the water first."

She threw her cloak around the lad's shoulders as the Highlander began to lift him.

"My . . . f-foot . . . my . . . foot," Gillie whispered, shuddering violently. "The d-d-d-devil . . . h-h-has a hold . . . on my f-f-foot!"

Glancing sharply at her as he pushed the cloak out of his way, Wyntoun reached one arm elbow-deep into the frigid water. "A branch. He has one foot stuck in a branch. Get him to stand if he can."

Adrianne did as she was told, and draped the boy's arm around her shoulder.

"You can do it, Gillie." Taking all of his weight, she pushed both of them to their feet.

" 'Tis a wondrous change to have you do as you are asked."

Adrianne looked up, feeling her temper flare as she realized that Wyntoun's reproach was directed at her. "I always do as I am asked."

His huff of disagreement was audible, and she stared at him. Shaking his head, Wyntoun took hold of the submerged branch, straining to dislodge it. On the third powerful heave, the branch loosened, and he carefully freed Gillie's foot.

In an instant, he had the boy in his arms and was moving toward the water's edge. Adrianne waded alongside of him, struggling to keep up with his powerful strides.

"Can you possibly follow instructions?" he growled, carefully climbing the bank of the stream.

"I always do." She ran a few steps to keep up with him.

For the first time, she could feel the bitter cold, her wet clothes heavy around her legs. She hid her shiver.

"Adrianne, the lad needs help."

"I know that!" she answered wearily, untying the horses' reins and turning back to the Highlander. She peered at Gillie, reaching up and touching his cold face. He appeared to be unconscious in the tall knight's arms. "We have to get him to the castle."

"There should be two blankets, one in the travel bag of each horse. Take them out and wrap one around yourself."

"I do not need one. Gillie is the one—"

"Do as you are told or, devil take me, I'll tie you with a rope and do it myself!"

"Churlish, ill-tempered boor!" She muttered the words under her breath and did as she was told. "You want the other for Gillie?"

"Put the other down, and mount your horse."

"Don't you think we should see to Gillie—"

"If you hurry up and do as I bid you—"

"Very well! I *am* doing as I am told." She positioned herself on the horse, pulled the blanket loosely around her shoulders. "Well?"

He handed Gillie gently up into her arms.

"I have him!" she said, pulling him tightly into her lap and wrapping him in the blanket as she grasped the reins.

"Now if you'll hold the lad for a moment, I will take . . ."

The Highlander's next instruction was lost as she spurred the animal into motion. Adrianne didn't need to wait. She knew what she had to do next. In a moment, they were splashing across the wide stream and up the far embankment. She could hear Wyntoun in the stream behind her, and kicked her horse into a gallop.

Shedding the lad's wet clothes and wrapping him in warm blankets. Making a large fire and letting Gillie's body gain back some of its warmth. Feeding him some hot broth and praying that the lad wouldn't come down with a fever. Adrianne's mind whirled with everything that she had to do as soon as she would arrive back at the castle.

Wyntoun's steed was thundering up behind them, but the

way he was barking her name at her back made her wonder for an instant if he'd had other plans. She closed her ears to his calls, spurring her horse on. In a moment they would be clear of this forest, and the black waters of Duart Bay would lead directly to the castle.

They would have time to talk once Gillie was safe and warm.

Chapter 16

"I was touched by the Treasure of Tiberius."

The lie came across as the absolute truth. The statement sounded as sincere and as authentic as any sentence Benedict had ever spoken in his life. And he could see the words work their desired magic. Every face gazing so intently on him turned from guarded suspicion to surprise and overt interest in what he had to tell them. A complete hush fell over the room.

Benedict knew why he had been summoned here. In the presence of the two Percy sisters whom he had tutored as children, the earl of Athol and William of Blackfearn intended to interrogate him about the dead fool, Jacob. Well, he had not so long ago suffered torture at the hands of true masters of pain, men who relished the cries of tormented souls as they plied their hellish trade.

Somehow, Benedict thought sneeringly, somehow he doubted that he would suffer quite so much here at Balvenie Castle.

He thought of Jacob. Listening to the man's whining, seeing the weakness and the fear that had overtaken the monk's soul, there had been no choice left for Benedict but to kill the chattering, squint-eyed fool. It had only taken a moment. A rope looped around his scrawny neck, a bit of a struggle, a twitch or two at the end, and 'twas over. Hauling his dead weight up so that it looked like a hanging . . . a suicide . . . had been the only difficult part, but Benedict had managed.

And now he had every intention of using Jacob's "treachery" and death as a means of gaining a secure place in the trust of the Percy daughters.

He'd stepped into the earl's study prepared for what was to come. He'd known exactly what to say and how to explain his "discovery" of the dead monk's disloyalty. Of Jacob's drunken mention of Tiberius the night he had hung himself. Aye, he'd told them, he had known then what Jacob was after . . . and had watched him carefully . . . dutifully.

And it hadn't taken long before they directed the question at him. What did Benedict himself know of this . . . this Tiberius?

The question had been uttered almost casually by William of Blackfearn. The Highlander was shrewder than one would suspect, Benedict realized. The Ross chieftain would bear close watching.

But as his interrogators had cast quick looks at one another, he had known that this was his moment to turn the tide. This was the answer that would convince them, assure his place in their confidence, as it had won him the confidence of the many clerics who had done his bidding over this past year. He would use their beliefs, their superstitions, to his advantage.

"Aye," he repeated. "I know the power of Tiberius. It holds the power of miracles within it, and it touched me."

"What do you mean by that?" Athol frowned.

The monk threaded his gnarled fingers together and met Catherine Percy's gaze. Of the two sisters present, Benedict knew his best chance to conquer lay with her—the dreamer of the family. It was she who always had been the most trusting.

"My presence here—the mere fact that I have been able to dedicate myself to a life of contemplation and study—is evidence of Tiberius's power."

"Are you speaking of your own spiritual well-being? Is this how Tiberius has affected your life? Please be clear, Benedict."

The monk nodded and bowed slightly toward Laura, acknowledging her words, but then directed his attention back at Catherine.

"I am speaking of a direct blessing . . . of a miracle as real and as physical as our ability to see and hear and touch."

"What do you mean? Have you ever seen the Treasure of Tiberius?" John Stewart asked bluntly. He turned to his wife and his new sister-in-law. "Has anyone?"

"Aye." Benedict spoke quietly. "I have seen it!"

"At last," Catherine said, relief evident in her voice. "Someone who has!"

Benedict's face showed none of the satisfaction he was feeling at that moment. This confirmed his suspicion that the sisters had not moved it after all. It was still waiting for him to claim it.

"Sit down, Benedict." William Ross's order was spoken sharply, hinting at the man's impatience. "Sit here and tell us everything you know about the Treasure of Tiberius."

Bowing slightly to the group, Benedict shuffled slowly across the chamber and took the chair offered to him near the hearth. "There is so much of my past that you already know." His words again were directed at Catherine. "But I do not know if 'tis my place to speak of the Percys' sacred trust with . . . with outsiders."

"Please tell us everything," Laura replied. "'Tis time our husbands learned what we know. We all need to know everything, so that we can carry out that trust."

"Benedict, we only know you as our tutor," Catherine said. "But you have known our father for much longer than that, haven't you?"

Benedict raised his eyebrows, feigning his surprise. "Countess, your father never told you the circumstances of how I happened to come and stay? Where do I begin?"

The monk considered for a moment. In all of his previous musing and plotting, he had never thought for an instant that the three girls would not know exactly what the Treasure of Tiberius was. Pondering it all now, he realized that—despite all their mischief and their secrecy—it was quite reasonable that Edmund Percy had never had the chance to advise his wife of the true nature of Tiberius. His arrest had been sudden and unexpected. And she, in turn, would never have revealed it to the daughters.

He peered thoughtfully at the women. On their faces he could see the thirst to know more about this treasure that they were given the maps to—and yet obviously knew so little about. This indeed had been the chance that he'd been waiting for. An opportunity to move once again inside the circle.

"I was once blind." Benedict paused and looked about him to study the reaction of his words in his audience's expression. He'd seen the same reaction before, among the monks and nobles he'd gulled in the past. The four simply stared, believing, intently awaiting his next words. "As a lad, my world was darkness for as long as I remember. And I grew up in that darkness ... until a most unbelievable event occurred.

"I was born a nobleman's son, but without sight I had no hope of becoming his heir. So I was sent as a young lad to the Cistercians at Jervaulx Abbey—only a half day's ride from your family's home. You two are quite familiar with that abbey, I know. Blind though I was, I was assigned to the monks who lived their lives among the books in Jervaulx's great library. They knew I would be of no help to the brothers who worked the farms and the kitchens. I had found a place where I might spend the rest of my life in the service of the Lord."

All of the monks who had known him during those early years were dead now. There was no one left to challenge his story. No one alive who could call him a liar.

"I come from strong stock—my father and one of my brothers fought and died with King Richard that day when that upstart Henry Tudor stole his bloodied crown at Bosworth Field. Aye, very good stock. My body grew straight and strong in spite of my lack of sight." Hiding his loathing, he glanced at Athol and William. "The broken old man you see before you is the work of this King Henry ... and his henchmen. But as a lad and later as a young man, all the time that I might have wasted in training my body for the battlefield, I used in training my mind. I used my lack of sight to my advantage by being everywhere and hearing everything. I had the others read to me from the volumes in that wondrous library. I came to know the work of the ancients and others so well. I can recite to you today the wisdom of Plato and Xenophon, Aristotle and Dio Chrysotom, Augustine and

Aquinas. I know the histories of Herodotus, the poetry of Virgil and Horace and Homer, the treatises of Galen—aye, especially Galen. And in spite of my blindness—nay, because of it—I learned the Sacred Scriptures by heart. All of them, I thought then."

Benedict watched carefully for any response to his words. Nothing changed in their expressions of interest and sympathy.

"But even as I slowly and steadily became learned in the arts and sciences and Scripture, I became more and more frustrated, more filled with sorrow and—aye, I can admit it now—fury that I would never be able to put that learning to use. More and more I seethed to think that I would never leave the familiar walls of Jervaulx Abbey. Never would I be of any service to others. There was no hope."

So much of this was true. Though teaching a few privileged nobles had never been a driving ambition for Benedict, the frustration and the fury that he had felt—that he felt now—were real. Very real. It was power that he wanted. Power he craved. Power he would have. And from early on, he had seen that religion was the way. There was nothing like the authority of the "divine." Nothing gave more mastery, more control over the two-legged sheep of this world. With religion, you could control them all, body and soul.

Benedict knew it was true, and he looked at his audience—as captivated as when he'd first begun to speak.

"I was a young man of twenty and he eighteen when Edmund Percy and I first crossed paths. 'Tis hard for you to believe that we were so close in age, but 'tis true. The years have gone hard for me, in some ways. Be that as it may, I had heard of the young knight. Then one day, word came that Edmund and an entourage were at the abbey gates, having undertaken some grave mission and traveling to the north. There were words that were whispered—secretive words like 'treasure'! The rumors told that Edmund Percy and his men were in possession of the most powerful and holy treasure in all the world! And they would be taking shelter at our monastery for one night before continuing their journey.

"'Twas true. Edmund Percy, swearing all to secrecy, would

even allow the monks to see this divine treasure. For centuries, this treasure had been protected . . . from the day the holy crusaders had found it in the town of Tiberius, on the Sea of Galilee." Benedict wrapped his bony fingers around the cross at his belt and forced a note of sorrow into his voice. "But such a gift would not be wasted on a blind monk."

"Was this truly the Treasure of Tiberius?"

The ever-impatient one, Benedict thought, casting a hasty glance at William Ross.

"Aye, 'twas Tiberius indeed! They laid it in the chapel in the great library for the night, with a coterie of knights around the door. Only because of Edmund Percy's kindness—aye, he heard of the blind monk Benedict who had been kept away—I was allowed to visit the chapel. I could not touch the ancient treasure, but I was at least allowed into the chapel, and given a chance to speak with the good knight into whose hands it had been given."

William Ross moved from the window to the hearth, and the earl of Athol was momentarily distracted, but Catherine and Laura did not take their eyes off of Benedict. The monk continued. He would not allow anyone to steal this moment of glory.

"Somehow, a fire started in the chamber beneath the great library." Benedict's body seemed to come alive at the memory of the blaze he himself had set. "'Twas late, many were sleeping. I myself had retired to my cell to pray. Suddenly, the cries of the knights and my brothers could be heard. I never remember experiencing greater confusion than I found when I reached the library doors. The smoke was thick, burning my lungs, and the air was filled with the shouts of men running to and fro, battering me about in my blindness. Everything I knew of the place, every doorway and every stair, every sharp edge on the floor, was thrown over in the frenzy of the moment. I was pushed ahead and turned round and round until I was dizzy."

Benedict's voice rose in the quiet of the room. "And then, suddenly, I was alone. I could feel the sweep of cold fresh air to my left . . . and hear the crackling sound of fire to my right. I turned, found the wall, a corner that I recognized. I started back. I could hear men coughing, crying out, trying desperately to get back inside. One voice called out to me, but I continued on. In a moment I was through the doors to the library. I did not try to breathe, for I could feel the inferno of heat and smoke on my face. I moved toward the tiny chapel. The heat was intense when I reached the door, but I pushed through it. I could feel the power of the treasure drawing me on, hear that heavenly voice calling me, leading me through the flames. Aye, there was a voice calling me on."

Benedict gazed down at his own hands. He'd meant to take the treasure that night . . . to make it his own.

"There was a power there far greater than anything I will ever experience again on this earth."

The monk's eyes snapped up to the group.

"I had no fear of death when I walked through the heat of those hellish flames. I had no regrets about my life, only joy in going toward that voice that could only have come from heaven itself. And then, suddenly, I felt no fiery heat. Cool air—sweeter than any I had ever breathed—swept into my lungs. I reached out my hand."

Benedict didn't wipe away the tears that ran along the deep furrows of his face. The excitement continued to build in his voice.

"I reached out and found the charred wooden casket. It was not even warm. Opening the top, my fingers touched the thick velvet wrap that protected it. Touching it . . . just touching it, I felt the power vibrate through my body, touching my soul. I closed the top once again, clutched the casket to my chest, and stepped back into the flames."

He'd had his hands around it. The most glorious chance of his life. How close he'd been to succeeding that night! How close! He could almost feel the heat around him again. He took a deep breath and continued.

"I walked through the burning library and out into the corridor. Though I could hear the wailing and shouting of voices in the distance, the corridor was empty now . . . but for one man—Edmund Percy."

" 'You've saved Tiberius!' he cried out. 'By the Virgin. You've saved the Treasure of Tiberius!' "

"As he took the charred wooden casket from my burned fingers, the only thing that I could think was that I could see!" Benedict met Catherine's gaze. "I could see, and your father's face was the first thing that I ever saw."

Thundering past them, Wyntoun raced ahead along the stony spit of sand and sea grass. As he drew near the walls of the castle, he shouted for the iron-banded portcullis to be raised. Frowning fiercely, the Highlander turned to watch Adrianne approach, Gillie perched precariously in front of her. Wyntoun didn't know which of the two he was more furious with.

The gate was open by the time Adrianne neared the castle, and as the two horses passed side by side beneath the low arch, Wyn could hear Gillie murmuring under his breath about protecting his mistress.

Leaping off his horse at the foot of the steps into the east entry to the keep, the knight reached up to take Gillie from her arms. The courtyard was empty but for a couple of half-asleep grooms trotting over from the stables to tend the horses.

Gillie's head dropped back, revealing his sadly afflicted face, now pale and deathly looking in the moonlight. The lad must have left the castle on foot after seeing them ride out. In the middle of winter, on foot at night, dressed as poorly as the boy was and then crossing a half-frozen stream . . . he deserved a whipping to beat some sense into him.

By the devil, Wyn cursed himself, he never should have gone out riding with Adrianne. And he should have known that the lad would try to follow them. Gillie had barely taken his eyes off her from the time they left Barra.

He shot her a glare. Concern was evident in her face, but not a trace of guilt over her impulsiveness. Instead of staying out of the water and having a dry garment to wrap Gillie in, she'd simply wrapped her cloak around him as he'd crouched in the stream. And then she'd just ridden off before Wyntoun could take the lad back! Why, Gillie weighed nearly as much as Adrianne herself, and yet she'd gone off at a gallop across unfamiliar terrain in the middle of the night . . . without even a passing thought as to the possible consequences! 'Twas only by some miracle that she'd been able to keep them both atop that horse.

Striding toward the keep, he ground his teeth together. He would deal with her later. She had to learn a lesson from this, but he didn't quite trust himself to broach the subject now. Forcing his temper back, he told himself that first they needed to get Gillie situated. He would discuss Adrianne's actions with her later. Aye, that was the better course of action.

"I'll have a talk with Gillie after he awakens," she said, running up the steps beside Wyntoun as he carried the boy into the building. "There is no reason why he should worry about me so much when I am here."

"*If* he awakens!" he growled under his breath, glancing at the still form in his arms.

"Surely, he will awaken!" she cried out in alarm. "He must!"

"A wee bit late to show your concern." Wyntoun shifted the boy in his arms and pounded his fist on the huge oak door. A bleary-eyed serving man yanked it open before the master could knock a second time. As he turned to edge through the doorway, Wyn glanced at Adrianne. From the look of pain and shock on her face, he realized he might as well have struck her, as spoken to her in such a way.

He pushed back a pang of regret for using such words on her.

Wyntoun turned to the servant and jerked his head toward the stairwell ahead. "Run up to the bedchamber above my chambers and see that a fire is started."

"For him, master?" the man said in disbelief, hurrying along ahead of the knight.

"Aye, for him!" Wyntoun roared angrily, sending the man scrambling up the stone stairs.

As the Highlander followed, Adrianne was suddenly at his elbow. "I see, now. Well, you can unleash your temper all you want, but I know you're only angry with me because I took charge by the stream and—"

"Responsibility, Adrianne! Is that a word that means anything to you, at all?" So much for holding back until later, he thought darkly.

"I am quite responsible when it comes to the welfare of others!"

"A pretty enough delusion, I'd say. But far from the truth."

"If you are speaking of the lies you heard on Barra, then I will only say there were circumstances that would well justify my actions . . . if someone cared to hear my side of things."

"I am speaking of here and now, Adrianne. I'm speaking about the half-frozen lad in my arms. Just consider the reckless path you've set this young one on, just since I've met you."

"Reckless? I didn't tell him . . . I didn't even suggest that he should follow us tonight!"

They reached the top of the steps, Wyntoun watched the serving man run from the chamber.

"I'll fetch more peat, m'lord!" he murmured as he raced by them.

"Nay . . . that you did not. Just as you never suggested that Gillie leave Barra along with you, swimming in dangerous and icy waters to reach my ship."

"That's true! I never did!"

The tinder the serving man had set ablaze in the brazier lit up the chamber. Luckily, the heat from his own chambers below kept this room fairly warm anyway. Wyntoun gently placed the boy on the bed.

"And you believe that is where your responsibility ends? Just because you didn't ask him, you think he wouldn't follow?" He shook his head as they both worked to peel the wet clothes from the boy. Gillie was moaning now, and Wyntoun knew a fever would be coming on. His voice was low as he spoke to her. "The fact is, you *did* ask him. *You* have set the course, and Gillie followed."

"I would never endanger Gillie's life . . . or the life of anyone!"

He snorted. "Foolish words, coming from the mistress of dangerous acts! Climbing from a cage suspended from Kisimul Castle? Swimming out to a ship in a winter storm?

Holding a knife to the throat of a warrior twice your size?"
He paused. "Marrying a man you have no intention of remaining with? Nay, Adrianne, you've set an example for the
lad. No thought before action, no consideration of consequences."

"None that *you* might see. But I have reasons for everything I do." Her eyes were stormy as she turned her gaze on
him. "And I've survived, have I not?"

"Aye, you have. But will he?" Wyntoun watched her gaze
falter, and then turn to the boy. "He adores you, Adrianne.
Whether you will admit it or not, Gillie has come to worship
the ground you walk on. The lad would follow you blindly
and happily to the ends of the earth without a second thought."

Together, the two tucked a heavy blanket around Gillie,
who was shivering.

"Therein lies responsibility, Adrianne! Responsibility for
others. It matters only a wee bit what you care to do or not
do for yourself. When others are depending on you . . . devoted to you . . . following in your footsteps . . . you cannot
jump off a cliff just to prove you can do it. Now you have
to think of who might be jumping after you." He straightened up from the bed and looked at her and at Gillie. "I cannot say it plainer than this. 'Tis time, Adrianne, you stopped
thinking only of yourself."

The Knights of the Veil!
Nichola knew that blue cloth as well as she knew her own
family's crest. The same blue cloth with the gold fringe had
been hanging in her husband's private study to the day he
had been taken away to London. She drew a deep breath,
thinking of him, of the vision she had just seen in the burning tower room.

Sighing, she hesitantly crossed the chamber and reached
up to touch the gold fringe of the cloth. It was of the same.
It was the sign of the Knights of the Veil—the same secret
order of warriors and priests that Edmund Percy had belonged
to from the time he was a young man. She knew that, like
his father before him, Edmund had taken vows to serve the
Virgin Mary. Vows to protect the Treasure of Tiberius. From

the time they were first married, Nichola had known that her husband would have forfeited his very life if he were called upon to do so.

She closed her eyes. Perhaps, in the end, he had done just that.

The sound of the door closing behind her jerked Nichola's head around.

"Sir Henry!" Her feeling of relief at seeing the familiar face of her husband's friend quickly dissipated as she gazed on the knight's grave expression.

"M'lady." Henry Exton—whom Nichola knew to be approaching fifty years of age—stood straight as a Spanish lance by the closed door and bowed to her courteously. His deep, gravelly voice was hardly unfamiliar to her. "I am extremely relieved to see you were unharmed by the fire."

"What's the meaning of any of this, Sir Henry?" She started toward him, but stopped abruptly as the Englishman held up a hand suddenly. His piercing blue eyes gazed commandingly at her, and she felt suddenly a sense of helplessness before the tall knight. Henry Exton had been a friend to her husband —a protégé, even, at one time—but the answer to her question was plainly visible in his expression. *Do you have to ask, m'lady? Do you think we do not know what you have done?*

Nichola tried to hide the blush of embarrassment that was burning her cheeks, but there was no relief.

"The fire has been extinguished. In a few moments your chamber will once again be ready for you to occupy."

"My chamber!?" Her embarrassment turned to fury in an instant. "You cannot think of returning me to that prison?"

"You must remain our . . . my guest, Lady Nichola . . . for the time being."

"Guest!" She drew herself up, letting him hear the anger in her voice. "Stealing me away, keeping me a prisoner for so long. Without human company. Without an explanation of any sort! Depriving me of even a breath of fresh air. Your standards of courtesy have declined, Sir Henry. Is this how you treat all of your guests?"

"Nay, m'lady. Your stay with me has required a few exceptions to the rules of courtesy. For that I apologize deeply."

She fought back the sudden urge to fly at him, to strike him, to tear out those steady blue eyes.

"Will you at least answer a few questions?"

"I fear I cannot, m'lady."

She glared at him, studying his solid, comfortable stance by the door. He had been a great fighter in his youth. His body, broad and muscular, still showed evidence of that physical prowess. If he were only to move, so she could go past him. She could run. Escape out the door. Fly down the stairs and disappear into the night.

Nay. She knew there was no hope of any of that coming about.

She decided on a different approach. "You were a trusted friend to my husband, Sir Henry. You were welcomed and entertained in my home. I was told by Edmund himself always to consider you an ally."

"I am sorry that you did not see fit to heed his advice earlier. But I pray that you shall continue to think of me as an ally in the future."

"But how can I? How could I possibly think of your actions in imprisoning me as anything but treacherous, when you have provided no explanation for the state of affairs in which I find myself? Is kidnapping now an act of friendship, Sir Henry? Is this how the Knights of the Veil now treat their allies?"

Before he could answer, a knock at the door drew his attention. She watched him open the door slightly, but Nichola had no idea with whom he spoke or what was said.

Suddenly, the reality of her situation struck her. She was no longer viewed as an ally! Nichola's mind raced as she considered just how the Knights of the Veil must have viewed her actions in the aftermath of her husband's death. She was a woman willing to risk the Treasure of Tiberius in exchange for the lives of her daughters. And that had been—for all practical purposes—exactly what she had done. Dividing the map into three sections. Sending them to the farthest reaches of Scotland, where she prayed her daughters would marry and settle. The maps had not been a dowry, but part of their past . . . part of their heritage . . . part of their father. Something to keep them tied together.

And that had not been the end of her "treachery." She had kept the truth from her daughters. She had not told them that the Treasure of Tiberius was not theirs to protect. She had not told them that it belonged to the Knights of the Veil, a group that—as far as Nichola knew—her daughters knew nothing about.

Her only salvation had lain in choosing Wyntoun MacLean for Adrianne. If her plans ever blossomed, if those two ever were to wed, then Nichola had the peace of mind that part of that map was back again in the hands of one of the Knights of the Veil.

But, in fact, none of this mattered now. No doubt these men saw her actions as treason against all her husband had lived for.

Sir Henry closed the door. Then, as the Englishman turned to gaze at her, she felt a tremble pass through her. Her face flushed with heat she hadn't felt in years. She knew he could see it, as well. It was there in his eyes. His blue eyes showed no hate or distrust. Nay, the look she read in his eyes was far, far from any of that. Stunned, she stood stock still, her ability to breathe suddenly gone from her body. Without uttering a word, though, Sir Henry pulled his gaze away and swung the door open wide, motioning for her to pass through.

Nichola took a step forward, pausing for only a heartbeat before gliding into the gallery. The corridor was now empty. A scent of smoke was present in the air—coming from the stairs that she knew lay to her left.

Welcome back to your prison, it seemed to say. And whatever Sir Henry had been thinking a moment ago, in spite of anything she had glimpsed, he was still her keeper.

"M'lady, allow me to escort you. I do not wish for you to suffer unnecessarily."

The knight's voice drew Nichola out of her reverie and she turned to meet her host's gaze.

"Will you say the same, Sir Henry, when you escort me to King Henry in London? That is your plan, is it not?"

"I cannot answer that, Lady Nichola."

"Am I to remain your prisoner for long, then? Surely you can answer that."

"I cannot, m'lady."

"So you are not alone in this, are you, Sir Henry?"

In spite of his silence, Nichola already knew the answer. Henry had to be acting on behalf of the Knights of the Veil. Instead of helping her, he had come after her.

The knight took her gently by the arm and guided her along the gallery. At the bottom of the steps, Nichola planted her feet and whirled on him.

"Please!"

She found her show of strength breaking down under the weight of this new discovery. She'd been so certain the fire in her prison upstairs would create enough of a distraction for her to get away. But now this!

Disappointment washed over her, cold and wearying.

"Please, Henry! I appeal to your honor and the friendship you felt for my husband. Answer this one question. Are my daughters protected from the fate that awaits me?"

The knight averted his blue eyes, fixing his gaze on the steps behind her.

"That, Nichola, is up to you."

Chapter 17

Adrianne needed no one to accuse her. With every shuddering moan from the young boy, guilt tore at her insides with the claws of some ravenous beast.

A fire crackled in the brazier. The wet clothing had all been stripped from Gillie's slender frame. Piles of blankets had been tucked around his frail, shivering body. But in spite of all Adrianne had done, the lad continued to shake like a willow leaf in a winter storm.

The sleepy serving man who had lit the fire for her had long ago gone back to his bed. Wyntoun, too, had stormed off. She looked about her, frantic for more blankets to pile on top of the boy. But there were no more left. She laid her hand on his cold, clammy forehead. Helpless desperation washed through her, draining her. The dawn still seemed hours off. She wondered briefly if getting something hot into the boy would help him. She shook her head. Leaving him alone while she ran to the kitchens was out of the question. She just couldn't bring herself to leave him alone.

The sound of someone at her door drew her attention. After another quiet knock, Jean's wrinkled face appeared from the shadows. Adrianne cried out with relief and ran to the older woman.

"Thank heavens you're here!" She moved forward to give the older woman a hand. Jean's heavy walking stick clunked loudly on the wooden floor. "How did you know to come?"

"Wyntoun came for me, of course."

"Of course."

She looked at Adrianne carefully. "This is not much of a wedding night for you two, lassie."

"This is all my fault," she blurted out. "I should have known that Gillie would be waiting outside of our chamber. I mean, the poor child always watches over me. He's always there at night. 'Tis so irresponsible of me—"

"Hush!" Jean said sternly, putting an arm around Adrianne and wiping away her tears with callused fingers. "That kind of talk does no one any good. You cannot be taking care of him if you are falling apart yourself."

Adrianne nodded and drew a breath to calm her tattered emotions.

"Now, first things first." She leaned on her stick and frowned at the younger woman. "I want you to go directly to your chamber and get out of this wet clothing before you catch your death yourself. And you'll do it this moment."

"But—"

"No arguing, child. Go!" Jean turned toward the bed. "I am going to look after the lad while you're gone. The sooner you go, the sooner you'll get back. And when you do get back, I'll have a number of things we'll be needing to put this urchin to rights. Now be on your way."

Adrianne rushed down the stairs and burst into the chambers that she had so carelessly convinced Wyntoun to leave before. The rooms were as they'd left them, and there was no sign of the knight. She went directly to a large chest containing the new clothes Mara had directed Bess and her helpers to sew for Adrianne.

She hadn't even realized how cold she was herself until she had cast aside the wet dress and shift and pulled on dry clothes. Reaching over her head to tighten the laces in the back, she raced out of the chambers. Adrianne took the steps two at the time and ran to Gillie's room. Jean was sitting beside the boy's cot. She had propped him up with pillows and was rubbing an oil of some kind on Gillie's chest.

"How is he?"

"Sleeping. But the fever has already begun. By morning, if he survives the night, the lad may begin to cough."

Adrianne moved to the side of the bed. "Please tell me what to do."

"Sit with him for now," she said, soaking a linen cloth

with another oil that she poured from a horn jar. Carefully, she spread the cloth over Gillie's chest. "Cover him when he has a chill and bathe the lad's face and neck with a damp cloth when he is burning up. Use this oil to dampen the cloth." The woman painfully pushed herself to her feet. "On my way out I'll stop in the kitchens and have one of the women bring you up some warm barley water. Spoon the liquid into him as much as you can. I'll make up a mixture of sorrel and honey when I get back to my cottage and send John back here with it. Give that to the lad when he starts to cough."

Adrianne listened intently to these directions as Jean handed her the two horn jars containing the medicinal oils.

"Let me walk you downstairs," she said when the healer was finished.

"I can manage." Jean waved a hand, pausing to look back at Gillie. "The lad's face . . ."

"He was born with it, I understand." The young woman gazed at Gillie's face, raw-looking with its scabs and open sores and scars. For a change the cheek was not covered by his wool cap. "But he is no bringer of bad luck, Jean. He is just a young lad."

"Nay." The old woman shook her head. "The lad wasn't born with those sores."

"What do you mean?"

"Never mind any of that now." Jean turned toward the door. "We'll talk more about it if the lad survives the fever and the cough."

Wyntoun was standing by the great arched cooking ovens and talking to John when Auld Jean limped into the kitchen. The two men both stopped and waited for her to speak.

"Only the Lord can tell," she said in response to their unasked question. "I've seen a few folk in that laddie's condition who've met their Maker in a day and others who've lived to a ripe old age."

She squeezed Wyntoun's arm and looked up into his face. "I think your young wife, though, is the one who is suffering the most right now."

"If she is, the woman brought it on herself."

Jean cocked an eyebrow at him. "Not like you to shrug off *your* responsibility."

The Highlander frowned and turned his gaze to the embers banked in the hearth. "I didn't mean it as it sounded. The lad has been my responsibility since the day I found him as a bairn and took him to Kisimul Castle. And I haven't done right by the boy. I left him out there to be treated with less care than they'd give a dog."

"That's the problem with both of you." Jean shook her head, moving toward the fire. There was a pot of water simmering at the end of a long iron hook, and she used her stick to pull it closer to her. "You and Adrianne are both so wrapped up in what is past that you are not paying any heed to the present."

The midwife turned to the Highlander. "This is your wedding night. The beginning of many things."

She watched him as he continued to fix his gaze on the fire. Wyntoun MacLean had grown tall and strong. To everyone else, he was the fierce Blade of Barra, their master and future laird. But to Jean, he was still the young lad with a bloodied knee. And, out of respect, he still wouldn't look her in the eye when he disagreed with her. Some things never changed, she thought.

"You are a great man, Wyn. A man of the world. An educated man ten years Adrianne's senior. You are also an understanding man."

"Jean, I have no stomach for this—"

"You *do* have stomach for it," the older woman scolded gently. "And you *will* hear me out."

Her husband John moved away from the fire and picked up a fat cat from a bench. He stopped by the door, far from his master's wrath.

"She is a young thing, Wyntoun. Young and restless and hungry for life. Aye, the lass is starving for life. She wants to learn . . . and help . . . and belong." Jean leaned heavily on her stick. "Just think of what she has been through. Losing a father. You know what it felt like when you yourself were a wee lad and Alexander was out at sea. But you had Alan and the rest of us. Adrianne was separated from her mother and her sisters. Who did she have on that godforsaken Barra? She had your aunt! You yourself could not stand her blustering for a day, John tells me."

Wyntoun didn't fight her. He didn't disagree. But she could still see the battle raging in his face. He wasn't convinced. He wouldn't let himself be convinced.

"Have a wee bit of patience with her, Wyntoun MacLean. See her not just for all that is wrong with her. Appreciate her for all that is good in her. I'm telling you, Wyn, few have a more compassionate heart than that one."

He gave her a curt nod, and she watched him go. There was trouble in this marriage. She could see it in the sadness that lay in Adrianne's soul, in the storm that brewed in Wyntoun's eyes. There was trouble, here. But there was passion, too.

Jean shook her head and looked into the fire as her husband joined her by the hearth. If she only knew more about healing. She needed a medicine that could make these two pour out what lay bottled up in their hearts. She sighed.

If only there were such a medicine.

Adrianne dipped a strip of linen cloth in the bowl, wrung it out, and patted away the beads of sweat forming on the lad's brow again. There was a small whimper. An incoherent murmur. Gillie's head moved jerkily from side to side.

Two nights and a day had passed, and Gillie was still burning with the fever. Jean had come back next morning, checking on the lad, leaving more medicines. Mara too had come up each day, her concern obviously more focused on Adrianne. Against the older woman's remonstrances, though, she refused to leave Gillie's side.

How could she, Adrianne had argued, when the boy continued to sweat profusely one moment and shiver like a winter leaf the next. He needed her.

And she needed some sign of improvement in him. She needed a reprieve from all the guilt she was feeling.

She gazed at the boy. He was so helpless. So sad.

Adrianne couldn't hold back her own tears as she watched the young boy continue to struggle against the fever.

" 'Tis all my fault," she whispered guiltily, caressing his face. Sitting on the side of the bed, she stopped him from pushing back the covers in a sudden thrashing frenzy. "I am sorry, Gillie. I am so sorry."

She laid the damp cloth across his forehead. The boy relaxed a little, but he mumbled incoherently and cried out softly in his sleep.

She had been blessed with the affection of loving parents for all of her life. Despite all of the troubles she'd caused, Adrianne had always had the comfort of being surrounded by those who'd watched over her, loved her, forgiven her—no matter how horrible her transgressions had been.

When her parents were taken away, then she'd had her sisters. She had not known what loneliness meant until she'd been sent to the Isle of Barra.

Loneliness. Rejection. The stinging lash of reprimand from one who does not love you. Adrianne had endured five months of it on Barra. Gillie had faced it for all of his ten lonely years of life.

Never to have been held in a mother's arms. Never to have felt the warmth of a proud father's glance. Never, ever to have been cared for or loved.

To be as lonely as this child had been for all of his life! The thought was crushing.

"I will look after you," she murmured, gently cradling with one hand the scarred side of his innocent face. "I promise never to be as careless as I've been before—never to endanger you as I have done. Please, Gillie! Please get better!"

The words caught in her throat, choking her, and her tears coursed down her cheeks. Adrianne reached up, impatiently wiping them away as she continued to watch the young face.

He looked too pale. Too weak. If his fever did not break soon, she feared she might lose him. Fear. For the first time, the emotion was taking control of Adrianne's mind. What happened if Gillie did not live through this? What if her carelessness should cost this innocent boy his life? What if Wyntoun had been right in all that he'd said?

"Please, Blessed Virgin . . ." Adrianne's prayer was hushed, yet wrenching. "Please, help him get better. Give him strength to fight this through."

"I think 'tis time you went downstairs and rested, young woman."

Adrianne hadn't heard the door open, nor had she heard Mara's approach. "I am well. I do not need to rest just now." She clumsily wiped away at her tears.

Mara's small hand rested on Adrianne's shoulder. "I disagree. You have not slept for over two days. You will get ill, as well."

"I have been resting as Gillie sleeps. Surely, Mara, you can see that I am fine."

"I see no such thing. And that's a lie, my dear, about resting. You know as well as I do that you've sent away each person I've sent up here to take your place. Whenever I've come up here to check on you myself, I see you steadfastly vigilant, caring for this foundling lad."

"I cannot leave him while he is like this, Mara." Adrianne leaned over and touched Gillie's face as he began fretting again. He seemed to quiet at her touch. "I am the reason he is here. I am the reason he is fighting for his life. The least I can do is to stay here and help him fight."

"Reason! Reason!" Mara huffed, sitting down on a small stool that had been placed beside the bed. "That is one area of your education in which I can see you are greatly lacking. 'Tis cold in here."

But Adrianne was in no mood for Mara's scolding. She was in no mood for anything but being left alone. Responsibility! That's what Wyntoun had said she lacked. Responsibility . . . and now reason!

"Have you seen your husband?"

"I have." Adrianne lifted the cup of barley water to Gillie's mouth and poured some of the liquid past his parched, chapped lips. The boy sputtered, but swallowed a little.

"When did you see him last?"

"I've been too occupied with other things to keep track of when he was last here." Adrianne knew she sounded short. But worrying about Mara's perception of their marital affairs was not high on the list of her priorities right now.

"He hasn't been back up here for two nights. The last time was when he carried the lad up to this room . . . and you know that as well as I do."

"Aye, but he went after Auld Jean that first night. And Alan stopped by yesterday . . . in the evening, I think 'twas . . . to check on us for Wyntoun." Adrianne knew the exact length of the Highlander's absence. Considering everything that had been said between them, though—remembering his appraisal of her failings—she could find no reason to blame him. "He knows that there is nothing he can do beyond what he's already done. Certainly, he has more important things—"

Mara snorted in a very uncourtly fashion. "Adrianne, you are his newly wedded bride. He should have come to see you a dozen times, if not more."

"He wished to come," Adrianne lied. "But I sent word to him that he shouldn't. I told him I didn't want anyone disturbing Gillie's rest. I told him that we shall have all the time in the world to see each other, after . . . after the lad is better."

"Aye, you'll have a lifetime together."

Although Adrianne nodded her agreement, she was not fooled by the words. Mara's tone was rife with mockery. The laird's wife was not easily fooled.

An uncomfortable silence fell between them. The young woman stared at the plastered wall above Gillie's head, trying not to think of Mara's steady gaze, fixed intently on her. There was a tiny hairline crack in the plaster. The recent whitewash of the plaster did not hide it. As she stared, she imagined the line growing, separating, a chasm forming that showed no light from the outside, only a darkness that threatened to swallow her up forever. She glanced quickly at Mara.

Please. Not now, she prayed silently. Please do not let Mara question me now about this false marriage to Wyntoun.

Adrianne wasn't sure she had the strength right now to carry on with such a terrible lie.

Mara broke the silence. "I suppose there is nothing I can say or do that would make you follow my advice and get some real rest?"

She glanced gratefully at Mara and shook her head. "I am truly quite well."

Another long moment passed before the older woman nodded resignedly and rose to her feet. She came around the bed and placed a pale hand on Gillie's brow. "Still hot to the touch. Auld Jean tells me you are doing everything that can be done, Adrianne. But give him more of that barley water, and I'll send Bege up with a tray of food for you. And more peat for that fire!"

"I am not hungry at this moment—"

"And I want you to eat it, child!" Mara ordered. "I may allow you to give up a good night's sleep for one more day, but going without food or nourishment will *not* be tolerated."

She stood over Adrianne. "Aye, I know that you've barely touched anything that I've had sent up to you. I am warning you, Adrianne. This time I will be checking the trays myself, so you'd better get something into you or you'll truly see the extent of my wrath."

"As you wish, Mara."

"Bah! And if you think that I believe that . . ." She pulled her fur collar tighter around her neck and turned haughtily to go. By the doorway, though, she stopped and threw a glance at Adrianne. "By the way, I am having Bess repair the nightshift you wore on your wedding night."

Adrianne smiled weakly, hoping Mara couldn't see her blush of embarrassment.

"Some of the serving women are looking forward to the two of you spending more time together."

Adrianne's gaze lifted in confusion.

"Aye. Cleaning up your chambers after your wedding night was a source of unrivaled entertainment, I believe." Mara opened the door but didn't go through it. "Not all of the lassies share that sentiment, though. That blue-eyed, blond-haired wench named Canny seems to have a few other ideas about your husband."

"I am certain I don't know what you're talking about, Mara."

"Nay? Well then, you might take time to have a few words with the hussy."

"Why?"

"Well, my dear, of all the clan's women, I believe Canny claims to have seen more of the scars on Wyn's body than anyone." Mara stepped through the door. "You might just learn a thing or two from the wench."

Adrianne turned and stared at the small fire burning in hearth. Suddenly, she felt quite ill.

The first golden rays of dawn appeared high on the tower room wall, filtering through wisps of smoke that continued to curl and dance amid the rafters. Nichola watched without joy as the light, shaped by the narrow form of the window, began to work its way downward along the far wall.

The acrid odor of the fire still hung heavily in the room, sickening her. It was the sharp smell of failure. Even the charred floor served as ugly proof of her failed plan. Nichola turned wearily on top of the clean blanket and stared blankly at the dark ceiling.

It was cold. Very cold. But she did nothing to cover herself.

Learning what she had—finding out that her plans for the future of her daughters could be at serious risk—had washed all of the fight out of her. For the first time since her capture, she was feeling the bitter cold barbs of defeat.

A knot formed in her chest, and she lay an arm across her face. She could feel the dampness of her tears, forming and escaping from the corners of her eyes. They scorched her skin as they tracked downward across her temples.

Guilt. Guilt. Guilt. Guilt.

How could she have felt that . . . whatever it was . . . that had passed between herself and Henry Exton?

She heard the sound of the door at the bottom of the ancient steps. The heavy creak of rusty hinges. More than likely, the mute old woman making her way up the winding steps. This time, though, Nichola didn't have the energy to sit up. What was the point, she thought, of watching her prison door swing open? It might be the only means of communicating with the outside world, but what was the point?

Nichola had first been introduced to Sir Henry Exton when

she herself had been but a young and blushing bride, only recently settled in Yorkshire with Edmund. Sir Henry and *his* newly wedded wife, Elizabeth, had been among the many visitors who had come in those first months. All she remembered now of that visit was the bright cheery face of the young and pregnant Elizabeth . . . and how attentive and protective she'd thought the handsome English knight had been toward his bride.

Aye, they had been an impressive pair, she remembered thinking. Beauty and strength bound together in a union that was sure to produce the most radiant of offspring.

How young they had all been then, Nichola thought. How curious that her own outlook on life had focused so singularly on the ability to produce heirs! How curious and foolish and young!

After that first visit, she did not see Sir Henry or Elizabeth for several years. Edmund, however, had kept her apprised of the sad events that seemed to batter their two friends unmercifully. Nichola had heard of Elizabeth's various ailments, of the loss of two bairns —one at birth, the other before reaching the age of four.

As the proud mother of three healthy daughters herself, Nichola had been almost ashamed of her own happiness and good fortune when Elizabeth and Sir Henry had visited their manor house a few years after the loss of their second child.

Nichola's recollections of this visit were far different from the first.

The loss of the children had proved extremely difficult for the two to bear. Sir Henry had aged—lines of grief, deep and hardened by his warrior's life, had given him a sterner visage. Elizabeth, however, had simply withered away. Entertaining them for more than a fortnight, Nichola had been greatly distressed by the constant, oppressive melancholy that surrounded the woman. It was clear to see that the husband's worries centered on his wife's physical frailties, but from what Nichola could see, Elizabeth's state of mind was the far more dangerous threat. There was little she could do, though, to cheer her guest.

They had stayed, and then they had gone. In autumn of

that same year, Nichola heard of Elizabeth's death. Neither she nor Edmund were greatly surprised.

Nichola saw much more of Sir Henry in the years following Elizabeth's death. He visited many times, delighting in the company of her own daughters. The images came back to her even now—Catherine on his knee, listening as she talked. Henry, following Laura through the storage cellars of the manor house, his hands clasped behind his back, his face sternly attentive as she explained how the household's grains and casks of ale and wine had been organized for the year's use. Nichola smiled vaguely, thinking of him backed against the courtyard wall, Adrianne's wooden sword pressed against his heart as he begged for mercy of the toddler.

Though still young, he had never chosen to marry again, and that had in itself impressed her. Instead, Sir Henry appeared to have focused his life on the matters with which her own husband was so involved. Matters of politics pertaining to the English court, covertly struggling against the tyranny of the Lord Chancellor Cardinal Wolsey, fighting valorously and sustaining terrible wounds at the Battle of Spurs, and later traveling to France again to participate in the meeting of kings at the Field of Cloth of Gold.

But that was not all. There were other matters. Clandestine affairs that pertained to the Knights of the Veil.

As close as Nichola and Edmund had been—in marriage and in life—when it came to the secrecy of his beloved group of knightly brothers, Nichola remained an outsider. There was never a time when she was invited or allowed into any of their meetings. There was never a word ever spoken to her about what took place in those gatherings. Loving Edmund as she did, and appreciative of his devotion and love as she was, Nichola had never complained or tried to find out more about these meetings. She knew that the Knights of the Veil were a force for good, and therefore never pressed her husband for more details.

She had held true to this belief for more than twenty years and would have remained that way for the rest of her life, but that was before the wolves came to her door. Everything changed when the king's henchmen took Edmund from her. Now she had to ensure her daughters' survival on her own.

But how could she explain away the steps she had taken to safeguard Catherine, Laura, and Adrianne after their father's arrest? Edmund had been the Keeper of the Map, a position of sacred trust in the order of knights. How could she ever justify the splitting up and dispersing of the maps that told the location of the Treasure of Tiberius?

Nichola knew that the treasure did not belong to her. No matter what she said now—no matter how she tried to justify it—it was clear her actions must surely have been construed as treacherous by the Knights of the Veil.

And this must be the reason why she had been captured and held a prisoner here. But her girls. Catherine was settled now. But what about Laura and Adrianne? Would her plans for them bear fruit as successfully as it had for Catherine?

Nichola Erskine Percy was a Scot by birth and, although she had spent many years in England, her connections were still strong with her native land. And it was from these people that Nichola had chosen the potential husbands for her daughters.

For her dreamer Catherine, the oldest and most scholarly daughter, Nichola had chosen John Stewart, the earl of Athol and the cousin to the king. Athol was an educated man and one, she prayed, who was worldly enough not to be threatened by the learning of his wife.

For her enchantress Laura, Nichola had chosen William Ross, the master of Blackfearn Castle. William's troubled soul and wayward lifestyle surely offered the perfect challenge for Laura's problem solving ways.

For her firebrand Adrianne, Nichola had pinned her hopes on Sir Wyntoun MacLean, the Blade of Barra—knight and notorious pirate. It was only with a soul more adventurous than Adrianne's own that Nichola believed her daughter could find happiness. That the Blade was a member of the Knights of the Veil was an added bounty, of course, and one that Nichola had also considered.

The hinges of the heavy chamber door creaked loudly, and

Nichola, shaking herself free of her thoughts, turned her face to the wall.

She could not face her silent keeper right now—especially after what she'd done, endangering the life of the old servant as she had. What would have ever happened if the woman had fallen, or if her old skirts had caught fire? How could she have called for help if Nichola herself had been overcome by the smoke? Shame washed over Nichola. How could she had been so callous to the possible dangers? How could she have been so foolhardy?

She heard the door close, but unlike the past, no familiar shuffling steps passed across the floor. Silence engulfed the room.

Every nerve of her body came alive, but Nichola continued to lie there, staring at the stone wall of her tower prison, listening.

Somehow, she knew who it was, and an undefinable thrill of anticipation swept through her. Nichola pushed herself up, swinging her feet to the floor, and stared at the figure by the door. Her visitor filled the doorway, his burgundy velvet tunic and leggings looked almost black in the dim half-light of dawn.

Aye, she knew him. The relaxed, catlike stance—balanced and sure, and yet ready to spring at any moment. He was a man who had spent a lifetime in control of his body. Powerful arms crossed a wide chest. She looked up and took in the strong and determined jaw. The weathered skin and the nose—broken who knew how many times—only managed to add character to his handsome face. She met the piercing blue eyes that were watching her with unveiled interest.

She scrambled to her feet and lifted a trembling hand to the neckline of her dress. "Sir Henry."

"Too many years, Nichola," the knight whispered, straightening from the door and starting toward her. "I've desired you for too many years to let an opportunity like this pass me by."

Alexander MacLean paused at the doorway of his son's chamber and watched as Wyntoun and Alan pored over the large chart spread out on the table. Listening to the hushed tones and watching them exchange their ideas, he could see the respect and trust that had always been so evident from the time they were lads.

The MacLean smiled. Not much had changed over the years.

True, they were now built quite differently. Alan, his hair going gray as his father's had at the same age, lean but strong with a mind as sharp as Toledo steel. And Wyntoun, he thought happily, tall and broad and smart enough to outmaneuver—on sea or on land—any man alive. Wyn was a son to be proud of—a strong-armed lad with a warrior's heart and scholar's brain. And above all else, these two cousins had remained the same steadfastly loyal friends that they'd been from the time they had wrestled together in the courtyard as toddlers.

Why, the two had always been hellions in their own way. Always thinking up the same mischief and carrying it out so damned efficiently. Like the time the two rogues stole and roasted the abbot's prize fighting cock. By the devil, Alexander chuckled to himself, he'd had to pay a price to get the old bastard to lift the sanction of excommunication from them. And the time they'd pelted Colin Campbell, the earl of Argyll, with snowballs. Colin had leaped from his boat onto the quay and chased the two halfway to Loch Dan, nearly burying the two in the snow when he caught them . . . and laughing about it for the rest of his visit.

Och, so many other times, as well . . . the rascals! And every time someone would haul them by their ears into the Great Hall, each of them would insist on taking the blame alone for the other. There had been many a punishment that Alexander had had to mete out in doubles.

His gaze narrowed slightly, thinking back on the dark days when his brother Lachlan had been laird. He shook off those thoughts, eyeing the two young men. There was something else that had not changed over the years. The two of them still were vying for the attention of the same lassie.

Alexander cleared his throat and strode into the chamber.

"Early risers and hard workers." The MacLean laird took note of his son's tired face as Wyntoun raised his eyes from the map. "I hear in the Hall that neither of you two have been in to break your fast with your kin, and yet here I find you already plotting and planning your next conquest. So, are you taking New Spain from Emperor Charlie this fine morning, or will it be Ireland from the haughty King Harry? Personally, I'd prefer you took Ireland—you cannot be too careful about your neighbors, I always say!"

As Alan deftly rolled up the chart, Wyntoun came around the table to greet his father. None of this disturbed Alexander in the slightest, however. For the last five years, he'd insisted that his son keep him in the dark about his pirating plans.

In truth, the MacLean had had little choice in the matter. Alexander believed Mara's threats about his continuing to ply his trade on the waters of the Irish Sea. He wasn't about to let himself to be affected by any longing over his own seafaring days. Nay, he'd long ago decided to sit back in the Great Hall and let these lads carry on the clan tradition.

"Good day to you, Father." Wyntoun sat on the corner of the table. "I had planned to be away from the castle for the better part of the day, so Alan and I thought we'd best catch up on our work now."

"Ah, so where will you be taking yourself off to, this day?"

"A few of the men will be riding with me west . . . to Glen Forsa."

"All that way!"

"Aye, there is a crofter there with a bonny colt, they tell me."

"A colt, is it? Well, your new bride will enjoy a ride like that, I'm sure." Alexander peered at his son closely. "You *are* taking Adrianne with you, are you not?"

What sounded like a snort from Alan earned the shipmaster a withering look from Wyntoun, but the laird was amused to see Alan look back challengingly at Wyntoun as he excused himself from the room.

"Nay, Father. I am not taking her with me."

"And why not?" Alexander asked bluntly, walking about the chamber. He took his time to look at everything as he continued to talk, making certain to add to Wyntoun's uneasiness. "From what I hear of her, the lass is an excellent rider. I understand you yourself saw fit to test her skill—on a horse, I mean—on the very night of your wedding."

Wyntoun's brow was furrowed, his eyes dark. "Adrianne is busy caring for the lad Gillie."

"Mara tells me the boy's fever broke during the night." He stopped and picked up a jewel-encrusted Spanish dagger from the table, gazing at it with feigned interest. "She tells me that your wee bride, on the other hand, is the one that looks to be ailing this morning."

"What do you mean? What's wrong with Adrianne?"

His undisguised concern brightened Alexander's mood considerably. "Perhaps you should ask Alan what's wrong with her. They tell me he makes certain to visit her every evening, just to make sure she eats some supper."

The flush of anger in Wyn's face was, to the laird, another satisfactory response. Alexander moved around the table and sat on the carved wood chair.

"Father, stop your meddling in my affairs. By the devil, you are starting to sound like Mara herself!"

"Aye, there is a ring of truth in that, Wyn. But have it your way, lad. And while you're at it, do not give another thought to what I said about Adrianne's health." He casually flipped the dagger over in his broad palm. "Of course, if you were to visit her yourself . . . Nay, lad, just ask Alan to check on her for you."

The MacLean leaned back against the chair, watching the agitation play over Wyntoun's handsome features. He himself hid his enjoyment of his son's discomfort, instead furrowing his brows and putting on a reflective demeanor.

"But then, hearing these gossiping wenches talk, the whole clan knows you and your bride had quite a night after the wedding feast. 'Tis very well, lad," he said, holding up a hand to silence Wyntoun. "And if you're no longer interested in the lassie, you need not be explaining to me. Many a man has sown the seeds of his posterity and then moved on to greener meadows. And we both know there are more than a few lassies here on Mull who are ready to open the meadow gates for you . . . in a manner of speaking."

The MacLean watched Wyntoun wrestle with a response. By the saints, he thought, this is very promising. He'd never seen his son tongue-tied before.

"Father, my men are waiting," the knight said finally. "A good day to you."

As Wyntoun practically fled from the room, Alexander smiled broadly in the direction of his son's belt and the sword, standing by the door. Aye, the lad did indeed have to be going, the laird mused. But where Wyn was headed . . . now, *that* was something worth thinking about.

Chapter 18

As the knight approached, Nichola stepped back, accidentally sitting on the bed. In an instant he was standing before her, towering over her, his grip strong and sure as he drew her to her feet.

"Sir Henry," she murmured, disengaging herself from him. "I do not . . . you . . . you should not . . . your word . . ." Nichola took a deep breath. "M'lord, your words are most unsettling. I suggest you make clear what you have just said."

"Aye, Nichola, that I will," he said quietly. "Allow me to do just that."

Their gazes locked for a long moment, and Nichola read nothing there to support any fear. She always knew Henry Exton to be a man with a strong will and powerful passions, but he was also a man of honor. She had nothing to fear, Nichola reminded herself. Not from this man, anyway.

But as she gazed into his blue eyes, she wondered at the strange fluttering sensations in her belly. Never had she felt desire for another man but her husband. It could not be that, she told herself, fighting the feeling. It must not be.

"I want you to know, Nichola, I would have stayed away if you had not learned in whose keep you were being held."

He reached out, his strong hands taking hold of her upper arms, holding her at arm's length. She could feel the strength of his fingers, the heat that seemed to radiate from the two points where his thumbs rested on her shoulders. She held her breath as the heat spread inward, through her chest.

"But you know who holds you," he continued. "And I am too old to waste more years pursuing you."

Nichola shook her head vaguely, not trusting her voice.

She could not swallow because of the incomprehensible dryness in her throat. By the Virgin, she thought, why must my heart beat so wildly in my chest?

She forced out the words. "What do you mean, 'pursuing' me?"

"I only speak what is in my heart, Nichola. Death took from me a good woman, a good wife. But since her passing, one woman alone has filled my thoughts, challenged my willpower. One woman alone has taken hold of my soul, Nichola. When I ride in the hills, I see one woman. When I find myself in a crowd, I look for one woman. When I close my eyes to sleep, I dream of one woman. You, Nichola. You alone."

"I scarcely believe my ears, Henry. How could you . . . how . . . ? All these years? I am . . . I was a married woman."

"True enough. But have I ever behaved dishonorably, in spite of my . . . my desires? Have I even once allowed myself to act or say or even hint anything that might be construed as improper, so long as my friend Edmund was alive?"

His hands slipped once along her arms, caressing her. Nichola closed her eyes, willing herself not to show the treacherous shiver that raced through her.

"But now, everything has changed. Edmund is gone, and you have been a widow nigh on a year. You are free to choose."

"Hardly enough time to—"

He took her hands in his own, interrupting her. "Nichola, 'tis no secret that you have been left with naught. Everything your husband owned—everything that you and your daughters should, by rights, possess—has been taken by the English Crown. Most women in your position would be planning their next marriage before their husbands are cold in the grave."

"I am not most women," she said shortly.

"Aye, that you are not," he said more gently. "Truer words were never spoken."

The fingers of the warrior moved to her face, caressing the curve of her cheek, the flesh of her bottom lip. She opened her mouth to protest, but no words formed.

His lips were on hers the next instant and, as the fiercest of the storms raged within her, Nichola managed somehow to remain steady on her feet while his mouth plundered hers . . . and then withdrew.

Her eyes were closed, but she could see him in her mind's eye, his rugged face a breath from her own. She felt as if she had been branded by him . . . inside and out.

And suddenly, with the force of a lightning bolt, she realized what she had known all along. Each time he had come to visit. Each time he had spoken her name. Each time he had touched her hand. All these years. She had known all along.

"Now that I have told you how I feel, m'lady, I only ask that you consider my offer. I will give you my name, my devotion, and all the passion that a man can feel for a woman . . . for as long as life allows. And I promise you, Nichola, I will protect you from every danger that lies in your path." She stared at his broad chest as he paused. She did not trust herself to look up. "Real danger is coming nearer each day, my love, and in the end I may be the only man alive who can protect you from it."

With a gentle touch, he raised her chin so their eyes once again met.

"Choose me for whatever reason suits you . . . but choose me." His eyes shone with feeling for her, feeling that she knew he had worked so hard to hide for so long. "I will await your answer, Nichola. And I pray you will not make me wait another lifetime."

Catherine refused to be intimidated by the three sets of eyes staring at her as if she'd lost her mind.

"Certainly, you should see that my idea makes sense," she said to her sister Laura, who appeared even more dubious than Athol and William. "Benedict is the only person we know who has seen the Treasure of Tiberius . . . who has touched it. Showing him the two portions of the map that we already have, might give him enough information to tell us where it lies hidden. He was close to our father. He might already have some idea of the whereabouts of the treasure. In fact, he might even have been the one who helped devise some of the cryptic notations on this map. We simply won't know until we ask him."

Laura shook her head. "I do not entirely trust Benedict, Catherine. And I am not certain Mother totally trusted him, either. If she had, she could have arranged for him to accompany any one of us when we left England." Laura placed a hand on Catherine's arm. "Though I know time is of the essence, I don't believe we should rush into such a potentially disastrous act. I say we wait until Adrianne arrives. It should not be long now, and everything may become very clear to us then."

"And what do we do when she arrives?" Catherine asked in reply. "None of us know what exactly 'tis that we are facing. What happens if, when we have the map, we send an army to retrieve the treasure, only to discover it missing? What will we do then to free our mother?"

"Something is already being done about the Lady Nichola."

William of Blackfearn's answer was an obvious surprise not only to Catherine but to Laura, as well. The Ross chieftain looked from one face to the next as he explained.

"Wyntoun MacLean did not only go to fetch your sister, Adrianne. He also went to begin searching for where your mother is being kept."

"But he was going to the Isle of Barra!"

William nodded to his wife. "Aye. And from there Wyn was going to Duart Castle on the Isle of Mull, where he was to begin collecting information through his connections in the Western Isles . . . and in the south, as well, to the Borders and beyond."

"Connections with pirates?" Catherine asked skeptically. "Connections that only the Blade of Barra would have?"

"Why did you not tell us of this, William?" Laura asked.

"Even without knowing for certain what he would do, I knew that Wyn would not let us down or further endanger your mother. But there is something else I know of Wyntoun MacLean that you should all know." He paused, glancing at Athol. "He is also a Knight of the Veil."

"A Knight of the Veil?" Catherine asked with alarm. "Who are these knights?"

The earl of Athol took his wife's hand. "They are a group of knights that answer to a higher power than any one king. 'Tis a secret brotherhood that is rumored to wield more power than Scotland, England, and France combined."

"How is it that we have never heard of these knights?"

The two sisters' confusion was increased by the look that passed between their husbands.

"Sometimes we do not know even those who are closest to us," Athol asserted. "I, for one, believe that your father was a member of this brotherhood."

"And I am certain of it," William asserted flatly. "Though Wyntoun is my friend, he would not have agreed to help us so quickly had he not been so interested in the well-being of Edmund Percy's kin. These knights protect their own. Wyntoun not only safeguards your sister. He will find out where your mother is through the Brotherhood of the Veil."

"Wait." Catherine glanced from one Highlander to the other. "How do you know this . . . about our father being a member of this brotherhood? None of us were told anything about such a group of men."

"What I know of them comes from . . . well, comes from Wyntoun." William sat himself beside his wife and encircled her hands with his. "The Knights of the Veil are extremely secretive. For many, their existence is considered nothing more than a shadowy illusion, an imaginary organization of knights, brave and true, who have sworn to fight for the weak and the needy."

"But they are real," Athol chimed in. "They formed in Palestine during the first great Crusade. While some knights were combining their forces to protect the kingdoms they had carved for themselves in the Holy Land, though, 'tis said that these men, the Knights of the Veil, formed to wield the sword of justice for those not strong enough to do it for themselves."

"How is it possible that our father was a member of such a group?" Laura asked.

"Because *his* father . . . and *his* father before him may have been a Knight of the Veil," William answered. "Merit and blood are the requirements for entry. Some who are asked, though, decide for themselves that they are not worthy."

The Ross chief stood up abruptly and went to the fire, and silence fell over the group for a few moments as they stared at his broad back.

"But . . ." Catherine said finally. "But our father was an Englishman; Wyntoun MacLean lives here."

"As I said before," Athol replied, "they are not bound by the borders of any country, nor by their allegiance to any one king."

"And that's another reason why they have to keep their existence so secret." William Ross cut in, facing the others. "There is nothing more threatening to a king than having a group of warriors in his kingdom who fear nothing and are unified under a banner not his own. Why do you think King Henry hates your family with such passion?"

Catherine and Laura gazed in silence at each other for a long moment, suddenly remembering things from their childhood. Small things, like the private chamber in their home that the three daughters were forbidden ever to enter. And the warlike, dark-visaged men who came—sometimes in large groups—to their manor house. These cloaked men were knights, to be sure, and always unaccompanied by families. Disappearing into the forbidden chamber, they would meet only with their father, riding out in the middle of the night and never returning.

"And you believe our father *was* a member?" Catherine asked, directing her question to William.

"Aye. Wyntoun MacLean met Edmund Percy on two different occasions that I know of . . . and probably more."

"Wyntoun knew our father?" Laura exclaimed.

"Aye, that he did."

"I cannot believe that our mother knew nothing of this," Catherine said suddenly.

"On the contrary," William replied. "I believe your mother *did* have knowledge of her husband's friends." The two men exchanged a look. "Though 'tis difficult to know whether she knew of Wyntoun's involvement when she was searching out husbands for the three of you."

"Husbands!" Catherine looked mischievously at Laura. "Did *you* suspect Mother of meddling?"

"Only after I was already married." Laura smiled at her sister. "I wonder if we *shall* hear of another marriage . . . from the Isle of Barra!"

"Adrianne? Married?" Catherine stared into the fire with a half-smile. "I can only imagine how tempestuous a household that would be."

"If the lass is as wild as you say, Wyntoun MacLean might just drown her in the Western Sea," William said, adding, "but at least I know he will send us her portion of the map."

The two sisters smiled at each other.

"Well," Laura said wryly, "just so long as we get her portion of the map."

Torches flared in the crisp night air, casting huge shadows on the stone walls of the keep as the three kilted riders spurred their steeds into the courtyard. Behind them, two foals pranced at the end of leather leads, flecks of sweat sparkling in the dancing light.

The early, winter darkness had reigned over Duart Castle for hours now, and from the sounds of revelry coming from the wee windows of the Great Hall, Wyntoun knew that the dinner meal must be well advanced. As he leaped from his horse, he could hear his father's laughter booming out over the rest. He wondered if Adrianne was there with them. Not bloody likely, he decided.

As the horses were taken in hand by a trio of stable lads, Wyntoun stood for a moment in the middle of the courtyard.

"Go on, lads," he said, slapping one on the back and nodding toward the doors leading into the Great Hall. "I've been listening to your grumbling bellies long enough. Go on in to your supper. I'll be along shortly."

He turned and watched the horses and his new foals disappear into the stables. Fine young animals. The filly, he thought with a frown, was a wee bit on the wild side, though. That one would take a steadier hand.

Filling his chest with the wintry air, he glanced up at the towers of the castle looming black in the starry blue over-

head. That open door into the Great Hall was a welcoming
sight to a tired and hungry traveler. But Wyntoun's gaze immediately shifted to the east wing. He stared up with furrowed brow at the closed shutters, where he knew a rather
headstrong young woman was sure to be keeping watch beside a sick lad's bed.

Riding out across the open moors of Mull, Wyntoun had
told himself over and over that what he was doing was the
right thing. By the Virgin, just staying out of Duart Castle
was a damned victory. And 'twasn't as if he'd needed these
young horses—the MacLean stables were the finest on the
west coast of Scotland already.

Nay, he'd successfully stayed away from her. He'd not
thought about Jean's words on her behalf, nor about his
father's prodding. He'd stayed away. He'd not given in to the
desire to court her, to woo her, to feel her in his arms, to
touch the smooth ivory skin and kiss those rose-colored lips.
Nay, he argued silently, 'twas a victory indeed that he'd not
been here, fighting a battle he was certain to lose—in the end
surely carrying her into that cold marriage bed and stripping
away all that lay between them until skin and flesh alone separated their beating hearts.

Strangely enough, though, standing alone in the darkness
now, he felt far from triumphant. How empty some victories
can be.

Wyntoun took a deep breath, expelling the air in a puff
of smoke. Stop right there, he commanded silently. He was
a man of reason. A man of self-control. He was proud of his
ability to plan and to direct his life where he himself chose
to go, and when it suited him to go there.

So what was happening to him? After spending but a few
short hours in Adrianne's company on that first night of their
wedding, he'd realized that the impetuous, hard-headed chit
had the *most* unsettling effect on him. When he touched her,
he no longer had the ability to think straight. His reason became clouded, and his will focused on one thing and one
thing alone . . . Adrianne Percy.

He stared up at the small windows of the keep. It had
truly been unfortunate finding Gillie when they had. Though

the Highlander genuinely hoped for the lad's speedy recovery, he still knew that the entire incident had saved him from himself. A second chance had been given to him to gather his wits and rethink his approach to this temporary marriage.

"She is still there."

At the sound of Coll's gravelly voice at his side, Wyntoun tore his gaze away from the building and turned to his seasoned sailor. The man scratched a bald spot on his head and then pulled his wool cap back on.

He squinted up at the window his master had been watching. "The lad is faring much better, though. The fever is near gone, and, though the lad is a mite weak, Auld Bege was saying in the kitchens that the wee fellow has calm seas ahead of him."

Wyn nodded. "Very well. The lad deserves a bit of clear sailing. He's survived being thrown overboard into the sea. He's lain half a night in an icy river." He snorted, and then paused. "Tell me, Coll, what do you hear about Gillie bringing bad luck?"

"Nary a thing, master." Coll scratched his head again and flashed a grin. "From what I hear, the lad has had none of that. Everyone knows that Gillie's a favorite with you and the Mistress Adrianne, though . . ."

The sailor hesitated and then nodded toward the high windows in the east wing. "But you'd best be speaking with your bride, Wyn, if you want things to stay that way. If Mistress Adrianne keeps carrying on as she's doing, the lad will surely have a bad name lashed onto him before he's even well enough to leave his bed."

"What do you mean, the way she's carrying on?"

"Everyone on Mull knows that the lassie has not left Gillie's side since you brought him back here half-frozen on your wedding night. Everyone talks about her not returning to . . . well, to her wedding bed." Coll glanced toward the kitchens. "And I nigh cuffed that blathering Makyn this morning when I heard her telling others in the kitchens that your wife must be under a spell. Not leaving the lad's side and not letting anyone else be left alone with him—not even for a moment—just ain't natural, says she before I take her by the ear."

"Some people just cannot mind their business. But Gillie will be back on his feet soon enough, and that should stop some of the tongue wagging."

"Aye, master. That's true enough. But the problem, as I see it, lies not with how the lad is faring. The problem lies with Mistress Adrianne. Every day the lass is looking more ragged than the day before."

Wyntoun could easily guess at the rest. At the rumors that must already be starting among these simple, superstitious folk. If Adrianne gets sick, then it will be Gillie's evil spirit taking over Adrianne's body. And whether she gets sick herself or not, the gossipers will have her withered and dying before the boy even puts his two feet on solid ground. Glancing at the window again, he wondered why was it that she couldn't guess at this new hardship she could be causing Gillie.

Wyntoun started for the building.

"Should I be getting one of the serving lasses to put up a trencher of food for you in the Hall?"

"Nay, Coll. There'll be no supper for me yet. There is something I need to be doing that's more important than eating."

Chapter 19

"Like lying on a puff of clouds," Gillie whispered sleepily, smiling at Adrianne before his eyes drifted shut.

"Dream of angels, Gillie," she murmured softly.

As the boy sank deeper and deeper into a restful slumber, her fingers played with the dark tendrils of his hair, her eyes studying the perfection of one side of his face and the scars of the other. She couldn't wait to talk to Auld Jean about the comment the midwife had made that first night in this chamber. Jean had said that Gillie hadn't been born with the scars and running sores and whitish crusty scabs. She'd meant that there was a cure for the boy; Adrianne was certain of it. How wonderful it would be to shake off the curse that he had carried with him since infancy!

Thanks to her parents' belief in the power of knowledge, she had been raised in the world of books. But even without the wisdom of the ancients, she just couldn't imagine herself behaving toward others who were different in the way that so many had behaved toward Gillie. From the time of his birth, with only a few exceptions, the poor creature had faced hardness and cruelty at the hands of people who were, in so many other ways, good people. It was beyond her how people's belief in fairies and in the other powers of the old religions could lead them to harbor within their hearts such a callousness toward the needs of others. Here, we call ourselves Christians, and yet we treat a child so unjustly.

What were we all so afraid of? she thought, gazing at the lad's scarred face. It was just a face.

She withdrew her hand and pushed herself to her feet. Only two steps lay between herself and the single chair that sat by the bed, but she could barely muster the energy to reach it. She slumped into the chair, laying her head against the carved wood back.

But Gillie's life, Adrianne silently vowed, would not be a waste. And neither would her own. It was just as her father once told her, " 'Tis not what we are born that matters in life, 'tis what we become." Adrianne was determined to shape the person Gillie would become.

And then . . . maybe . . . she would figure out something for her self.

The door of the chamber swung open smoothly, and Adrianne looked away as old Bege directed a disapproving glare in her direction upon seeing the tray of food sitting untouched on the small table where she'd left it earlier.

"Mistress!" the serving woman complained under her breath, seeing the lad was already sleep. "Do not even think to ask me to keep this to myself. Lady Mara will take one look at yer face come the morrow and she'll know that ye are still not eating or sleeping as ye should. 'Tis not right, mistress, I tell ye, and do not be thinking I'll be keeping any secrets. Nay, not I."

The woman continued to grumble and huff as she piled Gillie's empty trencher on top of Adrianne's. "I suppose ye'll be telling me ye helped the laddie eat this one."

"Nay, Bege. He ate that all himself. Is it not wonderful?"

"Hummph." She stopped and glanced at the boy before looking back at Adrianne pointedly. "And in case ye might be wondering, your husband is back."

"Is he?" Adrianne asked noncommittally.

"Aye, and he is not too happy, they're saying in the kitchens. Sir Wyntoun has been asking all kinds of questions in the Great Hall about what ye have and have not been doing these days."

One more day, Adrianne had promised herself tonight. At the most, perhaps two. She simply had to stay here until Gillie was well enough to leave his bed. Once the boy was fit, then she could carry on with the rest of this masque she and Wyntoun had devised. Right now, though, she was too tired to think about such complex issues.

"And who would blame him, I'm telling ye," Bege was saying as she crossed to the brazier. Adrianne watched the woman put another block of peat on the fire. "Whoever heard of a bride refusing her husband's bed? Staying clear of him? Tsk, lassie! Ye ought to be ashamed!"

Though Adrianne wasn't about to set Bege straight, in truth it was Wyntoun who was staying clear, she thought. A week had passed, and she was yet to catch a glimpse of him in this chamber. True, there were excuses. Alan cheerfully delivered them every day. Wyntoun had to go north, to check on the rebuilding of the gristmill that had burned. Or south, to see to the peat cutting. Or west, to look at horses, or at sheep, or to hunt, or . . . whatever. She had become convinced days ago that he would go anywhere to avoid coming up here and checking on Gillie. Or on her . . . not that it truly mattered.

She was just too tired to care. Too weary to take notice. At least, this was what she needed to keep reminding herself.

Their wedding night, apparently, did not exist. Their ride to the bluffs overlooking the moonlit loch was nothing but a dream. What she'd felt in his arms must have been just an illusion. And that matter that Mara kept reminding her of— the need to take a firm hand in curbing "those wenches" and their interest in Wyntoun—could only be a distressing nightmare.

She leaned forward with her face buried in her hands as the old servant continued to busy herself in the room. Her body ached from lack of rest. She hadn't slept in a real bed for days. The buzzing, jumbled mess in her brain would undoubtedly remain as it was for the rest of her days. No matter, she would just keep up the pretense of being a responsible individual. Maybe someday, she would truly deserve Gillie's devotion.

All of this should have been so easy, but she was just so confused . . . so tired.

"Bege, I would like you to spend the night here with Gillie."

Adrianne was jerked out of her stupor by the sound of her husband's voice.

"I will, m'lord. I have been making the same offer to the mistress here, every night."

Dried mud covered his boots and legs, and his tartan and shirt were spattered as well from the travel. But even so— she felt the tightening in her belly—Wyntoun MacLean looked perfectly magnificent.

Adrianne straightened in the chair as her husband moved across the chamber. He did not look her way. He did not even acknowledge her presence. Wyntoun strode to the bed, studying the sleeping lad for a long moment before running a gentle hand over Gillie's hair.

"How is he doing?"

Bege was quick to volunteer an answer. "He seems to be doing much better today, m'lord. Jean the midwife came by this morn, and she said so herself. In fact, the laddie ate some bannock soaked in barley water, and even managed to keep down a wee bit of oat brose while sitting up, he did." The woman frowned at Adrianne around the Highlander's broad shoulders. "Though I wish I could give ye the same encouraging news about this jimp-faced taupie ye married."

"Keep a civil tongue, Bege," he growled.

Then, for the first time since entering the room, he looked at her, and Adrianne felt her heart stop. The chamber walls swayed in an odd way for a moment, and suddenly she was aware only of the wild pounding in her chest . . . and him. Wyntoun's green eyes were gazing into hers, searching, on his face a reproving scowl.

It hardly mattered, though, that after so many days he still appeared to be angry with her. The sensation . . . the worry . . . that dominated her brain right now focused on the way her entire body had come alive at his mere presence. In the way her insides suddenly ached at the thought of how much she had missed him over these past few days.

"And you, Adrianne, are sleeping in *our* chambers this night."

"But Gillie—"

Bege was quick to jump in, her tone now curiously polite. "I've already told Sir Wyntoun that I'll spend the night right here beside the lad's bed, mistress. He is faring much better. Whatever he'll be needing, I'll be right here to give it to him."

"I—" She started to complain, but Wyntoun's glare was direct and dangerous. *Our* chambers, he'd made a point of saying. For her to refuse would be the same as openly refusing Wyntoun himself. The same as publicly renouncing her marriage. Adrianne gnawed at her lip a moment, considering the consequences. She would be leaving after this ordeal, but he would stay. It would be wrong to undermine his authority by refusing him now.

She sighed. And who said she didn't think her actions through?

"If you are quite certain that you don't mind," she said to Bege before slowly rising to her feet. "But you must promise to fetch me if his sleep becomes troubled . . . or if the fever returns!"

"Aye, mistress. That I will. Ye needn't fear at all." The servant cheerfully ushered her toward the door.

Adrianne was certain she knew the old woman's mind. Auld Bege surely couldn't wait to take this news to Mara. She puffed out her cheeks and cast a glance over her shoulder at Gillie . . . and at Wyntoun, still standing beside the bed.

"I'll be along, Adrianne," he said, nodding sternly toward the door. "You go ahead."

As she made her way along the corridor to the spiral stairwell, her weariness struck her hard. Her knees wobbled as she took the first step down. Her body felt sluggish and weak for lack of activity and the absence of food. Even her clothes felt weighted down, as if they were wet and her pockets filled with stones. Adrianne leaned one hand against the wall to control her descent as a strange wave of lightheadedness struck her suddenly.

"And would this not be another fine thing for the clanfolk to blame on Gillie?"

Adrianne let out a gasp of surprise as she found herself swept off the stairs and lifted into her husband's arms. She clutched at his neck as her head continued to whirl with the suddenness of his action. "What . . . what could Gillie be blamed for?"

She stared at his profile as he descended the stairs. Even in the shadowy darkness of the stairwell, she could see his furrowed brow, his brooding expression.

"Is it not bad enough that there are rumors claiming Gillie is sucking the life out of you to build up his own strength? Now, if you had fallen down these steps for any reason, there would be an outcry that the poor lad surely pushed you as punishment for leaving his side."

"What gibberish!" she cried incredulously. "What is this nonsense?

With a shrug of his broad shoulders, he continued down the stairs.

"You can put me down, you know," she said. "I am perfectly capable of walking on my own."

"Humor me. I am actually enjoying this."

Something softened inside Adrianne, but she tried to not read too much into his words. She held him tightly, and made no further comment about him carrying her. The masculine scent of the sea and leather was intoxicating, and it must have been exhaustion, she thought, for she laid her head against his chest as they exited the stairwell at the ground floor of the keep.

Her voice was quiet. "How could people think such foolishness about Gillie?"

"My people are simple folk—"

"I am no more than a simple person, myself," she interrupted, raising her head and looking into his face. "Tell me a reason."

His eyes were gentle, but he said nothing. A few more steps brought them to his chambers . . . *their* chambers. As he pushed open the door to the outer chamber with his shoulder, Adrianne again felt the threads of heat coiling and burning in her middle. Suddenly, she wondered if he intended to continue on from where they had left off on their wedding night.

She had not prepared herself. By the Virgin, she didn't

even know what she needed to *do* to prepare herself. Oh, this was all becoming so confusing!

"Naturally, you have been causing it all, unknowingly."

Instantly alert, she lifted herself in his arms and stared into his face. "What do you mean, *I* have been causing it?"

He pushed open the door to their bedchamber with his foot.

"Caring for someone and sacrificing yourself are not always one and the same thing."

He dropped her on the bed, and she scrambled to sit up as he stood over her.

"Now you are trying to rile my temper!" She pushed back his hands as they reached under her for the bedclothes. "Stop these riddles. Instead, explain yourself."

Ignoring her, he simply knocked her arms away, making her fall backwards again onto the down-filled mattress.

"And here, I thought you were so tired that I could just take advantage of you without any complaining."

Her mouth went instantly dry. "Take advantage of me?"

"Aye, of course, take advantage." The twitch at the corner of his mouth was too obvious to go unnoticed. "Lecture you. Push you about. Have you sit quietly and listen to my commands with the utmost respect and submissiveness." He reached under her and pulled back the coverings. She found herself lying on linens as he took one of her feet in his hand and began removing her shoe. Stunned, she watched in disbelief as he tossed one and then the other to the floor. Nonchalantly, he pushed back her skirts to the knee and pulled the tie of her garter, stripping off her hose in a single movement.

With a sniff, Adrianne gathered up all the dignity she could muster and sat up, tucking her bare feet under her.

"If you consider this lecturing, Wyntoun MacLean, then you must have been a poor student."

"Perhaps you should make that decision once you've heard the entire lesson."

Adrianne's face burned, a reaction that was unaccountable to her, considering the chills that were racing through her body.

"You're distracting me! Tell me whatever 'twas you were going to say about Gillie."

He stood over her, his fists resting on his kilted hips. "After your initial foolishness—behaving as you did the night we found the lad—what you have been doing for him has been most admirable. But"—he paused, unfastening his long sword from his wide leather belt and laying it aside—"but my people do not know you as I do. They cannot understand that there is no going part of the way in anything you do in life."

Adrianne raised an eyebrow. In a way, that all sounded somewhat complimentary. She shook her head. "I still don't understand what any of this has to do with Gillie sucking the life out of me. I am here, well and alive!"

"You do not understand because you are not listening," he said gruffly. "Can you not see that by spending endless days and nights beside the boy, by allowing no one else to take care of him, you are excluding those whom he will truly need in his life? Like it or not, Adrianne, 'tis the people of Clan MacLean that he will be living among and working with as he grows older. These folk—and not you—are the ones whose acceptance—whose affection—he needs to win. But more importantly, he needs to have their trust."

Adrianne didn't want to think about Gillie on his own again, and she fought back the knot that suddenly rose in her throat. Nay, even at the thought of Gillie, powerless against the buffets of a world that could sometimes be so cruel and ignorant, she would not give in to the hot tears welling up in her eyes.

His voice was softer as he continued. "Aye, you look away, but you know what I say is true. And to make matters worse, what do you do while you are up there caring for him? I'll tell you. You stop caring for yourself. You give no attention to your own health. And what are these castle folk going to think when all they know is that the new bride of their master appears bewitched? And not by her husband—as they would expect—but by a wee lad who looks as strange as any creature they have seen in their lives."

Wyntoun reached out and took a hold of her chin and drew her face around until their eyes met. "They think that Gillie is the cause, that there must be dark magic at work here, since not one of them understands the change in you."

She pushed away his hand as the tears finally escaped. "If they are all so blind, then they don't deserve to have Gillie among them."

"Tell me then, where *does* he belong?"

"With me!" she cried, stabbing away the tears. "I'll take him . . . wherever I go! I'll take care of him."

"And you think this is the way for a lad to grow into manhood? You think this will make a happier life for him? To go through life having no place to call as his own—having no clan that he can belong to?" As she heard him voice the echoes of her own thoughts, Wyntoun sat on the bed and leaned toward her. "Adrianne, do you truly believe that Gillie can be happy hiding behind your skirts anytime life rises up to challenge him?"

"I can protect him! I can keep him safe until he can fight for himself."

"Listen to me, woman. Gillie does not need protection as much as he needs acceptance. Hiding him away from all these people is not the answer. He needs to be a part of his people. They have to see that he is no different than the rest of them. 'Tis the only way for the lad."

The tears continued to fall, but through her misery she started to hear his logic. Despite all of her desire to protect him, she could see the sense behind his words. After all, she herself had been different from her sisters in so many ways, and yet her family had never tried to shield her from the world that she wanted to experience. True, she had taken some hard knocks, but she was better for them. Of course, no one had ever tried to feed her to the fish.

She found herself hugging her knees—her face buried in the soft wool of her skirts. Her breathing was growing erratic as hiccups and sobs began to wrack her body. Never in her entire life, Adrianne thought vaguely, could she remember falling apart as she was right now.

"I am a miserable failure . . . in everything I do!"

Even as he moved beside her, she heard his one, short, mirthless laugh in response to her desperate words of defeat.

She felt his arm wrap around her, and draw her head to his shoulder.

"There is only one thing in which you have failed miserably, and that is the way you have been taking care of yourself." With the back of his hand, he wiped the wetness from her face. "You need some sleep, Adrianne. Aye, a wee bit of well-deserved rest is just the thing, I'd say."

She continued to weep softly against his chest. "But what of all the damage—of all the trouble I've brought on Gillie? How am I to fix what I have done?"

"No need to worry about any of that now, lass." He placed a kiss in her hair and laid her back on the bed, pulling the blankets up to her chin. "Gillie has beaten the fever, but he needs more time to recover. This gives a fair opportunity for others to help. Quick enough, the rest of the household will get to know the lad, and all will be well. Now get some sleep."

Wyntoun started to get up from the bed, but she reached for his hand. His eyes were dark and his thoughts hooded as he looked down on her.

"Will you stay?" she asked hesitantly. "Just for a few more moments. Will you just stay . . . with me?"

She watched the planes of his face flicker as his jaws clenched and unclenched, and she held her breath until he gave her a nod of assent.

Adrianne didn't give much thought to the fact that she was fully clothed and beneath the blankets and he lay on top of them. What did register somewhere deep within her was the gentle way he put his arm around her, gathering her so protectively to his side, resting her head on his chest. In a moment, her hand found his, and their fingers entwined.

As she fell asleep, she could hear his great heart beating in his chest, and it formed the rhythm that reverberated in his quiet response.

"I'll stay."

Chapter 20

If she were a wee bit stronger, and taller, and perhaps a bit wider—or at the very least armed—Adrianne knew for certain she could have removed the man physically from her path. But as it stood now, she felt more like some sparrow looking into the face of a falcon. The man was a monster.

"What do you mean, I cannot go by?"

The sailor called Bull refused to meet Adrianne's direct gaze, staring at a spot just above her head.

"No trouble, now, mistress. 'Tis just as I told ye. The Blade says I canna let ye go by."

"Are you telling me that Sir Wyntoun has ordered you to block this flight of stairs?"

"Aye, mistress. Just so."

"Is Gillie still upstairs?"

"Aye, mistress. And getting haler all the time . . . I'm to tell ye."

She was glad to hear the news that Gillie's health was improving, but still she wanted to see the boy for herself. She stepped to the side to go past the man, but he shifted his weight, as well. If she was going to go up these stairs, she was going to have to take the man down.

"Is there another flight of stairs that I am ignorant of, Bull?"

"Nay, mistress."

"I only told Bege to look after him for the night, for certain the poor woman needs some rest."

"Oh, Lady Mara's seen to that. Auld Bege's watch finished up yesterday morn. And after that, Makyn took the watch fer half a day. And then there was that bonny scullery lass with hair the color of fire. And then—"

Adrianne raised a hand in front of Bull's face. "What do you mean 'yesterday morn,' Bull? How long have I been sleeping?"

"Well, mistress"—the man removed his tam to scratch his head—"I came over fer my watch at dawn, but afore me Ian stood a piece, and Tosh before him, and—"

"How long has it been?" she asked less patiently. No wonder she had been so hungry this morning. She'd eaten every morsel on the trencher left in her husband's antechamber.

"Well, I'd say ye slept away the day yesterday, and last night, as well."

Adrianne closed her eyes and put a hand to her forehead. She hadn't the time to dwell on staying away so long. Instead, she needed to focus on what needed to be done now. She put a hand on his forearm. It was rock solid and roughly the size of her waist.

"All the more reason for me to check on Gillie this morning. Don't you think so, Bull?"

The sailor's face reddened at her entreaty, but he went back to staring at that spot above her head. "The Blade says I wasna put on this earth fer thinking, mistress. I canna let ye by."

"But what if we just kept it as our own wee secret? All I'll do is poke my head in and—"

"Sorry, mistress. Blade's orders."

She *wasn't* going to be as protective as she'd been before. Adrianne thought she'd made Wyntoun understand that. She only needed to see Gillie. Just for a moment. And then she had things to do. She wanted to visit Auld Jean, to thank the midwife for all her help with Gillie and to ask her about the lad's face. There were others in the village that she wanted to see, too, now that she was on her feet—Agnes and Gerta, the widow Meggan and her wild brood of children.

"Bull, I have it! You can come up with me and make certain I keep my visit short."

The man shook his big head stubbornly. "Nay, mistress. Blade's orders."

"Am I the only one to be kept from visiting Gillie, or have you been ordered to hector everyone who wishes to visit the lad?" This was her last hope. Perhaps Wyntoun had meant to keep everyone out.

The man scratched his chin and took a half step backwards. "Only *ye*, mistress."

"Where . . . *is* . . . my husband?" she asked as civilly as she could, through clenched teeth.

"He . . . the master, that is, had a busy day, mistress. He did leave a message that perhaps ye might like to spend some time with Lady Mara, and he'll be looking fer ye there when he gets back."

Adrianne folded her arms across her chest and stared up at the man. "Bull, I am certain you know of my reputation when it comes to creating mischief."

"Aye, mistress."

"So you do know that if I am provoked to do it, I could easily climb the castle wall and go wherever 'tis I wish without the use of those stairs you so valiantly guard. Now, Bull, did I mention the word 'provoked'?"

"Aye, mistress."

"Now, climbing the wall hardly seems like mischief to me, but if I were to take the opportunity to do some damage in this new section of the castle . . . if I were to wreak so much havoc here, that my husband would have to rebuild this entire wing . . ." She looked about her with keen interest. "And do you know who would be responsible if there were some *serious* damage . . . ?"

"He's in the training yard, mistress," Bull blurted out quickly. "He was planning to ride out again, but with the heavy weather, the master is working with the men."

"Thank you, Bull. You have been most helpful."

"Ye willna burn down the keep now, will ye, mistress?"

"Not on your watch, Bull," she said, smiling sweetly. "At least, not this morning."

Steam was rising from the bodies of the muddy, half-naked warriors as they pushed through the open doors of the stables. They had worked hard with their weapons, and now sweat mingled with rain on their torsos and faces, beading up and glistening on every naked chest and back. The day was cold and gray and somber, with heavy mists giving way to occasional downpours, but the spirits in the stables were high as the men poured buckets of water over each other to the sound of shouts and laughter.

Wyntoun made his way through the boisterous group of men and took a bucket of water himself from one of the stable lads. His father's castle guard—many of them old sailors who'd fought under Alexander's sea banner for years—had provided good exercise for his sailors, and even now a number of the men were facing off in friendly competition inside the stable doors.

"I believe we've been away too long, master," Ian called loudly to Wyntoun. "Why, these old graybeards have aged so poorly, the poor auld buggers can barely hold a weapon aloft."

"Poorly aged, is it?" a broad-chested warrior of middle years responded, making an obscene gesture. "Well, I've got a weapon that stands aloft on its own, I'll have you know . . . unlike that wee and pitiful excuse for a thing you've got!"

Amid a burst of laughter and cheers from the two groups, the two combatants threw themselves at one another like a pair of battling bulls, grappling in the open space by the stable doors. Their friendly scuffle drew a wry smile and a shake of the head from Wyntoun, who moved down the row of stalls to a safe distance from the escalating battle. The knight sat himself on an overturned bucket and looked at his own upper arm and a long cut that—though not very deep—continued to bleed fairly steadily.

"Could I be looking after that for you, Sir Wyntoun?"

Looking up in surprise, he saw the blond-haired Canny approaching across the stable floor, carrying a clean shirt for him. Ten years earlier, as the Blade of Barra, he had saved her entire family from a Danish raiding ship off the east coast of Scotland. She'd been hardly more than a child then, but she'd grown into a strong-willed and lusty wench. It was no secret that the lass was not quite ready to give up her long-held crush on him, but her determination to ignore both Adrianne and the marriage ceremony gave Wyntoun pause even to talk to the young woman.

"Nay, lass. Leave the shirt and go on back to the keep."

"You must take better care of yourself, master. A cut can go very deep, sometimes." The young woman leaned forward, her hand brushing lightly over his muscled arm as her large, firm breasts practically spilled out of the low neckline of her blouse. Her voice dropped to a husky pitch. "And you know I'm quite capable when the blade goes deep."

Wyntoun would have been deaf and blind to not get Canny's not-so-subtle suggestion. He looked directly into her blue eyes. "Nay, Canny. I've a wife to look after these things now."

Her lips parted slightly as she let her gaze drop to his bare chest and even lower. Her eyes traveled back to his face, holding his gaze.

"I do not know how the Englishwoman is to care for you when you're hurt like this, Wyn, when she cannot even keep to her bed."

The young woman's frankness was as impressive as her body, he thought, but she needed to be set straight for her own good.

In a way, Wyntoun was relieved to realize that he wasn't in any way tempted by Canny. But even as that thought registered in his brain, he frowned, distressed to think that his feelings toward Adrianne were changing the way he might desire an attractive and very available lass. By the devil, he thought, he'd need to think about that a wee bit more when he had time.

Nonetheless, the Blade of Barra shook his head at the young woman and started rising to his feet, only to have Canny pretend to lose her footing and throw herself at him. With a crash of the bucket, the two of them tumbled into the straw and dirt, Canny's voluptuous body sprawled on top of him.

"By the devil, lass . . . !"

"I haven't forgotten how great a lover you are, Wyn," she cooed in his face before planting her lips firmly on his.

He had rolled her onto her back in an instant and was

peeling himself out of her grasp when he realized that the men's distant shouts and laughter had died.

Wyntoun knew somehow what was facing him before he even turned.

"Adrianne," he said casually. She was standing in the midst of a crowd of half naked men, most of them twice her size.

Like a number of the men, she stood with her arms crossed over her chest, watching the spectacle. If it weren't that her eyes were shooting arrows of fire, one might think she was calm and entirely unaffected by the sight of her lecherous pig of a husband tumbling in the straw with a hot-blooded wench.

Canny appeared at Wyntoun's side, but Adrianne's threatening half-step forward coincided with him shaking the woman's hand off of his arm. Coll, though, immediately stepped forward and took the young woman in hand.

"I believe ye have done enough damage here for one day, lassie." The burly sailor's words were hushed, but in the deadly silence of the stables, there was nothing said that went unheard. As he led her out, Adrianne's gaze nearly reduced Canny to cinders before returning to Wyn.

"Out! All of you men!" Wyntoun growled sharply, never taking his eyes off of Adrianne.

There was some grumbling as they moved off. The spectacle that was sure to ensue would be something to talk about over a cup of ale, but the lash of Wyntoun's temper was something none of them wanted to feel. In a moment the stables were empty of all but a few horses in their stalls and a bold-hearted sparrow chirping in the eaves overhead.

He hadn't done anything wrong, Wyntoun reminded himself. Seeing her unflinching glare, though, he guessed that Adrianne had already jumped to a most reasonable conclusion. He could handle that. It was the unpredictability of how she might immediately respond that had him on the defensive at the moment. He knew danger when he saw it.

Wyntoun watched her turn and walk to where his sword and sheath stood up against the wall. She picked up the weapon.

"We should be able to resolve our differences without that."

She whirled the sword lightly in the air as if to get the feel and weight of it. He was impressed, in spite of himself, with how easily she handled the weight of the weapon. She turned to him with the sword still in hand.

"Adrianne!" he growled. "There is no reason to behave rashly."

Her eyes flashed as she met his gaze. "I would have cut out that hussy's heart with a stone if I were behaving rashly. I would have dragged her out of these stables by her lank, yellow hair and let *her* hang in a cage from the Duart Castle's walls if I were behaving rashly." The sword cut another arc in the air, and she came a step closer. "Tell me, Sir Wyntoun, would you consider it rash if a woman—not even a fortnight married—were to react violently to the sight of her husband in the arms of another woman?"

The knight stood his ground, his arms crossed over his chest. "And is there a woman here who can make such a claim?"

"I *did* see a man sprawled atop a wench on this stable floor a moment ago, did I not?"

Wyntoun continued to watch her careful and practiced approach. The angle at which Adrianne held the weapon would easily thwart any attack.

He would *not* have allowed Canny to get any further in her attempt at seduction. But he could understand Adrianne's anger—she had to be respected while she was still seen as his wife. Still though, she was the only person who had ever raised a weapon to him twice without fear of the consequences, and this irked him to no end.

"I see you have already forgotten our arrangement regarding this marriage."

His tone was as cold as Wyntoun could make it, and he saw the immediate effect his words had on her. A shadow of disappointment flickered across her fair features. She didn't lower the weapon, though. Not a whit.

Her eyes narrowed. "Very well. Then you are free to do as you wish . . . and if I am free, as well."

"As you wish, wife."

She nodded. "So, for every wench you bed . . . including

this sorry creature . . . I am free to *summon* any man of my choosing."

Wyntoun's back stiffened, a cold feeling washing through him. And *that* man, he found himself vowing inwardly, would be searching till the Judgment Day to find all of his body parts.

"You didn't answer me, husband." The weapon cut through the air again.

"Of course. But I tell you now, the Blade of Barra's men value their lives much more dearly than to answer a summons from his wife."

Her eyes flashed with temper. "You don't believe I am a worthy enough prize. You don't truly think any of them would even be tempted."

Despite the raised weapon, Wyntoun took a threatening step toward her. His voice was low and menacing. "Adrianne, I am not issuing a challenge."

"I believe you are. And I will prove you wrong."

She threw the weapon aside and turned abruptly toward the stable doors, but he was beside her in an instant, her arm in a death grip.

"Let me go, Wyntoun!" She tossed her head. "Don't you see? I have places to go. Lovers to woo."

"Adrianne!" he growled, turning her in his arms until she faced him.

By the saints, she was a walking firebrand. Wyntoun stared at her a long moment, forcing himself to keep his wits about him. It was so tempting just to smother her in his arms and devour her frowning lips.

"By God, you are the most stubborn woman—the most infuriating creature—I have ever met."

"Don't start lecturing again. I am hardly the one who deserves a setting down, this time."

"Adrianne, if you would listen a moment and—"

"Don't start on me, Wyntoun MacLean." She pushed his hands away but held her ground, a finger pointed at his bare chest. "I don't care what agreement we made before we took our vows. I don't give a tinker's damn what your needs might be as a man. So long as you are my husband, you will remain virtuous, courteous, agreeable, and attentive. You will behave as is befitting a Percy husband."

"Is that so? Well I will, Adrianne Percy, only if you start behaving as is befitting a MacLean wife."

She raised herself on her tiptoes and yelled in his face. "I *have* been behaving as such, you lecherous clackdish."

"Only in your dreams, you ill-tempered banshee." He pushed her hand away and glowered down at her. "Locked away as you've kept yourself, you wouldn't have any way of knowing, but your failures as a wife are a favorite topic of gossip in this keep."

A deep blush crept up on her flawless face and she stood in silence for a very long moment.

"This is all about the marriage bed, is it not?" she asked finally, breaking the silence.

His mistake was allowing himself to be distracted by her beauty. The spark of light in those magical blue eyes seemed to throw him off every time.

"Is that it?" she repeated more sharply.

"Not completely," he said halfheartedly, realizing that he should not have let their argument reach this point. After all, he was the one who had tried to keep his distance, and here he was blaming her because he himself had been struggling to avoid spending any time alone with her.

And "struggling" was the correct word, he thought. Two nights ago had been pure hell. Holding her in his arms, watching her sleep so trustingly, while his mind had conjured so many images of how he wanted to have her. Hour after hour, his brain had fought a losing battle with his desire. He *needed* to take her, to make her his own.

He'd felt like a man possessed, and yet he'd forced himself to walk away from her and seek a safe distance once again.

"You hesitate to answer, so it must be true." Adrianne appeared calmer in temper, but her face showed flashes of emotions that he could not name. She took a step back. "I am tired of worrying about how many women are planning to lure you to their beds. I am ill from all the gossip. Married to an ice-maiden . . . I can almost hear them say it. The poor

Blade, deprived of marriage bed, rejected by his own foolish bride."

Her face was now an open window to her suffering, and
Wyntoun could not abandon her in such obvious distress.

"Adrianne, what you saw here was not what you—"

"Very well. Enough," she said flatly, ignoring his words.
"A married woman must give up her maidenhead sooner or
later. And as for me, I shall simply have to live without it
when this entire ordeal is over. I'm certain I won't miss it."
Without meeting his gaze, she turned down the row of stalls.
"Come on, Wyn! With any luck, the last stall on the left might
be empty."

A good long moment passed as Wyntoun stared after her,
gathering his wits about him.

"Adrianne!" he called, striding after her. He was unsure
if he understood what she had set her mind to do. And yet,
the prospect of having her now aroused him greatly. "Adrianne, I swear, you will be the death of me."

By the time he caught up to her, she was already inside
the empty stall at the end. Facing him, she was reaching back
to loosen the laces of her dress.

Standing in the stall door, he stared, tongue-tied and fighting to control the tightening in his loins. It was no use—he
could feel himself hardening beneath his kilt.

"As you already know, I have never done this," she said
falteringly, avoiding his gaze. "But seeing that you already
are half-naked, I suppose that is expected of me, as well.
Though I don't recall them ever shedding their clothes when
I was young and watched those scullery maids summoning
the men."

He watched as the dress loosened, the top of the white
undershift peeking through. He forced himself to swallow.

"I simply need to remind myself that this is only a body.
You expose yours to me without shame, so it must be ac-
ceptable for you to see mine." She pushed the dress off her
shoulders and worked it past her hips, letting it pool at her
feet. As she straightened, Wyntoun couldn't tear his eyes away
from the dark tips of her full breasts budding under the thin
fabric of the shift in response to the cold.

Her arms were long and smooth and strong, her legs like carved ivory below the thin stretch of linen. His gaze lingered on the play of the fabric across her breasts and stomach and the juncture of her legs as she raised her arms to shake loose the coil of dark hair on top of her head.

"When we leave these stables, we will hear no more complaints about my reluctance in giving my body to my husband. Just tell me when I should cry out—I should cry out, should I not?" Her ebony hair cascaded downward like a blanket of silk around her shoulders. "And after today, I shall continue to play the part of the seductress in the presence of all of your people, so there shall be no question about whose bed you crawl into every night."

He was aroused and beyond hope of any return to sanity. Still though, the truth of their future tugged at his conscience. A single tie held the garment together just above her breasts and she quickly pulled the knot loose. Crossing her arms, she grasped the garment at the shoulders and started to push it down her arms.

"Stop, Adrianne!" Wyntoun rasped out, his voice graveled and low. "Think for a moment, woman. We cannot go through with this and then simply walk away."

"Don't you want me?"

"Aye, but that is not the point. Any man would."

"Then you do want me."

"Of course! But my pleasure would mean your ruin. I cannot do this to you, Adrianne."

She was trying to hide it, but he saw the tears that immediately pooled in her blue eyes. "I don't believe you. You hate me so much that you cannot even bear a moment of intimacy. Am I so undesirable? So less worthy than all the legions of women that you have bedded in your life?"

A part of him wanted to laugh, but another part of him had the stronger hold. Wyntoun could control his actions no better than he could control the aching warmth in his chest. How did it happen that he could come to care for this woman so much?

Wyntoun closed the distance between them and in the next instant had her wrapped tightly in his arms. His lips were ravenous as they tasted her tears, caressed her face, and settled on her lips. This was just a sample of the flaming passion that burned inside of him.

"Tell me again that you want me." She tore her mouth away for a moment as her hand caressed the crisp curls of hair on his chest. "Tell me that you find me desirable."

"This should expel all of your doubts." He took her hand from his chest and guided it to his kilt, where their bodies cried so achingly to be connected. She hesitated for an instant before finding her courage and reaching beneath the wool. A low groan sounded deep in his throat as the Highlander drew her mouth to his own.

"Tell me again, Wyntoun," she said shyly, her hand gliding along his manhood in a journey of discovery for her and torment for him.

"I want to bury myself inside of you, Adrianne. I want you more than any woman I have ever known in my life."

"That sounds very promising," she whispered against his chest. "Well, I am yours to take. I am your wife."

This was a mistake, Wyntoun silently reminded himself. A mistake. A grave mistake. But it mattered naught what he told himself. He lifted her in his arms and closed the distance to the closest wall of the stable.

"Is standing against a wall the position that one uses in Scotland to begin such things?"

"One of many," he said hoarsely, taking hold of the front of her shift. The fabric tore easily, dangling at her waist. His eyes feasted for a moment on the fullness of her breasts, raising and falling with the uneven pace of her breathing. She was truly the most breathtaking woman he'd ever laid eyes upon.

"And is tearing the clothing off your wife's body another commendable start?"

Surprised, he couldn't help but look up into her flushed face and smile. With her wondering eyes watching everything that he did, she was obviously quite serious about her questions.

"Commendable? This is a desire that you yourself planted in my mind, Adrianne . . . the night of our wedding."

"I did that?"

"Aye. By tearing the sheer nightgown that you were supposed to be wearing for me."

He saw her blue eyes close slightly, a low moan escaping her lips as his thumbs played lightly over the rosy hardness of her nipples. He pressed his rock hard thigh against her, one hand moving slowly downward over the smooth skin of her bare stomach.

"Are you cold?" he whispered, feeling her small shiver.

She shook her head. "I am burning with heat. But the way I feel . . . I don't know how to put what I am feeling into words."

He kissed her lips, his tongue sliding into her soft mouth. He moved again to her neck, to the top of the creamy flesh of her breasts. As her fingers moved up and sank in his hair, he took one nipple into his mouth and devoured her sweetness.

"Wait! There is . . . there is something I must do," she whispered breathlessly as he reached for the torn chemise and started pushing it over her hips. "There must be some way that I can bring this . . . this kind of . . . of madness to you . . ."

He didn't wait, instead sliding a finger into her wet folds and watching her eyes open wide with the wonder.

"Truly . . . you'd better hurry and tell me what 'tis I can . . . or . . . or I . . . or so much like the night on the bluffs . . . I shall soar to the heavens and leave you . . ."

"Adrianne, when will you stop this incessant talking?" he asked softly, sealing her mouth with his lips. Her body was visibly quivering, her breaths becoming shorter and shorter, her little gasps becoming whimpers. Suddenly, with a cry she arched against his hand.

Sweeping her into his arms, Wyntoun lifted her up, and she clutched him about the neck tightly. He could feel her body continue to shudder as the waves of pleasure washed over her. He laid her down in the straw.

"I didn't want your first time be as rough as this." He knelt on one knee beside her, his hands fisted tightly as he tried to control the urgency of his desire to bury himself in her at that instant. She was perfection that he'd never known existed. Softness as in a dream. And more willing than he'd ever conceived in his most carnal imaginings.

"As I recall, Wyn," she replied softly, "the arrangements on our wedding night were more luxurious. But I quite foolishly forfeited that chance."

Her eyes clouded with passion, looked up at him. She made no attempt to hide her body from his hungry gaze. Instead, she raised her arms to him in invitation. He removed his kilt, throwing it to the ground beside them.

"Adrianne, this will change everything," he warned, watching her eyes focus on his fully erect manhood. She raised herself on an elbow and hesitantly reached out to touch him. "Adrianne—"

The words were caught in his throat as a silky hand stroked his hard and straining shaft. His engorged member throbbed against her touch. She moved her hand to the soft sack at the base of the shaft, and back up.

"This is most amazing. You are magnificent!"

"And you are setting me on fire. Do you know when you touch me, you destroy my control and good intentions?"

He lifted himself onto her body. Instinctively, her legs opened to accept him. He knew he had to go slow, he tried to be gentle, but she wouldn't let him. Instead, Adrianne squirmed beneath him. He could see the desire beneath the hooded lids of her blue eyes, in the way she parted her lips, only to gnaw on one as she arched up to receive him. His throbbing manhood teased her moist opening.

"This *will* change everything," he warned again, cupping her face in his hands. He gazed steadily into her face until he was certain she was listening to what he was saying. "From now on, Adrianne . . . this is forever."

He watched the haze of passion clear a little from the blue depths of her eyes. She nodded, and he entered her in one swift motion, penetrating her maidenhead.

Adrianne didn't cry out as he had expected, but the digging of her fingernails into his shoulders told him that he had hurt her.

She was incredibly tight, and Wyntoun, buried deep within her, remained very still. He waited, pushing himself to the very limits of his endurance, straining to control his own body . . . a body on fire.

"You don't appear to have enjoyed this mating as much as I enjoyed myself on the bluffs, Wyntoun."

The laughter began deep in his belly and then rose to his chest. In a moment, the tears were rolling down his face, though he still tried hopelessly to remain motionless within her sweet center.

"You did not find me desirable." She punched one shoulder as he continued to laugh, unable to speak. "I asked you to show me things . . . and I could have made it more pleasant for you. You have truly hurt my feelings this time, Wyntoun MacLean."

Sobriety came quickly as she tried to push him off her body. Still smiling, he caught hold of the fists that were now pummeling him and raised them above her head, holding them captive with one massive hand. Her breasts, lifting high, beckoned to his mouth, but instead he gazed into the blue depths of her eyes and the pool of unhappy tears that were straining to spill free.

He kissed her cheeks, her nose, he claimed her mouth for a long moment as he withdrew slightly and again buried himself deep within her. When he lifted his head, her eyes were wide with a new wonder.

"We are not finished with our lovemaking yet, Adrianne."

"Oh! But you stopped."

"Only to allow time for the pain to go away. For you to get used to the feel of me."

A deep blush crept into her cheeks, but he didn't let her look away as he again claimed the softness and heat of her mouth.

A moment later, he felt her hips move slightly beneath his weight. Still fighting his control, he broke off the kiss.

"The pain has already gone away. And for future reference . . ." She gasped as he pulled back slightly and slid deep inside her again. "You . . . you might consider me to be a wee bit tougher than you imagine . . . oh, my!"

"Is that so?" he groaned, straining for control as she arched her back and writhed beneath him. Her eyes were now clouded over as again waves of passion started to take charge of her body.

All his discipline crumbled in one instant as he saw her lips part and the shuddering gasps begin again. He could hold back no longer. He withdrew to the very tip of his shaft and plunged into her again. Letting go of her hands, he reached under her, cupping her buttocks as her ankles instinctively hooked around his legs. He kissed her mouth hungrily as the rhythms of the love dance overtook all conscious thought. Again and again he slid out and rocked into her, accelerating with each succeeding stroke. Out and in, again and again, he drove into her as she writhed and pulled, arching and crying out.

And then it came, an explosion of passions. A brilliant, mind-shattering explosion that consumed them both in a glittering moment of oblivion. And in that moment, as their bodies melded into one, as the two of them simultaneously spiraled upward, a heaven was created . . . a golden place for them alone.

An eon later, as Wyntoun held Adrianne in his arms, he smiled at the sparrow eyeing them with cocked head from the stable rafters. He touched her hair and gazed at her bonny face. In his heart he could feel the bliss, the utter satisfaction of knowing that he was now forever bound to the loveliest and most giving woman ever born.

His smile faded. Now, if he could only halt the passage of time.

Chapter 21

Restless, she paced across the chamber of her tower prison, listening for any sound that might indicate the knight's return.

After the unexpected visit from Sir Henry, Nichola Percy had spent two days and nights brooding over what had passed between them. Mired in guilt, she had tossed and turned, paced and prayed. And then, as a black night sky had edged into the gray light of dawn, her mind had cleared and common sense had finally prevailed.

It had only been by chance that Nichola had discovered that the bar no longer secured the heavy oak door. That morning, her silent keeper had brought Nichola her breakfast. When she'd left, the prisoner realized that the bar had definitely not been replaced on the outside. Indeed, when Nichola had pushed open the door, she could see that no guards watched the stairwell leading down from her tower prison. Closing the door quietly, Nichola had endured one more unending day of solitude. And each time the old woman came and went, the door had remained unbarred.

Finally, as evening drew on, Nichola summoned enough courage to pass through the door, descending the winding stairs as her heart pounded in her chest. How far would she be allowed to stray? Perhaps, she thought, Sir Henry had decided to treat her more as a guest than a prisoner.

She was already standing before the door to Sir Henry's study when she discovered the guard standing at the far end of the corridor. So much for her hopes of freedom, she thought, stopping dead in her tracks. The foot soldier stood by the stairwell at the far end of the corridor, staring into the fading twilight through the long, narrow window that opened out onto the castle courtyard below. He did not look up.

Nichola could not push herself to move forward, and she would not allow herself to retreat. She stood in silence for a long moment, and then turned and entered Sir Henry's study.

As it was when the knight had first found her there, the chamber was empty. She looked about once again, taking in the worktable—now neat and tidy—the gold-fringed blue veil and the shield hanging on the wall, the settle before the fireplace. The room was comfortable, a small fire burning in the hearth.

What would she say to Sir Henry? Surely, he was simply waiting for her . . . waiting for an answer.

Her face burned with her own thoughts. She had done no wrong, Nichola told herself. She had been faithful to her husband and to her marriage vows for all the years she and Edmund had been together. She had done nothing to encourage Henry Exton's attentions, then or now.

If their relationship had changed—as it obviously had—then *he* was the one to blame for initiating the change. Aye, *he* was the one to blame for the flurry of strange sensations that had plagued her, confused her, terrified her these past few days. He was the guilty one.

Nichola touched her mouth with her fingertips. Henry Exton had kissed her with a passion so startling that she could still feel the heat of his kiss on her lips. She fought down the butterflies stirring treacherously in her belly.

There were so many questions that had to be answered. Sir Henry's words had been too filled with hints of impending danger, of how time was of the essence. If she could trust the words that he'd spoken, words that bespoke his great interest in her, then by the Virgin, she deserved some answers.

She forced herself to focus once again on her surroundings. They had to be in a holding of Sir Henry's. In Northumberland, perhaps? She didn't think so. Farther south? Probably not.

She sat down on the settle by the hearth but leaped up at the sound of voices in the corridor outside the chamber.

Henry Exton himself opened the door, and for an insane moment Nichola had difficulty controlling that fluttery thrill in her belly as she looked up into his handsome face.

"Lady Nichola." His tone clearly conveyed his delight and his surprise. He paused by the open door for a moment, staring across the chamber at her.

As she hesitantly stepped forward, she noticed the presence of a cowled cleric in the doorway behind the knight. Although she did not know the priest, the look in his eyes told her that clearly *he* was cognizant of *her* identity. Her eyes flicked back questioningly to Sir Henry's face, and he quickly turned to the priest.

Clasping her hands nervously before her, Nichola waited in the center of the room as the knight and the priest exchanged a few hushed words by the door. In a moment, the cleric disappeared into the corridor, and Sir Henry closed the chamber door.

As she watched the knight turn toward her, Nichola's gaze dropped to her hands clasped before her. The room was glowing with a golden light from the fire burning in the hearth, and every detail of the chamber was suddenly sharp and distinct, from the curl of a vellum scroll on the desk, to her own shadow dancing on the carpet of woven rush on the floor before her. As she raised her eyes once again to her host, she wondered at the feeling of excitement that seemed to prickle along the skin of her arms and back.

He was watching her, but with none of the casualness that she'd hoped.

"Can I send for some food or some wine, m'lady?"

"Nay, Sir Henry. I am fine. I did not come here to be fed."

As he took a step in her direction, she pretended not to notice and turned to move toward the veil and the shield, putting the desk between them. There was no denying it, though. As strange as her feelings were, as unfathomable as her body's reactions were to his mere presence, being alone in the room with him was discomforting for her in a myriad of ways. Recalling his intentions now, she suddenly felt like the doe facing the hunter.

And yet, she reminded herself, she had come of her own accord.

"Whatever your reasons, Nichola, I am very glad you came."

Her gaze fixed on his blue eyes, studying her with enough heat and passion to set a body and soul on fire. Nichola knew she had to speak now—and quickly—or there would be no hope for her salvation.

"Henry"—she cleared her throat and turned to him, her hands tightly clasped before her—"I came here to seek some answers."

"I told you before, there is very little that I can reveal to you."

She shook her head and watched the knight cross to the hearth and stand with his back to it. "The questions I wish to ask you this day are different in nature than the ones I asked before."

A dark brow arched slightly as Henry waited for her to continue.

"These questions have to do . . . have to do . . . with what you mentioned . . . in my chamber."

"Questions about my proposal of marriage!"

She twisted her fingers together, trusting herself with only a quick glance at him. "I have given your words much thought . . . and there is so much of it . . . that I . . . that I do not understand."

"Then ask." His voice was quiet . . . even gentle.

Taking a deep breath, Nichola straightened her shoulders and looked across the room at him. "I ask you to put aside these present troubles for a moment."

He nodded.

"I have known you for many years, Henry, as a trusted friend of my husband. Over the past two days, I have thought long and hard about how, if Edmund were in your place, how he might have acted in a similar situation . . . in a situation where his friend's wife was being chased down . . . hunted . . ." She watched his expression. A cloud passed over his face, and she frowned. "Sir Henry, I want you to know, in no uncertain terms, that despite all the hardship . . . all the uncertainty . . . that I might face in this world, I shall *never* allow any man to take me as a wife out of pity . . . or out of chivalry . . . or even out of some warped sense of obligation!"

"Chivalry has never motivated my feelings for you, m'lady. Nor obligation. And certainly, Nichola, not pity."

"Then what is it that motivates you?" she asked shortly. "I pray you, sir, to explain to me what 'tis that you wish to gain by choosing me as your wife."

"I thought I made my feelings clear the other morning." He straightened to his full height and took a step toward her. "But I'd be happy to repeat—"

"Sir, keep your distance. I need to keep a clear head." She raised a hand to the knight, signaling for him to remain where he was. "I ask you, Henry, to place yourself in my position and consider this . . . this confusion that has all but left me amazed."

He didn't speak at once. But as he stared at her, a smile began to soften the edges of the lines around his eyes.

"I am delighted," he said finally in a gentle voice, "to hear of this confusion. But perhaps you should explain your doubts."

Nichola closed her eyes for a moment before continuing. "Henry, you know better than anyone that after Edmund's death became known, I was left with no land and no prospect of regaining it. My wealth is gone, and the king's men are searching after me. I have no friends to come to my aid in the English court. No one would dare even to speak my name aloud in the king's presence. None of that has changed."

"I have no concerns about any such thing, m'lady."

"Then *what* are you interested in, Sir Henry? I am not vain! I know that at my age of five and forty, I could hardly be called a beauty." This time she didn't dare to look up into his face. "And regarding what you, in your position, should truly be concerned about—with your own wealth and name— I have nothing to offer you. Henry, I am too old for bearing children. And that's exactly what you *do* need, a young woman who can give you heirs."

"Having no one to follow in my footsteps has been no torment to me these past years."

"But it should concern you," she scolded gently. "You are still too young, too handsome, not to contract a good marriage with someone more worthy than I . . . a lass much younger. In fact, I can perhaps be of service to you. Successful or not, I have been able at least to plan for potential marriages for each of my daughters. If you will allow me, I can certainly arrange something for you, as well."

"Nichola, I will not be needing any bride finder!"

She frowned, somewhat disconcerted by the way his blue eyes glinted with humor. "Very well, then, do it yourself."

"I am trying at this very moment to do just that."

She started to back up as he moved closer to her. "Henry, I thought I clearly explained myself. I am not the wife that you should seek."

"And I thought that I explained myself clearly, as well," he said, capturing her hands and arresting her retreat. "You, Nichola, are the only woman that I seek."

She opened her mouth to protest, but he sealed her lips with a kiss that scorched her with a lightning-like heat. When he finally drew back, her knees were weak, her body so limp that he had to support her weight in his arms. She struggled—with shocking difficulty—to regain her composure.

"I want you, Nichola. My affection . . . nay, my love has for years been yours alone."

"I do not understand . . ." She shook her head. "Consider my age . . . my—"

"At this moment I am, I believe, five years older than you. But if you were five years my senior . . . ten years . . . twenty . . . none of that would matter. For all the flaws you think you embody, you . . . my dearest Nichola . . . represent perfection in my eyes. You are the dream, the prize, I never thought I would ever be able to attain in real life."

His large hands framed her face, and she gazed up into eyes that she was suddenly sure were the deepest blue this side of heaven.

"Marry me, Nichola. Grant me this chance at happiness." He paused a long moment. "Give yourself the chance, at least, of one day growing fond of me."

One day, she repeated to herself. One day. How could she

tell him what she already knew in her heart, but could hardly even admit to herself? One day. Drawing a deep breath, she forced herself to shake her head.

"No matter what I might want for myself, two of my three daughters out there . . . their lives and safety, as far as I know, are far from settled. Henry, I cannot . . . nay, I will not think of my own future until I can be satisfied about theirs."

He frowned deeply, his gaze wandering to the blue veil hanging on the wall. Watching him, Nichola could see the internal battle playing itself out on his face. It was crystal clear to her that there were things about her daughters that Henry Exton was not revealing—could not reveal—bound as he was by his vows to the Brotherhood of the Veil.

"Then marry me for their sake," he said finally, fixing his gaze on her face. She could read the determination in his eyes.

"I do not know what you mean!"

"I have already kept you here far longer than I should have. Very soon, unless you accept me, I will have no say as to your future. And when you go"—his knuckles gently caressed her cheek—"I will not be able to remain in contact with you. You will be lost to me. Be that as it may, I now ask you to think of your daughters."

"What of them?" she asked with alarm.

"I am sure you must have already guessed that word of your capture has been taken to them."

"Of course," she lied, panic suddenly rising like bile into her throat.

"Then you also know that they will be coming after you."

"They will *not* come!" Nichola tried to sound confident, but she knew that they would come, stubborn and loving children that they were.

But Henry knew them just as well, and she understood his knowing nod. "No, of course not," he said, his tone wry and gentle. "But think, Nichola. Rather than having them search the English countryside, exposing themselves to the worst kinds of danger, would it not be better for them to find you here in the Borders, where they would most likely stop first, seeking my assistance?"

So that was where she was—in the Borders area between England and Scotland, in the small castle that Sir Henry kept in the Cheviot Hills, not far from the great dark forest of Kielder and its roving bands of brigands!

Her mind raced ahead. "And are you setting a trap for them? Is this what the Brotherhood plans? To bring them harm? And you"—she looked at him, aghast—"you are conspiring with them?"

"And would I be speaking to you as I am if I were a party to that?" His gaze was steady as he shook his head. "Nay, Nichola. My castle and my name will never be used to bring any harm to you or to your daughters. But if you agree to be my wife, do you not see that my protection of you extends to them, as well? I would value them as my own children."

He paused for a moment before lifting her chin until she was looking into his eyes. "So that is all the more reason for you to marry me. Do it for them. Marry me to protect them."

The conflicting messages battered at her mind. And so much of what Henry said, she knew to be true. Time *was* running short. And she *had* stayed here longer than any of the other places of her forced confinement.

Nichola took a deep breath and decided. "Very well, Henry. How long will it take? How long for you to arrange for this marriage to take place?"

Henry Exton's eyes shone with something beyond satisfaction. She wondered, with an almost desperate hope, if the feeling she was reading in his face could possibly be happiness.

"Wait here, my love, and I shall fetch the priest. We shall be wed immediately."

Chapter 22

All was not well in the healer's cottage, and Adrianne's brow furrowed with concern as she looked around her. All was tidy enough, she thought. The same gifts crowded the sills and the table. The same fragrant herbs and flowers hung drying above her head. But something was lacking. A vitality, a glow, a warmth.

Adrianne ladled out a cupful of broth from a pot simmering over the fire and brought it to Jean. The old healer struggled to sit up in the cot and took the drink gratefully from the young woman's hands.

"I should be up and about."

"None of that, Jean," Adrianne said, rinsing a pair of wooden bowls in large kettle of water and putting them up on a shelf. "You'll be staying right there and giving your legs a rest as long as it takes you to start feeling better."

"I will not have you fretting over me, young woman."

Adrianne tied up a loose bunch of herbs on the table, using one of the more flexible stalks to bind it. "I am doing no such thing."

"By the Virgin, you are a stubborn lass." Jean eyed her with an affection that belied her gruff tone. "But, to tell the truth, I wouldn't have you any other way. You have more goodness in you than the whole lot of them."

Adrianne didn't ask whom the healer meant, though she knew the older woman was not lumping her husband John in with "the lot of them." Coming here every morning this past week, she'd seen the aging sailor heading reluctantly toward the quay beneath the castle.

Inside the cottage, though, Adrianne had found an old woman who was declining rapidly.

And just yesterday she had realized what the healer's problem was. Perhaps it had been something in Jean's face as she'd gazed up at an intricately carved spoon on the shelf above her bed. Or perhaps it had been in the way she had said a particular word. Adrianne could not say exactly what had brought about her sudden understanding, but something had happened, for now she was fairly certain she knew what lay at the root of her friend's troubles.

Loneliness.

Her legs had been bothering her for some time. Suddenly faced with thoughts of her own mortality, Jean had—for the first time in her life, Adrianne guessed—stopped to look upon her life and her future.

She and John had never been blessed with children, so now she had no child of her own to come and visit. She had no grandchildren to play in the garden. Now there was no one to come to the cottage, unless there was a problem of their own they needed her assistance with.

This winter, with the cold and her age crippling her movements, Jean's spirit had been brought low.

As she hung the bunch of herbs, Adrianne glanced over at the woman lying back in her bed and wished she could think of a solution. Jean looked up and caught her gaze.

"Stop working at my hearth and come keep me company."

Adrianne quickly wiped the worktable and went and sat obediently beside the woman. Jean's wrinkled fingers took the young woman's in their own. "Tell me, did you give the lad the briony as I told you?"

"I mixed the root as you said, and even as early as yesterday Gillie was saying that his face is not itching as bad as 'twas before."

"But he is still wearing the wool hat against the skin."

"Aye, his clothes are all wool, like everyone else. And you were right, I did look at his elbows and the backs of his knees. He has scars and open sores there, as well."

"Well, there is nothing you can be doing about any of this now, lass. With this winter wind, no linen shirt will keep out the chill. So just keep putting the oils I give you on the lad's face. Come spring, see if you cannot get Wyntoun to allow the lad to wear leather."

Adrianne and Jean had had ample time to talk about Gillie during their days together. After seeing the boy's face that first night, the midwife had judged that the lad must have been born with only the pulled skin beneath his eye. The rest of it had developed later. Jean had seen it once before with another bairn whose mother had died in childbirth. The infant had been given cow's milk and terrible rashes had started immediately on the face. The bairn had started scratching it and wailing like a banshee. And there was a poor nun at the convent by the monastery overlooking the Firth of Lorn; she had broken out with similar scabs and sores anytime she wore wool against her skin. The pitiful creature had nearly lost her mind from the itching.

Knowing that Wyntoun had found Gillie abandoned, Jean wondered if the lad had a combination of the afflictions those two had endured—cow's milk and now wool. With that wool cap forever sitting against the boy's face, Gillie would never be free of the itching torment. For as long as Adrianne had known him, she remembered him scratching at his face, at his neck, at his leg—wherever the wool must had been touching the skin.

"And you are certain there are no other tanners on the island?"

Jean shook her head. "Dylan is the only one, and as long as he's been here, the MacLean has been sending him to the mainland to gather hides during the winter months."

Disappointed, Adrianne began to rise to her feet to busy herself with more work, but the healer's touch on her arm stopped her.

"Has anyone told you anything about Canny going off to Oban this coming week?"

"Aye, Wyntoun told me this morning." Adrianne took the cup from Jean's lap. "She must be blaming me, though, for tearing her away from her people—"

"She has no people here, lass," Jean interrupted. "This same Dylan, the tanner, is her own father, and the man spends more months in Oban than here at Duart Castle. Why, she knows more folks there than she does here. If it weren't for her . . ." She shook her head. "Never mind that now. You just believe me when I tell you 'twill be better for the lass to be where her da can keep an eye on her. She doesn't need to be here and getting into mischief the way she's been doing."

Adrianne put the cup on the table, in a way relieved that she wouldn't have to be worrying about the constant threat of the persistent young woman. A great deal had happened between herself and Wyntoun this past week. A great deal that she wanted to preserve.

"I can see from your face that the seas between you and your husband are smoothing out." Jean's words drew the young woman's mind to the present. "Just put Canny out of your mind, lass. 'Twill be no more than a fortnight before the wench is barely an unpleasant memory for you."

Adrianne nodded, but her mind was already racing beyond Canny. She was now thinking of the young woman's father. A tanner, Jean had said. A craftsman to provide leather to make new clothes for Gillie. This Dylan was the key to finding out if getting the lad out of his ragged woolen clothes could make a difference with the sores on his skin. Making Gillie whole again would be worth all the trouble she might be stirring up by talking with the woman.

Aye, indeed. She had to talk to Canny.

Double-cross. Treachery. Lies and lechery.

As the monk had stared morosely into the fire in the Great Hall earlier, the thought had come to him as clearly as if the angels had spoken.

Even now, standing before the door of the earl of Athol's study for the fifth time in the last hour, Benedict could hear the words. Aye, every sign pointed to double-dealing. And who—more than he himself—knew more about such matters.

The monk scowled and cursed inwardly once again, thinking of Wyntoun MacLean. Benedict already deeply regretted having told the Blade of Barra anything of his plans regarding Tiberius. And now the infernal spawn of Satan had certainly betrayed him. But he must somehow be sure. Benedict's gaze burned into the door. If only the muffled voices from inside the earl's study were just a little clearer!

When the Blade had met Benedict in the crypt of Ironcross Castle, a half-day's journey to the south, the pirate had sworn to help him take one of the Percy sisters. True, the monk had left Ironcross soon after Sir Wyntoun had traveled on to the Ross lands, where Laura Percy was hiding. Nonetheless, if any message had arrived, he would have heard immediately. And what had he heard? Nothing!

And then, only because of his own success in convincing Catherine Percy Stewart to confide in him, Benedict had learned about the trust that had been bestowed upon the Blade of Barra. Without a word, the faithless rogue had left for the Western Isles to find the youngest daughter and return with the last piece of the map to the Treasure of Tiberius. Without a word!

The voices in his head told Benedict that he had been betrayed by the villain. The Blade of Barra had already partaken of the fountain of knowledge.

Treachery, thy name is MacLean!

Benedict forced down the fury boiling just beneath the surface of his skin. How long were these bloody fools to remain in there?

It was still only mid-morning when he'd seen the weary strangers ride in. All the way from the west coast, a kitchen helper had told him as the men were quickly ushered toward the earl's study. Nay, he did not know from where exactly.

Within minutes, Catherine and Laura and her insolent husband William had joined them in the study. And there they had remained for the past two hours.

"Is there something you want here, monk?"

Benedict turned and looked up sharply at Adam, the bastard brother of the earl. Today, as always, the fierce Highlander's face did little to hide his disdain for Benedict. Looking at him now, the monk wondered vaguely if the man's hostility was rooted in the years he had spent in English dungeons. He shook off the thought with a frown. What did he care about one filthy Highlander's feelings toward him?

"I was . . . in search of the countess."

"And have you been in search of her all the other times you've passed by that door this morning, as well?"

"Aye," Benedict answered carefully, working hard to hide the anger that was again flaring up within him at the Highlander's brusque tone.

"Why not just have one of the servants bring a message in to her?"

"My message is important."

A suspicious brow went up. "How important?"

"Important enough that I felt I should deliver it to her, myself."

With a look akin to a sneer on his face, Adam took a step at his direction, and Benedict felt the hair bristle on the back of his neck. "Perhaps your message is so important that the two of us should barge into my brother's study and interrupt a meeting that is of no concern to you . . . or would you prefer to continue eavesdropping out here?"

Benedict's back stiffened and his hand moved furtively to the small dagger hidden in the sleeve of his clerical gown.

"There you are, Adam!"

Benedict stepped back as Adam's hard gaze shifted to the young woman coming down the corridor. The lovely Mistress Susan, distant kin to the earl, and this blackguard's intended. The monk hid his sneer, noting the difference in the Highlander's face now. So soft. So vulnerable. Well, there would be another time for recompense, Benedict thought, bowing slightly to the woman.

"Good day, Father Benedict. Adam, did anyone mention anything to you about whether the MacLean men would be sleeping in the Great Hall tonight? If they're to sleep in the guards' quarter, someone should let the earl's men know, I should think."

"No need. I was given to understand that they will be leaving again for the west, as soon as they are finished here." Adam's hand lingered on his intended's arm. "Incidentally, I was hoping to have a word with you on another matter . . ."

The monk had heard enough. So they were MacLean men! Proof enough that Sir Wyntoun had stabbed him in the back. Edging away from the two, Benedict moved quickly down the corridor. It would not be long before he himself was summoned to that chamber. And there would be no answering the accusations that the cursed Blade surely sent in his messages.

As he and Alan climbed the hill to Duart Castle, Wyntoun stared at the crystal ice that was forming where the dusting of snow had fallen just an hour or so before. Glancing backward at his carrack riding at anchor in the bay, he frowned with the thought of the ice that was surely forming on the lines and the rigging.

Well, he thought, no coating of ice would stop this journey. There was far too much at stake, and he and Alan had spent the morning making sure the ship was prepared to sail when word came from the Highlands. Nay, it would take far more than ice to stop him now.

"If you're thinking of the weather, Wyn, you shouldn't worry," Alan said, as if reading his cousin's mind. "I think those storm clouds that are blowing in from the southwest should be long gone before we set sail. But even if they settle in over us, that old wench has weathered many a strong buffet to her hull. We'll be ready to sail into the teeth of a gale, if you so choose."

The walls of the castle rose up above them, and the knight eyed the activity in the courtyard beyond the arched entry.

"We must be sailing . . . whether Adrianne's sisters agree to our proposal or not." He turned his face to the north and frowned fiercely. "Damn, if we only knew what was happening up there!"

"Do you think they might not give up their sections of the map?"

Wyntoun stared for a moment—considering the possibility for the thousandth time—and then shook off his doubts. "Nay, Alan. They'll go along."

"And what of Adrianne? Do you still think 'tis a good idea leaving her here when we go after the mother and the Treasure?"

The Highlander glanced up past the ramparts of the curtain wall at the upper reaches of the keep. In his mind's eye he could see his bonny bride as he'd left her before dawn, naked between the linen sheets. Her blue eyes had opened, revealing in their depths the snug afterglow of a night of lovemaking.

"Time to rise?" she'd asked. "Jean will be waiting for me."

"Nay, lass. 'Tis still too early. Go back to sleep." He'd kissed her gently and she had drifted back to sleep. A passion like nothing that he'd ever experienced before had taken over his life since he and Adrianne had made love in the stables a fortnight ago. He wanted her all the time. Desire for her ruled his body. Thoughts of her confounded his brain.

And at every moment they were together, in so many ways, she gave herself to him with an unbounded affection that he knew he did not deserve.

"Will you leave her behind?" Allan repeated his question.

"I have no other choice. The matter of her mother's captivity has to be resolved before she can be told the truth."

As they strode under the arched gateway into the castle courtyard, Wyntoun knew that his cousin had more to say on the matter.

"Wait." Alan put a hand out to stop him. His perpetually serious face was even graver than usual as he searched for the right words.

"Aye, Alan. Speak your piece. A politician you'll never be."

"Very well." He glanced around him before speaking. "Wyn, I know that you care for her. With all that is in the wind, I do not know how the Brotherhood . . ." He lowered his voice at the word. "I do not know how they might perceive your actions toward her. All that aside though, I know that your feelings for her have come a far pace from the day you formed your plans."

"What's your point?" Wyn asked darkly.

"Just this." The shipmaster gazed steadily into his cousin's face. "I do not think 'twill be so easy for you to let her go, afterwards. What happens if she does not forgive you, Wyn?"

The image of Auld Jean's cottage formed in Wyntoun's mind, and he thought of his bonny bride spending her hours helping the old healer amid the clutter of herbs and jars and baubles.

"I'll just have to make certain that she does," he said gruffly, turning away.

The reclusive tanner lived beneath the bluffs at the northern end of Glen Forsa, where the river ran into the sea.

Adrianne repeated the directions in her mind as she continued to push the horse forward over the ice-encrusted trail. An hour's ride, that's what Canny had told her the day before, and then Adrianne had watched the young woman climb aboard the small boat that was taking her to Oban and her new home across the water from Duart Castle.

When Adrianne had initiated the meeting, she'd wanted to be sure that no resentment would remain, festering and unresolved. Canny had spoken first, her tears and words of apology immediate and unreserved. Far different than the response Adrianne had expected. The talk with Canny had provided not only peace between the two women, but had given Adrianne a valuable piece of information.

Canny had heard talk about the castle of Adrianne's desire for a leatherworker. So in trying to put the past behind them, Canny said, she was giving the mistress directions to her father's cottage beyond Scallastle Bay, saying that Dylan often left pieces of finished leather there while absent from the island. Aye, there should be enough to cover a lad the size of Gillie. Of course, Adrianne was more than welcome to take what she needed; she was the master's wife. The distance to Dylan's cottage and back, the young woman said, could be covered in a day on foot. Nay, she didn't know how long it would take on horseback . . . an hour or two, she judged.

Adrianne knew that her decision to go this morning had been impulsive. She had been up early, visiting with Jean and making deliveries around the village and checking on Agnes, Kevin's blissfully pregnant wife. Then Jean had mentioned how she was a wee bit concerned that she'd heard "nary a word from Barbara," the wife of a young crofter whose farm lay "by a curve of shoreline folks call Scallastle Bay."

Adrianne's offer to take a jar of Jean's medicine out to the farm had surprised the midwife, but on the other hand

Wyntoun had been planning to spend most of the day on the carrack with Alan, readying the vessel for sea. True, she thought, the farm was on the way to the tanner's cottage, but there was no need to worry anyone here with those kinds of details. And as far as taking one of Wyntoun's horses to deliver some of Jean's medicine, no one in the castle's stables had dared to question the Blade's new bride.

The visit had been brief. The weather was worsening as the day progressed, and Adrianne definitely wanted to be back in the castle before her husband returned from his ship. The crofter's wife had been grateful for the medicine that was sure to help with the cough that had been troubling her husband for weeks.

Now, riding along the bluffs, Adrianne felt the sting of the icy rain against her face. An hour's ride. It had taken her twice that long to get to the crofter's cottage, and that long again to reach here. Still, she could see no sign of the river that flowed out of Glen Forsa.

The horse stumbled, but righted itself. The young woman tugged the reins to move the animal away from the bluff. Far beneath them, a furious sea crashed against the rocks with an incessant roar.

Pushing aside that possibility that Canny might have lied to her, Adrianne tightened her cloak around her and forged onward.

"From what Bege tells me, your bride left the keep not long after you and Alan left this morning."

With the rain still dripping from his tartan and kilt, Wyntoun ran a hand over his face and turned from Mara to one of the serving women. "Makyn, check the apartments in the east wing for Mistress Adrianne."

The woman curtsied and hurried off.

"She might have gone there directly to change." Even to his own ears, his words sounded like those of a man trying to convince himself.

"You might want to be checking Jean's cottage," Mara added as an afterthought. "Every morning, the lass . . ."

"I know. And I've already been there!" Wyntoun, hopeful

to see Adrianne, had gone there first. "Jean said that Adrianne was delivering medicines for her."

"Wyn, you know how your wife is," Mara said with a wry smile. "At this very moment, she is quite likely sitting before some villager's fire with a half-dozen urchins hanging on her elbow, as she stirs up stew made with mutton intended for her own dinner."

Any day but today, Wyntoun mused, he would believe that. But a gnawing feeling in the pit of his stomach told him that all was not right.

It was true that Adrianne was already welcome at the hearth of most members of the Clan MacLean. In many ways she had ingratiated herself much more than Mara had after close to twenty years of marriage to Alexander. And Wyntoun silently admired this in his wife. Though noble by birth, she never seemed to shy away from those lower born than herself, whether they be sick or simply in need. It was the Celtic blood that ran in her veins, of that he was sure. Why, just consider all she'd done for Gillie.

"Gillie!" he said aloud just as a breathless Makyn ran in from the east wing and shook her head in disappointment. Wyntoun turned toward the door. "She must be with Gillie in the stables."

In a moment he was crossing the sleet-covered courtyard toward the stables. The weather appeared to be getting fouler by the moment. In the time he was in the keep, the sleet had turned into a heavy, wet snow. Clenching the muscles in his jaw, Wyntoun swore under his breath that he wouldn't scold her or even lecture her if she was there. Anything, he vowed, he would be agreeable to anything, as long as she was safe.

The uneasiness that had gripped him became immediately worse at the sight of Alan striding out of the stables.

"I was just coming after you."

"Is it Adrianne?" Wyntoun asked, his heart hammering in his chest.

The shipmaster nodded before glancing toward the gates. "She took one of the horses out of the stables this morning. Alford says she has not returned."

"Where did she go?"

"To a croft near Scallastle Bay. Supposedly she was to deliver some medicine."

Wyntoun headed into the stables and toward his own horse. "If she went to Scallastle, she should have been back by now."

"Wyn, you know Adrianne," Alan said, following him. "Most likely she's visiting and forgot the time. Those folks wouldn't let her start back during this storm."

"I *do* know Adrianne." Wyntoun quickly threw a saddle across his horse's back. "But there is no way that I know what that blasted woman will do next. I sure as hell don't know that she arrived at that croft. I don't know that she stayed there to wait out the storm, though my guess is that they'd have to tie her to keep her, if she had a mind to go. By the devil, Alan, I don't know that she isn't wandering in that storm even now."

Wyntoun led his horse out of the stable and swiftly mounted up.

"If I could read that firebrand's mind, coz, my life would be far, far simpler!"

The winter sky was clear and blue above Balvenie Castle in the Highlands far to the north, and the two Percy sisters rose when Athol and William rejoined them in the earl's study.

Both of their husbands had insisted that the sisters take a moment in private to discuss Wyntoun MacLean's letter and his suggested solution to the finding of Tiberius and their mother. Catherine and Laura, however, needed little time in considering the proposal. They both had been certain from the first.

"If any one of us three is prepared to pursue this course, 'tis Adrianne," Laura asserted.

"Our only question would be her safety," Catherine added. "But that too is answered by this news of her marriage to Sir Wyntoun."

"And you are both willing to surrender your portions of the map to the man . . . and to your sister?" William asked.

"What's the use in keeping them when Adrianne and our

new brother are ready to go after it? In truth, Catherine should not travel, and I doubt that I would contribute a great deal."

Catherine nodded in agreement. "Our greatest concern lies in the conveyance of the maps from here to Duart Castle."

"We will have a group of our most seasoned warriors accompany Wyntoun's men back to Oban." The earl of Athol moved to his desk and picked up an open letter. "Something in the letter from Wyntoun, however, concerns me greatly."

He handed the letter to Catherine, and Laura moved to stand at her sister's back.

"What is it, John?" his wife asked.

"Wyntoun knew Benedict from the Knights of the Veil," he said, repeating the information in the letter.

"That surprises me, as well," Laura agreed, frowning over her sister's shoulder. "Sir Wyntoun's words, however, do not fill me with confidence about the monk."

William Ross nodded. "Considering that Benedict was the one who saved Tiberius from the fire, I can see why the trust of the Brotherhood would have been extended to him."

Athol strode to the door and looked out into the corridor. Closing it, he turned back to the others. "Wyntoun's letter is clearly a warning about the man. Even though he says that he himself is not totally certain of the motives behind the monk's actions, he clearly wants us to be wary of him."

"Benedict wanted the Treasure of Tiberius for himself enough to try to buy the Blade of Barra's services in secret," William Ross asserted angrily. "That is good enough reason for me to distrust him."

"But he knows what the treasure is, William. What would one man want with such a thing?"

William faced his wife. "This same man has witnessed the power that it wields. He has had a lifetime to plan how to use it."

"How did Sir Wyntoun know Benedict was here?" Catherine asked.

"I do not think he does . . . or at least, he was not totally certain of it," Athol answered. "But if the two last met in the crypts of Ironcross Castle, it stands to reason that the monk would come to Balvenie Castle with Laura and Catherine both here."

"We should question Benedict. There might be a simple explanation to all of this." Catherine's voice reflected her hopefulness, but the faces around her were grim.

"I sent for him before while you and Laura were discussing the proposal from your sister. But I do not know why—" Athol yanked open the door again, revealing a fierce-looking warrior standing poised to knock.

"Well, Tosh?" Athol asked. "Did you find him?"

"Nay, m'lord. We searched everywhere, but the ground appears to have opened up and swallowed the rogue whole. The monk is gone!"

The horse, tired from the day's travel, balked at the edge of the cliff. Below, the sea pounded the rocky shore, throwing up spray and foam in a wild display of nature's power. Adrianne knew that she would never be able to coerce the animal over the edge of the bluff, and in truth she doubted the steed was surefooted enough to manage what was left of the icy and washed out path leading down. The sleety rain, driven by the gusting wind, was now mixed with huge flakes of wet snow that clung to both horse and rider for an instant before melting away.

A stone's throw inland from the cliff Adrianne found a shelter from the storm for the animal. In a spot where two large boulders had provided a slight windbreak, a thicket of twisted pines had taken hold, and she tied her horse there. Returning to the cliff, she stared down at the top of the deserted hut for a moment before starting the treacherous descent along the icy rockface.

When she neared the bottom, she was surprised to see a more passable track leading along the shoreline at the base of the cliff. How curious, she thought, that Canny had forgotten to mention a word about it. Clearly, the tanner used that one far more frequently in his coming and going.

Adrianne was soaked to the skin, but excited as she made her way toward the door of the leatherworker's hut. She had spoken to Bess, the seamstress, days earlier about her plan.

Bess had told her she would have no trouble stitching up whatever the young mistress wanted for the lad. The woman had worked with leather before and assured Adrianne that she had the necessary awls and needles. All that was left was for Adrianne herself to provide the leather, and that task appeared to be all but accomplished.

There was no sign of smoke escaping the hole in the roof of the hut. A tanner's fleshing log sat on an angle by the open door of the hut. As a blast of wind stung her face, Adrianne pulled the hood of her cloak forward. All she had to do was walk in there, choose what she needed, and be on her way. From the hunger gnawing at her stomach, she knew it was growing late in the day, and she wanted to get back to Duart Castle and her husband before night had descended completely.

Coming to an abrupt stop, Adrianne swallowed hard at the sight of Wyntoun standing silently, accusingly in the doorway.

She would have preferred that he shout at her, that he scream at her. The silent, angry, look was far more threatening, far more damaging, sending a chill through her that was colder than the winter wind.

He looked as if he might break an icicle off the hut and drive it through her heart. The look in his green eyes cried murder.

"Wyntoun," she managed to get out, glancing toward the cliffs she'd just descended.

"I'll come up those rocks faster than you can climb."

Her eyes flicked at him in surprise before turning toward the furious sea.

"You'll have less chance there."

Guiltily gnawing a chapped lip, she turned to him and held out a hand to him.

"And don't try that, either. I won't believe you."

It was terrifying how well he was getting to know her. Adrianne lifted her head slightly and decided to face the storm straight on.

"Once again, I am guilty," she called out to him. "I set

out to do what I thought would be of some good, and instead made an error in judgment."

She wondered if he planned to stay there in the doorway and let her die in the storm.

"I should have told you where I was going. I should have asked someone to accompany me." She looked about her, trying to think how else he might find fault with her coming. "I should have waited for a better day to travel?"

She was running out of ideas.

"You believe I was reckless. You believe I reacted to my heart's whim rather than using my head. Very well, I admit it."

She shivered where she stood, this time daring to meet his angry gaze as her own temper flared. Before they had consummated their marriage, it had been easy to face him in a situation like this. She'd always simply attacked before he could start, reminding him that he had no power over her. Their marriage was in name only, after all.

That tactic would no longer work. Things were quite different, now, and she felt the change.

"Come inside!"

Like a sheep to slaughter, she thought, imagining the hides hanging in the tanner's hut.

He turned and disappeared into the darkness of the cottage, and for one insane moment she considered making a run for it. But her courage and her intelligence prevailed and she followed him.

When Adrianne entered the hut, Wyntoun was standing at the far wall, his back to the single shuttered window. A half-dozen heavy tubs of varying sizes sat around the ashes of a firepit in the center of the one room. More tubs stacked up along the walls, and stained large wooden frames used for stretching and working the hides stood with them. She pushed the hood of her cloak back and scanned the dark interior for any sign of the promised hides.

"Do you know what I would do to you if you were one of my men?"

Her eyes snapped up to his. "Let me follow my own path?

Wished me a good riddance . . . with the hope, of course, of at least getting your horse back?"

"I would tie you to the back of that horse," he snapped, "and drag your arse back to Duart Castle! And then I would leave you in one of the dungeons to rot . . . if I didn't hang you, first."

"You mean you'd hang me first . . . and *then* put me in the dungeons to rot?"

"Do not attempt to rile me any further than you have already, Adrianne."

"If that is what you would do," she said as casually as she could muster, "then 'tis a shame I am your loving wife. Think of the entertainment you're giving up."

She had to force herself to stand still as he closed the distance between them with a few long strides. He took hold of her shoulders with both hands, and his powerful grip hurt, but she willed herself to show nothing of what she was feeling.

"Could you be so completely unaware of the trouble you cause? The danger you put yourself in!" He shook her once, releasing her and stepping back. "And what a fool I was to think that, by taking you to my bed, you would change! No one ever changes. Everyone knows that. We die as we are born. We cannot change our nature."

Adrianne stared at him. Never had she seen him like this. Never had she heard him express his frustrations so passionately.

"You are wrong," she said quietly. "People do change. Gillie has. You have."

"Nay, we are the same people. Our nature has not changed. We only choose to close our eyes now and not see your flaws. We choose to tolerate you as you are."

"Tolerate . . . ?"

Wyntoun's hard words hurt her far more than she could ever have imagined. A knot rose in her throat, and she fought back the tears burning her eyes. She took a step back. Disappointment was etched on every line of his handsome face.

Tolerate. You tolerate a nuisance—a thorn or a pebble or

a smoky fire. She had no more meaning to him than that. So
this is the point they had come to.

Adrianne felt the strength to fight draining out of her, but
forced herself to face him before she shamed herself completely.

"We made a mistake," she managed to say. "Nay, that is
not correct. *I* made a mistake. I lured you—tricked you into
marrying me—and then later I convinced you to consummate
a lie."

His face was a mask, and he started to speak, but she
raised a hand.

"Let me finish." She took in a shaky breath. "You say I
am the same as the day I was born. You think I am the same
creature that terrorized my people in Yorkshire. That I am the
same wild thing that your aunt delivered to you in Barra."

She turned abruptly toward the open door and dashed away
a tear.

"Despite what you believe, Wyntoun MacLean, I am *not*
the same. I am not the same person who left my home so
long ago. I am not the same person who escaped an abbey
in Yorkshire in the dark of night. Nay, since I had to leave
my home, had to leave behind the love and the acceptance
of my family, I have had to reach out to people and beg for
them to accept me. I tried that in Barra, and for naught. Every
good thing I tried to do there was construed as wickedness,
and every attempt to help someone called disruption. So I
changed, and perhaps not for the better. But then . . . but then
something else happened."

Adrianne turned to him. The wind was no longer battering the hut, and the silence in the dimly lit dwelling hung
like a wall between them until she broke it.

"In coming to Duart Castle, in becoming your wife, I
thought I no longer needed to beg for acceptance. For the
first time since my father was dragged from our home, I felt
secure here among your people. More than that, I felt a new
purpose in my life. Here, Alexander and Mara and . . . and so
many others did not constantly feel the need to remind me
of my flaws. They accepted me. So I have tried to grow with
the changes happening within me. I wanted to help people

just for the sake of making their lives better. I've had no expectations of any reward for this. In some ways, I've found that I could be more like the woman that Auld Jean is. A healer. A giver. And yet, now you tell me so eloquently that I still have failed. I am tolerated, you tell me."

Her hands shook as she wiped away at the tears.

"But I am not weak. I have found a home and a purpose . . . right here." She touched her heart. "So I *have* changed. I am far different than the person I was in Yorkshire . . . or even in Barra. And if you cannot see that—if you cannot recognize this new me—then I have wronged you more than anyone else in my life."

She turned away again and hugged the wet cloak against her arms. "We will just go on as if this marriage was never consummated. We will end it as you had originally wished—just as you had planned. 'Twas foolishness . . . aye, recklessness and pride on my part to think I could be a wife to the great Blade of Barra. 'Twas wrong of me to assume that you'd ever see me with—"

Momentarily choked by the knot that had formed in her throat, she pulled the cloak over her head and glanced toward the door. "I found my way here; I'll find my way back. And when this is over, I will leave Duart Castle, and your life will once again be your own."

Chapter 23

As Nichola unhooked and pulled open the wooden shutters, the winter wind swept into the chamber like a conquering hero.

She closed her eyes at the brightness of the sun, drawing the air deeply into her lungs. The cold wind felt good on her burning skin, but did little to calm her distraught mind. But there would be no relief in the wind, and she already knew it.

Marriage! Intimacy! The pleasure of skin against skin. Of a man's body, hard and demanding . . . and yet so giving, too! She had not forgotten the pleasure of the marriage bed, the feel of a man within her. By the saints, she had never expected her life to travel this path. Guilt and pleasure so inextricable bound together, intertwined like the branches of a thistle and a rose.

She moved away from the open window and stared at the damask-canopied bed. For two weeks now they'd shared that bed. And for a fortnight Henry had honored her wish, not demanding intimacy. Throughout this time, he'd been the most courteous of knights, the most agreeable of companions, the most generous of men, showering her with gifts she had neither expected nor sought. During these two weeks, he'd become once again the friend to her that she had once known.

But something had happened last night. A moment of weakness. A yearning she couldn't turn her back on. A fire—kindled by some unknown force—had flared up between them. A desire so strong that she had not been able to keep him away.

She had not wanted to keep him away.

Nichola stared at the empty bed, and sensual images flashed back into her mind. Henry slowly peeling away her clothing. She blushed even now at the shock of seeing his arousal, so potent and alive for her. And yet his actions, so gentle and coaxing. Henry had succeeded in peeling away her restraint, as well.

There were other images, far more carnal ones. Henry, buried deep inside her, holding her on his lap as he suckled her breast. She remembered her own moans and felt the heat in her own belly stirring again. Over and over again, he had sent her into a realm of quivering rapture, driving her ever higher into a world she had never before experienced . . . even in the arms of the man she had loved and cherished for so many years.

Finally, they had risen together on a joyous wave, riding a crest of bliss until she was sure she would go mad. Even now, Nichola could hear their cries in the night. Even now, she could feel him driving into her again and again until the two of them had burst in a flood of ecstasy, melting finally in each other's arms.

And then, they had simply begun again.

Nichola covered her face with her hands and shook her head. What was wrong with her? Moving again to the window, she once more filled her chest with the icy air, trying to cool the madness that was rising within her. Where had this need come from? How had this man so easily seen it in her . . . and known how to answer it so passionately?

Nichola turned and leaned her back against the sill. How could she go on living with this? The marriage was not the problem, but the intimacy was unfathomable. The innocent faces of her daughters moved before her eyes. What disapproval they each would feel—and rightly so—for her betrayal of their father! Why, she had sold herself—body and soul— in a marriage to another man.

There was a gentle knock on the door, and Nichola jumped, hurriedly closing the shutters. She had sent a word to Henry this morning, after waking up and finding he had already left their bed. She wished to see a priest. She wished to confess her sins and shed some of the weight that was now beating her to the ground.

There was another knock, and this time she called the person to enter. The creaking of the door on its ancient hinges drew Nichola's gaze to the face of her visitor.

She gasped with delight at seeing the familiar face. "Benedict!"

Vivid memories of three days sitting off the coast of Africa came back to Wyntoun now. It was four years ago. He and Alan had just taken a cargo of gold from a Portuguese treasure ship too badly damaged to take as well. As they'd turned for home, he remembered his cousin saying that if Wyntoun's luck held, the new university in Glasgow would be one of the finest—or did he say richest—in Europe. That was when the wind died.

For three days they had baked in that sweltering heat. No breath of wind stirred. Not a ripple could be seen on the water from horizon to horizon. Never, never had three days dragged on so slowly.

Until now.

The three days since Adrianne had walked out of that tanner's cottage had easily been the longest of Wyntoun's life.

She had gone out of the hut and climbed the rocky bluff without so much as a look back. She'd returned to the castle without any assistance from him.

And he had stood there like a stone. Like some witless fool, he had said nothing, simply watching her as she walked away. Why had he not been man enough to tell her that he was moved by her words? He was a knave, a villain to the core for not cutting into her speech, making her understand that their pact was finished, though not as she thought. They had consummated their marriage, so there would be no walking away.

Wyntoun MacLean realized now that he had never known what the word *frustration* meant until he was forced to deal with his wife's resolve.

She'd deserted their bed. Why, she'd shunned him entirely. The only time he saw her was when she was in the Great

Hall, breaking bread with the rest of the household. Once, she had rushed past him out the castle gates. He'd watched her move across the hills toward Auld Jean's cottage.

And damn him if he hadn't tried to break through the wall between them. Damn him if he hadn't gone to extremes to win back even a shred of her affection. He'd brought back enough leather with him to make ten outfits for Gillie. He'd made a point to send Bess, the seamstress, up to Adrianne. He'd directed Coll to start training the lad to fight and to sail. Why, he'd even assigned Gillie to serve as his own page.

When he'd seen her in the Great Hall, he'd been his most congenial, chatting and grinning at her like a jackanapes until his jaws ached. But other than a damned letter that she had written to him—the thing was more formal than a papal bull—she'd not spared him so much as a blasted smile.

Wyntoun MacLean was a cursed man. He missed his wife . . . desperately.

"Are you going to stand there for the rest of the evening, staring into that fire? Or are you going to look at these maps?"

He turned and glanced at the three sections of the map sitting on the table in front of Alan. The other two sections of the map had arrived that morning. The two sisters had sent them from Balvenie Castle without any qualms, at all.

Now, Wyntoun was even considering the possibility of taking them to Adrianne. To bask in the glow of her smile, of her renewed trust, would be a gift from heaven. But how long would that trust last, considering all that he'd held back from her? How long would that smile last when she found out that the Knights of the Veil had been the ones behind her mother's capture? Or when she found out that Wyntoun himself had been the one who had directed the Brotherhood to take Nichola Percy?

He walked toward the desk. It would be best if he waited. Waited until he could set Nichola free and return Tiberius to the protection of the Knights of the Veil. Then he could return here and work diligently on winning back his wife.

If she would have him.

The door to the antechamber was shut and barred, the shutters closed as well. As Wyntoun bent over the desk with Alan, he tried to be deaf to the sounds of the crowd in the Great Hall.

Adrianne had been arranging something for this night. Something with Mara. Whatever it was, she had been planning and working and planning some more. Wyntoun had been watching the preparations going forward, but had finally decided to turn a blind eye to it all. Whatever it was, he would have no part in it unless his wife told him about it herself. A number of messengers had come to him from Alexander and from Mara during the day, insisting that he join them in the Great Hall. But he could be stubborn, as well. If they wanted him, he'd told Mara finally, then they could send Adrianne to bring him.

And that, Wyntoun knew, was not about to happen.

Before him on the table the three portions of a map sat—the edges aligned to form a whole.

"The damned thing is so vague."

"I would expect no less from Edmund Percy." Wyntoun moved a burning candle closer and tried to focus only on the map. "The Treasure of Tiberius lies in Glasgow, of that we can be certain. The drawing of the salmon and the ring on Adrianne's portion tells us that."

"By the time we drop anchor in the Clyde, most of the others should have gathered there. With a wee bit of help from the older knights of the Brotherhood, you should be able to sort out some of these cryptic scratches."

The green eyes of the Highlander remained riveted to the map. Solving it was not a problem. Keeping his mind clear and keeping his heart free of the growing ache—those were the more challenging problems.

Wyntoun and his men were sailing the next morning, going away for as long as it took to get the treasure and return Nichola Percy's freedom.

By the devil! He was missing her already, and he hadn't even gone away. He again tried to focus on the task on hand. He frowned at Alan.

"Have you heard anything, any rumor around the village or in the keep, that might give the true purpose of our trip away?"

Alan shook his head. "Nay, meeting the earl of Athol's men in Oban worked very well, Wyn. No one on Mull knows that the men sent to Balvenie Castle have returned."

Wyntoun glanced down at the map. "I want someone to tell Adrianne that our journey tomorrow shall take no more than a week . . . that we'll be back before her sisters' response arrives from the north."

Alan's gaze was thoughtful. "Why not tell her yourself?"

"I would if she would listen!" Wyntoun snapped, pushing himself away from the table. "I'll have Alexander talk to her tonight. And after a week, he could speak to her again. Tell her about the tricks of the wind and the difficulties in predicting the length of a sea journey."

If she would only talk to him tonight, Wyntoun thought. If she would only give him a chance to rephrase his harsh words. He hadn't been wrong, by God, but he also hadn't expressed himself very well.

Alan's voice broke into his reverie. "I've been watching the lad, Gillie. I think he'll be strong enough to come on this trip."

Wyntoun nodded as he carefully folded the maps and put them in an oiled leather pouch on his desk. "He is my only source of redress with Adrianne. I'd make the lad king of Jerusalem if that would buy me her affection."

Alan laughed. "A word of warning, though. The lad is no sailor yet."

"I know, but he'll do very well. He is healthy, and on our trip here from Barra, he handled the rough seas like an old salt," Wyntoun asserted. "And I made no empty promise when I vowed to take Gillie on as my page. The lad needs all the advantage he can get in life."

The knock on the door brought the two men's heads around sharply. Wyntoun walked toward the door and lifted the bar. The big head of one of his sailors poked in.

"Ye're needed in the Hall, master."

"Who needs me, Bull?"

The man took the tam off and scratched his head. "The laird is going to be there soon, and there is Mistress Mara—"

"Who sent you after me, Bull?"

"I'm not supposed to be telling, master."

"You have started thinking again, Bull."

"Say what ye will, master, but yer wife's threats are far more frightening. So, begging yer pardon, I'll not be telling."

Wyntoun nodded thoughtfully. "Well, why don't you go back to the Great Hall and tell her . . . whoever sent you after me . . . that your master is not coming."

"But ye cannot, master! There'll be all sorts of hell to pay, and I—"

"A better idea. What don't you go and tell Mistress Adrianne that I am surrounded by my people in here and that I am planning to work here for the rest of the afternoon . . . and this evening, as well."

Bull looked suspiciously around the chamber. "But there's no one here but Master Alan."

"You are thinking again, Bull."

"Aye." The man scratched his head again and stepped back.

"Tell her that I want no more messengers disturbing me again. Do you hear me, Bull? No more messengers!"

At the sailor's quick nod, Wyntoun shut the door in the man's face.

"I thought you *wanted* to see the lass."

Wyntoun turned to his cousin. "Of course. Bull is the tenth person she's sent after me today. I'm hoping she'll come herself."

"I can tell you what this is all about," Alan offered. "That way, you can—"

"I don't want to know," Wyntoun warned. "Now, if we—"

There was another knock on the door. Softer than Bull's huge knuckles were capable of delivering. The Highlander moved to the side of the door and motioned for Alan to open it.

"Just a moment," the shipmaster called out, taking his ship's charts in hand before lifting the bar to the door.

"Alan . . ." Adrianne's voice was quiet. "I was hoping you would relay a message for me to—"

"I cannot, mistress. He is far too busy in there with all these people." Alan swung open the door wide and stepped out into the corridor. "You can go in there yourself and do the asking."

The moment she peered into the room, Wyntoun reached out and took a hold of her wrist, dragging her in. He swung her around behind him, at the same time kicking the door shut with his boot.

"What are you doing?" she asked breathlessly, trying to wrest her hand free. He let her go but stood with his back to the door, blocking her exit. She took a few steps back, her blue eyes stormy. "There is no one here."

By God, her face was a balm to his aching heart. "I thought I was the only one that you wished to see."

"I was . . . I needed to speak with you. But Bull said you were in here, surrounded by 'a hundred folk, at least.'"

Her cheeks were flushed. Her eyes were avoiding his gaze. He wondered what she would do if he just took her in his arms and devoured her lips. If he just picked her up and carried her to their bed. He glanced at the small dagger that she'd taken to wearing at her belt. He'd probably feel the point of it between his ribs.

"A hundred people . . . ?" she asked.

"They must have passed you in the corridor."

She frowned at him as he barred the door.

"Adrianne," he said, taking a step toward her, "we need to talk."

Her frown disappeared, but as she looked steadily at him, Wyntoun could still see the hurt in the depths of those blue eyes.

"We have said all that needs to be said between us," she said, backing away from him until she was against the desk. "Unless you want to send me away until—"

"You are not going anywhere." He took another step and she went around the desk, making it a barrier between them. "You belong to me as I belong to you. We are joined for life—forever."

"I refuse to belong to someone who does not want me." Her voice caught, and Wyntoun could see the sheen of the tears in her eyes. "I'll not stay with someone who finds me so riddled of faults. I'll not be 'tolerated.'"

"I was angry, and"—he stepped closer—"and I could not think straight. I have never felt as helpless as I felt looking for you. Not knowing where you had gone. Whether you were in danger. Visions of you hurt in some ditch . . . or set upon by outlaws on the moors . . . I . . . I . . . Adrianne, this is all so new to me. I have never cared for someone so much that it hurts me."

He watched her chin drop to her chest. Tears, shimmering like tiny crystals, were rolling down on skin as smooth as silk. He went around the desk and forced himself to stop a step away.

"I knew you were in search of leather for Gillie. I even knew the reason. But you never asked me for help. You never found me worthy enough to tell me what you needed. And then when I found you missing . . ." Wyntoun's fingers ached to touch her. "I want you, Adrianne. I need you. I was more than harsh in what I said in Dylan's cottage. I said those words to hurt you—to make you suffer, too. But I have suffered far more since that day. I cannot live without you. It is as simple as that."

"I've suffered, too," she said softly, still looking down. "And I should have sought out your help. I just thought your time more valuable—"

"There is nothing more valuable to me than you." He touched her cheek and brushed away the tears. He lifted her chin and looked into her blue eyes. "I am asking you to forgive me, Adrianne."

She closed the space between them, walking into his arms. "I am the one who should seek forgiveness."

"By God, I have missed you," he growled, his arms gathering her so close that there was not a breath of air left between them. "I have missed you at my side—and in my bed."

"I have, too," she whispered against his lips before he took her mouth in a kiss. She pulled away a moment later, breathless. "I slept in the room above this one, thinking of you every moment, soaking my pillow with the tears of longing. And then this morning, hearing of you going away, of your journey—"

"Enough talk of that." His lips tasted the delicious skin of her throat. "I want to make love to you."

"But we cannot," she said with alarm, putting a hand to his chest. "At least, not now. There is something I have planned for tonight, and I need your help."

"'Tis only afternoon. There are hours left until tonight."

"But there is a great deal that still needs to be done. But I have to tell you about what has been planned, for I—"

"You can tell me now!" He leaned back against the desk and drew her to him. "But I'll die if you deprive me of the pleasure of holding you."

Reaching up, she threaded her fingers through his short hair, and her gaze drifted over his face, settling on his lips. "There *will* be time for this later."

"Not enough time." His hands moved down her back and over the curve of her bottom. He could feel the flesh, firm and smooth, through the green velvet cloth of the dress. He pulled gently until she was snugly pressed against his body. "Three days. You have made me suffer for three days."

"And do you think you have suffered more than I?" She smiled up at him. "Do you think I can just forget the way you make me burn?"

"Do I make you burn, my firebrand?" He slid his hands upward, reaching for the laces of the dress.

Her soft hands framed his face. "You are a rogue, Wyntoun MacLean, for you very well know the answer to that."

"My memory is not what it once was. Why don't you remind me." He tipped her toward him and pressed her lips to his.

Words were forgotten. Angling her head she took charge of the kiss as he opened the back of the dress and touched the bare skin beneath. As he slid the dress and shift over her shoulders, Adrianne's tongue tangled with his, teasing him. His desire grew as he heard the quiet murmurs of pleasure in her throat.

"Let me see you," he said huskily, breaking off the kiss and forcing her to stand away from him. He tugged at the front of the dress and watched it slip down just beneath her breasts, pushing the delicate buds upward. "By the saints, Adrianne, you are perfection."

"You only say that because I am your wife, and you have missed me. I have many physical flaws. A scar on my knee. A cut on my back. A small birthmark by my hip."

"Och, such a negligent husband I am. So much that I have missed." He kissed her mouth again as her fingers dug into his hair and he felt her shiver with delight as he trailed a line of kisses from her jaw down the length of her neck to the swell of her breasts.

She leaned against him, her eyes smoky with passion. "You are right! Tonight is not enough."

He suckled one breast, and her fingers dug into his shoulders. Wyntoun used one hand to unfasten his sword belt, dropping it to the floor.

Taking her by the hand, he led her to the carved wood chair by the hearth and drew her down onto his lap. She shivered again as he lifted her skirts and slid one hand along her leg, lightly touching the inside of her thigh. "I wanted to do this to you last night when you were so intent in ignoring me during the supper."

She gasped sharply as his fingers entered her, finding the sensitive nub of her womanhood. "It would have been my undoing."

Wyntoun shifted her on his lap, turning Adrianne until she straddled him. Pulling his kilt out of the way, he pressed his erect manhood into her moist folds. He watched her lips part slightly as he slid into her.

He kissed her chin, trying now to think of anything but his intense desire to drive repeatedly into her. Adrianne's hands gripped his shoulders, and her skirts billowed like a blanket around the two of them.

"Never do that to me again. Never walk away."

She moved closer as her lips settled on top of his again, tormenting him. He throbbed within her.

"I never will," she whispered a moment later.

Lifting her easily, Wyntoun slowly eased back into her, more deeply this time. He smiled as she gasped with pleasure at the sensation.

"We are made for each other. Here . . ." He reached down and touched where their bodies joined. "And here." He touched their hearts. "Everything else we will work out."

She blushed, drawing back to look into his face. The movement made his control slip another notch. She slowly lifted herself on his lap and lowered herself again, taking him even deeper.

"Forever!" she whispered.

He held her by the waist and gazed into her incredibly blue eyes, smoky now with desire. As if by some unspoken agreement, the two had resisted uttering words of affection before. Their lack of a clear future had called for such restraint, and they both knew it instinctively. But now, hearing the warmth in her voice, suddenly those utterances were the very things Wyntoun too wanted to say to her . . . and hear from her. Whether he deserved them or not.

Indeed, there was another desire, stronger than the carnal one that held him in thrall at this moment. It was a dream that had been nagging him—plaguing him—since he had made Adrianne his own in the stables more than a fortnight ago. It was the burning desire to end the war between his head and his heart.

She squirmed on his lap despite his tight hold on her waist. Framing his face with her hands, she brushed her lips gently across his. "You already know me better, Wyntoun, than anyone else ever has. I cannot hide my feelings. I have to do and say as my heart bids me."

"That is who you are, my love."

He saw the welling of tears in her eyes.

"I know you consider me rash and reckless. But I will try." She paused and took a deep breath. "I will try to be a deserving wife." She moved again on him. Her lips again brushed lightly across his. "I love you, Wyntoun. I love you more . . ."

Her proclamation was his undoing. He took possession of her with the force of a tempest. His mouth was bruising as it took hers in a deep and searing kiss. But she punished him back. Her fingers were insistent. Her body arched as she strained to take him deeper into her body.

With smooth and agile power, Wyntoun rose to his feet. With her legs wrapped around his waist, he took the few short steps to his desk. Placing her gently on the edge of the smooth wood surface, he abruptly withdrew from her. Wordlessly, he knelt on one knee and kissed the inside of her leg before moving his mouth to the juncture of her thighs. She cried out with a startled gasp at the shock of the intimacy, and her entire body jerked up toward the ceiling. But he pushed her back and continued his sweet torment.

He could not tell her everything that was in his heart. He would not reveal a truth that was so tainted with fraud. For now, at least, he had to wait until the wrong he had done would yield a better situation. Only when her mother was returned to her would his guilt be washed away. Then—only then—could he declare his love for her.

But for now she would know of the passion he felt for her.

"Oh, Wyntoun!"

Her body shuddered in wild waves of release and her hands clutched desperately at the edge of the table. Kissing the inside of her thigh once again, he stood up and guided his throbbing manhood to the place where his mouth had been. As he buried himself deep within her, Adrianne's cry of pleasure rang out in the chamber. Holding her hips steady with two hands, he slid out and thrust into her again and again. Faster and faster he drove, and when his own release came, he heard himself call out her name.

As his breathing slowed, he found her wrapped in his arms. Her lips placed kisses on his neck.

His eyes focused. Just above her head, the pouch containing the maps to Tiberius lay on the table. The oiled leather gleamed in the firelight, accusing him of the treachery that he'd brought to this marriage.

Wyntoun MacLean held her tighter in his arms, knowing the time was running short for setting that wrong to right.

Chapter 24

The appreciative cheer of the gathered clan continued to ring from the rafters of the Great Hall, and the look on Auld Jean's face was one that Adrianne knew she would cherish until the day she died.

Standing between Wyntoun and her husband, John, the midwife stared in disbelief at the full Hall for a moment before her emotions broke through. The tears that sprang from her eyes ran down both cheeks. Shaking hands reached out to hug the first person who approached her from the throng of smiling and laughing clan folk that now encircled her.

Adrianne stood at the side of the Great Hall and wiped away her own tears as the older woman was led to the dais and the seat of honor at the laird's table. Jean sat beside a beaming Alexander MacLean, and John sat beside Lady Mara.

"When you asked me to tell Auld Jean a lie for you, I never guessed the extent of your plans."

She smiled at Wyntoun as he brushed a tear from her face with his thumb.

"Was it difficult to get her up and about?"

"Not once I told her you were ill. John and I put her up on my horse, and she started giving orders like the abbess herself. As I started up to the castle, she had John run back into the cottage for a dozen herbs and a satchel of oils. Told him not to stop and chat with anyone on the way up, either."

Adrianne laughed at the thought of it.

"Oh, this is for you." She held up a necklace of silver-painted acorns on a leather thong and looped it around Wyntoun's neck.

"Silver acorns?"

She gestured to her own necklace. "All the people who Jean ever helped or healed or cared for are wearing silver." She pointed to the large number of clan folk wearing gold acorns as well as silver. "And all the folk that she helped to bring into this world are wearing gold-painted acorns."

"I see. 'From the tiny acorn the mighty oak doth grow.' It signifies all she has done to make the clan thrive." His fingers entwined with her own, and she blushed at his look of admiration as he raised her hand and brushed a kiss on her fingers. "Well done, Adrianne. You've planned well and carried it through. You've done so much to make Auld Jean see that she is still needed and loved."

She looked down. "I didn't do it all. I had plenty of help. But this gathering . . . this is not only for the purpose of Jean to see the faces of her real children. 'Tis for them, as well."

Adrianne turned to face the dais as an oak tree twice the height of the MacLean was dragged into the Hall on a pallet and placed before the healer's chair. John and the laird supported her, and Mara accompanied them to the edge of the dais.

"'Tis like the old beliefs and the sacred oak. She stands for the mother of the world, and we are her children." Wyntoun nodded and grinned at her. "I think, my dove, that you did not learn this from the monks in Yorkshire."

Adrianne smiled and clutched her husband's arm tighter as all the people with gold acorn necklaces approached the tree first. Young and old, women and men, they all stood before the healer and kissed her hand before hanging their necklaces on the branches of the oak. There were words of gratitude spoken. Laughter would ring out as Jean would remember something or other about the time when someone had been a bairn or a child. There were invitations made for Jean and her husband to come and visit someone's croft or cottage.

"And they all mean it," Wyntoun whispered to Adrianne. "These are good people. They just had to be reminded of the treasure that they have taken for granted."

She nodded but then felt the heat of his gaze. She looked up and found his green eyes looking on her with more passion than she'd seen in his chamber this afternoon. In those eyes she saw more affection than she'd thought he could ever have for her. She felt something flutter in her chest.

"'Tis your turn, master." Someone's voice behind them broke the moment. They both looked at the dais and found that the clan folk with gold-painted acorns had finished presenting themselves.

"Ready, m'lady?" Wyntoun offered her his arm.

Adrianne, suddenly unwilling to trust her voice, nodded through a blur of tears as she moved beside her husband to the dais. They hung their necklaces on the tree with the others.

But as the healer joined their hands together and touched their faces in a silent blessing, Adrianne knew that they had crossed a threshold toward a new beginning.

As the candle beside the bed flickered, Wyntoun looked one last time at the beautiful curve of Adrianne's bare shoulder showing from under the blankets. A black lock of hair curled across her cheek as she slept, and he fought the urge to push it back and kiss her lips one last time. Memories of their fervent lovemaking by candlelight rushed back, filling his senses and causing his loins to tighten by instinct.

But it was not just that. There had been real love between them in the night. It was in her words, her sighs, her actions. The feeling had surfaced, taking hold of them both like some great hungering need.

He had known this would be their last night together for a long while, and he had savored each precious moment.

Adrianne Percy was his treasure. His love. In a lifetime of searching, he would never find another like her. She had captured him with so unexpected a passion . . . that it still surprised him. He looked forward to the day when this journey would be behind him. That would be the day when he would open his heart to her.

It was Wyntoun MacLean who smiled at his wife one last time, a sadness ripping at his chest. By God, he didn't want to lose her. Ever!

It was the Blade of Barra, though, who turned away and strode from the chamber.

Alan's crew was hard at work readying the ship by the time Wyntoun arrived on deck. Small boats were continuing to run in and back from the shore with last minute provisions. Gillie, eager to be useful, was at his master's side the moment Wyntoun had deposited the maps in his cabin and climbed to the high, stern weather deck.

"I will be assigning you to work with Master Coll again," Wyntoun told the lad as Alan made his way toward them. "No one knows more about sailing than Coll, Gillie. There is a great deal you can learn from the man."

Gillie nodded, barely containing his excitement and holding his new leather cap in place as a predawn breeze buffeted him slightly. He was quite the dashing figure in the clothing Adrianne had had made for him. All leather with undergarments of linen. Wyntoun slapped him on the back. He himself would be interested in seeing whether the clothes would make any improvement in the lad's sores. Without a word, Gillie turned and scanned the deck for the seasoned sailor.

"Coll is still ashore, but we've a couple of new lads joining the crew," Alan announced, arriving at their side. He pointed toward a couple of boys carrying carefully rolled sails below decks. "Why don't you go and give them a hand until he comes aboard."

With a quick nod of the head, Gillie scrambled off to do as he was told.

"The lad looks eager enough."

"Why is Coll still ashore?" Wyntoun asked, surveying the readiness of everything else on deck. "The tide will turn shortly."

"Aye. He'll be here. The laird called for him."

"I wonder what my father is up to now?"

"Who could say? Ah, good." Alan pointed as Coll and another boy climbed aboard. "Here he is . . . and he has the smith's son. That should do it."

Wyntoun glanced at the lad who had followed the old

sailor on the deck. From this distance he couldn't put a name to the boy.

"Damn this breeze!" Alan said, looking toward the entry to the bay. "We'll have to sail further west than we'd originally planned, Wyn. But once past Colonsay Island, we can tack to the east past Islay . . ."

Wyntoun found his attention drifting from Alan's words and instead focusing on the boy who had climbed aboard with Coll. The lad's hesitation and the old sailor's careful attention as they moved forward caused Wyntoun's brow to furrow.

Adrianne wouldn't do this now, would she? Abruptly, he stepped away from Alan. The rising wind stung his face as he approached the railing of the aft weather deck. The voices of the lads and Coll barking orders rang out.

"Here, lad! Not like that!" Coll shouted at the new boy. "I told yer pa ye'd be earning yer keep, and ye will, devil take ye! If ye think I'm . . . here, hold the line this way! Keep this up and the Blade will have ye lashed to the ship's anchor and use ye for fish bait. Do ye hear me, now, lad?"

"Aye, sir." The boy's voice had that cracking quality of one approaching manhood.

Coll slung a net satchel at the boy and shoved him farther forward. "Take my gear below deck and be quick about it, or ye'll have the master calling for a whipping before we clear the harbor mouth."

The lad quickly ran off, and Coll turned to see the knight standing at the railing.

"Who is your new helper?" Wyntoun asked as Coll crossed the main deck to him.

The old sailor turned his wrinkled face away and ran a weary hand on it. "Och, bloody worthless, I'm thinking. 'Tis the blacksmith's lad . . . from Ulva."

Wyntoun watched the lad clamber down the ladder. He remembered the old blacksmith, but he couldn't remember anything about his son.

"The laird says the smith's wife was over this past week complaining about all the trouble the lad was getting into and how she'd wished there was a way he could be of some usefulness, as he had no interest in working at the shop at his father's trade and—"

"Let me guess," Wyntoun growled at his man. "And my father quickly offered the lad a position on the ship."

"Ye know how the laird is, Wyn." Coll gave him a guilty grin. "He thinks there's no better way to make a man of a lad than on a ship's deck."

"And what was all that you were telling the boy about getting a beating from me?"

"Keep the fear in them, and they are sure to behave." Coll was looking up into the rigging at the men taking their places. "I'll keep the lad busy and out of harm's way."

Wyntoun looked over his shoulder as Alan called out for the sailors to raise the anchor and unfurl the sails. "What's the lad's name, anyway?"

"Adam!" Coll replied, giving Wyntoun a quick nod and turning away. "I'll be sure to send the lad in so ye can have a talk with him after we set sail."

Wyntoun watched as the aging sailor moved off. He glanced skeptically down the ladder where this lad named Adam had disappeared. There was something that did not sit well about the boy. He shook his head. He trusted Coll with his life. The man had served Wyntoun for as long as he'd been sailing. And before that, Coll had sailed with Alexander.

He shook his head again and glanced ashore. She wouldn't do it. Not after last night. She trusted him. She had set her mind that Wyntoun would go and return for her before her sisters' message came from the north.

His eyes were drawn to the ladder as Gillie surfaced from below decks and excitedly ran toward Coll for his next set of orders. Gillie would have passed this Adam on his way up from below.

Wyntoun smiled at the boy. If Adrianne were on board, Gillie would not have left his mistress's side for all the gold in New Spain.

Alan called Wyntoun's name from the stern railing, and the Highlander cast one last glance in the direction of the ladder. Nay! Adrianne was no sailor. She would never come aboard unless she thought it was time to go after her mother . . . and Wyntoun was certain she had no suspicions in that regard.

He strode across the deck toward his ship's master. Adrianne was probably just stirring from her sleep at this very moment. Wyntoun smiled somewhat wistfully at the image of her rising from that bed.

The old sailor wearily eyed the young woman dressed in a lad's ragged clothing as she retched the contents of her belly into the bucket.

"I'm telling ye, mistress, I should be taking ye up there to yer husband's cabin, right now. If I had the sense of a jellyfish, I'd—"

"Nay, Master Coll," she groaned, barely lifting her head from the edge of the bucket. She had taken the oversized tam from her head, and tendrils of hair—so tightly braided on top of her head before—had escaped and were now framing her greenish-hued face. "You said yourself mid-afternoon should be the earliest we tell him. Sooner than that and he will be turning the ship around to take me back to Mull."

"Aye, mistress. But he'll be doing that only after he throws my carcass into the sea."

She heaved into the bucket again. A moment later, wiping her mouth on the back of the coarse sleeve of her wool shirt, she looked up at him. "You are not the one to blame, and I'll be sure to tell him that. You were only following the laird's orders in taking me along."

"And ye think that's some kind of an answer?" Leaning next to her, the man pried Adrianne's fingers off the edge of the bucket and handed her a clean one. "Knowing how angry the Blade will be, I'd say there'll be no mercy for anyone . . . and I do mean for *everyone*!"

A small shudder in the ship had her doubled over the bucket again. Coll shook his head.

"I cannot believe I let myself get drawn into the middle of this. I should have said 'nay' to the laird. I serve his son, now. And *you*, mistress"—he glared accusingly at Adrianne—"I don't know what kind of magic you used on the laird and his wife, for I've never known Himself to go along so willingly with such knavery."

She just couldn't let him go without her. Not now. Not after all that had happened over the past few days. She had to be with him . . . beside him. In a moment of madness last night, while the celebration of Jean was proceeding in high glee, Adrianne had approached Mara about this. Everyone in the castle, it seemed, was well aware of the rift that had formed between the newlyweds, so Mara had embraced the idea with characteristic energy.

Now, however, as Adrianne continued to retch into the bucket, she chided herself for acting so impulsively. Someday, she thought sourly, she would listen to Wyntoun.

"I shouldn't have . . . shouldn't have done this, Coll. I am no sailor."

"Trust me, it shows, mistress." Feeling genuinely sorry for her, Coll picked up a blanket off the floor and wrapped it around her shoulders.

The ship heeled over as it slipped into a trough, and Adrianne groaned again. "Are you certain I'll not be discovered down here?" She glanced about at the dimly lit hold of the ship. A few barrels were lashed to an aft bulkhead, but other than a few extra sails and some rough-hewn timber secured in a forward stall, the hold was empty.

"Aye, mistress." Coll got up and dragged some of the sails over. "But just in case someone comes down, just cover yerself with these. Ye'll be safe at least until nightfall. One of the lads will be sure to come down here looking for a place to sleep, but I'll keep a close eye out."

"Hopefully, we won't have to wait until nightfall."

"Nay, mistress. The ship is moving along at a goodly clip in this wind." He frowned as she started shivering violently and throwing up in the bucket again. He hoped she would make it to midday. "But let me send Gillie down, so the lad can keep an eye on ye."

She shook her head vehemently. "He knows nothing about me being on board and I want to keep it that way. The poor lad doesn't need any more trouble." Her one hand reached inside the pocket of the wool shirt she was wearing. She took out a small pouch. "Lady Mara gave this to me this morning. A powder to mix in a wee dram of water and drink to ease my stomach . . . in case I became seasick."

"Well, I'd say now is the time to use it, mistress, as I haven't seen anyone sicker than ye in all my years of sailing." He took the pouch from her trembling hand. "I'll go and mix this for ye and be back right quick."

Chapter 25

The Spanish-built galleon was closing quickly on the Blade of Barra's smaller carrack. Standing at the bow railing with Alan, Wyntoun peered across the rolling waters.

"Look at those colors, Wyn. Scurvy, dog-faced Danes!" the shipmaster muttered. The midday sun had burned through the gray morning mist, and the flags on the larger ship were easily visible in the rapidly diminishing distance. "And a wee bit insolent at having taken such a fine prize of a ship. Look how low she's riding in the sea. The bastards would have been smarter to stay their course and head for home. I don't believe they know who they're dealing with."

"Any voyage but this one and I would have been quite happy to take that ship and its belly full of gold. But I don't want a battle now. We've got another treasure that we're seeking."

"Well, Wyn, I don't think they're giving us much choice in the matter. They've picked a course to take us on, for sure, and you know we can't outrun them in this much wind."

Wyntoun stared out at the ship again. The galleon's cannons on the bow weather deck had clearly been positioned to fire on his ship. He could see men on board, as well, armed and ready. He quickly scanned the horizon for the Danish ship that had taken the galleon, but there was nothing in sight. That meant that there must be more than a few Spaniards still on that galleon who were being forced to sail the ship for the Danes. Not a fighting force with a great deal of heart.

"Then so be it, coz. Even from here you can see they smell blood."

"Aye, but 'tis their own blood they're smelling."

Wyntoun grinned. "Well, Alan, 'tis time we added a galleon to our fleet."

The Blade of Barra quickly assessed the situation. In just a few moments, the ships would be close enough for the galleon's guns to open fire. Judging from the speed and direction of the larger ship, Wyntoun was willing to wager that the galleon would then tack slightly and take a course parallel to that of his carrack. That would give the Danes ample opportunity to blast away at them until they decided it was safe enough to board.

"Hard to port, Alan. They've worked so hard moving their cannons to this side, we might as well hit her from the other! Cross through her wake as close to her stern as you can get her."

"Aye," Alan replied, his eyes gleaming. "Prepare to take some paint off that stern post!"

Orders were quickly passed, and within moments, the agile carrack swung over, now seemingly on a collision course with the galleon. The panic aboard the Dane's ship was immediate and evident. Men scurried in the rigging and on the decks.

"Coll!" Wyntoun shouted. "Prepare the guns on the bow weather deck and the lee side of the main deck. And get those men ready with the grappling lines!"

"Aye, m'lord," the aging sailor shouted back, turning to his duties. From where he stood on the stern deck, Wyntoun could see his warriors were prepared to swarm onto the galleon's deck.

"Wyn, we're going to take some fire from the—"

Alan's warning was cut off by the sound of the galleon's guns opening fire on the approaching carrack. A ball skipped once on the crest of a wave before crashing into the hull of the ship. Wyntoun looked up as two more ripped through the rigging above.

"Fire!" he shouted.

The sound of the returning cannon fire was deafening, and as the ships converged, the smoke became thick from the constant barrage. Then, when the carrack was no more than a ship's length from the foe, the galleon's guns hit the smaller ship with a combined blast that knocked a dozen Highlanders to their knees.

There was no time to assess the damage. The two ships were so close, Wyntoun could read the varied looks of shock and fear and exultation on the Danes' faces. An instant later, the galleon shot by the bow, and as the carrack crossed its wake, the bowsprit of the Scottish ship ripped through the Danish flag flying from the enemy's sternpost.

"Hard to lee!"

The carrack swung around like a hammer on a chain, banging alongside the galleon with great explosive cracks of wood on wood. The foe's ship—its wind momentarily robbed by the carrack's blocking sails—slowed and the grappling hooks arced through the air. The Scottish guns blasted away, cutting bloody swaths across the enemy's decks.

With the wild battle cry of their Celtic ancestors, the men of Mull swept across the divide and onto the galleon. Wyntoun had been correct. The Spaniards had no stomach for a fight, and the Danes were too few to offer much resistance. In moments the fiercest of the fighting was done, and the Blade of Barra stood on the stern deck of the captured ship, surveying the damage.

"Sir Wyntoun!" Gillie cried out from the deck of the carrack. "Master Coll is hurt!"

Firing orders at his warriors, Wyntoun grabbed a line and swung back across to the carrack. Alan and Gillie were crouching over the prostrate form of the old sailor.

"Coll!"

Alan looked up at him. "Appears the old seadog took a wee ding to the head."

Coll groaned, tried to sit, only to fall back, unconscious again.

"Will he be well, m'lord?" Gillie asked anxiously.

" 'Twill take more than that to keep Auld Coll down, lad," Wyntoun replied with a reassuring nod. As he turned to order two nearby sailors to see to Coll, a young lad ran up from below.

"Master Alan, the sea is coming in below!"

"What's that?"

"Aye, Turk sent me up to tell you that the ship is going to sink. He says to tell you the whole bow hull is smashed in at the waterline!"

The two men hurried below, only to find the lower third of the ship filled with seawater. It took Wyntoun only a moment to give his order.

"Damn them!" He scowled fiercely. "Alan, move all you can to the galleon. When you're ready, we'll cut free." He started up the ladder. "I've got the maps and a few other things in my cabin that I need to be getting."

In less than an hour, all had been moved to the galleon's deck, and the wreckage nearly cleared away. The Spanish-built ship had sustained little damage to its masts and rigging, and the surviving foes had been placed under guard below.

"You were right about the treasure, Wyn," Alan said with a rare grin as the knight climbed aboard. "The hold is bursting with gold and silver and chests full of emeralds and rubies from New Spain."

Wyntoun clapped his cousin on the shoulder with a satisfied nod, and then turned his attention to his new ship. "Well, do you think we can sail this wee gem?"

"Aye, Wyn . . . with our eyes closed, we can sail her."

With a smile, he handed Alan the oiled leather packet containing the Percy maps. "Secure these. And take a count of the men and the lads. We need to be cutting the carrack loose as soon as possible."

Wyntoun crossed the deck to where Gillie now sat beside Coll. The injured sailor's head was now bandaged, and his coloring and breathing were much improved. The old man was moaning and trying hard to regain consciousness.

"He'll be fine, Gillie." He gave the boy a reassuring pat on the back before rising to his feet. "Leave it to this old rogue to find a way to get out of helping with the cleaning of this mess."

Wyntoun moved to the railing where lines still held the carrack fast. He frowned at the damaged vessel. No matter how valuable this prize was, it saddened him to watch the carrack die. Many a storm had he ridden out on the smaller vessel. Many a battle had he fought from her decks.

Climbing over the side of the galleon and dropping onto the main deck of the heavily listing ship, the Highlander cast a despondent glance at the empty stern deck.

The carrack had served two generations of MacLeans. First Alexander and then Wyntoun. Walking toward the steps that led to his cabin, the Highlander's mind was crowded with memories of the past. He stopped and looked up into the rigging.

There was no saving her—he knew that. At least, she would die as a warrior should, he thought.

As Wyntoun climbed back aboard the galleon, Alan's face was the first one that he saw. "Everyone's accounted for. We lost only Jock—poor devil—and young Jemmy is missing a couple of fingers. But other than a few cuts and burns and bruises . . . and Coll . . . we're sound and hearty."

"Coll still insensible?" the Highlander asked, putting one leg over the railing.

"Aye. Gillie is still watching over him like a mother hen. But the old dog keeps moaning about someone named Adam."

"Aye. Adam, the smith's lad." Wyntoun said.

"Who?"

"Adam . . . the old blacksmith's son . . ." The Highlander's eyes narrowed as he surveyed the deck. "The lad that Coll brought aboard."

"I don't know of any Adam. The smith's lad is named Robbie." He, too, looked around. "Aye. There he is . . . by the windlass."

Wyntoun's face clouded over in an instant.

"The devil take her!" he growled, leaping back over the railing and landing on the carrack's deck.

"Adrianne!" he bellowed.

The Highlander ran to the forward castle where the crew quartered. As he moved down into the bowels of the ship, the sinking vessel groaned and lurched farther to port.

Perhaps it was the tightness that gripped his chest like a vise. Perhaps the sudden queasiness that churned in his belly. Whatever it was, Wyntoun knew that she was here—dressed as a lad named Adam—and about to go to the bottom of the sea on his own ship.

"*Adrianne!*"

The forecastle was empty, and he quickly returned to the main deck. The hatch cover was open and he dropped down into the gloomy hold. His boots splashed into a foul smelling mix of bilge and seawater.

"*Adrianne!*" he called out again.

Barrels were floating in the rising water, and Wyntoun pushed past them. In a moment he was waist deep in the icy water. The ship heeled over again, and the water rose higher.

"Wyn!" Alan's shout came from the deck above. "We need to cut her loose now!"

"Adrianne, where are you?" the Highlander shouted, ignoring his cousin.

Wyntoun thought he heard a weak cry.

For the briefest of moments his entire body went still. His heart hammered in his chest. Where had the noise come from?

Time was running short. Taking a chance, Wyntoun charged through the chest deep water, pushing toward a large group of barrels that were bobbing and banging hard against a bulkhead.

"Adrianne!" he shouted her name again.

There was a small whimper and that was all he needed. Summoning all his strength, he shoved away the casks. Only murky water greeted him.

An icy hand touched him somewhere below the knee, and he dove beneath the waters.

She was there. Her legs and arms were moving sluggishly as she struggled to push her head up in between the crowded barrels.

Wyntoun's arm wrapped around her waist and he dragged her back against his chest. She struggled for a moment in his arms, but in an instant they were both on the surface. Adrianne's intake of breath was the most welcome sound Wyntoun MacLean had ever heard. He turned her quickly in his arms, touching her face, checking her breathing, making certain that she was not hurt or injured in any way. He knew his hands were clumsy, his actions rushed, but the almost paralyzing fear that he'd nearly lost her dominated all other thoughts.

"Wyn!"

Alan's call from the deck above penetrated Wyntoun's brain. The water was sloshing back and forth in ever increasing waves. Adrianne was sagging like a dead woman against his chest. Lifting her high in his arms, Wyntoun pushed toward the ladder.

"What the devil . . . ?" Alan asked, leaning into the opening as Wyntoun climbed the ladder and handed Adrianne up. "By the—"

"Meet Adam, the smith's lad—or rather, my wife!"

"Not again!" Alan held Adrianne in a sitting position as Wyntoun climbed on deck after her. "Did anyone know she was here? By the saints, we could have left without her. She would have drowned, and we would never have known!"

"Save some of that until we have her on the galleon. It looks like this vessel is ready to go."

Their departure from the carrack was speedy, and Wyntoun ignored the commotion around them as they boarded the new ship, carrying her to the cabin in the stern, with an open-mouthed Gillie on his heels.

"Cut her free, Alan," the knight called over his shoulder as he disappeared below with his wife.

Below, he ordered Gillie to turn around as he stripped off Adrianne's wet clothing and wrapped her in warm blankets. She opened her eyes once and looked up at him and smiled. After that, she simply closed her eyes and dropped off to sleep. Peacefully, trustingly, she slept.

And, damn him, all he could do then was just sit beside her and hold her hand—feeling like a fool for not following his instincts when she'd come aboard—but thankful to have been given a second chance. He didn't want to even imagine what life would be like if the carrack had gone to the bottom with her aboard.

Adrianne had become more important to him than life itself. And the devil take him if he wouldn't work harder to make her understand the magnitude of his love. May he burn in hell, he told himself, if he didn't grow to be a better husband.

Chapter 26

Adrianne opened her eyes and stared vacantly at the dark oak beams of the ceiling. Scrolling vines of ivy leaves and roses had been painted in bright greens and reds and yellows along the exposed portions of the beams, and she smiled at the thought of some rough sailor devising such a lovely image.

She raised a hand to her forehead. It was a miracle. The headache that she had felt while she was just waking up was now gone. The floor no longer moved in great heaving swells beneath her. No longer could she taste the bile rising in her throat with each lurching slide of the vessel. She stretched her arms above her head and moved her feet. Her toes wiggled beneath linen bedclothes and she smiled.

And then the panic seized her.

By the Virgin, she'd intended to tell Wyntoun that she was aboard his ship. But it was too late! She sat up abruptly and looked around her. This chamber, though, was not the ship's cabin, and it was certainly not the carrack's dank hold!

The truth came back like a bolt of lightning. She'd been in the hold. Auld Coll had returned with a jar of water. She even remembered taking all Mara's medicine and feeling the sleep that had crept up on her shortly after. Adrianne even remembered thinking, as she'd dozed off, that the sleep would be a blessing after the relentless heaves that had been tearing her insides to shreds.

She remembered dreams of sea battles and the firing of cannons. And then the water. The incredible rush of cold water pushing her down with its weight. Serpents had risen from the depths, tangling her arms and legs and dragging her down. Her lungs had burned for air, but she had struggled against them. And then, she had been just a soul without a body, floating above the dark sea and watching her own physical form drifting in the ocean currents.

But then . . . the sound of Wyntoun calling! Like an archangel sweeping up from some distant earthly paradise, his voice had called her back from the very gates of heaven.

There had been no hesitation in Adrianne. She had known that she had to go to him. She had to help him find her . . . save her. And she had reached out a hand, and her husband had taken hold of her!

Adrianne brought trembling hands to her face. Vaguely, she recollected his hands upon her, wrapping her in warm blankets. She could remember opening her eyes and seeing his anxious face—such care and concern etched in the lines around his green eyes. She had known then that she was safe. That he was nearby to protect her.

So she had let herself drift back to sleep.

She lowered her hands and looked about the unfamiliar room again. A large bed, a carved wood chair with an embroidered pillow upon it, a large chest sitting against an inside wall. The peat fire in a brazier looked as if it had been recently tended. She turned her head and looked at the single, shuttered window of the room. The whirring of a sea wind could be heard outside.

Adrianne pushed the covers back and stepped onto the braided rushes that covered the floor. She was barefoot. Instead of the boy's clothing she had been dressed in when she'd left Duart Castle, she was now wearing a warm, long-sleeved, wool nightgown.

She was grateful for the warmth of the garment as she moved to the window and opened the shutter. The blast of wintry air hit her full in the face. She pushed her long black mane over her shoulders and peered out at the steep slope of land that dropped away below her window. Just below a series of defensive walls, a broad and gray-green river stretched from left to right, and a rolling moor dotted with bracken and pine rose beyond it.

It seemed that she was on top of a rock. In a castle on

top of a rock, she corrected, leaning out the window and looking from side to side at the impressive stone structure perched so high above the river. Looking up and down the river as far as she could see, Adrianne perceived no sign of Wyntoun's ship.

"He has left me behind," she whispered with dismay. He must have stopped at this place—wherever it was—and simply dropped her off before continuing on his journey.

Not that she had any right to complain about what he had done. She had been at fault again. Irresponsible—thoughtless—impulsively going where she shouldn't have, with no thought of the consequences.

But the ship, she thought in panic. Muddled memories of the carrack taking water through gaping holes in its hull. Whatever happened to Wyntoun's ship? Was it all a dream? And what of the rest—the other cabin where he had taken her?

She moved away from the window and frantically searched the room for something to wear. Running to the wooden chest, she was about to open it when the chamber door opened, and Adrianne whirled to face a well-dressed, silver-haired woman.

Adrianne gathered her unruly hair to one side and nodded hesitantly to the new arrival.

"Good morn," she said cautiously.

"Good day, mistress. But I'm afraid I must tell you 'tis afternoon already." The woman's gentle smile was warm and welcoming. She held a gray, woolen dress draped over her arm, and carried stockings and shoes in her hand.

"My name is Bridget. I run the household here." Following Adrianne's gaze to the dress, she smiled. "Hearing that your own clothing was lost in the voyage, I brought one of Lady Celia's daughter's dresses for you to wear. She wouldn't hear of us bringing you any other. Just about the same size as you, too, I should say."

"Lady Celia?" Adrianne asked, as she gratefully accepted the dress from the older woman and carried it to the bed. She looked steadily at Bridget. "Where am I, if I might ask? And who is Lady Celia?"

"Why, Lady Celia Campbell! You are at Dumbarton Castle, mistress. This castle belongs to the earl of Argyll, Lord Colin Campbell. Of course, Kildalton Castle is the place where the family spends most of their time." Bridget moved across the chamber to the open window. "'Twas very fortunate that the earl and his wife were here when you arrived. That's the River Clyde down below."

"Near Glasgow?"

"Aye, mistress. Not even a couple of hours away, with a good small boat and a favoring breeze."

As the woman closed the shutter, Adrianne quickly donned the clothes and stared at her visitor. She had heard so much about the powerful Colin Campbell and his influence in Scottish politics. She had also heard so many stories about his courageous wife—the woman warrior who had saved the life of the infant King Jamie in the aftermath of the fatal battle at Flodden Field.

But how had she ended up so close to Glasgow?

"Was I brought here by my husband?"

"Aye, mistress."

"But I thought . . . I thought the MacLeans and Campbells are not on the best of terms."

Bridget averted her eyes. "All I know, mistress, is that there are some things that can bind even the fiercest of enemies."

"Do you know where my husband has gone?"

"Gone?" The older woman went to the chest and withdrew a shawl of Campbell plaid for Adrianne. "Why, he's still here, mistress. Lord Colin and Lady Celia have been receiving a number of other visitors for the past week."

These were the best words that she'd heard the woman utter yet. So, Wyntoun had not been so angry that he'd left her behind. She excitedly pulled on the hose and the soft leather shoes. She had to see him. She had to explain everything. Finding her on board the ship the way he had . . . there must have been so much confusion.

Master Coll! Her heart sank. The poor old sailor must have taken the brunt of Wyntoun's anger.

The words she must say all jumbled in Adrianne's mind as Bridget calmly laced up the back of the dress. Adrianne knew she herself was completely to blame. Aye, completely to blame for loving him too much. She had to see him. She had to explain.

Wrestling her hair into some semblance of order was a challenge. Again, however, the older woman came to her aid, forcing Adrianne to sit while she braided her hair.

"Lady Celia is anxious to meet you in the Great Hall when you are ready. Since arriving from Kildalton Castle, she's been quite busy, but I know that she expressly asked for you . . ."

Bridget continued to speak as she worked, but Adrianne's mind was reeling with all that she had to explain to her husband. He had to be angry with her. In stowing away on his ship, she had all but slapped him in the face and said that she didn't trust him. Indeed, in going along, she'd betrayed his trust.

As the old woman tucked the last strands in place, Adrianne was out of the chair and moving toward the door with a murmur of appreciation. Adrianne paused at the open door just long enough to glance back at the amused Bridget.

"But which way do I go?"

"The levels are a wee bit skimble skamble at Dumbarton, due to the rock we sit upon. But you'll find only one flight of stairs going that way. 'Twill take you down to the first floor. Keep to your right, and you'll be in the Great Hall before you know it."

"I cannot thank you enough," Adrianne replied with a quick smile.

"And pay no mind to the dogs. They're old but frien—"

The rest of Bridget's words were lost as the young woman ran down the narrow corridor.

The castle appeared much older than Duart Castle, but from the smell of mortar and whitewash in the air, Adrianne had a feeling the old keep was undergoing repairs. At the top of the stairwell, she almost ran into a surprised serving boy, about Gillie's age, loaded down with an armful of peat. A black dog trailed after him.

"Good day, mistress!" The lad peered at her over a freckled nose.

"Good day to you, too." Adrianne smiled, pressing against the wall so the young fellow could get past her.

"Can I help you with anything, mistress?"

Adrianne thought for a moment and then she nodded.

"As a matter of fact, you can. I am in search of my husband, Sir Wyntoun MacLean. Would he be in the Great Hall?"

"Nay, I've just come through there, mistress." The lad adamantly shook his head. "He and Lord Colin and all the other men are still gathered in the armory in the White Tower."

"And where is the armory in the White Tower?"

"At the bottom of these steps, you'll find a door out into the courtyard. If you follow the wall and walk up the hill a wee bit, you'll see the tower straight on."

Adrianne frowned, thinking aloud. "If there are others there, then perhaps 'twould be best if I wait in the Great Hall."

The serving lad chirped in. "They've been at it since mid-morning, mistress, with nary a thing to eat. I'd say by the time you got up there, they could well be out and about."

Adrianne had to speak with her husband in private. She had to convince him—nay, force him to understand that she hadn't meant any disloyalty. And perhaps waiting outside—until those men were finished with their meeting—was the answer. She could talk to him there, once the others had all returned to the Great Hall.

She thanked the freckled serving boy and headed down the stairs and out the door of the keep.

The air was crisp, the day bright beneath the afternoon sun. On the far side of the courtyard, a number of sail-like tarps had been hung on wood frames like market stalls, and dozens of warriors milled about three or four cookfires. None looked her way, though, as she followed the wall.

In a few moments Adrianne spotted the tower up the steep hill, though it was hardly white. The stone was the same brownish gray as the rest of the castle, but it was the only tower in sight. There were no signs of anyone leaving the building, and no one stood guard at the base, so Adrianne climbed the hill, hesitating a short distance from the oak door that led into the tower.

The wind was gusting intermittently, and she could feel it cruelly through the wool dress. Even with the shawl wrapped around her, Adrianne was starting to feel a little weak from the exertion of her walk, and the cold was not helping. Running her hands up and down her arms, she shifted her weight from one foot to the other.

She couldn't let herself get sick and come down with a fever. This was certainly trouble that she didn't need to add to her husband's worries.

She stared at the door of the tower for a moment more and then strode directly to it. Pushing it open, she peeked into the dim entry level of the building. There was no one inside, so—building her courage—Adrianne slipped in, closing the door on a blast of icy wind.

Up a narrow stairway that followed the line of the wall, she could hear the sound of muffled voices. The words were not quite intelligible, but the tones were clear as they alternated between excited and calm, agitated and reasonable. And then she heard Wyntoun's voice.

Climbing the stairs, Adrianne found herself on a landing outside a stout door of studded and ironbound oak. No sounds came from the chamber, and she looked up the stairs toward the next level. The oak door in front of her was closed, but the air was warmer here. She gnawed her lip, undecided whether to wait in the warmer chamber or just stay where she was on the landing.

Suddenly, the discussion began again, with a number of men trying to be heard over the others.

Borders . . . Henry . . . Percy . . .

Her family name was one of the words being tossed about, but the gist of the discussion was unclear. And then one deep voice rose above the others.

"We cannot let you go about this alone, Henry."

There was some rumbling and a smattering of "aye's" among the group.

"Nichola might have left willingly."

Adrianne found herself flush against the door, her hands on the latch.

"She would *not* have. Not after our marriage."

"But she had been taken as a prisoner. Betrayed by those whom she trusted."

"She would not have gone with that monk of her own free will. She was taken, I tell you!"

Before she knew it, Adrianne was standing inside the chamber. A brawny knight wearing a chain shirt turned with a look of surprise, considered for the briefest of moments, and then stood aside for her to enter. A smell of incense hung in the air. Knights and warriors and priests alike stood and stared at her for a long moment of silence. On the wall, above a storage rack of halberds and spears and swords, a large cross had been hung. Upon it, a blue veil fringed with gold had been draped with obvious care.

Her gaze lingered on the veil, a memory stirring in her brain. A feeling of familiarity tugged at her consciousness . . . a feeling of trust. She turned her focus on the faces of the men in the chamber.

"I heard you mention Nichola Percy." She couldn't stop the strange quiver in her voice. Her knees felt suddenly weak. She took a step forward and spoke more forcefully. "If you have news of my mother, I need to know it."

Silence was the only reply she received. As she looked from face to war-scarred face, coldness and sometimes disdain were all she could read there.

"The information that my sisters and I received was that she was already imprisoned in England, but now I am hearing something quite different . . ."

The words withered in her throat. Never in her entire life had Adrianne felt more like an intruder than now. Never had she felt more unwelcome—more disliked—even in the company of the abbess on Barra. And yet, these were men who so much reminded her of Edmund Percy, her father. Her gaze fell on the cross again.

Ah . . . that was it! Women were forbidden here! Adrianne didn't know how she knew it, but words of admonishment from her childhood rattled in her head.

"She has every right to know."

The voice, strong and confident, spoke from somewhere to her right. Wyntoun! Adrianne took a deep breath and fought back the tears of relief that were pooling in her eyes. A murmur of surprise rippled through the throng.

"Adrianne and her sisters are the ones who have suffered the most. They *must* be told."

She didn't realize that she was trembling until she felt Wyntoun's warm and steady arm encircle her waist. She felt him beside her, but she didn't dare look up with the fear of losing what was left of her composure.

"Haven't these Percy women done enough damage?" Adrianne's attention was drawn to the hostility in the words and the tone of a gray-robed priest standing near the cross.

"'Tis hardly fair to blame them for their misfortunes, Sir Peter." She knew this voice. The same man who had been speaking Nichola's name earlier. A very familiar voice. She didn't dare, though, to turn and put a face to the man. "There has been no damage done that we know of. And if there is blame to be allotted, then let it be spread here, among us. Aye, *we*—the Knights of the Veil—must bear the blame for not taking better care of our brother's kin after his death at the hands of Henry Tudor!"

A rumble of dissension among the group followed his heated words. Like a statue, Adrianne remained where she was. It was a miracle that she could manage to draw a breath.

"Take the woman out of this pious assembly," one of the older knights called out. "We can send a message to her with whatever information we deem appropriate."

"Out with the woman!" another shouted.

"The daughter does not belong here."

"She intrudes on holy work!"

"She stays!" Wyntoun's sharp words silenced the chamber. Adrianne closed her eyes for an instant to fight away the tears. Her fingers entwined with his at her side. "'Tis her family that we have been discussing. 'Tis the very life of her mother that we speak of now."

"This breaks with all tradition," chided the priest who had been called Sir Peter. "As a woman, she does not deserve to be given leave to speak before the Knights of the Veil."

"My wife *is* deserving! Adrianne Percy *deserves* to be standing here with any one of you." A quiet fury laced Wyntoun's words. "She is worthy of standing here *instead* of some of you."

She glanced up to see Wyntoun's piercing green eyes sweep the chamber.

"She is a woman, true. But she is a warrior at heart. She is a fighter as well as a healer, a guardian of good as her father before her proved himself to be." As a murmur went around the room, Wyntoun's words gentled, his gaze resting on individual faces. "We should all be as indifferent to our needs as this woman has proved to be. She is brave, self-sacrificing, and as true to our cause as we each strive to be."

Adrianne felt a renewed sense of life and energy seep into her as she listened to Wyntoun's words. She felt his strength pour into her as she continued to hold his hand tightly at her side.

"There was another woman, once, who lived her life to those same standards." She saw her husband's eyes focus on the cross and the blue veil. "I appeal to the Knights of the Veil to allow Adrianne Percy MacLean to stay."

A loud murmur rippled across the chamber.

"I second that appeal." This time Adrianne turned to look at the knight who had spoken before on behalf of her mother and her family. She couldn't hide her joy at seeing Sir Henry Exton push through the group and come to stand beside her.

"I also support the appeal," a deep voice called out from somewhere among the assembly. Adrianne watched as an older, powerfully built Highlander pushed away from an outside wall and made his way toward them. From the elaborate brooch at his shoulder to the confidence in his step, she had a feeling that her latest ally must be Lord Colin Campbell, the earl of Argyll.

As strong as the surge to reject her had been earlier, the swelling current of acceptance was even more forceful—more potent. The faces became a teary blur as the men called out in her support. Adrianne knew, though, that this time was not one for a show of emotions or even for a display of gratitude. This was the time to show the strength that her husband so had eloquently credited her with.

Sir Peter, the warlike priest standing by the cross, was the last one who finally gave her a nod of acceptance.

Adrianne forced herself to absorb as much as she could as various members of the assembly spoke to her. Gradually, the information about the Knights of the Veil and her father's lifelong involvement became known to her. It all made sense, now. All the memories from her childhood. All the visits by scholars and priests and knights from all over Europe.

They told her, then, that the Treasure of Tiberius did not belong to the Percy family. Her father had only been a guardian of the sacred trust—the *Keeper of the Map*, they called him. What clearly distressed many of them was the way her mother had divided the map to Tiberius and sent the three sections into three remote corners of Scotland, where Adrianne and her sisters had been sent. Instead of condemnation though, many of the knights simply expressed their commitment to securing the treasure, while others assured her that they would find Lady Nichola and deliver her from their enemies.

There was one bit of information that struck Adrianne with the force of a blow. Her mother's abduction had been planned and executed by the Knights of the Veil themselves as a ploy to bring back the maps to Tiberius. From the start, there had been no intention of handing Nichola to King Henry of England. Moved from castle to castle, her final stopping place had been at Sir Henry Exton's keep in the Borders region.

"And there, Adrianne, your mother accepted my proposal of marriage. We were wed nearly a month ago." Sir Henry's blue eyes showed his inner torment. "But the very protection that I promised her with my vow of marriage, I failed so miserably to provide. Lady Nichola vanished one day in spite of my diligence."

"Sir Henry, you have no idea where she went or who abducted her?" It seemed as if these were the first words she had spoken since entering the chamber.

Henry's gaze cleared as it met Adrianne's. A silent message passed between them that both understood. In his eyes she could see gratitude for her acceptance of the marriage.

He had always been a true friend to her family. Adrianne knew he still cherished that position.

"It appears she may have been tricked into going. The morning of her disappearance, she had requested an audience with a priest." He frowned fiercely. "Though I had no knowledge of his arrival, I believe the priest who went to see your mother was Benedict, the monk well known to your parents and your family."

"Benedict was, until recently, a trusted member of this Brotherhood," Wyntoun added. "We have strong suspicions now, however, that the monk has only his own interests at heart."

"We received word that Benedict secretly met with Thomas Cranmer, the Archbishop of Canterbury, during your father's imprisonment," one of the knights said.

Sir Henry Exton gazed steadily into Adrianne's face. "The Treasure of Tiberius has always been more myth than truth to those outside of our circle. We believe that Benedict went to Thomas Cranmer to confirm the existence of it and to seek assistance—and funding—in his quest to possess it. The glory of possessing such a treasure would shine equally on all of them."

"Though his early efforts to take your sisters failed," Wyntoun said, "he must have decided that taking your mother was an even better target than you or your sisters. The monk thinks his abduction of Nichola will be the key to bargaining successfully for Tiberius."

"But where would he take her?" As fury burned in her cheeks, Adrianne found her strength returning, as well. "Do you think he's turned her over to Henry Tudor or Archbishop Cranmer?"

"Not yet. In fact, the word we get from friends of ours who are close to the English king is that Henry Tudor is completely unaware of both Tiberius and Archbishop Cranmer's dealings with Benedict." Colin Campbell stood outside the group surrounding Adrianne, and all eyes turned to him. "Keeping Nichola is the monk's only chance of wresting the maps from you and your sisters. Though we're not certain of the truth of it yet, we received a message this morning that

Benedict was seen in the company of a group of outlaws who recently served under the banner of the late Sir Arthur Courtenay. They were traveling southward, toward Kilmarnock in Ayrshire."

"Is there no way to stop him?" she asked with dismay, taking a couple of steps toward the earl and then turning back to Wyntoun. "Surely, they cannot be too far ahead of us."

Wyntoun nodded in agreement. "But there are a number of well-fortified keeps in Ayrshire where they could be hiding your mother. And the first thing we must do before cornering Benedict is to make certain that Nichola will not be injured in an attack. Benedict is as ruthless as he is cunning. He surely will use your mother to ward off any direct assault by us."

Colin Campbell agreed. "We also need to consider how committed Thomas Cranmer is to the pursuit of Tiberius. From what we've learned, I believe the archbishop is waiting for Benedict to bring him the glorious prize, so Cranmer himself can present it to the king. But we cannot be sure, and the last thing we want to do is create a situation that will bring English armies up against Scottish warriors. We are not quite ready to engage in another bloodbath."

Adrianne knew that the earl of Argyll was talking about the battle at Flodden Field, where ten thousand men had died in a single day. She was well aware of this history from her mother.

"He will not harm Nichola Percy," another knight put in. "Not so long as there is a chance he can trade her for Tiberius."

"Benedict knows better than to think that the Knights of the Veil will ever part with Tiberius again . . . no matter what the loss of life might be!"

Wyntoun nodded in agreement with Sir Peter Wrothsey, the fierce-visaged priest. "But he also knows the stubbornness of the Percy daughters and their husbands. He knows they will do anything to save Lady Nichola's life."

Adrianne stared for a moment at Wyntoun's face. His steely expression showed nothing of what he was thinking. She knew, though, that her mother would never be saved by turn-

ing over the Treasure of Tiberius to Benedict, or to Thomas
Cranmer, or to anyone else.

The daylight filtering in through the high, narrow win-
dows was growing dim when the meeting finally adjourned.
Adrianne stayed behind with Wyntoun and Sir Henry and
Colin Campbell, though, after the others had filed out.

The graying hair at the temples of the earl bespoke the
maturity of Argyll's years, and yet something about the man's
latent strength hinted at the vitality of eternal youth. He
clasped her hand warmly in his own.

"I was as proud of you as I know your father would have
been, were he here among us this day. You have his spirit
and his courage." He let go of her hand and clasped Wyntoun by the arm, giving him a fatherly smile. "You've done
well, Blade. Better than any of us would ever have hoped
for you."

Argyll nodded to Sir Henry. "Celia is anxious to meet all
of you. Come as soon as you can."

As the earl left the chamber, Adrianne felt Sir Henry's
hand upon her arm.

"Adrianne," he said solemnly, "I know that among your
sisters, you were the closest to your father. I remember your
mother saying that you were the son Edmund never had. "

She smiled sadly. In her heart she sometimes wondered if
this, perhaps, was part of the reason for her impulsiveness,
for her recklessness in the face of danger, for her sheer enjoyment in going where her sisters would not go.

"I want you to know that I respected Edmund. I cherished
his friendship. And for all the years that I was invited to
spend time with your family, I never harbored a dishonorable
thought regarding Lady Nichola." Henry's words rang out
with the weight of his confessions. "But the years have passed,
and my affection for your mother has grown so deep . . ."

She shook her head and moved toward him. "You don't
have to explain any of this to me, Sir Henry."

At seeing the surprise on his face, she moved closer and
hugged him tightly. His hands were bands of steel as they
closed around her. "I know what a true friend you were to

my father and to the rest of us. And I know how valuable your companionship could be to my mother now. So please don't explain." She looked up until her gaze met his. "Nichola chose you, and that's all the explanation my sisters and I would ever need."

As she stepped out of his arms, Wyntoun was there to take her hand.

"I'm riding south immediately," Sir Henry said. "My men are hunting for Benedict now. We will keep our distance, but we will be ready when the time comes to get her back."

"I know you will." She nodded reassuringly at Sir Henry, feeling her husband's strength feeding her own.

When Henry left the armory, only Adrianne and Wyntoun remained. She looked about the ancient chamber—the sacred cross, the cloth of blue. She remembered the respect the Knights had shown her husband. The Blade of Barra was clearly a hero to them—a leader in their cause—and Adrianne felt shame for all she had done to make his life difficult.

There was too much that needed to be explained. Too many errors she'd made that she had to mend. What she had heard clarified so much for her—Wyntoun's motive for wanting the maps, his right to bring them back to the Knights of the Veil. And then, there was her false scheming that served to make him take her as his wife.

Aye, there was so much to explain, and yet she didn't know where to start—or how she would dare to start! What would happen if there were no forgiveness left in him?

"Adrianne!" His large hand lifted her chin until their gazes locked. "We need to talk."

"There was no ship," she blurted out, deciding to start from the beginning. "At least no ship that would be of any use to you. 'Tis true . . . I lied! I am sorry, Wyntoun, but I had to lie to convince you—"

"What ship?" he asked, his brow furrowed.

"The galleon that I promised you . . . the one that belonged to my father. The one I said was still anchored on the Isle of Man." She could feel her face burn with the weight of her guilt. "I told you that it would be waiting there for you, after you helped me rescue my mother."

"Adrianne—"

She shook her head, refusing to meet his gaze. "I was deceitful. I know I said that my sisters and my mother would agree to give up the ship to you. I said that they would gladly relinquish their claim on it." She wrung her hands before her. "Don't misunderstand me. My family would gladly have let you have it, if there *were* a ship left worth having."

He opened his mouth, but she pressed her fingers to his lips. She had to tell him all of this now. Suddenly, she couldn't live another moment without unburdening herself of the guilt that had been weighing on her for so long.

"You see, there was a new-built galleon at one time, one that had been specially built for my father. But he never had the chance to sail it. A mishap on deck caused the vessel to burn at the quay just as the builders were nearly finished with it." She stared down at the tips of her shoes. "I lied to you, knowing you were in search of a new galleon and—"

"Adrianne, I knew your father through the Knights of the Veil . . . and I knew about his misfortune with the burned galleon." Wyntoun reached for her hand, his voice softening. "'Twas no secret to me that there would be no galleon awaiting my men once our search was finished."

She stared at him, openmouthed. "Knowing my lie . . . you still agreed to marry me?"

"Aye. And I have a confession, as well. Before you even asked me, I knew I would be marrying you. 'Twas the only way to gain the trust of your sisters and secure the maps that your mother had sent to each."

Anger flashed through her, but dissipated instantly as she looked into his eyes. Adrianne could see that Wyntoun was determined that no more secrets lay between them, and she felt the same way. He was choosing his words with great care, and she could feel his hesitancy. Wyntoun touched her cheek and held her gaze.

"But I would have married you, anyway. I think you knew I was enthralled by your beauty and your wit and your passion for life. And then later . . . I fell in love with you. Hopelessly, madly in love with you. You are my life, Adrianne. My very existence."

The pooling of tears in her eyes and the gentle heat rising in her cheeks was a sweet picture of victory. But Wyntoun knew he couldn't stop there. She had to know it all. He placed his arms around her and drew her closer. He would give her no chance to escape him until she'd heard this last confession.

"Adrianne, the actions I have taken have served to put your mother in jeopardy."

"Nay. The Knights of the Veil ordered her capture," she replied softly.

"At my bidding." He felt her back stiffen, and he held on tighter. "I was staying at Blackfearn Castle, and your sister Laura was marrying my friend, William Ross. Already, I had been contacted by the monk Benedict and had discovered his twisted plans. Time was running short, and if we were not to find those maps ourselves, then Benedict or any number of treasure seekers like him could have succeeded before us."

"You could have asked us for it, and we would have given it to you."

"Would you?" he asked. "Why would you have trusted us—a group of men unknown to you? Why would you have trusted the Blade of Barra, a pirate whose motives must surely be mercenary?"

She continued to stare at him—without an answer.

"I was chosen by the Knights of the Veil to bring back the treasure, but so far as I could see, my only chance lay in convincing you and your sisters that Lady Nichola was already at the mercy of King Henry."

"*You* ordered my mother's abduction!"

"Aye. I knew that you and your sisters would go to any lengths to gain her freedom." Wyntoun looked steadily into her eyes. "But I never intended her any harm. Although she was kept unaware, the people who initially took her were the very friends from the manor house she had just left. Later, we arranged for her to stay only in the households of people who had been allies of your father. She was a fugitive from the English king, so we made certain that she be moved

often. We wanted her to fall into no hostile hands. That is
how she came to stay at Sir Henry Exton's castle in the Borders."

He reached out and wiped away the single tear that
splashed onto her cheek. "I do not absolve myself of the guilt
of losing her to Benedict, but I truly believed she had a greater
chance of safety among us."

Adrianne's chin dropped for a long moment, and Wyntoun
held his breath waiting for her response. He needed her to
trust him—but more so, he wanted the chance to earn back
her love.

"You already had the three portions of the map with you
when you left Duart Castle, didn't you?"

"Aye," he said, nodding. "The messengers I sent to Balvenie Castle came back with the maps. But I couldn't tell
you about it or take you with me. I had planned to clear up
the matter of Nichola's captivity first, before involving you."

She finally looked up. "Have you found the treasure?"

"Nay! We came ashore only yesterday, and I've had no
chance to decipher the symbols on the map."

"Will you let me stay and help you with the rest?"

"The gates of hell could not separate us now!"

Her eyes narrowed. "And on which side of the gates of
hell do you envision me, might I ask?"

He grinned, relief washing over him at her response. "You
tell me on which side my bonny firebrand belongs . . . for that
is where I will be, as well!"

She continued to scowl, though he could see the glint in
her eyes. "If you think this is the way to win me over—"

"Why not tell me of some other way, hellcat." Desire for
her surged through him. He moved to put his arms around
her again, but she placed a hand on his chest.

"Very well. To start with, never, ever, ever—under pain of
death—ever scold me over being a stowaway on your ship
on this last trip."

"Hmmm." His temper flared at the memory. "Do you know
how dangerous a thing 'twas to hide aboard a sh—"

She rose onto her tiptoes and glared into his face. "Never!
Ever! Remember?"

Though he resisted the urge to smother her lips beneath his own, he could not help but smile.

"And anything else, my fiery one?"

"You will never, ever, ever—also under pain of death—go without me on any lengthy sea journey?"

"But you are no sailor, my love."

"I will learn to be," she said flatly.

He shook his head. "As there were on this journey, there are too many dangers that I cannot predict."

"Were there dangers?" she asked.

"Only a wee battle with some Danish blackguards who shot our carrack out from under us!"

"Oh! And how did the battle turn out?"

"As a matter of fact, we are now the proud owners of a new Spanish-built galleon, courtesy of the Danes."

"Were there any injuries?" An immediate frown of concern creased her brow.

"We lost a sailor named Jock, and there were a few missing fingers."

"I am sorry," she whispered quietly. "Gillie? Did he fare well?"

"The lad took to the battle like a hawk. I think the only thing that had him nervous was Auld Coll getting dinged in the head early on . . . but Coll has a skull nearly as thick as Bull's."

She nodded with relief. "Where are your people now? Where is the ship?"

"Alan took the galleon . . . and Gillie . . . back to Duart Castle. The entire crew seemed eager to put the ship to rights."

"Was it a fierce battle, Wyntoun? Was there a great deal that I missed?"

He laughed. "'Twas nothing. Hardly worth waking you for, I'd say."

"You see then? Having me along was no problem, at all." Adrianne smiled shyly as another thought struck her. "I think you should always take me along. Just consider the added bounty of having me on board the ship with you."

"Bounty, you say." Again his body was taking control. He reached for her, and this time she stepped into his arms. "Let me see. Keeping an eye on you night and day. That's an added bounty, to be sure. Curtailing your mischief. Aye, that's an added bounty." Her hands crept up his chest and encircled his neck. "Taking you to bed and ravishing you anytime I desire . . . that is a tremendous bounty, now that you mention it."

She rose again onto her toes and kissed him with such passion that all of his doubts were washed away. Before he lost complete control, though, Wyntoun broke off the kiss and stared into her deep blue eyes.

"So does this mean you've forgiven me?"

Wyntoun had heard it said that a person's eyes are the windows of the heart. Looking into Adrianne's now, he knew this to be true.

"Wyn, there was nothing that you could have done that I would not have been able to forgive . . . not after what you did for me this day." Her arms were still wound tight around his neck. "You stood beside me. Defended me. Fought for my right. By all that is good, Wyntoun MacLean, I love you more than life itself. And this day you showed me your love. There is nothing more to forgive!"

Chapter 27

"The Treasure of Tiberius is another gospel. It is a gospel told by the Virgin Mary herself!"

Adrianne stared into the face of her hostess.

In person, Lady Celia Muir Campbell was just as Adrianne had always imagined her to be, the very picture of beauty, bravery, and grace. And she obviously had a wealth of knowledge to share. Stealing Adrianne away from all the activities of the castle, Lady Celia had brought the younger woman to her own sitting room.

They both knew that Wyntoun would be coming for Adrianne in a few short moments, for several Knights of the Veil were to meet once again to try to decipher the cryptic symbols on the maps. She was grateful for her husband's continued insistence that she should be included in these meetings, but for the moment nothing would tear her away from Lady Celia.

"What I know of Tiberius is a collection of gossip, myth, and snatches of information that Colin has over the years shared with me." Lady Celia's voice lowered despite the closed door. "Believers and dreamers insist the very parchment itself has power."

"What kind of power?"

"Mystical power. Miraculous power. The power to heal," Celia answered. "Whether it does or not, though, it certainly has temporal power. For the person who possesses it and uses it for his own gain, can control masses of believers all across Europe."

"A manuscript." Adrianne found herself barely breathing. Her skin felt feverish. "In all the years my sisters and I studied Scripture, we were never told of the existence of a gospel according to Mary."

"No one is told. No one knows." Celia's intelligent dark eyes shone despite the shadows of the room.

Adrianne ran her clammy hands over her skirt. "And is it truly the Virgin Mother's words?"

Celia nodded. "My husband saw the manuscript many years ago, before 'twas hidden away again. The story is Mary's—told to a scribe in the last years of her life. It begins at the point where she found herself with child but had no husband. 'Tis a record of everything—the struggle, and suffering, the rise and fall and rise again of her son and his teachings, the years of great uprisings, the years of change and finally . . . the days of peace."

Amazed, Adrianne sat staring at her hands and listening as Lady Celia continued to speak, telling her of the turbulent history surrounding the treasure and of Edmund Percy's role in that history.

The young woman thought of the importance of such a manuscript in the present time. With Henry Tudor's men burning and looting the monasteries in the south, with the church in Europe in disarray as it was, Adrianne could see the power that such a relic could wield. If you possessed it, you could control vast numbers of people. You could control their spirit. Their very beliefs.

For the first time, she could understand Benedict's true motives. It was so simple. He wanted power.

Adrianne could see now the betrayal that some of these people must have seen in her mother's actions, dividing and sending the maps into the farthest reaches of Scotland. But she fervently believed that Nichola had wanted to keep the sections safe. With Wyntoun helping them Adrianne knew her mother's name would be cleared at the end. Nichola Percy . . . or rather Nichola Exton . . . was no villain.

"Lady Celia, do you know how was it came about that my husband joined this Brotherhood?"

Celia laughed. " 'Tis good that you ask me this question, for I cannot see Sir Wyntoun boasting of his good deeds."

"Good deeds?"

"Aye, of course. Aside from his prowess as a warrior, Wyntoun MacLean has been providing huge sums from his pirating to build the new university in Glasgow. 'Tis a special interest of my husband's, so I know for a fact that most of what the Blade of Barra has gained on the seas has gone into education. But what I like best about Wyntoun's efforts is that he has never given to the university at St. Andrews, where he himself was educated. Instead, he and my husband have been working together to build an institution that educates the children of ministers, burgesses, and farmers here in the west. Without question, it was because of his generosity and bravery that the Knights of the Veil had invited him to—"

The knock on the door of the chamber silenced the women, and they both smiled at the tall knight who eyed them with suspicion as he entered the chamber.

The armory in the White Tower glowed with the light of a dozen torches. In the center of the chamber, three figures huddled in deep thought around a table.

Adrianne glanced with interest at the group before smiling politely at the short thin man standing next to her. The Baron Avandale was not only a Knight of the Veil but also a distant relation of John Stewart, her sister Catherine's new husband.

"How much do you know, m'lady?"

"Some." Adrianne replied tactfully as she moved away from the hearth and edged closer to the trio in the middle. The baron stayed beside her.

"I have been given leave to tell you that the Treasure of Tiberius is a sacred manuscript, written in the ancient language of the Aramaeans. The manuscript was found in the city of Tiberius in the Palestine by Fulk of Anjou, King of Jerusalem in the seventh year of his reign, the year of Our Lord 1138."

The young woman nodded, her gaze fixed on Wyntoun, who was transcribing a list of the symbols on the maps on a sheet of vellum. Colin Campbell and the priest, Sir Peter Wrothsey, looked on, commenting occasionally as he worked.

"Many years ago, the Knights of the Veil became concerned about the manuscript itself breaking down, crumbling away to dust," the baron continued. "The decision was made . . . it needed to be translated. Edmund Percy was given the task of taking the manuscript and relocating it for the purpose of translation and preservation. Always in the past had a member of the Knights of the Veil preserved it, protected it, and kept the manuscript's history alive. They were planning to continue the tradition for the next five hundred years . . . or until the Second Coming. Being a member of the Brotherhood and being the expert in ancient languages that he was, your father was assigned as the next keeper of Tiberius."

Adrianne's father, though still a young man, had been the perfect person to carry out the task. He was a scholar as well as a Knight of the Veil. He was given the task of overseeing the translation of the text into Greek and Latin and—after a great deal of discussion—into English.

Though Adrianne already knew most of this from her talk with Lady Celia, she chose silence, moving closer and glancing at Wyntoun's list as the baron continued. A cross planted in the ground. An M with a cross over it. The letter A repeated . . . ten times. A decorated number 7 in a square . . .

"Edmund Percy was to hide the treasure and secure this map you see before you." The baron pointed to the pieces that the other three were intently poring over. "There is one other copy of this map, and that is buried beneath the crypt of St. Peter in Rome, under the altar of the great church that is being built there . . . that is, when the French king and the Holy Roman emperor allow the work to continue."

Adrianne continued to watch her husband work. A drawing of a hound. A heart. A bell and a bird. She was surprised to see that Wyntoun did not seem at all perplexed by all the symbols.

"As you probably know, after the translations were complete, your father moved the treasure north. 'Twas then that he stopped at the monastery where Benedict supposedly managed to save it from the fire. After that, Edmund Percy carried it here . . . and became the *Keeper of the Map*."

"Very interesting," Adrianne murmured as she moved to

stand beside her husband. Wyntoun looked up and gave her a reassuring smile before going back to his list.

She stared at the map and a thick black line curling about what looked like a hook with a point at the long end. So many symbols.

"Does the M with the cross signify a church . . . or even the Cathedral, do you think?" The priest spoke for the first time.

"This is not a map of Glasgow," Wyntoun said with quiet confidence.

"What?" Sir Peter said, looking up nervously.

"'Tis a map of Glasgow Cathedral," the knight replied. "The series of repeated SCS's represents the open timber roof."

"And the elaborate '7' in the square?" Colin Campbell asked.

"The carving of the Seven Deadly Sins of the Seven Ages of Man on the screen above the Quire."

Adrianne felt herself filling with pride at her husband's knowledge.

"The hound, the heart, the bell and bird?" Sir Peter questioned.

"The hound and the heart? They are two symbols for the same word . . . Mungo. The word can mean either 'my hound' or 'dear heart.' The bell. The bird. The salmon and the ring. These are the miracles of St. Mungo." Wyntoun's green eyes flashed, giving away his restrained enthusiasm, as he looked at Adrianne. "The Auld Hound himself is buried in Glasgow Cathedral."

A long silence fell over the group. Adrianne watched each man's expression. Wyntoun—confident and at ease. Colin Campbell—solid, serious, and aloof. The priest, Sir Peter Wrothsey—agitated, hardly able to hide his excitement.

"Would Edmund bury the treasure in a saint's crypt?"

Adrianne had nearly forgotten about Baron Avandale. She waited to see who was going to answer the man's question. No one did. She turned to Wyntoun and found him studying a depiction on the map. A thick line curling around the pointed hook.

"We cannot open the crypt," he finally answered. Adrianne stared at him with disbelief.

"The Archbishop of Glasgow's blessing and presence would be needed." Colin Campbell agreed solemnly. "'Twill probably take a week to arrange it, I would think."

"Then a week 'twill be," Wyntoun said, frowning as he squeezed Adrianne's hand. "After all the time we've waited, though, a week is nothing."

The irony of it all was just too delicious.

The haughty Blade of Barra and the omnipotent Colin Campbell had both failed. Plain and simple. They had failed.

These two filthy Highlanders, with arrogance and condescension, had lorded their power over everyone for years. Well, now they were both ruined.

Benedict felt a chuckle rise up in his chest, but the sound of laughter never emanated from his throat. He smiled fiercely into the face of the priest before him.

Sir Peter Wrothsey barked out a laugh. "The saint's tomb!" he said again. "The fools think the treasure is hidden in Mungo's tomb."

Benedict sat down by the hearth and focused on the glowing embers. Finally, after all this time. It was almost within his grasp. "And you are certain of the other symbol?"

The priest nodded confidently. "The thick line curling around the pointed hook."

"A snake!" Benedict hissed. "A black adder."

"Aye, 'tis the Blacader Aisle." Sir Peter said. "The fools overlooked the obvious. The hook is a shepherd's crook . . . a bishop's crosier. The other symbols identify the cathedral, but the pointed end of the crosier indicates the location of the treasure. I am certain of it!"

The monk's gnarled fingers entwined with excitement. "Archbishop Blacader built an extension to the transept about thirty years ago. Just about when Edmund Percy was moving the treasure north!"

"'Tis there. Waiting for you to save it, just as you saved it thirty years ago."

Benedict smiled at Wrothsey. "You've done well, my

brother. Archbishop Cranmer will be pleased to hear of your efforts on our behalf. You will be well rewarded for this."

The priest clutched the cross at his belt and nodded his head in acknowledgment. "The time is running short, though. On Friday they'll have Saint Mungo's tomb open. And when they don't find the treasure, they'll be looking again at the symbols on the map."

"If not before. But we'll not wait that long. By this time tomorrow, I'll have my hands on the blessed Tiberius." Benedict's gaze was drawn toward the door, where the voice of a complaining Nichola Percy could be heard from a barred chamber down the corridor.

"And what are you going to do with her?" Sir Peter asked.

"Together we will bring her back to England and allow the Archbishop of Canterbury to present her to the king." An evil grin slowly spread over Benedict's face. "But why should we go to all that trouble? Perhaps we should just take her head."

Wrothsey's knuckles were white around the cross at his belt. "Her head?"

"Think of what a nuisance she would be to travel with. The king wants her head, and that we will provide." Benedict's eyes glowed with satisfaction at his ingenuity. "I am leaving for Glasgow now. You, my warrior priest, shall kill the traitorous wench and bring her head in a satchel. Take the Lanark road north toward Glasgow. I'll meet you on the road when I am finished at the cathedral."

"Very well, Benedict. We will meet on the Lanark road, then."

The monk stood up and limped toward the door. He turned and looked at the priest.

"'Twill be magnificent, Sir Peter. I will present the Treasure of Tiberius. You will offer the head of the king's most hated enemy. 'Twill be sublime, I tell you. Glorious! This will be our triumphant moment!"

Chapter 28

An hour before dusk, a fog descended, thick and gray as a monk's cowl, upon the city. Shortly before midnight, the heavy mists enveloped the silent men crossing the Clyde, hiding them and dulling the sound of the boatmen's oars. East of Bridgegate, where the English cannons had battered down the walls twenty years earlier, the silent men slipped into Glasgow.

A dozen men in all, they moved through the sleeping town. Skirting the market cross, they moved northward, stealthily climbing the long hill toward the darkened cathedral. Armed and well paid, they were mercenaries prepared to kill for Christendom's most precious treasure.

By a side entry all but one dispersed. In no time at all the men had taken up their assigned positions. In an alcove of a door. Behind the grove of trees. By the ancient wooden bridge that crossed the ditch.

Benedict waited until they were gone, and then he alone stepped into the Glasgow Cathedral. This moment he would share with no one.

Once inside, the monk moved quickly. He knew the way. Even at this hour, the cathedral was lit by dozens of candles, though without the daylight coming through the great stained glass windows, it was dark and cold. Above him, arches created a cavelike feeling. He stopped only once as the sensation of being in a crypt or a catacomb passed through him. Benedict frowned fiercely and looked about him, his hand clutching the dagger at his waist. The cathedral was empty. Pressing on, the lone figure reached the Blacader Aisle in a matter of moments.

To anyone else, the graceful white arches of the Blacader Aisle might had been a distraction. But for Benedict, a treasure of another kind had enthralled him. He took a torch from a sconce on the wall and lit it from a candle.

The monk stood in the middle of the aisle, looking above him at the colorfully painted, carved stone bosses forming a line along the uppermost point of the arches. From what he could see, there was no hiding place above him. But then his searching gaze lit on a large, gold plate that decorated the front of a marble altar. Above the altar a statue of the Virgin Mary stood in an alcove. She had been depicted wearing a blue veil with gold fringe.

"Of course! 'Tis here . . . here!" His voice echoed off the stone walls, coming back at him. "You are mine . . . mine!"

Benedict limped to the altar and knelt before the gold plate. His hands trembled as he touched the insignia of a black adder curled around a bishop's crosier. He smiled. The long end of the shepherd's crook was pointed like a quill.

And the point of the quill lay on an open book!

The monk sneered upward at the statue above the altar. "Thirty years wasted . . . wasted . . ."

Impatiently, he pulled at the gold panel. Laying the torch on the stone floor, he used his dagger to pry the heavy plate free. That was all it took. The plate slid straight outward on iron pins. He dropped it behind him on the floor, the crash reverberating through the cathedral.

Benedict held up the torch, and he saw it. There, in an open space behind the plate. His eyes glittered as he looked on it . . . the object of his desire. The end of his search. It was his now!

He reached out for the charred, wooden casket.

A steady rain was falling when Benedict slipped out of the side door of the cathedral with the casket tucked beneath his arm.

The kirkyard was silent as death. Tendrils of mist curled around the dark objects before him—the low wall, the grove of trees, a stone crypt by the wall.

Holding the torch in one hand, he whispered into the night.

Silence was his only answer. He moved along the perimeter
of the stone walls, where he knew at least two of his men
had been posted. They were not there.

They had to be here. They would not leave him. He had
paid them, true. But he had promised them more . . . much
more. Uneasiness gnawed at the monk. Benedict could feel
his heart hammering in his chest, but he ignored it and continued on toward the bridge across the ditch. There were more
men in the graveyard on the hill beyond. He tightened his
hold on the wooden casket as he crossed the bridge. As he
climbed the narrow path, the sound of his own footsteps was
all that he could hear.

A moment later, a sharp cry cut through the night, stopping the monk dead in his tracks. It sounded like a cry of a
woman. The shriek of a woman in pain. Of a woman dying.

Dogs barked in the distance, but there was no other cry.
In the fog, it was difficult to judge where the sound had come
from. The monk could not be sure if it had come from ahead
of him or from behind.

This time, he called out loudly for his men. Silence was
his answer.

Adjusting the casket under his arm, Benedict turned and
charged back down the hill. There were more men waiting
for him with the boatman at the Clyde. Men trained to kill,
waiting to serve him.

He just had to get there.

He saw the dark shape on the path too late, stumbling over
it and kicking it ahead of him as he fell. The casket landed
with a dull thud, and the torch lay flickering on the frozen
ground beside the path. Whatever he had fallen over had not
been there a moment before.

Panic-stricken, he crawled on his knees through the fog,
reaching for his treasure. Instead, his hands touched a cloth
bundle. It was a bag containing the object that had tripped
him. He moved closer, peering at it. Not a bag. A tartan . . .
tied about something heavy. He pushed it and it rolled slightly
into the light of the torch. Strands of dark hair stuck out of
the tied opening.

"Nichola!" he whispered, rising to his feet and stepping back. "Dead."

He looked around wildly. Up the hill, the dim shapes of gravestones. Though he could not see it, in front of him lay the bridge. There was no sign of Sir Peter Wrothsey or anyone else. The monk's legs suddenly felt like lead, and his hands trembled as he bent to pick up the casket that was lying on the path. He straightened up and listened again for a sound.

Benedict despised the fear that gripped his stomach, but he could not shake it off. The fog that had hidden him before now seemed like a shroud. A shroud for him alone. Forcing himself to step forward, he cursed himself.

"Sir Peter!" he called out. "Where the devil are . . . ?"

The words withered in his throat as the figure of Nichola Percy suddenly appeared before him. Like an avenging angel on the Judgment Day, she came out of the mist. Panic gripped him, and he gaped at the accusing form. Dead or alive, spirit or human . . . it didn't matter. Nichola Percy stood before him, blocking his path. Benedict could not move his feet. He could not speak a word. The sound of his ragged breathing was the only noise. Neither broke the silence for a seemingly endless moment. And then she spoke.

"This is the end, Benedict."

He shook his head, forcing himself to think clearly.

"Nay, Nichola. You are not real! You are a spirit. You cannot hurt me." She was a trick of his mind, he told himself, but he could not will his feet to move forward. "Begone, you vile, accursed wretch!"

"One should never molest the mother when she has her babies in the nest."

Echoes of his own words came back to him. He shuddered uncontrollably. He had spoken those very words to Sir Arthur Courtenay.

"Through all the years of my marriage—through all the years bringing up my family—you lived among us. You were one of us, and still you lied to us. You sold your soul to the devil, and you betrayed us. For what, Benedict?" Her finger extended accusingly toward the charred box. "For *this*?"

He hugged the wooden casket to his chest. "'Tis mine.

Mine . . . as 'twas supposed to be so many years ago. Edmund started this. He shouldn't have stopped me that night. I started that fire in the monastery. I walked through the flames and saved it. I had the Tiberius in my hand, but he took it away."

"He gave you glory in place of it. He made you a hero. He saw that you were accepted as an honored member of his brotherhood."

"I hated him for that, too. I hated them all. Wealthy, privileged knights of a degenerate order. You think I needed them? I scorned them. Compared to my own lineage, they were all base, lowborn curs."

"Edmund gave you a chance to be part of something good and virtuous."

"He took away my chance for power. He shattered all of my plans." Benedict's voice shook as anger steeled his will again. "I had to destroy him after that. I waited and planned. I would destroy him, destroy his family, destroy everything that was important to him."

The weight of the casket in his arms brought him courage. He held it. It was his now. The treasure was his, quickening the spirit that had been dead for years.

"Edmund had no chance against me. I knew all his secrets. I was privy to all his activities. I cultivated my friends. I waited for my chance. When the time was right, when my ally Thomas Cranmer became Archbishop of Canterbury, I struck!

"Aye, Nichola! 'Twas I who brought ruin on your house. 'Twas I who brought the king's Lieutenant, Sir Arthur Courtenay, to your door. 'Twas I who harried you and your brood of sluts all across England and Scotland." He stepped closer to her. " 'Twas I, Nichola, who arranged for your noble husband to die like a dog in the Tower. 'Twas I."

"This is the end, Benedict," she said again quietly.

"Aye, the end for you. The end for all who oppose me. With this I shall have all that I desire. With this relic—more precious than the Holy Grail itself—I shall have my rightful place. Inside of a month, I shall be Archbishop of Yorkshire.

Inside of a year, when King Henry takes Rome, I shall be Pope!"

"You are mad," she whispered.

"Do not confuse ambition with madness, spirit."

"Only a madman would stand and converse with a spirit, Benedict." The younger woman's voice came out of the mist, and the monk drew back at the sight of Adrianne stepping up behind her mother.

"You!" he rasped, his fingers closing around his dagger.

He drew back another step as Wyntoun MacLean moved out of the mist to stand by his wife.

Others appeared as well—Sir Henry Exton with his warriors behind him, and even Benedict's "ally," Sir Peter Wrothsey. The monk cursed his bones with all the fervor he could muster. He spat on the ground and looked about him defiantly.

"'Tis mine, now," the monk whispered fiercely. "Mine."

Wyntoun's voice cut through the graveyard. "'Tis not yours. It belongs to all. To all humanity."

"You cannot take it from me." Benedict backed up another step. The torch lay at his feet. His gaze darted to the side. He turned around. On every side, the grim faces of warriors gazed back at him. He was surrounded.

"'Tis over, Benedict," Nichola repeated.

The monk pulled out his dagger and drove the blade under the lid of the casket, wrenching the top open.

"I'll not give it up!" he screamed. "I'll destroy it first."

Benedict looked into the charred wooden box. It was empty.

Wyntoun stepped forward. "Your own villainy has entrapped you."

As the monk threw the casket at the knight's feet, the circle around him shrank. He whirled around, flashing his dagger at his enemies.

"Yield, Benedict," Wyntoun said. "Yield and you will find mercy yet. "

The monk's gaze went from Nichola to Adrianne, and then fixed on Wyntoun's face for a long moment.

"Never," he rasped, turning the blade on himself and plunging it into his own heart.

Adrianne watched the mask of death steal over Benedict's face. Silently, they all watched him die, and then she saw her mother turn away from the corpse.

The circle of warriors appeared to come alive instantly, but the young woman's gaze remained fixed on Nichola's face and on the tears that were glistening on her cheeks.

Nichola opened her arms, and Adrianne moved into her embrace. As she held her mother, memories of her father drifted through her consciousness. Edmund Percy had died for his beliefs. The evil of this one man, Benedict, had only hurried the process along.

But that was over now. Her mother had insisted on being here. Nichola had insisted on facing the monk and hearing his words. And now it was over.

As Wyntoun had explained to Adrianne as they had waited, Sir Peter Wrothsey had always been true to the Knights of the Veil. Just as Wyntoun himself had done, the priest had maintained a covert connection with Benedict during the past year. Knowing of Benedict's alliance with Thomas Cranmer, it was critical for the brotherhood to retain some direct link to the monk. Through Sir Peter, the Knights of the Veil had been able to relay to Benedict what *they'd* wanted him to know. The monk's cunning had kept him a step ahead of them, but it had been this same connection that had ultimately saved Lady Nichola's life. With Sir Peter inside the keep where Nichola was being held and Sir Henry waiting in the hills surrounding the place, Nichola's rescue had been an easy one . . . once Benedict and his men had departed for Glasgow Cathedral.

Adrianne kissed her mother's cheek softly and drew out of her embrace upon seeing Sir Henry approach them.

"I believe this man needs to feel your arms around him as much I," she whispered, smiling into her mother's face. "Sir Henry has been a man all but ruined with worry. Perhaps you could show him some mercy."

Nichola squeezed Adrianne's hand before letting go.

The young woman turned and found her own husband waiting a few paces away. Her heart beat proudly at the way he'd planned the monk's capture. The information about the treasure being in St. Mungo's tomb had been a ruse all along. The day before, with Adrianne looking on, Wyntoun had taken the manuscript out of the charred box and turned it over to the earl of Argyll. From that moment forward, the task of protecting the Treasure of Tiberius would fall on Colin Campbell.

Wyntoun's arms wrapped around her like bands of steel. "I am sorry you had to witness this. It didn't have to end this way for him."

"We had to be here. My father's memory required it."

"And did it also require a block of wood wrapped in a tartan and a lock of your hair in the knot?"

She looked up at him. "Thank you for letting me give him back a taste of the fear he has inflicted on my family. 'Twas a wee bit impulsive, I know—"

"Say nothing more of it, my love. Don't forget I have changed. From here on, I will have absolute trust in everything you say and do."

She jabbed him playfully in the ribs and pulled away. "None of that, Wyntoun MacLean. I demand that you keep your common sense. After all, I don't trust everything I say and I do."

Wyntoun's face glowed with affection as they started down the hill toward the horses that would take them back to Dunbarton Castle.

"Do you think the earl of Argyll and Lady Celia have already gone?" she asked.

"Aye. They were to leave at dusk. With the number of warriors accompanying them, taking Tiberius to its new hiding place should be uneventful."

The fog was beginning to lift as they arrived at the place where the horses had been tethered.

"Wyntoun, what of those men who were with Benedict?" Adrianne asked, relishing the feel of her husband's protective arm around her.

"They were not men serving the Archbishop of Canterbury. Sir Henry questioned the ones who didn't manage to run off. They were simply hired hands, paid by Benedict . . . though probably with the archbishop's gold. I believe Thomas Cranmer was keeping a safe distance from Benedict. If the monk succeeded, he would benefit immensely. If Benedict failed, Cranmer would be no worse off."

"But still the archbishop must have lost a small fortune!"

"Aye, a fortune stripped from the monasteries they've been raiding in the south. Cranmer had nothing to lose, really."

Adrianne's frown turned to a smile as she saw her mother being assisted by Sir Henry over the slippery ground. The affection that glowed in Nichola's eyes, the love that was so obvious in the English knight's touch, brought a feeling of warmth to the daughter's heart.

"And so this is the end," she found herself whispering.

"Only the beginning," Wyntoun murmured as he placed a kiss beneath her ear.

She smiled broadly and turned in her husband's embrace. "The beginning?"

He gave her a satisfied nod. "The beginning of our journey north to Balvenie Castle to meet the rest of your family."

She raised herself on the tips of her toes and placed a kiss on his chin.

"And the beginning of our return to Duart Castle and a marriage we left there."

She placed a kiss on his right cheek.

"And the beginning of starting our own family."

She placed a kiss on his left cheek.

"And the beginning of change in one particular man and in one particular woman. The beginning of love and trust that is so strong that 'twill overcome any obstacle in our path. This is the beginning, my love, and forever is the next step."

Adrianne kissed her husband with all her heart and soul.

And that, they both knew, was only the beginning.

Authors' Note

We hope you enjoyed the *Highland Treasure* trilogy. We *loved* writing it for you!

As most of our readers already know, we delight in occasionally bringing you glimpses of characters from our past novels, and we loved doing it here. In *The Dreamer*, we had the pleasure of introducing Catherine and John Stewart. In *The Enchantress*, you met Laura and William of Blackfearn, chieftain of Clan Ross. It was also a special treat for us, in *Firebrand*, to bring back Colin and Celia Campbell from *The Thistle and the Rose*, our first novel.

As in our past novels, we have tried to stay true to the descriptions of historical sites of England and Scotland, as well as to the time period. For those of you who are (or want to be) familiar with the Isle of Barra, Duart Castle, Glasgow Cathedral and the Necropolis, and Dumbarton Rock . . . well, we certainly hope you enjoyed the tour!

As always, we love to hear from our readers. You can contact us at:

May McGoldrick
P.O. Box 511
Sellersville, PA 18960
e-mail: mcgoldmay@aol.com

May McGoldrick is the pseudonym for husband-and-wife team Jim and Nikoo McGoldrick. Nikoo is an engineer, and Jim is an English professor who has also had a career in submarine construction. Their novel *The Thistle and the Rose* was nominated for Best First Historical by *Romantic Times*. They live with their two sons in Pennsylvania.

*Three sisters each hold a key to their family's treasure—
and to the hearts of three Highland warriors....*

THE FIREBRAND

Adrianne Percy was hidden in the
Western Isles, safe from her family's
enemies—until her sisters sent a
notorious pirate to return her to the
Highlands. But when she hatches a plan
to free her kidnapped mother, it requires
her to marry the handsome rogue—
and what begins as a simple
matter of business quickly
flares into an uncontrollable
desire. As Adrianne's heart
smolders, their calculated
arrangement threatens
to ignite into a
burning passion....

http://www.penguinputnam.com

ISBN 0-451-40942-6

40942

0 71162 00599 8

UPC
S

$5.99 U.S.
$8.99 CAN.